ABOVE
THE
NOISE

the in too deep series

MICHELLE KEMPER BROWNLOW

Above the Noise
Copyright © 2014 Michelle Kemper Brownlow

The characters and events in this book are fictitious. Names, characters, places, and plots are a product of the author's imagination. Any similarity to real persons, living or dead, is coincidental and not intended by the author.

ISBN-13: 978-1499619126 (paperback)

Cover Design: Michelle Kemper Brownlow

Cover Image: Captblack76
Cover Model: Lorenzo C

Editing: Book Peddler's Editing
https://www.facebook.com/BookPeddlersEditing

Formatting: Fictional Formats
https://www.facebook.com/FictionalFormats

Original lyrics: Michelle Kemper Brownlow ©
http://michellekemperbrownlow.blogspot.com

praise for
ABOVE THE NOISE

One of the greatest talents Michelle has is getting the reader to feel and experience her storytelling and Above the Noise is a perfect example of that. I could feel the music, the atmosphere, the emotions... all of it. Never has music and reading gone better hand-in-hand than with this book and Michelle continues to shine with Above the Noise.
~Jillian Stein, Read-Love-Blog

A beautiful story that will leave you emotionally attached to the characters and fanning yourself with some incredibly sexy scenes. Calon made it very hard to stay faithful to Jake!

~Jenee Gibbs, Jenee's Book Blog

Calon and Becki's story is one filled with emotion, passion, and absolutely scorching hot chemistry. Yet another must read from the very talented Michelle Kemper Brownlow.
~Holly Baker, Holly's Hot Reads

This is a series that will stay with you for quite some time. I love how this group of characters' lives intertwine.
~Heather Davenport, Naughty and Nice Book Blog

To everyone who makes music.
From those who play alone to those who play for tens of thousands, you're speaking a
universal language that has the power to heal the broken.
Don't. Ever. Stop.

ABOVE THE NOISE
playlist

The Keeper by Chris Cornell
Skeletons by Yeah Yeah Yeahs
Lie in the Sound by Trespassers William
American Music by Violent Femmes
Lump by The Presidents of the United States
Tsunami by Dvvbs & Borgeous
Crazy Train by Ozzy Osbourne
All of Me by John Legend
Suds in the Bucket by Sara Evans
Eat for Two by 10,000 Maniacs
Drive all Night by Glen Hansard and Eddie Vedder
Laid by James
Counting Stars by OneRepublic
Lips Like Sugar by Echo and the Bunnymen
What if by Five for Fighting
State of Love and Trust by Pearl Jam
Crash by Sum 41
Criminal by Fiona Apple
The One by Static Cycle
Wings by Birdy
Paralyzer by Finger Eleven
Accident by Emily Wolfe
Arms Wide Open by Creed

Find Michelle Kemper Brownlow on Spotify.com
for this and her other novels' playlists
http://open.spotify.com/user/124106530

ABOVE
THE
NOISE

one

"CHANGE OUR IMAGE? Are you fucking kidding me? This is ridiculous! Guys, Becki, we're out!" Calon's voice was sharp, and his stance was on the verge of threatening. It was unusual to see him that way. He'd been nothing but sweet, sensitive, passionate, and gentle since we'd first met. I'd heard him get loud with Gracie when they practiced new songs at Mitchell's, but that was usually because she held back what he tried to pull from her. *That* kind of passion was a cool thing to see. The clenched fist thing in Greystar Management's conference room teetered between passionate and dangerous, which was a first for me.

Mr. Barnes sat with his eyes fixed on Calon but seemingly unshaken by my new boyfriend's outburst. I sat with the band on an eccentric couch across the room from Mr. Barnes. I looked around at the other guys to see if they were as thrown by Calon's booming voice as I was. They didn't seem fazed. Spider leaned back into the couch with his arm up over the back behind Manny, whose elbows were on his knees. Manny rubbed his forehead then turned his head away from Mr. Barnes, looked passed me, and grinned at Bones. Bones nodded, straight-faced, then looked back at Calon. Since it seemed I was the only uncomfortable one in the room, I was the odd man out. I felt like I should stand up to leave, as per Calon's directive, but no one else budged.

"Mr. Ridge, listen. It's common practice in this industry for management to help you create an image. Your image is what sells your music, that's no secret."

"Funny! I like to think it's our talent." Calon wasn't about to let this go. It was incredibly sexy to watch him take charge and stand his ground, but I would have rather had toothpicks shoved under my fingernails than spend any more time in that meeting.

"Calon, think of the bands you know off the top of your head. You can picture the band members, right?"

"Of course, I can, but that's not what sells a record, Mr. Barnes. The passion for the craft, the investment in the art of taking an emotion and slinging words around it then folding in just the right beat and melody is what sells, not my hair or the style of my clothes. I don't even think about that stuff before I go on stage. All I think of is how I'm gonna move my fans. And I sure as hell think they're longing to be moved… by my voice—not my image." Calon added air quotes at the end of his rant.

"Honey, what's your name, again?" Mr. Barnes pointed at me with his pen as he stood and walked around the back of his chair. I hated that he called me that, but I decided to ignore it, so as not to add to the stress level in the room. He nodded in my direction, and that proverbial pin dropping against the silence in the room would have split my eardrums.

"Becki." My name came out of my throat like it'd been dragged across sand paper first. I hated that this cocky man had me so worked up.

"Becki, you're Alternate Tragedy's manager."

I nodded. "Yes, sir."

"Which means you must be a fan of their music, correct?"

"Of course." I nodded again and rubbed my hands on my knees to try and keep my body from shattering from the nervous energy that ran through it.

"Are you also a fan of their look?" He raised his eyebrow at me and slowly turned his head to Calon as if he was drawing an imaginary line between us, challenging me.

I took a slow deep breath and gathered my thoughts before I spoke. I stood and walked toward a bookshelf where a framed photo of Mr. Barnes and the members of his company sat. Mr. Barnes blinked a couple times as though I caught him off guard with my decorum. I made it obvious that I would use that photo as a means to turn the table on him. I nodded in the direction of the well-dressed, exclusively male executive team posed around a boardroom table in the frame.

"Mr. Barnes, image sells, you're right. So, we can agree that people may not take your company seriously if your trademark photo had been taken on a beach and you were all shirtless and in Hawaiian swim trunks. Correct?"

"Sure." He remained behind his chair, an obvious comfort zone. He only looked a little nervous. But I told myself I *made* him nervous as I tried not to pass out.

"There is no doubt in my mind that women will fall in love with these guys, as they have for years, for their music and what it does to them while they listen. I'm sure they'll each have their very own groupies." I heard a loud slap and looked over my shoulder at Spider, who threw a dirty look at Bones then rubbed his arm. Bones looked up at me like a scolded child. Dork.

"That's exactly what—"

"Excuse me, I'm not finished making my point, Mr. Barnes." I nodded when he motioned with his hand to continue, and I walked back over and stood behind the guys on the couch, next to Calon, who'd stepped out of my way when I stood up to go head to head with Mr. Barnes. "As an avid music fan and former 'groupie' myself, I have to stand behind my clients and support Calon's concerns. There needs to be an authentic match between appearance and music. If there's even a slight shift, it will appear orchestrated and unnatural to the fans, who've followed them for years, just as it would if the professional reputation of your company was challenged by a beach bum photo. Do you see what I'm saying, Mr. Barnes?"

Mr. Barnes folded his arms across his chest and reached up with one hand to rub his chin. He walked around the front of the table and sat on the edge.

I took my phone from my pocket and scrolled through my music while I struggled to keep my trembling under control. I pressed play. The acoustic guitar that sprung forth would not only prove my point, it would help to calm my nerves immediately.

"Mr. Barnes, you know this artist." The guys instinctively kept the beat with their feet on the expensive oriental carpet under their shit-kickers.

"Chris Cornell."

"Yes. When you close your eyes and picture him performing this song 'The Keeper' live, can you feel the vibe he has?"

"Of course. The man's an icon."

"But that's not why you can picture him. You can picture him easily because he wears his music. Everything about who he is, what cuts his soul, how deeply he loves, and how passionate he is about his fans is externally evident in his image. If I saw Chris perform in anything other than his signature combat boots, jeans, and t-shirt it would be a distraction. If he walked out on the stage in a pair of Justin Bieber's saggy leather dance pants, a flat brim hat, and a wife-beater I wouldn't appreciate what he had to offer that night. It would seem contrived. I would feel cheated out of what I should've received from him in the form of an artistic experience."

I looked at Calon for approval of my calm rant. He smiled his crooked smile that never failed to cause the bottom to drop out of my stomach. But he tried to hide it by scratching his forehead. Then he nodded.

"Mr. Barnes, what you see in front of you, how these guys dress and how they wear their personalities, is what you get on stage. Calon couldn't take a handful of short hair in his hands to show the ache in the words he's singing. Spider couldn't throw it down on the drums the way he does if he wasn't comfortable in his own skin. Manny and Bones light up the stage with those guitars if you asked them to morph into something they aren't. They wouldn't suck the crowd in like they always have. Listen, it's smart marketing. You can look at a photo of Alternate Tragedy and know the kind of music you're getting, just like you can with Chris Cornell. Asking them to become something they're not, would be cheating everyone out of what they have to offer. And, in my honest opinion, that would be a huge mistake for you and this tour."

Mr. Barnes looked a bit stunned, but kept his eyes locked on mine. He wasn't going to admit that I'd just put him in his place. "Becki, you raise a good point. Let me mull this over, and we can get together tomorrow to discuss my thoughts. Sound good?"

"Sounds great." Calon's voice was calm and relaxed. However, I was about to throw up, but I plastered a classy smile across my face and nodded. We all shook hands and left Mr. Barnes's office in a single file line; Calon right behind me, bringing up the rear. We walked silently to the elevator, and once we were in and the doors closed, all four of them let loose. Whoops and yells that I'm sure could be heard two floors away were showered down all around me. All I could do was laugh. My very first official day as Alternate Tragedy's manager, and I rocked it like nobody's business.

Calon turned his body to mine and crowded me into the corner of the elevator. He pressed his hips into me and slid his face next to mine until his lips touched my earlobe. I could feel his hot breath on my neck as he spoke. "That was the hottest thing I've ever seen, Becks."

"Oh, here they go again. Good grief, get a room, would ya!" Bones was always the one to complain about me and Calon. The other guys didn't seem to mind all that much, and it's not like we were all PDA all the time. We'd been stuck in a van with all of them since we left Knoxville for Los Angeles. Calon hadn't gotten anything from me in all that time except a few stolen kisses.

"Becks?"

"Yeah." It was the breathiest word I'd ever spoken, but the sexual tension between the two of us turned me inside out.

"I can't wait until we have our own room." Calon spoke loud enough for everyone to hear.

"We can't wait either." Bones's voice was harsh. "God, you're making me horny. Would you put your dick away, man? All this sexiness is really starting to be a problem for me." He grumbled something else under his breath. Calon chuckled and turned toward Bones in the cramped space.

"Bones, man, I'm sorry my dick is such a problem for you."

"Shut up, jackass."

The elevator erupted into celebratory laughter. When the doors opened on the ground floor of the posh LA office building, we stepped into the glass atrium and the late afternoon August sun stung our eyes. Manny spoke the words forming in the back of my mind.

"Let's go get some drinks."

summer flashback

THE FIRST TIME Calon and I drank together was after one of their shows when he walked me back to my dorm. The guys didn't usually drink during a show, but a big storm rolled in that night just as their first set started. The atmosphere inside Mitchell's unexpectedly turned from a slamming rock sound to an acoustic vibe when the lights went out. Gracie ran around and gathered as many candles as she could from the back room, and we all helped her light them and place them on the silent speakers all around the stage. Calon and the guys enjoyed beer after beer and did a show like I'd never seen from them. It was rustic with a little folk-funk. The bar's patrons sang along in the glow of about forty container candles of all different sizes. Calon sat center stage on a stool and sang away the hours with his guitar resting on his thigh. The whole night was ethereal and quaint and very fucking sexy.

He asked if he could walk me home again, which was exactly what I'd hoped for. When we crossed the road right outside of Mitchell's, Calon grabbed my hand, and we ran for the opposite sidewalk that led across campus and up to my dorm. Electricity ran through the hand he held, I was sure he could feel it because he didn't let go.

He told me groupie stories for the entire length of our walk to my room. I was laughing when I pushed my door open. Being a little tipsy, I tripped and fell into him, pinning him against the open door. My hands landed on his chest, and, in an attempt to keep up both upright, his strong hands grabbed my hips. My mind shot back to the thoughts I'd had earlier while watching his deft fingers move on the strings of his guitar.

His t-shirt was damp from sweat, and his curls tickled my forehead when he laughed. It was one of those moments you see in movies when the couple finds themselves in a compromising position and they freeze; chests heaving, mouths agape, and hearts racing. His eyes searched my face, but for what I didn't know.

I pushed off his chest and, a bit shaken, walked to the mini fridge and grabbed the bottle of vodka from the top freezer portion.

"Shots?" I spun around and took in all of him; dark curls, sultry green eyes, an intense stare, and lips I could entertain for days.

"Absolutely." He let the door close, plopped down on my bed, and leaned back against the wall, his legs so long they hung at a weird angle not quite touching the floor. He had a hole in his jeans just below his front pocket, which puckered when he sat. I had a hard time diverting my attention from it.

I was completely oblivious to what my heart was capable of at that point, so the alcohol was an attempt to loosen up before we started making out. This was the token third time he'd been to my room, and that's just how it typically worked. The guy comes back the third time after not getting laid the first two, you know they want it, or they'd have given up after the second night of blue balls.

We did a couple shots and laughed about random shit, and then there was the uncomfortable silence; it was deafening. I decided to make the first move before it got really awkward. I turned on the twinkling lights that hung above my bed and turned off the overhead fluorescents. I climbed onto the bed on my knees facing Calon and reached for his face to pull him in for a kiss. He stopped me and held me still by the wrists.

"Becki, I'm not here for that." He loosened his grip on my wrists, and I dropped my hands in my lap.

"Oh." Fuck. He wasn't interested. It was one thing to be turned down by the conceited freak from my study group, but to be turned down by a hot rock star who probably hits every piece of ass offered to him sliced a little deeper. I brushed it off like it didn't bother me, but it did.

"No, no. Listen." He took my chin between his thumb and finger and pulled my face a little closer to his. "I am extremely attracted to you, Becki. I love your personality, and you're gorgeous, so my comment wasn't a rejection." He smiled, and I felt like a complete idiot, a slutty idiot.

"It's okay, I get it. It was stupid for me to—"

"Shh. No regrets, Becki. You're attracted to me, too, and I'm glad. I'm just not one to rush into that kind of thing." He dropped his hand from my chin, and it joined my hands in my lap. I held his hand with both of mine.

"Wow. I'm pretty sure you're the first rock star in history to turn down a groupie." I rolled my eyes and got up to pour more shots. Calon followed me over to the mini fridge, put his hands on my waist and spun me around. His thumbs touched my skin when my Marilyn Monroe tank flounced with my spin.

"I don't see you as a groupie, Becki, and I'm technically not turning you down. I can't explain it, but I feel like there's more here between us, a connection that we should pay attention to." He rubbed the outside of my bare arms with his warm, strong hands. Those fingers...

I didn't know what to say. I suddenly felt mute. He had all the right words, and I didn't have a single word in my head. He left me speechless, which was no easy task.

"So, am I crazy? Or, do you feel it, too?" He tilted his head.

"Yeah." It was all I could muster, but admitting just that much sucked the air from my lungs. I wasn't the sappy, talk about your feelings kind of girl. In my experience, it just made life messier. But there was something about those green eyes and sexy grin that pulled the sap right out of me without even trying. He was so incredibly intense, and, even though it took years for me to build the walls I had around my heart, he'd already knocked away a couple bricks, and something told me he could get through to my whole heart if he really wanted to. Calon may be ready for me, but what if I wasn't ready for Calon?

two
Calon

"CALON, IF I have anything else to drink, I can't be responsible for what happens when we get back to the room." Becki spun around and leaned back into me. My chest rumbled with a groan, and she looked back at me and grinned, which told me she very well may have been picturing the same thing in her mind that played out in mine.

"Mmm, Becks. You'll have to control yourself as long as we are sharing a room with those punks." I nodded in the direction of Manny, Bones, and Spider, who were wallowing in the LA groupie attention that came as soon as the word had spread around the bar about our upcoming tour with Smiling Turkeys. I finished the last of my beer and set the bottle on the bar then laced my hands around Becki's waist. I clasped them across her belly and rested my head on the top of hers. We swayed to a beat much slower than the one that pounded in the hotel bar. Her clean but sultry scent gave me a buzz no alcohol could touch.

She loved when I called her Becks. And I loved that no one on the planet smelled as good as she did. But I didn't love that we hadn't yet had a moment without 'the punks' since we'd left Knoxville. It had only been a couple of days, but it felt like a lifetime since we'd been alone. Our regular late nights in her dorm had grown more frequent just before we left

Tennessee, so I was hoping for our own room once we finally got to LA and the management company started footing the bill.

"So, do you *want* another beer?" I leaned down and whispered in her ear. As I pulled her closer to me, she laid her head back against my chest and closed her eyes.

"You have to ask?" She spun within the circle of my arms and gripped the sides of my t-shirt, stood on her tip toes, and crashed into my mouth. I bent slightly as I tightened my grip around her waist and lifted her until her feet dangled toward the floor.

"Bartender," I called, motioning for another beer. Shit, Becki was hot. I tried to convince my dick I wanted to take things slow, but, she was naked in my mind so often, it was hopeless.

It felt like years since Gracie was all I thought about. The connection Becki and I had hit me like a freight train. That first night we met at Mitchell's, when the two of them snuck into play on our stage before Buzz opened the place, my heart was tugged in a new direction for the first time since the night I kissed Gracie two years before. When Becki introduced herself to me that night, it was like something from her soul reached right inside me. I remember I winked at her and something about her reaction was different than the typical groupies. She said something about being daring and pushing the limits, and I knew she'd be a challenge. So, I decided to accept the challenge.

Each time I saw her, it was like she crawled deeper inside me. The first night I walked Becki home after she and Gracie came to see us play at Sid's, I felt like a love-struck teenager on his first date. My palms were sweaty, and my heart beat a mile a minute, but something seemed off kilter. I still hadn't shaken my feelings for Gracie, and, at that moment, both beautiful girls took up space inside my heart. It was just a matter of time before one squeezed the other out.

It had been years since Chloe passed away, four to be exact, and she'd moved from taking up space inside my heart to simply inhabiting the man I'd become. I never wanted her to look down from Heaven and see me as a man-slut musician. I stayed grounded, didn't do drugs, or fall into the party scene, just played my music, wrote lyrics, and drank a little when I felt like it. As a band, we'd pretty much walked the straight and narrow, and we owed that all to Chloe, my first love.

Over the last three months, my heart bounced all over the fuckin' place. Gracie caught me off guard when I ran into her at the beginning of the summer. She had me all torn up, and when we started working on her music, all I thought about was taking her face in my hands and kissing her like I did the night we met. But then I'd walk Becki home from one of our shows. Becki and I would spend hours lying across her bed, propped up on pillows, laughing at some ridiculous story one of us told, or standing our ground on some inconsequential argument. Becki and I connected on a very different level, and that intrigued me.

I'd dreamed about Gracie and what we could be together. I was in love with someone that was born inside my head, held captive inside the memory of a single night. Once I could see it was all a fantasy and began to dig down deep to translate my feelings for Becki, my emotions intensified and came at me like a tidal wave.

Becki slammed her beer bottle on the table, which shook me out of my own mind. She stood on her tip toes and looked me in the eye.

"Calon?" She batted her eyelashes at me.

"Becki."

"We are dancing. Now."

I chuckled at her bossy nature. "Lead the way, Becks."

She took my hand and pulled, but lost her grip and flew chest to chest into some drunk muscle-head. *Shit.* My fists clenched. I walked up behind her and held onto her waist.

"Whoa, babe, I got women fallin' for me all over the place, but you're a little pushy."

I could only see the back of her head, but the way she moved it assured me she'd just rolled her eyes at him.

"Falling for you? Passing out *because* of you, maybe. You smell like ass. Ever heard of a shower?" She pushed past him with a grunt. I followed.

The guy made eye contact with me as he passed. "Good luck with that one, dude. She's a handful."

I realized then, Becki was going to handle touring with us just fine on her own. I also realized that I wanted her to know I'd protect her. I'd been in enough fist fights to not fear them. But, it appeared she didn't need my protection, even toe-to-toe with a guy she could fit inside. Both Chloe and Gracie were delicate, almost breakable, because of all they'd been through. Becki wasn't delicate. I got the sense she'd never had anyone to rely on to protect her, so she learned to do it herself.

She spun in front of me, and I had to catch her when she lost her balance again. "Dance, rock star."

"I think you're too drunk to dance," I teased.

"Oh, really?" She stood perfectly still and brushed her golden-brown hair from her face. She took a deep breath and started to move. She dragged her hands up her body from her hips to the underside of her arms, then her hands went in the air. Those hips moved in small circles. Holy fuck, she was gorgeous and so incredibly sensual. I firmly grasped her hips and pulled her into me. Her head fell back, and I leaned down and kissed her neck. Our bodies were so close I felt like she was climbing inside me, when, in reality, all I could think of was being inside her.

I slid one of my legs between hers, so she was gently perched on my thigh, which wasn't going to deflate the wood that'd formed behind my zipper, but I was too busy feeling her dance to care. She moved against my leg, and I held her there with my hand on her lower back. She leaned back, and her cropped top slid from her shoulder, baring enough of one of her breasts to catch the admiring eyes of a few of the men around us. I scrambled to cover her back up. In a quick, sharp move I wrapped my arm around her waist and pulled her into me again, which knocked the wind out of both of us. She looked up at me with her mouth open. Her tongue peeked out at the corner of her mouth then slid across her bottom lip. I wasn't sure if she was doing it intentionally, but it was hot.

"Let's get out of here." She was breathless.

"Lead the way, baby."

summer flashback

"THANKS FOR WALKING me home." Her words slurred a little, and she leaned against my chest with hers.

"You're welcome, Becki. Are you sure you're okay?" I'd walked her home before, but I was pretty sure she hadn't been this drunk any of those times. I didn't want to assume I was to follow her into the building, but I did want to make sure she didn't pass out before she got to her room.

"I'm fine." She hiccupped and shushed me like I was the one making all the noise.

"Listen, let me walk you to your room, or I won't get any sleep."

"Deal." She tried three times to swipe her card through the lock on the exterior door; however, not one of those times did she actually swipe it with the stripe facing the right way.

"Here. Let me." First try and we were in.

"Wow. Calon Rockstar, you are magic. But Gracie already told me that." She giggled and tripped into the lobby. "You know, Gracie says you're pretty good with your lips. Can I try them?" She spun toward me and puckered while fighting to keep her balance.

I laughed at the one-of-a-kind come on. The comment about Gracie broadsided me, though. Reuniting with Gracie had been unbelievable, but it hadn't turned out the way I'd imagined it would. Her heart belonged to Jake, and mine was left calling out to someone who would never hear it. But, then there was Becki. She intrigued me. She was cocky and forward, which was refreshing and fun. Something pulled me toward her. As much as I wanted to kiss her, I knew she would never remember it, and I wanted her to remember it.

Up until that moment, I'd never heard anyone but Gracie speak about the night we kissed. I had a feeling the guys never mentioned it because of the accident that sent me crashing through the windshield less than an hour after kissing her and stole my memory for so long. And now, the girl I felt drawn to spoke of a kiss that had once kept hope alive that I would someday fall in love again.

"Let's wait for a night that we haven't had so much to drink to try out that kiss." I followed Becki down the long hallway all the while wondering if her kiss could wipe Gracie's from my mind.

"Damn you, rock stars, always so logical." She giggled and fell hard against a door that I hoped was hers.

"Let's get you inside, and then I will leave you alone." I helped her with the key, and we walked into a room that was nothing less than what I would have expected. There was a brightly colored tapestry draped from the ceiling on one side of the room and what looked like Christmas lights taped to the ceiling above her bed. She had a poster of Audrey Hepburn from Breakfast at Tiffany's on her closet door, and the quote that ran across the middle seemed like a window into the psyche of this girl I was a little more than fascinated by, 'You mustn't give your heart to a wild thing…'

"Could you tuck me in?" She sat down on a bed completely void of covers and pushed her bottom lip out into a pout. She could barely keep her eyes open, let alone sit upright.

I took off her shoes for her, and she fell over onto her pillow. I lifted her legs onto the bed and covered her with a blanket from a pile on the floor. She snuggled in, eyes closed, and with a smile that spread across her face slowly. She hummed a contented sound, then her breathing slowed, and her lips parted a little. She was out. I stayed crouched next to her for a little bit and just watched her sleep. Her hair fell across her pillow like someone had placed each tendril just right. Her bottom lip was full and pouty, and her cheeks a little flushed, probably from everything she'd had to drink.

I stood and turned off the glaring overhead light, walked to the door, and turned back to see her sleeping under her twinkling lights. That's when I realized I couldn't lock her door from the outside without her key, and I couldn't take her key with me. The space under the door wasn't big enough to slip a key through from the outside. So, I couldn't leave without waking her up to lock the door behind me. I didn't want to wake her.

I chuckled to myself and flopped down into the well-worn, oddly shaped, pink overstuffed chair in the corner. I covered up with what looked to be a 'Made by Grandma' afghan and watched Becki sleep until my eyes forced themselves closed.

The sun pouring through her windows woke me the next morning. Becki was in the exact same position she'd been in when my eyes closed. It was daylight, so I felt better about leaving her alone with her door unlocked. Folding up the afghan and placing it carefully over the back of the chair, I knew she'd never know I'd stayed, which was fine. I'd stayed to keep watch over her, not to get credit for doing something thoughtful. My only intention had been to keep her safe.

three
Becki

CALON AND I stumbled out of the bar and headed toward the elevators. I'd been hot for Calon for years. Gracie, Stacy, and I were technically Alternate Tragedy's first groupies. We'd been going to see them play at Mitchell's since the night we first tried our fake IDs. Stacy and I even lied to our parents and drove to Chicago to see them once.

Gracie and Calon's musical connection had Calon closer to me than arm's length for the entire summer. He and I started something the moment he winked at me back in June. I couldn't explain our connection then, but there was no doubt we both felt it.

I liked music and all, I just didn't 'get it' like Calon and Gracie did. I simply hung out with them to enjoy the view. There were times they'd speak in their special music lingo and discuss things like motif and tempo. *Whatever.* I just sat there thinking, *blah, blah, blah, lick those lips one more time, Rock Star, and I will be in your lap.*

It felt like Calon and I had known each other longer than a couple months. Not to mention, I'd just travelled half-way across the country with him and the band. And now I was headed toward an empty hotel room with Calon *Fucking* Ridge. The thought made me dizzy.

"Let's race, but no running." Calon took off like an Olympic speed walker, wiggling his ass like a pro. It was all I could do to not piss myself laughing at how ridiculous he looked. I was so fucking tired I could've probably fallen asleep standing up, but I'd have to be able to stop giggling at the dork in front of me to do that.

We were exhausted. Spider had driven the last leg of the trip, which was the longest. We'd met with Greystar Management and checked into one of their hotels in Los Angeles. Mr. Barnes was a cheapskate and, much to our chagrin, put us all up in one room. We'd been down at the hotel bar since Happy Hour, and when it comes to drinking, I have a hard time with moderation. It's usually balls to the wall for me, which was another reason why Calon should've gotten us our own room.

"Becks, shh!" Calon swiped the key card and aimed one finger toward his lips but completely missed, which made me giggle even harder. He turned toward me.

"Go! Dork!" I pushed him through the doorway, making him stumble backwards. When he fell, I tripped and landed right on top of him.

Oh, damn. Our noses touched, and if we hadn't already been out of breath from our race, we would have been at that point. His body felt hot against the weight of mine. His hair was splayed out under his head, and his hands were on my ass. *Fuck!* As much as I enjoyed our lengthy and sometimes deep conversations, I'd wanted to move past talking and, well, just fuck for a while. There was no doubt it would be mind-blowing. No man could be as panty-melting sexy as Calon Ridge and not know what he was doing in bed.

"Calon?" I tried to catch my breath.

"Becks?" He raised one eyebrow and started to smirk. I loved when he called me that. There's no way he hadn't pick up on how sexually attracted I was to him. Our relationship, if you could even call it that yet, had moved slower than molasses in January. We'd spent many nights in my dorm, snuggled up together talking about… life, really. We talked a little about our pasts and our beliefs and the things we stood for. I found out he believed in God. I told him all the reasons behind my choice to become a vegetarian. Our conversations were easy and sometimes very intimate. Intimate on a level I'd never been while keeping my clothes on. Getting to know each other on a deeper level had been great, but now I needed to cross that line with Calon, or my ovaries would explode. Boom! Done.

"Calon, I really need to be alone with you." My hair feathered against his face, and he reached up and tucked both sides behind my ears.

"Becks, we *are* alone."

"Yeah, but just until the guys get here. I mean *alone* alone."

"Ohh, *alone* alone." He chuckled and smacked my ass then pushed himself up so I was sitting in his lap with my legs wrapped around him. *Yeah, this was going to calm the fierce throbbing going on inside my panties. Not!*

His eyes didn't leave mine, and I could feel his hot breath on my face. He moved his hands up my back. One grabbed the back of my neck while the other cradled my face. He rubbed my nose with his, and we just sat there. Staring. He closed his eyes and licked his lips, then he sucked in a slow, deep breath. His eyes opened, and when his lips touched mine, the pit of my stomach clenched. I swear I felt my heart stop for a split second. His lips were full and soft but strong at the same time. He tasted the corners of my mouth, his tongue ran across my bottom lip, and he moved his hands to the sides of my head. He'd only kissed me this passionately once before; the night before we left Knoxville. Since then, we were conjoined with Thing 1, Thing 2, and Thing 3. We'd stolen a couple more-than-a-peck kisses over the past few days, but nothing like the way he was kissing me at that moment. What he was doing now—yeah, that's what I needed.

His tongue slowly dragged across my bottom lip again. My hands shot to his head, and my fingers tangled in his hair when he crashed his mouth into mine. I could barely breathe. His mouth was so needy, so hungry to taste every part of mine. His chest heaved in the same rhythm mine did. We were lost—truly lost in a moment of passion that felt like an extension of the intimacy we'd shared during those long talks. It was a natural step; a deeply passionate connection that stemmed from our souls connecting so slowly.

He pulled his head back. His pupils were so big I could barely see the deep green irises that seemed to be exclusively Calon's. He grabbed me around the backs of my thighs and maneuvered the lower half of his body so he could stand. He steadied himself slightly with his hand on the wall directly behind me. I laced my hands around his neck, and it only took one step until my back was against the wall. He rocked his body into mine and kissed me again but this time a little rough and hurried, like he was running out of time and couldn't get enough of me.

"Becki. God, your mouth." He spoke against my lips and slowly let go of my legs. My body slid down his, and I felt the excitement hiding beneath his cargo shorts. And, that's where he stopped me. The seam of my jeans crushed against me where I throbbed the most, and just the mere thought of his huge hard-on being only a couple layers of clothing away from me drove me insane. I just wanted to feel him. Not his clothing. Him.

"Calon, I need to f—"

The door flung open and slammed against the wall behind it, and, at first glance, I thought it was a crowd of people that rushed in.

"Yo! Cal! Look! We just won a bottle of Jack Daniels in a bet! Whoa, you guys were gonna do it, weren't ya? Sorry, man." Nope, it was just Bones. He was the crudest of all the guys and always the drunkest. He fell onto one of the two beds, face down and hugging his bottle of Jack. Manny and Spider stumbled in, not as drunk and pretending not to notice what they probably assumed Bones interrupted. Using my body as a human shield to hide his giant boner, Calon backed me toward the door and called out, "Guys, we're gonna go get some ice." He grabbed the ice bucket from the shelf, and we rushed out the door.

Once in the hallway, I spun with my back against the wall and tried to catch my breath. Calon leaned in toward me with one hand next to my head. His curls brushed my face and tickled. I blew them away, making us both laugh.

"You were saying?" He tipped his head, resting his forehead against mine.

"Huh?" I didn't know what freakin' planet I was on, let alone what I'd been saying.

"You said, 'Calon, I need to' just before the idiots burst in."

"I was going to say that I needed to feel you—closer, ya know?"

"Whoa, Becki Mowry, are you saying you want to move past first base? Wait. Is kissing first base?" he whispered it sarcastically as if second base would a huge step. I hoped it wasn't a huge step for him, because I'd never even slowed down at second base. Shit, I'd touched Gracie's boobs within the first week I knew her. Of course, I was drunk, and it was one of our middle school friend's stupid dares. But it was faster than Calon was moving, which frustrated the piss out of me.

"Yes and yes." I took my hairband from my wrist, threw my hair up into a messy bun, and then shot him my best puppy dog eyes.

"Are you propositioning me?" His eyebrow arched as his thumb brushed my jaw lightly.

"Yes, thick-as-a-brick rock star, I am. Geez. What's a girl gotta do to get into your pants?"

"Oh, honey, what's in *these* pants… we may need to work you up to it." He kissed me on the cheek and grabbed my hand. "Come on, let's go get some ice."

Shit.

summer flashback

"I'M CLEAN. I'VE been tested twice since Shawn and I broke up." I reached up and turned the overhead light off, which left us snuggled up on my single bed, joined only by the moonlight that shone through the window. We were in the middle of one of our stream of consciousness conversations. I couldn't even remember how the conversation of exes came up, and I was still trying to wrap my brain around something Calon said that made me think he wasn't the typical groupie-slut rock star.

"Twice?" Calon picked his head up off my pillow and looked down at me.

"He said things were getting too serious, but I found out later he'd been cheating."

"Well, I'm clean, too. Only been tested once, though." He rested his head next to mine

"Slacker."

"Yeah, that's me—big ole slacker." He pushed me in the shoulder, almost causing me fall off the narrow bed. He pulled me back into him, and I swore I felt something in his jeans that hadn't been there before. It could have been wishful thinking, though.

I needed to calm the hormones that had me ready to strip for him down, so I changed the subject to something that was sure to deflate all boners. "What about kids?"

"Do I have them?" He sounded shocked that I asked. For a second it made me wonder if he did and just didn't want to tell me.

"No, dummy, do you want them?"

"Umm… I don't like to think that far ahead. I'm more of a 'live each day like it's your last' kind of guy, ya know? How about you? You want kids?"

"No way. I guess I'm a little too selfish for that."

"Selfish?"

"Yeah, I like my body the way it is… not fat. I like to spend my time the way *I* want to. I'm impulsive and love to do spur of the moment things. Kids kinda disrupt all of that."

"Yeah, I guess they do." He brushed the hair from my neck and let his hand gently fall there. Goose bumps prickled over my entire body, and I hoped he didn't notice.

"Besides, when I was twelve, I got really sick and was diagnosed with Leukemia. I had to have chemo as part of the aggressive measures to rid me of what lurked inside my body. The doctor said I would most likely never conceive because the kind of chemo I had pretty much leaves you sterile. So, I've grown up with the mindset that kids aren't part of my future, which is just fine. I look forward to all the shit I can do that all my preggo friends won't be able to. They'll be jealous."

"You've got it all figured out, don't you?"

"I like to think I do." My eyes fluttered. I was so tired, and it seemed the more personal and intimate our conversations got, the more exhausted I felt.

"Well, be careful what you're absolutely sure of. Because life has a way of throwing you into situations you never dreamed of." He kissed me on my nose and climbed out from under my blankets. "I should go. Lock the door behind me, okay?" He winked and then was gone, and all I could think about was what it would feel like to make love to his tender soul. I was falling. It was way too soon to let down my walls. *Shit fuck.*

four

Calon

WATCHING HER SLEEP, I could barely breathe. It was weird. I let my guard down that first night I walked her home, and it was like Becki completely took up residence inside me. Everything about her left me splayed open. I would be remiss to think I could've ignored it. There was no hiding what I felt for her.

After Chloe died, my heart became guarded and didn't let anyone in. Sure, I entertained groupies, but, unlike a lot of musicians, my entertaining was done with my clothes *on*. Recently it started to feel like my heart had a mind of its own and all this time had been revving up just waiting for me to let go, so it could throw itself at someone. Well, my heart apparently has good taste because it would be hard to find someone more perfectly attuned to my soul than Becki. It was unbelievable. Quite simply, I was overwhelmed by how hard I slammed into what felt like love. The feeling was so strong it hurt sometimes, and there was no turning it off. I just wondered if she felt anything near what I did. It was way more than just sexual attraction for me.

Becki and I had gotten accustomed to staying up and talking all night long when I walked her home. It really was inconvenient that we had been surrounded by Bones, Manny, and Spider since we left Knoxville. Her dorm was artsy and cozy. It was rare for me to be so at ease with someone so quickly. Traveling across the country with the whole band wasn't conducive to those late night talks.

I always left her dorm before I fell asleep, except for the night she passed out, and at that moment we were sharing a bed for the first time. I was afraid if I closed my eyes, she'd disappear. The guys were completely passed out. Bones and Spider in the other bed, and Manny on the pull out couch. It took every ounce of willpower I had to let Becki sleep.

"Stalker." She peeked up at me through one squinted eye then rubbed it with the heel of her hand. "What time is it, Calon? Why aren't you sleeping?" A sleepy smile spread across her face.

"Because you're here." I brushed some hair from the side of her neck.

"You can't sleep with someone else in your bed?" She crossed her arms over her chest and rolled into me with a deep breath.

"Apparently, not tonight." I draped my arm over her and pulled her into me. "I'm having trouble taking my eyes off you." And my mind couldn't get over the predicament the guys found us in just a couple hours earlier. I was so unbelievably attracted to her and feeling her body react to mine, hearing her soft grunt when she felt how hard I was, would replay in my mind for days. That is, unless we outdid that scenario, then an even hotter memory would replace it.

"Well, no sense in you staying awake alone." She reached under her pillow and pulled out her ear buds, which I assumed were attached to her phone. She fumbled blindly with her hands then gently pressed one of the buds into my ear and one into hers. Music filled my head.

"You listen to Yeah Yeah Yeahs?" For some reason I didn't peg Becki as an indie rock fan.

"Why does that surprise you?" She looked up at me with sleepy eyes.

"I don't know. I just wouldn't have thought you'd like 'Skeletons'."

"So, you've been pigeon-holing me? You think you know all about me, Mr. Calon whatever-the-hell-your-middle-name-is Ridge?"

"James. My middle name is James. And, I'm shocked that, after all the time we've spent talking, you don't think I could figure out some of your details on my own."

"What's my favorite food?" She raised her eyebrow.

"Vegetarian Chili."

"Nicely done." She propped herself up on her arm, all full of herself and ready for a good challenge.

I licked my finger and made a tally on her forehead.

"Eww. That's gross." She kept her voice low and hushed and rubbed my spit away. "Let's see… what's my favorite band?"

"Let me think about this one." I thought back to all the times we were in her dorm. She always had music playing, but what band played the most? "The Cure."

"Dammit!" She was so cute when she was mad. Becki had this don't-mess-with-me vibe that I think most people fell for. I knew better. I could tell someone had hurt her in the past. Her outward demeanor was just a tough front. "Where do I want to go someday?"

"Los Angeles." I knew that wasn't the right answer, but I had no idea, and LA seemed like a good guess since we were there.

"Exactly." She rolled her eyes cluing me in that she was lying through her teeth. Her mouth flew open, and she sucked in a huge yawn.

I laid my head on the pillow and pulled her into my chest. She snuggled in, as though it was a familiar position, and I kissed the top of her head. I really wished we had our own room. All this skin and closeness was driving me mad.

"G'night, Becki."

"Goodnight, dork."

My phone blared an obnoxious alarm up through the pillow and into my brain. I flailed to shut it off. For a second I thought I was still in my apartment in Knoxville, but then I remembered I was in bed with Becki, and my dick flinched with morning wood accentuated by Becki's presence.

I looked down at Becki, still curled up tight against me. I ran my fingers through her hair and kissed her on the forehead. We hadn't moved from the spot we fell asleep in. Everything that happened for the band over the last couple months had us all spinning. Slowing down was a nice change, even though everything was about to speed up again.

There I was in a hotel room with the three guys I'd known since fourth grade, and we were getting ready to go on tour. We'd formed a band just so we could beat Alan Simmons in the talent show. He kept badgering us that he would win because girls loved the saxophone. He didn't bug us much after we won first place with our original punk rock song "Say No to Sax". That was the day I signed my first autograph, and Manny got his first kiss. I'd been through everything with these guys; we survived detention and some serious brawls together. We got drunk for the first time together with Spider's older sister, Beth. And Spider, Manny, and Bones physically held me up seconds after Chloe died. We were closer than brothers.

"What are you thinkin'?" Her voice moved me in a way I couldn't begin to describe.

"Are you a jealous person, Becki?" The words fell from my mouth before I could second-guess them.

"I've busted up a bitch over a guy, if that's what you're asking." She said it so calmly, like it would be no surprise to me, and it wasn't. "Why do you ask?"

"You asked what I was thinking. If you can handle it, I will always tell you the second you ask. But you have to promise the same."

"Deal. Hit me. I can take it."

"I was thinking about the day Chloe died." My heart still stung when I said those words. "I was just thinking about how these three idiots and I have been through a shitload of stuff together. Big stuff. It's amazing that we haven't killed each other."

"Calon, I am so sorry I've never asked you about her. I was afraid to make you sad." She wrapped her arms around me and pulled me as close to her as she could get me.

"I'm sad she's gone, but I keep the happy memories close to drown out the sad ones, if that makes any sense."

"It does. How long had you and Chloe been together when she…" She moved her head in a way that finished her sentence for her.

"Four years. Chloe and I grew up together. We were neighbors. When we were younger, we were more like siblings. Digging in the creek together, looking for crawfish, laying in the grass watching meteor showers, and stuff you do with your grade school friends, ya know?" Becki looked up at me as if I was telling her the secrets of the world. She smiled, letting me know it was alright to continue. "One summer, I think we were fourteen, we were hanging out on her back porch, and her mom and dad got into it. We could hear them screaming upstairs and things breaking, doors slamming. It was awful. Chloe lost it and ran inside to the kitchen and dialed 911 and let the phone off the hook on the counter. She took off into the woods, and I followed her. We ended up at our favorite little grassy knoll by the creek."

"Oh, God. What happened with her parents?" Becki was glued to the glimpse of my memory of that night.

"We could hear the sirens from the woods. Her dad busted up her mom's face pretty bad. She was in the hospital for a little while, and he went to jail for a couple months. But that night, Chloe and I made a pact that we would be together forever, because we'd never let anyone hurt the other. We turned in our v-cards that night, too."

Becki's mouth moved, and she took a couple staggered breaths, but no words came out. Her eyebrows arched and dove into some pretty crazy shapes. I couldn't tell if she was just overwhelmed by Chloe's home life, or stunned that I lost my virginity at fourteen.

"Becks, you promised."

"Calon, I don't have a problem with you telling me your first time was with Chloe. It's just the story as a whole just took my breath away. It's like one of those movies you sob through." She shook her head and pushed herself up onto her elbow. "I'm sorry, that came out all wrong. I didn't mean—"

"Relax, I know what you meant. It's okay. It was an honest answer. That's all I ask. That you're honest with me."

"I don't pull punches, Calon. I tell it like it is. Sometimes, it's my biggest fault." She let her head fall back onto her pillow, as if she was preparing for me to see it the same way.

"It'll never be a fault to me." I leaned down and kissed her on the forehead.

"Calon, what is this thing we're doing?" She motioned between us with her hand.

"What do *you* think it is?"

"I asked you first." She smiled and snuggled back into my chest.

I rubbed her back and sucked in a deep breath and prepared to blurt it all out. "Becki, I think this is something big. This might make me sound like a freak, but ever since you introduced yourself to me in the basement of Mitchell's, a strong connection has been building. Like a force far bigger than we are knew we needed each other."

"Yep, you're a freak." She kept a straight face and looked directly into my eyes.

I stammered for something else to say, and she burst out laughing. "I'm kidding. I mean, you *are* a freak, but, honestly, I've felt like something bigger than us was hard at work to get us together. I've never felt drawn to someone the way I'm drawn to you. I know that sounds super sappy, but it's the only way I can explain it."

"Look at us, Freaky and Sappy. What a pair we are."

"Gag! If the bottle of Jack doesn't give me a hangover, you two will. Shut uuup! Go to sleep." I squinted to see through the dark. Bones hadn't moved anything but his mouth during his rant.

"We were whispering, weren't we?" Becki spoke through her hands that had slapped into her mouth when Bones scolded us.

"I'm pretty sure we were. Guess we're going to have to be quieter if we want to keep talking." We situated our bodies so we faced each other as closely as we could possibly get and still focus on the other's face.

"Calon, as long as we're being honest, this whole thing scares the shit out of me. It got big and intense really fast."

"Agreed. If I let myself think too hard about it, it's more than I know what to do with. So, maybe it's good that we've been moving slowly, I guess."

"No. It's *not* good. That part is really, really not good." She flattened her hands on my chest.

"Yeah. My body isn't immune to you being so close to me under these covers, and no matter how hard I try, I can't stop picturing what this night would have been like if we had our own room."

"Oh, thank God. I was starting to worry you hadn't let your mind go there yet."

"Are you kidding me? Becki, I've been celibate for four years. You. Are. Driving. Me. Mad." I ran my fingers through her hair and let my hand rest on the side of her face.

"Celibate?!" The volume of her voice made us both wince. We froze waiting for Bones to flip out. Nothing. He was passed out again. "Celibate?" she whispered the word this time. "You haven't had sex in four years?"

"I have not." I smiled, knowing I'd just added shock and awe to our late night chat.

"How? You're like a rock god." She struggled to keep her voice at a whisper.

"But, I'm not a slut." I feigned offense, which made her giggle. She buried her face in my chest to muffle her laughter. Her body froze, and she pulled back to look me in the eyes.

"Wait, so, that means… Chloe… and that's it?" She tried so hard to lace her words together, but she obviously had a hard time picturing me as a sexless rocker.

I took her face in my hands and kissed her once between every couple words. "Just one. But," kiss, "hoping to make," kiss, "that short list," kiss, "one name longer soon."

Her eyes fluttered a little, and she growled out, "Shit, that's hot."

five

Becki

"YEAH, ONE PERSON! Can you believe all that sex god mojo has been pent up for four years? Gracie, I'm not even sure I can keep up with that. It could kill me!"

"Holy shit, Becki! I would have thought—"

"You're thinking of Calon in sex situations? Stand down, bitch!" I laughed so hard I snorted. Gracie was just what I needed. If I couldn't be hanging with her on campus, the phone would have to do.

"You're funny. So, tell me, how is everything going? You all survived the trip, I guess. Any news about the tour?" I knew she'd find a way to quickly change the subject. I didn't fault her. You couldn't look at Calon and not picture him naked. Yeah, he was that hot.

"The trip was long and smelly. Four boys in a crowded van for a couple days is disgusting. But, yeah, it was uneventful. We met with the management company yesterday, which was interesting. The guys had to go back there this morning, so I stayed here to call you and just be alone for a second. If you would have told me last month that I would be in a hotel room with four rock stars and wanted alone time, I would have said you were high."

"Pretty intense personalities, huh?" She yawned, and I could hear Jake and Sam in the background. I pictured them still sleepy-eyed and making some big man-breakfast. Classes hadn't started yet, so they were all sucking up all the sleep-in time they could get.

"Well, you know these guys. I mean, they're cool. Gorgeous, too, but they're guys… they can be pretty gross. And they don't feel the need to hold anything back when I'm around."

"Hmm. Sounds—fun?" Gracie's voice trailed off and got muffled.

"Wait! Are you talking to me from inside Jake's mouth?" I rolled my eyes, even though I knew she couldn't see me.

"Yes, she is, Becki." Jake's voice always made me smile.

"Hi, jerk."

"Nice."

"I'm kidding, Jake. You know I love you."

"Yeah. Yeah. I'll let you two ladies alone. I'm gonna go have half a pig with my chicken embryos."

"GROSS!" That thought actually made my stomach churn.

"Ha! That was for calling me a jerk, Veg-head!" Jake he howled with laughter.

"Why does he say that like it's an insult?" I giggled. "So, Gracie, any news about Noah and the guys?"

"Yeah, Detective Peterson called yesterday. They're going to need Ashley, Chelsea, and me to testify… and they will be using the DVD as evidence. Oh, Becki, I wish you were here. Dammit, I miss you." I heard a sniffle, and I knew this was probably the worst possible time for her to have to give up her best friend.

"I miss you, too. A lot! You're going to keep hanging with Sylvia through all this, right?"

"Yeah. I will probably hang with her until she dies of old age. It's hard, Becki, because I feel guilty for some of the stuff I've talked about with her." She turned her volume down to a whisper. "It's stuff that I wouldn't ever tell Jake. Not because I want to keep secrets, but it's just stuff about Noah did to me that he doesn't need imagery for, ya know?"

"But that's all the shit you gotta work through and get out of your head, so you can lessen all those triggers, and, it would do Jake no good to know those things." I sat up and leaned against the slotted headboard that was bolted to the wall and closed my eyes.

"Wow. You sound like you've been talking to Sylvia, too."

"Yeah, we hang out. She's a wild one, Gracie."

"Dork!" She giggled, and I felt the bed shift under me. My eyes darted to the end of the bed.

"Hey." Calon's sultry voice folded around me.

"Was that Calon?" Gracie's voice was so shrill it stung my eardrum. I loved that she and Calon had such a cool relationship. Gracie was the only human I would trust to be so close to someone I was so into.

"Sure was." I put my hand over the end of my phone and whispered to him, "How'd you get in here so quietly? I didn't even hear you." He just wiggled his eyebrows and climbed up the bed toward me.

"Hi, Gracie! We miss you!" Calon spoke in a sing songy voice near my phone, but his lips were barely an inch from mine. His breath smelled like coffee, and his hair tickled my forehead.

"I miss you guys, too. But, I'm gonna let you go. I… uh… I need to go eat with the guys." I knew she was lying. I knew she figured that Calon and I were finally alone with a bed, and she wanted to let me have at it.

"Bye, Gracie. Talk soon!" It was hard to hang up. I really missed her.

"Geez, Becki. Hang up already! Go!" Yep, she knew what I was hoping would soon go down.

I ended the call and put my phone on the side table between the beds, then slid down so I was lying under Calon's lion-on-the-prowl stance.

"Hi." His deep voice, those eyes. My God, those eyes. He lowered his head and rubbed my nose with his.

"Hi." I could barely speak. Images that would make Hugh Heffner blush ran through my mind at the speed of light.

"What are you thinking?"

"Fuck. Calon, that's totally not fair!"

Calon burst out laughing and fell onto the bed next to me. He folded his arms under the pillow I'd slept on and propped it up so we were eye to eye.

"Listen, I'll let you off the hook this one time. But, that's just because I'm feeling generous."

"Thank the Lord!" I let out a big sigh. "So, did you not go to Greystar?" I wanted to change the subject before he changed his mind, and I'd have to tell him about the X-rated fantasy I was having.

"Mr. Barnes met us in the lobby, so we didn't even have to go to his office. He told us we didn't have to change a thing about our image. So, thank you for that." He kissed my nose. "Then he gave us a fat pile of papers with addresses we'll need, contact numbers, and a bunch of stuff we needed to have filled out for our next meeting then he left. The guys decided to do a little exploring."

"And you decided to explore a little, too?" I bit my bottom lip and held my breath. *Please, say yes. Please, say yes.*

"Somethin' like that." He licked his lips and moved toward me so slowly I thought he'd never actually reach me. It was like someone lit fireworks between my legs, just that quickly. My body ached to know what he felt like. *Holy shit.* I wasn't sure I'd ever been so turned on and he hadn't even touched me.

Calon slid the top half of his body onto mine. My chest heaved for breath and not because he was heavy. He had this way of looking at me that made me feel bare, like he was already partially experiencing what I hoped we'd soon be doing. The throbbing in my panties was unbelievable. I felt like my entire body was pulsing with each pump of my heart.

"Becki, I've never been so captivated by someone in my life. I can't explain what you do to me." He brushed some hair off my cheek and placed his hands on either side of my head.

"Well, the feeling is mutual. And I can't seem to find the words for it, either." I slowly moved my hands up his body and across the shirt that stretched across his back. He shivered and dropped his head to my shoulder.

"My emotions are hitting me all at once, from all sides. I'm trying to control myself, but it's getting harder and harder, Becks."

"Don't control yourself on my account," I said in a sexy way, but the truth was, I wasn't sure I was ready. I'd always been ready for sex, but something was different with Calon. It wouldn't be 'sex' with him. It would be something deep and overwhelmingly spiritual. Something I'd never known sex to be.

Calon laughed and moved the rest of his body onto mine. I spread my legs apart, and he settled between them. I was commando in thin pajama pants and a cami, he was fully dressed including a tight t-shirt, jeans, and his big black boots.

"Becks, look. I don't want to control myself. It's just this thing we're doing has moved so slowly, and it's been so comfortable and easy while at the same time, intense and incredibly passionate—sublime, even. I'm scared out of my mind to move too fast and ruin it. Does that make sense?"

"It does. Can I ask you something?" I couldn't believe what I was about to say.

"Anything. Always."

I took a slow deep breath. "Calon, are you sure I'm not just the girl that'll help you get over Gracie and Chloe?

"Becki." He put his hands on either side of my face and kissed my lips. "You aren't 'just' anything. Look, yes, it took me a long time to deal with Chloe's death, and I believe my teenage heart was in love with her. And with Gracie, I was holding onto something I thought I felt for so long that she became this untouchable entity. So, then when I ran into her at the beginning of the summer, it all came back; our kiss, the sadness I was feeling for Chloe. But, what's here..." he patted his chest, "what's here is bigger than anything I've ever felt. And it's clear to me now that finding Gracie was proof there is something bigger than me orchestrating my steps so you would cross my path." He kissed me on the mouth very gently; it left me feeling satiated and cheated all at the same time.

"Wow." I blinked a couple times, surprised by the moistness in my eyes. I wasn't a crier.

"Yeah. Now, can I ask *you* something?" I knew what he was going to ask, and I wasn't sure I could communicate it as perfectly as he just had.

He spoke the same way he wrote lyrics, simply but tangled and deep at the same time.

"Of course." I knew I'd just given him permission to ask me something that I didn't know how to answer.

"What's *your* heart telling you?"

"Calon, there's no way I can describe it as beautifully as you just did. So, you're gonna have to bear with me." He nodded. His beautiful eyes were still, hopeful. "I've had a lot of boyfriends. There's been a lot of sex. A lot." He chuckled and shook his head. "But, that's all any relationship I've ever had has been based on. I was with Shawn for less than two years, and that's the longest I've ever been with one guy. All… *all*… those relationships, though." I picked my hands up off his back and tangled my fingers in the hair at the base of his neck. "All those relationships were shallow. I've never experienced anything this deep before, and it's blowing my mind. I never would've entertained all our nothing-but-talk nights with any of those other guys, but it's been so different with you, Calon. You've moved in far deeper than my surface, and it scares the shit out of me, but, at the same time, it feels like something I've wanted all along but never even knew."

He fisted my hair gently with both hands and kissed me with an eagerness that had me melting beneath him. It was like the flood gates opened and any walls we'd had started crashing down around us. I tried hard to keep up my tough exterior over the last couple months. I rebuilt my walls every time he'd leave my dorm in the wee hours of the morning, but I never seemed to get them as high or as strong as the one before. Finally, the night we kissed the first time, I knew it was futile. He'd wrecked me.

"Becki?" He sighed my name as a question, and his hot breath enveloped my mouth just before his lips took their place on mine.

"Yeah?" It was all I could muster from inside his kiss. His lips were sucking the life right out of me. The guy could kiss, holy shit, could he kiss.

"Can you remind me where second base is?" I felt his mouth curl into a sexy smirk against mine.

"Honey, if you have to ask, you're not ready for what's there." My mouth burned from his passionate kisses and the wayward scruffy traveler look.

"I'm ready, Becks." He straightened his arms until he hovered over me. He looked down at my cami and tossed his head to the side.

"You want it, you gotta get it yourself, rock star." I raised one eyebrow and tried to keep my cool when really my insides quaked. The look on his face when he realized it was up to him to get me out of my shirt was a cross between sheer panic and unadulterated lust. He sat back, took each side of my cami in his hands and gently pulled it up and over my head.

I smiled, and his eyes raked over my body, like he was preparing to memorize every square inch. "You're. So. Beautiful."

He laid his hands on my stomach and drew them up to my ribcage until each of his hands cupped one of my breasts. I watched every move he made; every shiver, every breath. His thumbs moved across my raised nipples, and then he gasped. My eyes shot to his.

"I've never… I want… oh, Becki." I had no idea what he was trying to communicate and at that moment, it could wait. He leaned down and lightly kissed my lips then kissed my collar bone. He dragged his face across one of my breasts, and as I watched, his lips parted. They touched every part of me, but he didn't take me into his mouth. Then he repeated the same with my other breast. My eyes closed, my fingers dug into his shoulders, and I arched my back, which increased the pressure of his mouth on me. Still he just touched, didn't taste. I closed my eyes and with each brush across my overly sensitive skin, I silently begged him to taste me.

"Oh, Calon." I tangled my fingers in his hair and tried to chase away the nervous feeling in the pit of my stomach. Sex for sex's sake didn't make me nervous, but what Calon Ridge could do to me would make me lose control. And *that* made me nervous.

He continued down my stomach with his light kisses. My core pulsed. He slid farther and farther down my body until he was almost to the end of the bed. Warm fingers curled inside the waistband of my pajama pants.

He revealed one of my hip bones then the other. He christened each with his mouth just as he had my breasts. My chest heaved so much he disappeared from my view as breath filled my lungs. I exhaled, and his face came into view just as his eyes flashed to mine and a sexy grin spread across his face.

"Becks, do you want me to stop?" His curls fell from behind his ears and danced around his face as he looked back and forth from my face to my hips.

I shook my head and reached for the slats on the headboard. I couldn't speak. I was so turned on I could barely breathe. I could do nothing but focus on *not* coming before he got my pants off.

His legs made their way off the end of the bed, and he stood. His hands left my body for a mere second, and it was like someone stole all the oxygen in the room. I needed his hands on me as much as I needed my next breath. He combed his fingers through his hair then grabbed a handful with each hand. Calon stood perfectly still, his eyes never leaving mine.

I propped myself up on my elbows and tried to slow my breathing, but it wasn't easy. My body desperately craved him. I watched his face and tried to read his thoughts. He shook his head a little, took a deep breath, shook it again then let his hands fall to his sides. He took his phone from his back pocket and tapped on the screen a couple times then threw it on the other bed. A soulful sound drained from the speaker, and then a beautiful voice softly sang about love. Trespassers William was a band hardly anyone knew, but it shouldn't have surprised me that Mr. Music knew who they were. "Lie in the Sound" gave me goose bumps all over every single time I let my guard down enough to swallow the lyrics.

"Becks, you're cold." Calon's voice was hoarse, and he grabbed one of the sheets to cover me.

I knocked it away. "It's the song. Please, don't stop."

Calon smiled and nodded then breathed a sigh of relief. He leaned over and placed his hands on either side of my hips. His head hung between his shoulders, and his curls tickled my stomach between my hipbones. He curled his fingers around the top edge of my pants again and pulled them toward my feet. I don't think he realized I had nothing under them, because he gasped when he realized he had just exposed all of me. He pulled my pants the rest of the way off and leaned over me again, shaking his head.

"Becki, you're gonna kill me."

"Come here, rock star. I'll be gentle." *What was I saying?* I wasn't ready.

He grinned and crawled up the bed until he hovered over me again. He lowered just enough for our lips to touch, but he didn't touch me with any other part of his body. His tongue took over and a quiet moan left my mouth. He kissed my neck just under my ear, which caused even more goose bumps. His mouth travelled down my chest. His lips once again brushed up and over each of my breasts. My nipples screamed for his tongue. I knew what he could do with it when it was in my mouth. I longed to feel it on all the other parts of me. He kissed me in a straight line all the way to my belly button. His tongue grazed around its rim, and I shuddered. He was so close to the part of me that literally ached for him.

"Is this okay?" His head lifted, and his hooded eyes stared right into my soul, and then he smiled, knowing he didn't need to wait for my answer.

There was a part of me—a very small part, mind you—that felt hesitant to let him go any further. I couldn't explain it. I was completely overwhelmed. I'd never let myself become so invested in a guy that I felt fearful.

Calon's lips brushed the skin below my belly button. The guitar in the song whined one pluck at a time, and the soft tapping on the cymbals matched my heartbeat. I was lost in Calon and the music when I felt his hot breath trickle down over me. He gently pressed my legs apart and looked up at me again. I couldn't take my eyes off him; the curls, the eyes, the broad shoulders, and the defined arms. That's when I realized, he was still fully clothed.

"Stop." A pang of relief ran through my chest when he immediately stood and ran his hands through his hair again. I wasn't sure I could handle all of what I knew he could give me and still guard my heart with the little piece of wall that was still left.

"I'm sorry, Becki." He licked his lips and rubbed the back of his neck.

"It's fine. I… I was just going to say, you're still dressed. I'm feeling a little selfish here." I pushed myself up the bed a little, smiled, and nodded toward my nakedness to make light of the situation, but the nervous tension in my gut wouldn't let up. My body wanted him so badly it ached, but something in my heart was scared to take it all in. To take *him* all in. I closed my legs a little.

"I just wanted to kiss you. I wasn't planning on going any further than what I've already been doing. Just kisses. But, I'll stop if you want me to."

Oh. My. God. He wasn't 'priming the pump' as Shawn used to call it. This was a selfless act. This was all for me. He was getting to know my body. It just so happened Calon Ridge used his mouth to navigate.

"Don't stop." I growled out the words and hung my head backwards and drew in a deep breath. There was no way I was laying down again. I needed to watch what he was about to do. I had no idea how a guy goes below a girl's waist without taking it any further than kissing. How do you—

A deep groan interrupted my thoughts. "Becks, you're beautiful. So fucking beautiful." He pressed my legs open again and bent forward. His breath heated my already hot center. He maneuvered one of my legs farther than the other and shifted so his body was almost perpendicular to mine. His face moved closer to me, and he tilted his head a bit. He breathed in a deep breath then placed his lips on the ones he hadn't kissed yet. Long, soft, caresses. He kissed me there like it was my mouth but again without his tongue. It was like true a first kiss all over again, complete with that anticipation of the guy slipping you the tongue and being unsure if he was going to. Each peck brought me closer and closer to coming without him doing anything more than lightly touching me with his lips. Just then, his mouth pressed against me with just enough pressure to enflame me. I could feel the roll of the tension growing like a wave about to crash.

He left that spot and kissed the insides of both my thighs, one at a time. He continued down from my knees to my ankles then stood at the end of the bed and kissed the tops of my feet and each toe one at a time.

"Mmmmm. Becks." He lifted his eyes to mine, climbed up the bed, bringing the sheet along with him. He lay on his side next to me and covered us both up. "Thank you for trusting me. I just wanted to kiss you."

six

Calon

I WASN'T SURE I was digging the vibe I got from the guys of Smiling Turkeys. We probably should've met them prior to signing on to the tour, but we were so stoked about getting the opportunity to open for them, we just sort of pounced.

Becki had warned us against jumping into something too quickly, because we'd been screwed over so many times and lost big gigs and possible contracts before. But, we just wanted to sign on that line and live it.

One of the band members of Smiling Turkeys called mid-week to tell us they added a date to their tour and we needed to be ready by Friday to follow them out to some night club on the outskirts of town for some secret celebrity birthday. They were all hush-hush about who the celebrity was, like they couldn't trust us with the information. Dicks.

We sat in their studio for an hour past what was supposed to be the start of *our* studio time. Instead of playing, we listened to them argue over which cover they were doing for their encore.

Their studio was over the top. First off, it was huge with not only the set up for the band but enough space to have a small house party. There were two big sitting areas with black leather furniture placed perfectly around the edges of geometric design throw rugs. There were framed photos of the band with famous people in the industry and a signed electric guitar displayed under a small spotlight that hung from the black drop ceiling.

It was beyond me why you would need all of this crap around you while you rehearsed. I couldn't imagine what it cost them for the space. Maybe they thought all the extras would inspire their music. We practiced at Mitchell's when the bar was closed, and Buzz never charged us a dime. For me, the smell of stale beer and the history of all the bands that had ever played on that stage were my inspiration. Luckily, all that came for free.

"Dude, fuck you. Everyone wants to do 'American Music', so let's just agree on that." Frank played guitar, he seemed pretty cool, but he and Max, their lead singer, rubbed each other raw the whole time we were there. I got the feeling no matter what Frank wanted to play, Max wouldn't have agreed to it.

"Oh, so because you, Troy, Ben, and Steve want to play Violent Femmes, that's everyone? Well, Frank, I counted and there are five of us, not four." Max walked over and got in Frank's face.

Frank didn't flinch. "Well, if we're voting, I'd say we have the majority."

Max had wild black hair, short but all over the place. He wore a long black leather coat everywhere and always had half a snarl on his face. I'd seen him enough times on the sleazy tabloid news clips that ran on the local LA stations. I wasn't his biggest fan. I couldn't understand why they couldn't just sing both songs for their encore. Crowds love lengthy encores.

"Nope. We're playing 'Lump', and that's it."

"Fine, Max." Frank threw his hands in the air. "I just think that crowd we're playing to may not even know that song. The Presidents of the United States didn't really make it onto a whole lot of 'Best of' lists. But, whatever."

Are you kidding me? Dude with tough looking coat rules the roost? That's bullshit. Spider, Manny, Bones, and I had been together since elementary school and never had stupid arguments like that. Not even when we were twelve. What a dick.

"You guys need to practice?" Max looked over at us like we were an afterthought.

"That's what we're here for." I didn't try to make nice. He could tell by my flippant attitude that I was pissed. I knew he was going to pick a fight with me before this whole tour ended. *Whatever. Bring it, bad ass.*

Max smirked and shook his head before he counted them off. They played their single encore song then started packing up their stuff.

The guys and I got the space set up while Max continued to antagonize Frank about their encore. It felt so good to be playing again. Just a couple days without amps and mics and I felt like a part of me had been amputated. I loved acoustic, but there was nothing like a hard riff through an amp to bring your soul to life.

"You guys wanna do all five songs in the order we picked for the set?" My sentence was barely finished when Spider's eyes flashed to something behind me. I turned just as Max walked up to me and shouted.

"Five songs? This isn't your concert. You're just the opening act. You get three songs. Got it?"

"Yeah, cool. Three songs because you don't want us to show you up, we get it." I turned to walk back to my mic.

"You fuckin' with me? You wanna start somethin'?" He followed me, and when I stopped walking, he slammed into my back. I turned, and we were eye-to-eye. The size of his pupils told me he'd puffed up his attitude with some illegal substances, so I decided to give him a break.

"Look, man, I'm not trying to start anything. We just wanna play." I rubbed the back of my neck just to give my right hand something to do so I didn't take a shot at him. This guy was such an ass.

"Three songs." He turned and flipped his coat like it was a fucking cape. What a tool.

They hadn't left the studio when we started to practice our set. They grabbed a couple beers and took up one of the seating areas like uninvited guests. We planned to play two songs from our *Fallen* album and one new one we were working on. It was so new we hadn't even titled it, yet. That was Bones's thing. He usually picked our titles.

"Hey, Cal, what do you think of this for the bridge in the new song?" Manny played something that had a bluesy twang to it but kept a rock tempo. I loved it.

"Dude, that's –"

"What?! You're still *writing* the songs you're performing for the tour? Are you kidding me? Where did we get these guys? Come on. Fuck!" Just Max's voice alone grated on my nerves. Add his inflated ego and I couldn't help but fantasize about beating the shit out of him. I'd knocked out guys twice his size before.

I tried to speak without clenching me jaw, because all I really wanted to do was throttle him. "Listen, Max, you worry about your music, and we'll worry about ours. Last I checked, you don't have a say in what we play." I shoved my hands in my pockets to control the urge to bust his face wide open. Not many people could even see the small vicious thread that hid deep down inside me, but Max was picking at it, and it was just a matter of time.

"Then you didn't read the fine print, hair boy."

Hair boy? That made me chuckle a little. "Come on, man. Let's not do this. We're gonna be spending a hell of a lot of time together. You really need to bring it down a notch."

"I read the fine print, Max." Becki's voice came out of nowhere, and she said his name like it burned her tongue. "And I assure you there is nothing in the contract that gives you any say in what songs Alternate Tragedy plays for their set." She slowly sidled over to where Max and I stood.

Holy shit, she was hot. Immediately, my mind was thrown back to earlier that day when I was between her legs. My stomach rolled, and my dick swelled. I had to put those thoughts out of my head if I was going to stay connected to the conversation that played out in front of me, because if he pulled his condescending attitude with her, I'd take him down.

"Well, well, well. And who do we have here?"

"Hi, Max, Frank, Ben, Troy, Steve." She smiled and tipped her head to each of them as she said their name. "I'm Becki Mowry, Alternate

Tragedy's manager. All contracts and deals go through me. We had a long chat with Mr. Barnes about the details of our contract, and I can assure you, they can play what they want." Becki walked up to Max without an ounce of hesitation. Her balls were huge.

"So, Becki, you wanna talk about this over dinner tonight?" Max raised an eyebrow, and the hair on the back of my neck stood on end. I shoved my hands in my pockets again and looked over at Manny. He winked and nodded his assurance that Becki had the situation under control, which helped me breathe a little deeper.

Becki smiled and took two steps toward Max. She reached up and put her hand on the lapel of his fuck ugly leather coat. "Max, I will let you take me to dinner, under one condition."

My fists clenched inside my pockets. What the hell was she doing?

"And what's that, beautiful?" He reached up toward her face. She took a step back and calmly blocked his hand with her forearm.

"You can take me to dinner tonight if you get down on your knees and blow Calon."

"WHAT?!" Max and I yelled in stereo. The visual in my head made me want to puke. I had no doubt Max felt the same way.

"No fucking way!" Max acted as though he actually thought she was serious. *Idiot.*

"Well, sorry, Max, but our deal's off. And I guess *I'll* just have to do it for you." She winked and walked toward me. Gene Krupa would have been proud of the *badum-ching* Bones banged out on Spider's snare drum, signaling Becki's score over Max. The guys all lost it! Even Max's guys laughed.

Becki's hands came up to my face and held me still. My jaw still clenched, I glared at Max over Becki's head. I was ready to rip his throat out.

"Calon, down here." Her voice was so calm and sultry, almost like she got off on putting Max in his place. "Calon, take your eyes off him and put your lips on mine this minute."

She didn't have to ask twice. She kissed me deep, and my mind went somewhere else. We could have been standing in the middle of a busy intersection, and I wouldn't have noticed. Becki Mowry stole my heart right out from under me. Her hands went to my ass, and she squeezed and pressed me into her.

"Come on!" Bones yelled and threw Spider's sticks. "This is getting ridiculous!"

"Bones, grab Spider's sticks. Let's practice our set. You stayin', Max?" I looked at him while still inside the loop of Becki's arms. He scoffed and shook his head. Frank, Troy, Ben, and Steve shook all of our hands, and they all headed out.

"Well, look at me, won't ya." Becki fell back onto the black leather couch that sat about six feet from my mic. "Private show by the hottest guys in LA."

"You think I'm hot?" Bones's chest puffed out. "Cal! Your girl wants me." Bones had himself so excited he tripped over the cord to his bass and fell on his ass.

WE PRACTICED FOR over two hours and then decided to head out to the nightclub we'd be playing on Friday to check out the vibe, see the stage and introduce ourselves to the management.

The line outside Paisley almost wrapped around the building. Bones drooled as his eyes raked over all the bare legs in line. There were definitely more women than men, which was good to know. Playing to a mostly female audience was very different than playing for a bar full of dudes.

"Dammit, Cal. We'll never get in here." Manny was the partier of the group. Bones could drink like it was an Olympic sport, but Manny loved everything about the nightlife. The dude didn't need sleep.

"Hang on, guys." Becki dove into the big hobo bag she always carried, pulled something out and spun on her heel. She looked back at us and smiled. "I got this. Hang tight." But before she walked toward the front of the line she adjusted her bright blue top to show just a little more cleavage and shimmied her form fitting black skirt further up her thighs. The gait she took off with was sexy and every guy in line thought so, too. I made a mental note to talk to her about that technique when we got back to the room later.

She returned in less than five minutes fanning herself with five bright blue cards on lanyards. She got to us and handed us each a V.I.P pass for the celebrity lounge on the second floor of Paisley.

"How'd you do this, Becki?" Spider asked.

"Well, while you guys were having a pissing contest with Max, I was at the printer having some business cards made up. The guy at the door recognized the band name from the posters hanging inside. He was happy to let you guys in.

As we followed her to the front of the line, I reached down with both hands and pulled her skirt down to a more acceptable length.

"Prude." She giggled, grabbed my hand, and snuggled into my side.

The entrance was a tubular hallway of neon lights. We made our way through, only getting stopped a couple times by people who knew who we were. The flashing tunnel opened up and the quiet hum grew louder and louder by the second. By the time we got to the bar, there were girls all around us. We were used to girls digging our music. We used to hang out with our female fans on our breaks at Mitchell's. They were fun girls we could laugh and joke with. Don't get me wrong, we'd been propositioned more than once, but we always respectfully declined. Well, except for Bones.

The term *groupies* always seemed seedy and dirty to me. I, personally, didn't like the word. But the girls at Paisley, yeah, they were closer to the groupie end of my measuring stick. We were being touched and groped and, as far as we knew, not one of them had ever seen us play. They were all over us, I assumed, just because our faces were plastered on the walls of the entryway.

"Cal, I feel like a piece of meat—and I love it!" Bones was grabbing and groping right back. He, of course, then followed a couple girls away from our group.

Spider and I both called, "Not it!"

"Shit!" Manny was always slow at that game. We all knew there had to be a chaperone assigned to Bones, or we'd lose him. It'd happened one too many times that we left a bar and headed to the van only to realize we were one man short. We'd eventually find him in someone's back seat, or he'd call from someone's apartment, but it always dragged the night out longer, and, quite frankly, it got annoying.

"You must be Calon." A beautiful blonde stood before me in a skin tight black tank and boobs that held their own zip code. I felt awkward because Becki was right next to me with her hand in my back pocket. I didn't want to flirt back, but at the same time I knew blowing off fans wasn't a good idea for any musician, especially an up and coming band. Becki's hand slowly slid out of my back pocket, and she slapped my ass.

"Go get 'em, rock star." She winked and linked arms with Manny. "Come on, Manny, we've got a bandmate to babysit." She was so fucking cool.

"Dude, I'll get us some pitchers." Spider headed to the bar.

I looked back down at the blonde, smiled and winked. "I am. And you are?"

"Adrienne." She whined her name then leaned in toward me and stood up on her toes. Her face was just a couple inches from mine, and I could smell about twelve tequila shots on her breath.

"Who are you here with, Adrienne?" I'm sure she took it as my way of finding out if she was available, but I truly just wanted to know who to drop her off with when I was ready to end our conversation.

"Just a couple friends of mine, but I'd like to go home with you." She winked and fell into my chest. I steadied her with my hands on her shoulders.

"Well, darlin', I really don't think that's a good idea." I felt like a dick, but, even if I wasn't madly in *something* with Becki, Adrienne wasn't my type. As old fashioned as it sounded, I wasn't made for one night stands or a quick fuck in the coatroom, and nothing, not even Adrienne, was going to change that about me.

She started to say something, but I noticed a head full of messy black hair out of the corner of my eye. The hair on the back of my neck stood on end even before I turned to see who it was.

Max had one hand on each of Becki's shoulders as if he was trying to hold her still. There were too many people crowded around Adrienne and me to see Becki's face, but I worried. My fists clenched and released then clenched again at my sides. I was more concerned about Becki's reaction to me stepping in than I was about taking a few hits from Max.

"I'm sorry, Adrienne, my friend needs me. It was really nice meeting you." Just then her drunk friends barreled up to us, which reminded me at the beginning of our short conversation I'd been concerned about just leaving her alone in such a crowded place. I had almost done that exact thing. It was obvious Becki trumped my chivalry. I smiled and nodded at her friends' giddy behavior just to be polite, but when I turned back around, Becki and Max were gone.

I stormed toward the edge of the dance floor where Max and Becki had been standing and looked around. Drunk people bumped me off balance, and a couple girls ran their hands along my back, but I didn't pay attention to anything except searching the room for Becki's bright blue top. I was livid. I was ready to strangle Max with my bare hands, but only after I beat the hell out of him with it first.

I had tunnel vision. I was panicked. God, if anything happened to Becki, I would never forgive myself. And where were Manny and Bones? Why were they not all sticking together like I thought they were going to? I must've spun around in that same spot ten times, each time scanning the room for Becki. I saw Bones and Manny step out of the men's room, and I took off. I bolted between kissing couples, I pushed people out of my way, all the while trying to get the guys' attention. They appeared to be looking around just as frantically as I had just been.

"Becki! Where is she?

"Dude, we were only in there a second. We told her to hang out at the bar."

"Max is here. I saw him with his hands on her, and then they disappeared."

I couldn't catch my breath. My grey t-shirt clung to me as sweat came to the surface of my skin. I ran my hands through my hair, and the three of us stood there like idiot dads who'd lost their kids at the toy store. *Shit.*

"Manny, were you guys anywhere else in this place? Are there any other dance floors or anything?"

"Yeah, the VIP rooms are upstairs. Maybe they're up there?"

"I'm gonna fuck him up. Where are the stairs?"

"Cal, listen, maybe it looks worse than it is. Becki's not gonna do anything with that douchebag." Manny was the eternal optimist.

"Not willingly. Go!" My heart pounded so violently, I was sure it would burst through my chest at any minute.

I don't remember going up the stairs. Suddenly, we were there at the top, all scanning the room for Max. The bouncer at the door nodded when he saw our VIP passes and granted us permission to be there. It was a big room with small seating areas partitioned off with sheer fabric.

"Cal!" Spider was about fifteen feet from us, standing by a tall table with three pitchers on it. "Becki's with Max, over there. I followed them up here. I was just about to text you." It was so loud, I'm really not sure if I actually heard him or just read his lips. Spider and I were the closest of the four of us. We were all super close, but Spider and I really tuned into each other's brains. He knew by the look on my face that I was ready to go ape shit if I didn't lay my eyes on her.

"Thanks, man." I grabbed one of the pitchers and sucked down what felt like half a six pack. It travelled cold and stinging down to my gut. I slammed the pitcher back on the table and bent a little at the waist with my hands on my thighs. I needed to handle this the right way. I had to calm down first. I couldn't get my head out of my heart, though. Max was with Becki, and I was pretty sure she had no interest in being with him.

Manny and Bones stood at the table with Spider as I watched what was happening behind the sheer fabric that was lit with pink and red recessed floor lights. Becki's back was to me, so I couldn't see her face, but her body was completely still. Her back was straight, and she sat sideways on the couch facing Max. One arm rested on the back of the couch, and her head leaned against her left fist. Her head flew back, and her laugh travelled back to where we stood. What the hell? I grabbed the pitcher again and barely swallowed, just poured the amber liquid into my blood stream. I didn't need to be wasted to kick someone's ass, and it would take more than a pitcher of beer to get me buzzed. But, there's a level of numbness that comes just before the buzz creeps up on you. Punches don't faze you in the least when that numbness sets in. I didn't *need* to be numb to fuck Max up, but I needed to be cool and not instigate anything when I approached them. Trouble was, I didn't know what it was Becki and I were doing, so there was a small part of me that worried he'd enamored her.

"Dude. Listen." Bones yelled over the techno vibe. "She's our manager. She's supposed to be schmoozing with the big guys, right?" Bones rarely had a good point but that was one.

"Right." I didn't take my eyes off them. I blinked hard a few times then took a couple deep breaths to calm my pulse, which was out of fucking control. I felt like I'd run three miles between getting to the top of the stairs and where we stood.

It was a strange duality. It was like everything in the room moved in slow motion, but, at the same time, everything my body did was revved up to Mach speed. I saw Max lean in, and I saw Becki plant her hands firmly on his chest. She leaned back into the arm of the couch, distancing herself. The wide neckline of her top slipped down over her shoulder, and the fucker leaned down and licked her uncovered bare shoulder.

I traveled across the room to their little nook in no time at all. On my way to her, there appeared to be a struggle. Max had the advantage and with one knee on the couch, he leaned over her. His hand moved up the inside of her thigh and under the edge of that short damn skirt she wore. He was about to have his liver removed through his nose when I got my hands on him.

"You fucking asshole!" I tore the sheath from the ceiling and threw it to the side, and in the same swoop with my arms I pushed Max off Becki. She screamed, and he regained his balance and stood and smiled. Smiled.

"Becki! The guys are over there. Go!"

Becki stood up right next to me. "Don't you bark at me, Calon Ridge!" My face spun to hers, and the disgust that flared in her eyes was vile.

"Becki! Go! I don't want you near this!" I turned back toward Max.

I'd allowed my eyes off him for way too long.

"This? What is *this* about, Calon?" Max was a dumbass for challenging me with semantics.

"You're hands all over Becki. That's what *this* is about, Max!" I motioned between us with my hand.

Just then the beat of "Tsunami" by Dvvbs and Borgeous bounced the floor. The music was so loud it's all I could hear. Max's mouth flapped, but I had no idea what he said. I didn't need to hear anything to read his cocky swagger as he walked toward me or the two middle fingers he shot up when he got within reach. That's when it all went down.

Max threw the first punch, seemingly in response to what he knew was coming his way. He caught me in the jaw, and I heard Becki shriek my name, but my head sprung back instantly, and my eyes locked on his. My fist connected with the side of his head right at his temple, and I felt something in my hand crack, but I felt no pain.

"Calon James! Knock it the fuck off!" Becki's voice was garbled, like it was coming at me through liquid.

I wanted to just leave with her and keep her safe, but the cocky motherfucker in front of me needed to *feel* the line I was drawing in the sand. He came at me again, this time he ducked and ran straight into my chest with his head. I curled my arms under his and brought them up violently and made contact with his chest with a deep thunk. I could feel the hit reverberate through my forearms. He staggered back, but his feet caught up with his body and he kept his footing.

"You think you're such a fuckin' hot shot, don't you?" He was calling *me* the hot shot?

I shook out the hand that hit him, and then ran it through my hair. I shoved the other hand in the pocket of my jeans. "Are we done, Max?" I had to yell over the music, and he was less than three feet from me. I drew my line. He needed to understand his boundaries if we were going on tour together, but I didn't need to kill him. We could be done as soon as he got the point.

"Dude, we're done when I walk out the front door with Becki." His lip curled when he said her name, which sent a shock through my body I'd never felt before. I could only imagine what went through his mind as her name rolled off his tongue. We weren't done.

I lost it and caught him in the head again with my fist. No doubt, I felt that one. I took another shot and made abrupt contact with his jaw then another. Becki was yelling, but I couldn't make sense of anything she said, the music was too loud. Someone grabbed me from behind and pulled me back. "Dude, he's not worth it, let's bounce. C'mon, Cal, don't do this." Spider, always the voice of reason.

I nodded and wrestled my arms back from him. I took a deep breath and calmly walked back over to where Max was crouched, trying to get up.

"Max, you were out of line." I crouched down in front of him and watched him wipe the blood coming from his nose with the back of his hand. I didn't want to apologize. I wanted to continue smashing his head with my fist, but that wasn't how I wanted people to see me. "Stay away from her. She's not yours to take."

"And I'm not yours to *take* either!" Becki's voice was loud and clear as the song ended. I stood and turned to her. She didn't say another word, but her eyes said it all. I'd disappointed her. That revelation stung way worse than if she'd just punched me in the gut.

seven

"ONE SINGLE ROOM, please." I cleared my throat so the vibrato of my voice would appear to be something other than the betrayal of my tough exterior.

The elevator doors closed, and when it lifted I got that familiar wave in my stomach. I thought back to one of the nights in my dorm with Calon. He and I were in my dorm talking. On that particular night I challenged him to a duel of sorts. I bet him a back rub that in just three sentences I could describe a sexier scene than he could.

summer flashback

"LADIES FIRST." HE raised an eyebrow and shifted his body so I fell back into his lap. He lightly touched my hair and all I could think about was the part of him my head was resting on. I had to cross my legs to ease the pulsing between them. I had no idea what the hell was wrong with me, it was so odd that I had not yet undressed this god that shared the space on my bed with me. I wasn't shy or awkward when it came to letting a guy know what I wanted. Gracie did that good girl thing way too well; made me look like a slut. She always laughed when I said that.

"They sat at the corner table with the least amount of light." I held up one finger, signaling the end of my first sentence. "She reached under the table, and he'd already freed his cock from his jeans, which just added to the wetness already soaking in her panties." I raised my second finger. "As she reached for him, his hand shot up her skirt and in one movement, pushed her panties to the side and entered her with two thick fingers." I held my three fingers in his face and made a cocky clicking sound with my mouth.

"Not bad for a beginner." Calon chuckled.

"Beginner? I do believe I felt my headrest rise during those three sentences."

"Nah, just so much in there—"

"Yeah, yeah, don't change the subject, rock star. Gimme what you got."

He cleared his throat, laced his fingers, stretched his arms out in front of him, and cracked his knuckles. He bumped his head to either shoulder and took a deep breath. It was all I could do to not crack up. He really was a goof ball. He silently raised one finger, counting his first sentence before he even spoke.

"He pressed her tight against the mirrored wall of the elevator, leaned down just far enough to reach under her thighs and lift her so her tight ass was above his hips. His pants fell to the floor, and before the change that jingled across the floor stopped spinning, he was inside her. With each thrust he pounded into her, she let out a whimper until the thrusts quickened and they shattered from a climax so intense they crumbled to the floor, spent and drenched in lust."

I stared up at his face. He waved three long fingers between us. My mouth hung open like an idiot, and I had no smart comeback, no sarcastic stab. I was speechless, and my panties were soaked. I sat up and continued to gawk.

"Roll over, you cocky son of a bitch, you won." He flashed that flawless smile that undid me a little further each time I saw it and lifted his shirt over his head then laid face down on my bed. I straddled him to rub his back. I knew just a few rolls of my hips and I'd come right there as I sat on his ass.

I SMILED AT the memory, swiped my keycard, and walked into my room. It was dark and cold inside. My smile faded when I caught a glimpse of myself in the mirror that took up most of the wall of the entry hallway. My face was sad, and my eyes held a confusion I wasn't sure even I could pinpoint. I threw the bags I'd grabbed from the guys' room onto the floor and kicked off my shoes. I bolted both locks on the door and walked across the cold tile of the bathroom. Another mirror. *Dammit.* I turned on the water and looked at my reflection staring back at me. I watched as the steam erased me completely.

I stood motionless under the hot water. I wished the water that streamed down over me and left red hot trails, could erase the confusion in my heart as easily as the steam had erased my reflection. Part of me loved that Calon took on the knight in shining armor role, but a bigger part of me was pissed that he assumed I *needed* him to do that. I don't need anyone. And I don't ever want to feel like someone's belonging. There was a big difference between belonging and *being* a belonging. I didn't mind the former, but I despised the latter.

I could hear my phone vibrate on the bathroom counter, but it wasn't going to pull me from the state I was in. I'd never felt so into someone, but, at the same time, I felt so alone. I never expected I'd allow a relationship leave me feeling on edge and unsure. Maybe it was just me. I needed a good Gracie fix. I finished my shower at a quicker pace than I'd started it. I wrapped my hair in one puffy white towel and my body in another then grabbed my phone. There were thirteen missed calls, all from Calon. I dialed Gracie and jumped under the covers of the one lonely bed in my lonely room.

"Becki? You okay?" Her voice was gravelly, and I realized what time it was.

"Gracie, I'm so sorry. I had no idea it was after two o'clock. Go to sleep. I'll call you in the morning."

"Becki, it's okay. We were watching a movie, and I fell asleep on the couch. It's a blow 'em up, blood and guts one, anyway. I'd be happy to leave Jake and Sam to their testosterone fest." I heard her whisper something, then it sounded like she jogged back to his bedroom. "Okay. I'm all ears. I've had a quick power nap, so I'm wide awake."

"So, tonight, Calon beat the shit out of Max, the lead singer of Smiling Turkeys, because he saw him make a move on me at a bar tonight."

"Oh, Becki, that had to be the hottest thing ever." She made a *Mmm* sound under her breath.

"It wasn't. Well, it was. But I got pissed and left. Took a taxi alone back to the hotel and got myself my own room. I am livid. Like I can't handle a lanky guy with wandering hands?" I leaned forward and rested my forehead on the duvet cover that draped across my bended knees.

"Becki, stop. You realize where all this is coming from, right? You can see that, can't you?"

"I… huh? I don't know what you mean. Do I? Should I?" My head pounded, and I was lost in the thought that I could be so unaware of what was going on inside me while Gracie could hit it right on the head.

"Becki, think about it. Remember how Jesse was?" A set of deep brown eyes flashed into my mind, and I could almost hear his voice saying my name. Jesse was my high school boyfriend, and he was incredibly possessive. He beat up more than one guy just for looking at me for too long in the hallway. He sent Jonathan Terrence to the hospital after he went into a seizure during one of Jesse's insane smack downs. It disgusted me.

"But, Gracie, Calon is nothing like Jesse. God, Jesse was sixteen. Calon's twenty-two." I rubbed my head and tried to focus.

"You're right. He doesn't even compare to the man Calon is. But what happened tonight may have triggered your memories of Jesse, which in turn triggered a Jesse reaction. You've gotta let your guard down with Calon, Becki. You'll destroy him if you don't let him in. He's super intuitive but also doesn't believe he deserves good things, and, trust me, you are the goodest thing he knows."

"Goodest? Really, smart girl?" I laughed out loud and wiped what looked a lot like a tear from my cheekbone.

"Just seeing if you're paying attention. Becki, promise me that if you can't bare your soul to Calon, you'll let him go before he gets too tangled up in you. The guy can't handle any more heartbreak in his life."

"Gracie Ann Jordan, don't guilt me into staying with your second favorite guy just because you want him to be happy."

"Get real. Chicks before dicks. I'd never put his heart before yours. But, just be careful, you both deserve the big love I know you both have just under the surface." She giggled, knowing what my reaction would be.

"Gag." I rubbed my eyes on the sheet and looked at the streaks of residual mascara I left behind. "So you think I overreacted."

"I do, Becki, but not because you chose to. It's just something you're gonna have to get through together. Calon's reaction was based on his past, too. He's had to protect the women in his life from some pretty nasty situations, and I am sure it was a gut reaction for him to want to kill someone who was overstepping what should've been a respectable, professional boundary."

"I get it. I just don't know how to turn it off. I was really pissed."

"So, you're not now?"

"I'm not. Ugh. I'm such an idiot. I'm going to screw this boy up more than he already is if I'm not careful."

"Then *be* careful, Becki. There's something big just around the corner for the two of you. I just know it. I can see it in yours and Calon's eyes when you're together. You just have some walls to scale, that's all."

"Yeah."

"You good?"

"I'm good. Now go finish your movie." My voice was more upbeat after such a short conversation. It took Gracie five minutes to translate what would have taken me days. Thank God for Gracie… every girl should have one.

"I'm not going back out there. I'm gonna strip and get under the covers and wait." She was absolutely giddy over her seductive self.

"Thatta girl! Love you, G."

"Love you right back, B. Now, call Calon!" She giggled and hung up.

Shit. Now I had to straighten everything out with Calon. *Dammit.* I lay back on the pile of pillows I'd stacked behind me while I was talking to Gracie. My heart was racing, and my stomach felt like there were a thousand butterflies inside. I usually didn't let guys do this to me. In fact, I'd never let any guy do to me what Calon had done.

I guess after my dad left, my heart secured itself inside my chest and decided that's where it would stay. I wouldn't give it away again. So, Jesse and Shawn only got my surface. My relationships with each of them could have been considered long term but, as far as boyfriends go, they really were just convenient place holders until someone would steal my heart right out of my chest. That's exactly what Calon had done. I just somehow always thought I'd have a say in it, but I didn't.

Calon was beautiful, inside and out. He wasn't tainted by the pain he'd endured so far in his life, at least not as tainted as I'd been. He was kind and receptive and open to the love that was blooming between us. At least it seemed that way. Maybe he was as tormented by his feelings and scars as I was but was just better at swallowing all of it. I didn't swallow well. That thought made me giggle, because that was true in all areas of my life with boys. My phone buzzed with a text. When I saw his name and the thirteen missed calls again, my stomach flipped over itself.

Calon: *Hey*

Me: *Hey*

Calon: *You ok?*

Me: *I think so.*

Calon: *I was worried.*

Me: *No need to worry. I can take care of myself.*

Calon: *That's obvious.*

I just sat and stared at his short sentences on my screen. I pictured him sitting on the end of the bed in their hotel room, head down, elbows on his knees. My fingers hovered over the keys, and I tried to think of what to say next. I felt like I owed him an explanation, but he really deserved more than a texted conversation.

Calon: *Are you at the hotel?*

Me: *Yeah. You?*

Calon: *Yeah.*

I wished I could see his face.

Calon: *Becks?*

Me: *Calon?*

Calon: *I'm sorry.*

Me: *Thanks. Me too. Are you mad?*

Calon: *What are you sorry for? And no, not mad. Confused.*

Me: *I'm sorry for freaking out. I don't think I'm mad anymore.*

Calon: *I want to see you.*

Me: *Room 227. Hurry.*

I hopped up, threw on sweats and a t-shirt from my bag, ran to the bathroom and put my hair up in a bun, then sat cross-legged in the center of the bed and waited. And waited. What the hell was taking him so long? The other room was just a couple floors up, not across town,

The knock on the door made me jump and woke up the damn butterflies in my stomach. When I stood, my legs felt unsteady beneath me. I stopped and took a deep breath to calm my nerves. I wasn't sure which emotion would make its way out first.

I peeked out the peep hole. His face was so sad, his eyes looked down toward his feet. One hand was shoved into his jeans pockets, and he shifted his weight to the left just as his other hand drug through the curls on the top of his head. I unlocked the door and opened it slowly, my face matching his in discontent.

"Oh, hi, rock star. You wanna come in?" I tried to smile to ease the tension.

His head still bowed, he peeked up through his thick top lashes and smiled slightly. I moved to the side and motioned with my hand. He dipped his shoulder and walked into the room and sat on the edge of the bed. His t-shirt was torn on one side, and his knuckles were bloody. He planted his elbows on his thighs and clasped his hands between his knees and winced. His face still aimed at the floor. I hated how ashamed he seemed to feel.

"Calon—"

"Don't, Becks, I owe you an apology. I acted like a dick, and I embarrassed you. I'm really sorry, it's just, Max. Fuck! He was using you to try and prove something, and I wasn't going to let him do that to you. Ya know?"

I got down on my knees in front of him and sat back on my heels. "Calon, if what you did was to prove a point to Max, then that's childish bullshit. But I think you did it to keep me safe, and that's something entirely different."

"He almost copped a feel under your skirt. I saw his hand on the inside of your thigh, and I knew what would happen next if I didn't make him stop. Becki, I'm sorry for my comment about you not being his to take."

"Calon, look, I'm such a mess, and I didn't even know it. I thought I had all my shit together and, apparently, I don't. See, I had this boyfriend in high school, Jesse, who was insanely possessive and would beat guys up on a weekly basis if they looked at me, talked to me, helped me with a project, or anything else. When you flew into Max, all I saw was you proving a point, I was yours to keep."

"But, Becks, I want you to be mine. Not mine because you *belong* to me but mine because you'll let me hold your whole heart. Does that make sense?" He was nervous, and I wasn't used to seeing this side of my sure-of-himself boyfriend.

"It does make sense. The thought of handing you my whole heart makes me panic because then what happens when you walk away? What does it feel like to put a used heart back in my chest?"

"Becki, listen." He reached for my face. His warm hands cradled my cheeks, and his thumbs rubbed my cheekbones so lightly I shivered. "I'm not asking you to turn your entire life over to me. Maybe I'm not even asking you to *give* me your heart. I just want you to trust me with it."

I smiled. His face was perfect, his bouncy curls dropped down in front of his evergreen eyes each time he spoke. His eyes sucked me in. Their color unlike any I'd ever seen. They were mesmerizing. I took a deep breath, closed my eyes, and said three words I'd never said to any male in my life. "I trust you."

He sat up straight. The smile on his face grew, and there was an ornery twinkle in his eye that I found myself completely turned on by. I stood when he did, my face still cradled in his hands.

"Becki, I have never felt for anyone what I feel for you. Tonight, when you left and I had no idea where you were, my chest actually ached. It was like someone carved a part of my heart from my chest. I thought I'd just lost the best thing that ever happened to me. My chest hurt worse than my hand did when I punched Max."

My stomach rolled. I took his punching hand in mine and brought his knuckles to my lips and kissed then gently. He winced. "Oh, God. I'm so sorry! Your knuckles."

He cracked up. "Becki. Chill. It's fine. I'm just messing with you. It really doesn't hurt."

"Oh, so your chest really didn't hurt all that bad when I left the club."

"Huh? Yeah it did. Why?"

"Well, you said your chest hurt worse than your hand did when you punched Max. So, if your hand doesn't really hurt then…" I smiled, I was just being corny. I got what he was trying to say.

"My hand *did* hurt. When I hit him the first time, I felt it crack. That hurt like a bitch. But, then the adrenaline just takes over and everything goes numb, ya know?" He pulled me in for a hug. I turned my head and pressed it to his neck. I took a deep breath and almost died. Fuck. He smelled incredible. I could have thrown him down on the bed, stripped him, and rode him until the sun came up. But, shit, the guy was practically a virgin, so that wasn't going to happen.

"Calon?" I tipped my head back and looked up at him.

"Yeah?" He gently brushed the hair off my cheeks. He tried to tuck some behind my ears but failed, and it fell right back in front of my face.

"Are we okay? I mean, we didn't just take a step backwards, did we?" I kissed him on the chin.

"If anything, Becks, we took a step forward. We're breaking down walls and being bare ass honest with each other. That's definitely a step in the right direction."

Bare ass. He said those two words, and I barely heard the rest of what he said. Dammit. "Pinch me."

"Pinch you?" He cocked his head to the side and raised an eyebrow.

"I need to snap out of something. No one's ever done this to me." My eyes fluttered when I said it. It was such a cliché thing to say, and I was so not cliché. I usually hated those terms and catch phrases that you read about couples saying to each other in those sappy romance novels. But maybe there was something to be said for being sappy and cliché. I mean, sometimes there was no better way to say it. So, there must be some validity to it. "Was that weird?"

Calon practically cackled. "Weird? Was *what* weird?"

"The thing I just said. Oh, shit. It was so weird, wasn't it?"

"Becki, you've got to stop worrying about every single thing you say and think. Just be who you are. Just be."

Just be who you are. Kind of cliché, but so much depth to it. Did I know how to just be? I didn't. I knew I didn't. I didn't even know who I was. Maybe that was my problem. I took a deep breath, and the words just fell from my mouth. I didn't plan them, just said them. "When my dad left, I needed to step up and help my mom. I didn't let myself get caught up in all the typical teen girlie things all my friends did, because I felt like I was solely responsible for my mom's sanity. I've never been one to 'just be'. But it sounds nice; so healthy and pure and real. Calon, I'm really not as tough as I let people think I am. I think I even have Gracie snowed for the most part."

"Just be… with me. I don't care if you fake it with the rest of the planet. I want you to *just be* with me." Oh, there was nothing more I wanted to do than *be* with him right that minute. Like, *BE* with him.

I wrapped my arms around his neck and crashed into his mouth. He chuckled a little into my mouth as he tried to match my fervor. He tasted of beer and Calon. Our heads tilted in opposite directions as our lips slid over one another's. His tongue danced with mine; a gentle but persuasive dance. He kissed me deeply. His hands left my face and landed on my hips. Strong fingers grasped the fabric of my sweatpants, and he grunted softly as if he were wishing them away. I dropped my hands from his curls and looped my thumbs inside the waistband. Warm hands and strong fingers kneaded my hips, his thumbs on my hipbones.

"Becki," he spoke my name against my mouth. It was barely audible as it fell from his lips, more like a breath with a tune.

I didn't answer, just pulled away from his mouth and looked up at his strong smooth face. His eyes were closed, and his long dark lashes rested against the top of his cheeks. They slowly opened, and it took him more effort to lift them than it should have. His eyes focused on mine, and I didn't need to say anything. He knew what I was giving him permission to do. I wanted all of him. I was ready to just be.

He took a step back, reached inside the back neckline of his shirt, and pulled it up over his head. I was frozen, and my jaw dropped when his shirt hit the floor. I couldn't help it. I'd imagined what his bare chest looked like, but, until that moment, I had never actually seen it. It was firm and defined but not too much. And, oh my fuck, his abs. It was obvious he worked on his abs, too. My eyes raked down across each ripple of muscle. Everything inside me clenched when I reached the dark hair just below his belly button that disappeared behind the button of his jeans. I longed to feel his skin against mine.

As I closed the space between us, I smiled at all the times I'd stood in the front row at Alternate Tragedy's shows and practically came in my shorts just watching how sensual Calon was when he sang.

"What's so funny?" He rested his forearms on my shoulders and made a ponytail at the base of my neck with his hands.

"Just thinking of all the times I fantasized about this happening." I suddenly felt shy about him knowing that.

"Really?" The look on his face was honest disbelief, but how in the world could he not know that every girl in the bar was having inappropriate thoughts as he sang?

"It's your voice, Calon. You could peel the clothes off a roomful of women if you wanted to." I could no longer control myself. I placed my hands lightly on his chest and brushed each one up over his collarbone and down his strong shoulders, down his forearms and to his bare stomach. The pulsing happening deep inside me got stronger, more intense.

"I could sing to you right now, Becks. I mean, if you wanted me to." That damn crooked curl at the corner of his mouth melted me. I was so mesmerized by this man I had to consciously make an effort to keep my walls down and take him all in. I needed to focus on how I felt and give myself permission to react instinctively.

"I would die." I took a step past him and sat on the end of the bed.

"Okay, you ready?"

I nodded my head as I mouthed 'no', and he smiled, rubbed his face with both hands then put them in his pockets. It was Calon's signature stance, and it was hot. His one leg bent and unbent just the tiniest bit, keeping beat to a song that hadn't made its way out of him yet. He closed his eyes and dropped his head back as his whole body moved seductively to that quiet beat. He hummed a soft tune then closed his eyes and sang.

Girl, my body aches.
My head, it spins.
Everything about you wrecks me.
I long for you more each day.

His voice was deep, smooth, and sultry. His eyes still closed. As he continued to sing, I was melting.

My heart, it's pulling you in.
Don't leave me. Don't walk away.

He opened his eyes, and they met mine. The sadness that usually floated just under their surface had turned to hope.

Girl, you wreck me.
My heart, it's singing our song.
Let me hold you, touch you...
I wanna be inside you.

After that verse, a fire burned in his eyes that only one thing could extinguish. And that one thing was about to happen. *Holy shit.* I stood and walked over to him, tucked my fingers in his waistband, and unbuttoned and unzipped his jeans. Unable to help myself, I looked down. Tight gray boxer briefs stretched over something I coveted.

"Show me, Calon," I instructed breathlessly. My heart raced and my hands trembled.

He flashed that cocky smirk again, but then it turned into a shy grin. He pushed his jeans down and let them fall to the floor. He stepped out of them then ducked his head and looked at me through his top eyelashes. "Becks, it's been a long time—a really, really long time."

"Calon, it's okay," was all I could force out. Every pump of my heart was so intense everything that could throb throbbed. I wanted to comfort him somehow, so I did what made the most sense. I pulled my tank over my head and shook my hair out when its length got tangled. I stood and dropped my sweatpants. I had nothing under them to block his view of all of me. I slowly lifted my eyes to Calon's. His eyes were hungry. I stepped out of my sweatpants and draped my arms over his broad shoulders. "Just be."

I kept my hands on his shoulders as he bent forward and dragged the briefs down over his hips, down past his strong thighs. They fell to the floor when they got to his knees. He stood slowly and nervously rubbed his forehead and winced with one eye when his face reached mine.

"I don't know… I'm not…"

"Show me how to touch you, Calon." I leaned up and kissed him.

The hand that rubbed his forehead slid slowly down his chest. My eyes followed that hand. He was going to show me. I watched as he touched his abs from the top ridges down past his hip to the front of his thigh. I felt him take a deep breath and hiss it out through his clenched teeth. He took himself into his hand with a firm grip. His long fingers wrapped around and barely met his thumb on the other side. It sent shivers up my spine when I realized how thick that made him. He slowly pumped himself. Once. Twice.

My eyes fluttered, and I reached down to cup his balls. When my palm touched his warm skin, he sucked in a sharp breath. Grabbing my wrist, he gently restrained me from moving while he caught his breath. Calon shook his head, let his hand fall from my wrist and then moved his feet apart just a little, so I could get my hand all the way around. We were both panting. I lifted my eyes to his, and there was a second we just stared. That stare was a whole conversation between us.

"Touch all of me, Becks."

I reached and covered his hand with mine. I squeezed a little, and he gasped. His hand slowly slid out from under mine, and he cupped my breast. His thumb rubbed my nipple hard as I gently pulled my hand toward me, and he let out a low growl. I felt him get harder in my hand, which made him thicker than my grasp. I was dizzy, probably from the heavy breathing.

"Becks, your body… I've thought about this so many times."

I let go of him and put my hands on my hips to lighten the mood enough to catch my breath. "You were picturing me naked?" I hated how breathy my voice sounded, but I pushed that thought from my mind in yet another attempt to relax and just be.

Calon's hands dropped to his sides, and his head bobbed. "Really? You think I could lay in your bed and on your lap and under your covers all those times and not imagine how a scene like this would go?"

"You did? 'Cause I was doing the same thing." I blushed and reached around and grabbed his ass cheeks, pulling his hips into me hard and quick. He grunted and ran his fingers through my hair and down my back.

"So, if you thought about me naked, and I thought about you naked, you think we both did the same thing after I left your place?" A grin spread across his face quickly.

"Ew. You jacked off outside my dorm? That is super creepy, Calon."

"No!" He was adamant, but then his expression turned slightly guilty. He dropped his chin a little. "Well… not outside your dorm. In the privacy of my apartment, I may or may not have pretended your hands were on me." He guided me backwards toward the bed.

"Oh!" God, that was hot. The bed hit me on the backs of my legs, and I fell back onto my elbows with Calon standing between my knees.

"Now it's your turn. Show me what you did after I left, Becks."

So, there I was, completely naked and now he was asking me to… touch *myself* for *him*.

Just be.

"Well, Calon, let me show you." I slid back, so my legs were no longer dangling off the end of the bed. I propped myself up on my elbow, bent one knee and stuck my thumb in my mouth and sucked. His eyes rolled back but not all the way as though he was afraid allowing them to do that would keep him from seeing everything I was about to do. I took my entire breast in my hand and brushed my wet thumb across my already peaked nipple. The tingling that it caused ran from my nipple in a straight line to where my hand was headed.

He was breathless. "Becks."

My hand left my breast and trailed down my ribs, then my stomach, and stopped on my hip bone. I let myself fall back onto the bed, and, without a second thought, I brought my hand back to my mouth and sucked my forefinger then let it glide back down my stomach.

My eyes flashed up to Calon, and he was standing motionless at the edge of the bed between my ankles, my legs spread open in front of him. I could see the hunger in his eyes, but I was going to take this further than he expected. My right knee fell to the side, opening me up even more for him. There were uncontrollable spasms inside me, and I couldn't stand it any longer. My hand shot down between my legs and into the pleats of wet skin that burned with Calon's gaze. A moan escaped my lips, and my finger circled the tiny nub that was the center of the universe to both of us at that very moment.

My eyes slid up Calon's thighs to his hand that was once again grasping himself, but this time he wasn't shy. I almost came. I pushed myself up on my elbows again.

"Calon, I can't do this." My chest was heaving, and I could hear the blood pumping in my ears.

A sudden disappointment crossed his face, and the hand he was pleasuring himself with stopped moving. "I… I—"

"No, Calon, I meant, if I touch myself while you're touching yourself, I'm going to explode before we even go any further."

Relief washed across his face, and he chuckled softly. "Tell me what you want."

I felt like the walls were pulsing along with the sound in my head.

"Make love to me." I gasped as soon as the words were out of my mouth. It was just a matter of seconds until every fantasy I'd ever had about this beautiful man standing over me came to fruition.

"I was hoping that's what you wanted, beautiful." He dropped forward with his hands on either side of my hips. He dipped his head and kissed me on those lips again, very gently but with just enough pressure to make me unravel. Then, without warning, his tongue broke the surface and skimmed down through my folds, and then his face was buried deep.

I thrust my fingers into his hair and grabbed two big handfuls of curls. "Calon, wait!"

He lifted his head, and I could see the sheen of my wetness on his lips and chin. I grunted at the sight, and he laughed. My eyes closed, but I felt the bed dip in enough places to know he was climbing up toward me. When my eyes sprung open, he was mere centimeters from my face. I could smell me on his mouth. He didn't move, but his eyes flitted around my face. He glanced at my eyes, my lips, my nose, and then back to my eyes. "You wanted me to wait. Well, I'm waiting." His voice was smooth and deep.

I wrapped my legs around him and pressed my heels into his firm ass. He didn't budge. I glanced down at the space between our bodies and peeked one more time at the large part of him that hovered just above my hips. He slowly lowered his body into mine and held himself up on his elbows right by my shoulders on the bed. He used his hands to brush my hair back. He was taking all of me in one bit at a time, as though he wanted to make sure he would never forget one second of our first time. He licked his lips.

"Becki, I want you to know that it's not just happenstance that's kept me from going this far with anyone over the past few years. I need you to know that it was a purposeful decision, one I didn't make lightly. I'm positive what I'm feeling right now wouldn't be nearly as intense if I hadn't waited for the perfect soul to crash into.

"I knew there was someone out there, someone who would one day cross my path that deserved as much as I could give her. Becki, that someone is you. I want to make love to you so bad it hurts but not because I've been horny for the last four years and not just because you're a beautiful naked women lying on a hotel bed underneath me. I wouldn't want to share this moment with anyone else but you. What I feel for you runs so deep I barely have words to do it justice. I love you, Becki Mowry. I love you."

You love me?

He leaned down and kissed me so passionately it sent shivers through me. Our breathing increased again, and I could feel his heart against my chest. Holy fuck, he loved me.

He tilted his hips just enough that I could feel the hot skin he pressed against my opening, and then he pressed into me so achingly slow I could feel my insides grabbing for him. The stretching that needed to happen for my body to accommodate the size of Calon was the most perfect pain I've ever endured. He slid the rest of the way in, and then his entire body stilled.

"I just want to feel you."

"God, Calon. You're... really... big... you... know... that?" My words came out in staccato similar to the rhythm body squeezed around him.

"Did I hurt you, Becks? That's why I went slow, so it wouldn't hurt." He rubbed my cheeks with his thumbs and kissed me on my nose.

"It's the most beautiful thing I've ever felt, Calon. It's never felt that way before." I picked up my head, so I could reach his lips to suck his bottom lip into my mouth. He groaned.

"So, it's the first time for both of us, just not in the conventional sense of the phrase." He wiggled his hips a little and took my breath away.

I nodded and tried to hold back the tears, or he would really think he hurt me, when he'd actually done the opposite. In that short sentence he peeled away years of tough skin and healed a part of me I wasn't proud of. There were times in my life I used sex to self-medicate: I barely even remember my first time it was such a non-event, and I regretted that. The words he spoke were a mirror into his heart, a mirror that reflected a love that didn't give a rat's ass about how many guys I'd been with. He really was my first, because sex had never, not once, touched my soul like it did with Calon, and we'd only just begun.

There was a beautiful burn as he pulled himself almost completely out of me and then gently and ever so slowly entered me again.

"Calon. Oh. My. God. You feel so incredible." I could explain the physical feeling of him, but, when paired with the deep emotional connection that accompanied our bodies becoming one, there were no words in the English language that would do that feeling justice.

"Becki, you're grabbing me, pulling me in. I've never dreamed it would feel like this."

The rhythm of his thrusts picked up speed, and I squeezed him harder with my legs that were still wrapped tightly around him. I tilted my hips up, and he slid his arms under me and grabbed onto my shoulders from behind. He pulled against my body each time he pumped into me. My body slid down his, and his body raked over mine headed in the opposite direction, which opened me up to his body grinding across my most sensitive spot and bringing me closer and closer to a torrent of sensations with each movement.

"Calon. Oh, Calon. Slow down. I don't want this to be over yet."

His body immediately slowed, and then he did something I would never have expected. First, he moved his arms out from under me and placed them back beside my head and took my face in his hands. A look washed over his face that took me somewhere else. We were all that existed. His body and mine, intertwined and fit together like we had searched our whole lives to find each other.

He brought his face to mine and kissed me deeply. His tongue tangled with mine, and he tasted me in a way that kept everything around him clenching. Then he pulled back a little, so he could look into my eyes as he softly sang.

Baby, this is it.
What we've craved all along.
I've got you in my grip
We're singing a brand new song.

With each verse of his beautiful song he moved in and out of me slowly. He caressed my face and sang to my heart

Your eyes are my peace.
Your heart's got mine in tow.
Your body is my release
Like it's all I've ever known.

He stopped completely after the last verse, and then while completely inside me, he began to roll his hips in a circular motion, which took the sensations to still another level. I closed my eyes and lifted my chin toward the ceiling as a means to try and control what I felt so I didn't come yet.

This is beauty defined
Our hearts sharing one beat
Our souls intertwined
You're all I'll ever need.

I was convinced I was dreaming. There was no way it was really this unbelievable in real life. Holy shit! Every pore was craving him. I needed more of him. I needed to come with him.

"Calon. I have no words." I was breathless. He smiled and continued to stare into my eyes. What he was doing to my body was incredible, but the way he just touched my heart and awoke my soul… this was what all the hype was about. This is what had Gracie gushing. This was it. It was real.

I put my hands on either side of his strong and beautiful face. I rubbed his nose with mine. I parted my lips to speak something I didn't know I could feel so soon. But, he captured my mouth in his, and as he kissed me deeply, he began thrusting into me again, faster this time. He spoke the next four words against my mouth.

"Come with me, Becki."

He straightened his arms and threw his head back. My eyes rolled back in my head, and we lost all control. Together. There was a twinge of nervous energy as we passed into territory I'd not experienced. The swell of pure ecstasy overwhelmed me, but I wanted this so badly I rode the wave no matter where it took me.

We panted. Our bodies bucked, and our voices growled and whined. We called out each other's names, and then as if our bodies spoke to each other, our rhythm increased and the sensations intensified. I opened my eyes just as Calon looked down at me. His eyes fluttered, and I could tell he was just as close as I was and the explosion of what we were together was about to happen.

"Calon! I'm… I'm gonna come." I thrust my hips up against his and unintentional sounds made their way from my lips.

He wrapped his arms under me again and held onto my shoulders, pulling me into him. "Yeah, baby. Come with me. God, Becki. Now!"

When Calon started grunting, and I could feel the strain of his back muscles under my fingers, I let go. Waves crashed over me, and I lost all control. We thrust harder and harder as we chased something bigger than the two of us, and with each thrust we came closer and closer to climax.

I dug my nails into his shoulders, and he clenched mine. I felt him swell inside me, and that was my undoing. I started to come, and he followed suit. We writhed. We were wild and loud, and it was so real, so raw, and so right. We bucked against one another and both came so hard, my legs and arms sprung from around him. My feet slammed into the bed at the same time my hands slapped the mattress beside me and captured handfuls of sheets. At that moment he was fucking me, I had to let go in surrender to an orgasm that threatened to shatter me, but he held on and pumped the rest of what he had into me. Then he slowed just as I hit the end of my climax and after a couple shakes and twitches our bodies went lax, and we tried to catch our breath. The sheets were wet underneath me, our bodies slick between us from sweat, and there was as scent that hung low in the air that was primal.

He slowly rolled off of me and onto his side. I couldn't move. I couldn't speak. I wasn't sure I could even see. I turned my head toward him and forced my eyes open. He reached over and laid his hand on the side of my face and touched my lips with the pad of his thumb. Unspoken words hung in the air between us. At first, I hesitated, but then I took a deep breath, licked my lips, and spoke them.

"I love you, Calon Ridge." His eyes fluttered, and he gasped. Hesitant tears burned my eyes, and we both laughed. We were in love. Real love for the first time. Calon was my first in so many ways.

eight

Calon

I COULD HEAR Becki singing in the shower, which made me smile. She had damn good taste in music, but she couldn't hold a tune to save her life. I lay in bed, overcome with the excitement of the beginning of something big but, at the same time, an overwhelming sense of desistance. Somehow in the act of making love to and professing my love for Becki, my past became just that, my past. Never in all my life had I experienced a love like what I felt for Becki, and it came on so strong and so quickly. It had left me emotionally flailing to make sense of any of it for the past few months. My emotions were all over the place, and I was glad to have a moment alone to sort out what I was feeling. Not because I wanted to hide my emotions from Becki, I just wasn't sure I could put what I felt into words, and I just needed to work through that myself, alone.

There were tears but not tears of sadness. Simply four years of tangled up emotions pouring from me and leaving room behind to fill the ache in my chest for what I could safely assume was the love of my life. I was comforted by the closure I felt. I didn't need to forget my past or where my heart had been and how it had been hurt. I just needed to be able to let go of those emotions and move on. My past was still part of where I'd been and who I was because of what I went through with Chloe, the abuse

I'd suffered at the hands of more than one of my mom's boyfriends, the accident, and my confusion over Gracie, but it wasn't taking up any of my heart anymore. Realizing I was in love with Becki, being forthright with those feelings, and having her reciprocate them had given my soul permission to move on and finally let go and accept all that life had thrown at me.

When Becki walked out wrapped in a towel, I realized how long I'd laid there trying to sort out the tornado of emotions coursing through me.

"Hi." Her voice was timid, and her smile sweet.

"Hey there, beautiful." I winked and patted the bed next to me.

"You're very naked. Don't you wanna cover up or something?" She sat and looked me up and down.

"Do you want me to?" I folded my arms behind my head and stretched out a little. She shook her head and raked her eyes up and down my body one more time. Her eyes passed more slowly over my cock than any other part of me, which brought it to a more firm state, and that made her giggle. She leaned down and kissed me.

"Calon, I have never... I don't have... just, wow." She climbed over me and slid between the sheets. I pulled my arm out from under my head, so she could use me as a pillow.

"Yeah, me too, Becks. I love you." I loved the way that felt rolling off my tongue.

"You said that already." She giggled.

"I know I did. I just want you to realize that, although I was completely caught up in the moment, I would never have said those words if there was even the tiniest sliver of uncertainty. There's none. I love you, absolute!"

"I like that you absolutely love me." She smirked.

"No, I meant it the way I said it—I love you, absolute." I turned and kissed her forehead. She flipped onto her stomach and propped herself up on her elbows. She reached across my chest and grabbed her phone from the night stand. She tapped the screen a bunch of times, and then looked at me out of the corner of her eye then back at her phone.

"You do know what that means, right?" She smiled, knowing I was a pretty damn good lyricist, so challenging me on my vocabulary was a moot point.

"Try me." I winked at her, and her breath caught ever so subtly.

"Okay, some synonyms are—without limit, infinite, no catch, no fine print, no holds barred, no ifs ands or buts, no joke, no strings attached, pure, unconditional, unlimited, and unrestricted."

"Sounds about right." I rolled over and draped my arm over her.

She wiggled upward so her face was right at my ear and whispered, "I love you, absolute, too."

THE NEXT COUPLE days were spent almost exclusively in the studio practicing with Fuckhead and his band. Becki spent her days learning the ropes with Cyan, Max's publicist. She and Becki hit it off immediately and were really enjoying each other, so it kept her out of Max's line of vision during those long practice days. I tried to be civil to Max, but just seeing his cocky ass face took me back to the night at Paisley.

It was Friday, and we had been at it for hours to nail our set list and practice a cover song we'd never performed. We were beat, but the adrenaline of playing an LA show started to hit us on the drive back to the hotel to get showered. We were the entertainment for big time recording artist, Ryan Flowers's niece's Sweet Sixteen party. It was a cool set up. Jordan's party was upstairs in a private room that had a large balcony that would give her and her guests a clear view of the stage, but no access to the bar below. The rest of the bar would be packed with patrons ready to rock. That was boss. We were stoked.

"Dude, so you ditched us for your girl? Already?" Bones's tone was tactful, but a hint of offense came through in his body language.

"Nah, man. Listen, she needs her own space. I'm sure it's a lot to take in, ya know? She's been living alone in a single dorm for a couple years, and all of a sudden she's thrown into a one room hotel room with four guys."

"And now you have a sex room," Manny said it with a friendly chuckle.

"Yeah, that, too." I felt my face get hot. I hoped to God I wasn't actually blushing. I'd never live that down.

"You guys fucked?" Bones, King of Crude, would give you the shirt off his back but had absolutely no friggin' filter on his mouth.

"Let it go." I looked right at him and spoke in a stern, but not condescending, tone.

"All right, so, we're ready for tonight? Shots when we get to our room?" Leave it to Spider to cut in and assist in getting Bones off my back.

"Sounds good. Now, listen, guys… I want to surprise Becki with the last song, okay. So, don't spoil it."

They all nodded as we parked and hopped out. I texted Becki on our way up in the elevator and then hopped in the shower while the guys set up some drinks on our small table by the window that had collected more than a couple fifths of top shelf booze we'd received at Glam, the bar in our hotel. Seems word had gotten out that we were staying at the Phoenix, and the bar was packed every night. It was our first taste of the celebrity treatment in the form of bottled tokens of appreciation from Miranda, Glam's stunning manager. She had coal black hair and legs all the way up to her arm pits and wore clothes that left nothing to the imagination. I would have put money on the fact that she was barely legal. There was no way she could be our age. I guessed it was a hand-me-down opportunity from a rich daddy.

Becki and I hadn't been naked together since the night in her room. Our practice schedule was crazy, and Cyan had her out late hobnobbing with some big names in the business. On those nights, she'd come up to our room hours after I had been asleep, climb into bed with me, and we would hang onto each other, exhausted, until the sun came up.

As I washed the day's sweat and grime off, I realized how much I missed being so close to her. Just thinking about her lying next to me in my bed had a half-boner rising into the stream of water. I ducked my head under the water and closed my eyes. Goose bumps lifted across my whole body when I thought about her body writhing under me when she came.

My body shuddered. I rubbed my face with both hands and opened my eyes to find the shampoo when my eyes landed on something that took my breath away. Her face.

"Mind if I join you?" She was naked, and her voice was so low and sultry I had to remember to breathe. I took her hand and helped her in. She pressed her cool body flush against mine.

"How did you get in here without them throwing a fit?" I took her face in my hands and kissed her deeply.

"I just told them I had to grab some stuff I left behind. So, if you wanna fuck me you need to make it fast."

"Oh, it *could* be fast, Becks. But that's not nice."

"Listen, nice boy. I'm all about you being respectful and shit, but if I ask you to fuck me in the shower and we only have a couple minutes, then I am giving you permission to be quick and not worry about being polite."

"Turn around and hold on." I took her hips in my hands and spun her. The intense ache she gave me was primal and urgent. She smirked over her shoulder and grabbed hold of the faucets. Her back was heaving with deep breaths, and she was making small, incoherent sounds. "Becks, you're gonna have to be quiet."

She nodded.

I bent my legs and came up underneath her ass, holding myself at the right angle to slide inside her, and I did, hard. She whimpered and threw her head back. I grabbed her hip with one hand and her shoulder with the other and pumped into her, trying to alleviate some of the ache that came from being so damn hard.

I felt her adjust the way she was standing then felt her hand on my balls. She had reached between her legs to hold me in her hand. Just then her hand moved away, her pussy clamped down on me, and I knew she was touching herself. I felt it building, an explosion that was going to be hard to control.

"I'm… I'm there… Becks, I'm gonna come." I was breathless and so dizzy I threw one hand over to the hand rail for support.

"Come for me, Calon. Fuck me and come for me." I could tell by the guttural sound of her voice that she was on the edge, too.

There was no control. We lost it. We called out in what probably sounded pained from outside the bathroom, but there was definitely no pain involved. Over and over the sensation rocked me deeper inside her, and, when she'd wrung me dry, I slowly pulled out of her and sank to the floor of the tub. She carefully sat back between my bent legs, and we caught our breath under the hot rain of the shower.

"Becki?"

"Yeah?"

"You can talk dirty to me every day for the rest of my life, okay? That was so incredibly fucking hot." I wrapped my spent arms around her and squeezed.

"I'd be happy to entertain your dirty mouth, too, should you ever feel the urge." Her head fell back on my shoulder, and she sighed.

Someone banged on the door, and we both jumped. "When you two love birds are done filming your porn in there, we have a show to play. Come on! Getting her stuff, my ass!"

Becki and I stayed seated under the water for a couple more minutes, kissing and chuckling at Bones's antics. I helped her dry off, and she quickly dressed then quickly and quietly ran out and headed down to her room to get ready. She and Cyan were headed to meet with Paisley's management ahead of us.

I planned on Becki standing off in the wings of the stage, so I could get her attention just before we did the last song. But after christening the hotel shower, I wasn't sure I could keep it together. I knew my mind would take me right back to the moment she turned and bent over.

I was undone, splayed open for all the world to know. I was madly, insanely, and absolutely in love with Becki Jane Mowry.

THE STAGE WAS dark, and the crowd was restless, just how we liked it. We waited in the wings as a few shrill whistles bounced around the people who stood beyond the edge of the stage. This was it. A soft hand slid into mine.

"So proud of you, Calon. Now, go rock this place!" She smacked my ass and stood on her toes to kiss me. Her warm hands on the sides of my face calmed the few nerves that were out of whack, and I was ready.

"Let's go!" There were shrieks and applause when those up close saw the guys make their way onto the dark stage. When I walked out, I looked around to see that everyone was in their place, and then I nodded. Spider called out through the mic, "All aboard!" Then Manny broke out with a cackle that sounded just like Ozzy. Bones came in with the recognizable bass beat, and when the lights flashed down onto the stage, I grabbed the mic and belted the "Aiy-aiy-aiy-aiy-aiy," and then came Bones with the bass and Spider with the rattle. Manny made his guitar scream as we warped into our own version of the classic "Crazy Train" intro.

The guys pulled the volume down a couple notches and instead of going into Ozzy's lyrics, I used their muted instrumentals as an opportunity to introduce ourselves.

"Hello, Los Angeles! We are so thrilled to be touring with Smiling Turkeys and even more thrilled to start that tour right here at Paisley! Give it up for Bones on bass, Spider, our percussion specialist, Manny on lead guitar." The crowd yelled and whistled. "I'm Calon Ridge—" The place erupted with a deafening roar, which made me lose my train of thought. I chuckled and looked around at the guys. What that hell was that? "And we're Alternate Tragedy! Thanks for coming out tonight."

I looked over to the wings, where Becki beamed. I laughed in response to the crowd's hyper-enthusiasm. Her smile wrapped all the way around her head. She drew a heart in the air with two fingers and blew me a kiss then ran off with Cyan, I assumed to do some more hobnobbing.

We started with our title track, our love song "Fallen", which always made me think of Gracie, then we moved seamlessly into "Tried". It had more of a nineties Pearl Jam angst to it. Max had given us a three song limit, but the crowd was unbelievable. We just couldn't walk off the stage after the next song. We had discussed the alternate plan prior to hitting the stage, so the nod of my head gave my band all they needed to tuck two more songs in before we did the cover I was so anxious to sing to Becki.

"Flames" was an acoustic ballad about love and how it sometimes burns out of control, like a flame. I pulled a stool to the mic, grabbed my guitar, and took a deep breath. The lights dimmed, except the spotlight right over me. I closed my eyes and drained my lyrics of the emotions I'd written into them. The crowd swayed, couples kissed. It was one of Becki's favorites from the album.

I waved to thank the audience for their appreciation and caught sight of Max headed to the steps that lead to the wings. He was going to have to wait. There was no way he would risk looking like a dick by throwing one of his tantrums and kicking us off the stage. So, we had him by the balls. I nodded toward him and introduced our fourth song "Trip You Up", a classic punk sound mixed with some hard rock beats. Spider lit up the drums with a machine-gun style drum solo that led us into the lyrics that had a *don't fuck with me* kind of edge. It was a high energy song, so I was all over the stage. I could hear Becki screaming down front and saw daggers coming from Max's eyes. All was right with the world. We ended the set, and when I lifted my head, it looked as if the number of occupants on the dance floor had doubled.

I grabbed the mic and used my hands to tell the crowd to hush. I'd always been amazed how the guy with the mic at a concert could get a crowd of tens of thousands to be silent. It was quite a powerful feeling. My heart pounded with adrenaline. I was so pumped that this dream we'd had for over half our lives was really happening right before our eyes.

"We love to write and perform our own music, but we also enjoy paying homage to those musicians who have inspired us. At one time, not too long ago, we did covers exclusively when we played for the students of UT Knoxville." There were a couple of whoops, I assumed from alums. I shot them a thumbs up. "We have missed doing covers of our favorites as we promote the *Fallen* album, so, tonight, we have a cover for you. This one goes out to someone very special, my absolute." My eyes found Becki immediately. Her hands covered her heart, and her mouth was agape. The smile on her face was priceless. My girl. "This is 'All of Me' by the one and only, John Legend." Manny prepped the keyboard and gave me a nod.

I sang of a feisty love of two imperfect people who found magic when their hearts collided. I wanted Becki to know, publicly, that I was giving her all of me. All. Everything I had. The words tumbled from my mouth, and the melody happened effortlessly. My voice was fluid and strong but gentle and sincere. Becki looked like she might cry, but that beautiful smile never waned. I used one hand to stealthily wipe a tear that escaped my eye and managed to make it look like it was one of my habitual hair tucks. When the song finished, I was spent. I could have laid on the stage and slept. I lifted my head and addressed our fans one last time before we left the stage.

"Thank you all for coming out and for the warm welcome us Los Angeles. Happy sixteenth birthday, Jordan! And now, the band you've been waiting for. Please, welcome Smiling Turkeys!" I hopped down off the front of the stage and into Becki's arms.

Max opened immediately with a slower song that wasn't typical of their band but perfect timing for me. I pulled Becki's face to mine and kissed her hard and long. Our bodies slowly moved to the soft tone of Max's voice. We danced, drank, and I signed autographs for what felt like hours.

"Want to head up to the VIP floor?" I was drunk, and all I could think about was Becki in the shower. I knew it was poor taste to leave the club early, but I needed to have some Becki time. Ducking into a closet and fucking like animals was even poorer taste, so hanging out together in one of the private lavish spaces upstairs would have to do.

"Lead the way." She smiled.

We found an unoccupied space and flopped down on the expensive white couch. I threw my arms over the back, slid down so my ass was right on the edge of the cushions, and laid my head back. I was drunk, exhausted, and the room wouldn't stop spinning. Becki straddled me and sat right on my crotch a bit harder than I would have liked, which caused me to buckle and her to laugh.

"I'm so sorry." She hugged my head to her chest as I groaned in pain.

"I think you broke it." God, that hurt.

Becki took my face in her hands and spoke into my nose. I think because her head was swimming in Patron shots. "Don't say that. I would never forgive myself if I broke Walter."

"Walter? You named my dick Walter? He's not a geek, Becki." I sat up and scooted back and gave her my best pouty look.

"I like the name Walter, it's very formal. I feel like it's a name that commands attention. And, let's face it, your dick commands my attention." She licked my bottom lip seductively and then bit hers.

"Commands it, craves it. Yeah, he digs ya."

"Well, good, because it's about time he and I meet face to face… if you know what I mean." Her eyebrows waggled, and a naughty smirk curled the corner of her mouth.

"Fuck you! Asshole!" Max's voice hit me at the same time his fist hit the back of my head. My face crashed into Becki's, and I had to catch her before she fell backwards off my lap. When I pulled her up to me, her nose was bleeding and she had a small cut on her lip. I grabbed a handful of ice from the water pitcher on the coffee table that was situated between the two couches in our space, wrapped it in a linen napkin, and pressed it against her mouth. She stood, so I could get up, and then she flopped back down and held the ice to her face.

"What the hell is your problem?" I spun around and took two steps toward Max, which put us eye to eye. "You wanna hit me, fine, have at it but don't FUCK with my girl. She's bleeding because of you!" I slammed him hard in the chest with both my fists, which caused him to stumble back into a support pole. I took two more steps, and my body had his pinned against that pole.

"You don't want to do this here, do ya, big shot?" His cocky ass grin made me want to knock every one of his veneered teeth out.

"Where do you suggest we do this? Or were you just in it for the cheap shot to the back of my skull? Pussy." My teeth were clenched so tightly, my words came out in a long hiss.

"I won't waste my time with you, Ridge. I just need you to know who's boss. Three songs, that's it. So don't pull that shit again with your extra-long set. Three songs. Got it?" He pushed me out of his way with his shoulder as he turned to walk away. Mistake number one. Never turn your back on someone you just sucker punched.

I grabbed the shoulder pads of his long leather coat and spun him around. Before he had a chance to react, I caught him in the jaw with a right uppercut and a quick left-handed hit to the gut. When he bent over, I smashed him in the face with my knee and threw him to the ground.

"That's for what you did to Becki's face. Come at me all you want, bro. But you touch her again, and I will fuck you up! Got it?" I glanced over at Becki, and she winked from behind a handful of napkins and ice.

He stood and slinked back over to me slowly. He shook his head. Damn, this guy was an idiot.

"Listen to me, you cock-sucking shit, you should be bowing to kiss my ass because I got you on this tour. But, now I'm warning you, you can be removed. You need coat tails to ride on to get anywhere in this business, and I gave you mine. You keep fucking up like this, and I'll find someone to take your place." He slammed into my shoulder as he walked past me then took two steps toward Becki and held out his hand for her. She looked him up and down but didn't budge.

"Look, babe. Bad call on my part by cuffing your guy to the head with you in his lap." He leaned in closer and whispered something in her ear then turned to me, smacked her ass and chuckled. "I'm truly sorry you got hurt in all this. I hope you'll forgive me."

I couldn't see straight. I could have killed him with my bare hands. But I'd learned my lesson last time. I didn't want to insult Becki again. She made it very clear that she could handle herself in the kind of situation Max had her in once again. My fists clenched at my sides.

Becki glared at him. He smirked and stared back but soon gave up waiting for her response, and he slowly walked toward the stairs. She looked up at me, moved the napkins from in front of her lips, and mouthed the words, "Fuck him up."

Instantly I was filled with both elation and anger. I lost it. He was almost at the steps when I got to him. I saw both bouncers nod at each other and turn their heads, as if to give me the clear to pound on him for a short period of time with no interruptions.

I spun him around and fired a shot to the side of his head with my clenched fist. When he went down, I threw myself on top of him. I got in two or three good shots to the face before the bouncers pulled me off. I struggled to get in just one more hit. The bouncers each held us, so we couldn't get at each other, but we were still face to face.

"You can let someone else ride your ugly ass coat tails. We're out. You're on this tour alone, asshole."

"Your loss, Ridge. You'll get nowhere, now. This will be front page news tomorrow. There are paparazzi everywhere in this place."

"Oh, don't you worry. We will have no problem getting gigs without you."

Becki walked passed me and right up to his face. I saw the bouncer holding Max size her up, but he didn't budge.

"And if you ever, EVER, touch my ass again, I will rip your dick off and shove it down your throat! Got that?"

Max just smirked and rolled his eyes.

Mistake number two. Don't fuck with Becki, especially with your hands held behind your back.

Her knee shot up between his legs with such force it lifted him at least an inch off the ground. He folded in on himself and cried like a baby.

Becki and I were escorted out without any fuss. We called a cab and headed back to the hotel.

When the guys rolled in later, still high on the vibes of our kick ass show, I had to tell them we didn't have a tour. Yeah, I'd almost rather take a knee from Becki than crush their dreams like that. But, I would risk it all to protect her. This was the first time in my life anything came before my music. I just hoped they understood.

nine

Becki

"CALON, I'M SORRY. I never should've given you the okay to beat the crap out of him. I'm glad you did, though. I'd never sacrifice my dignity just to get ahead, and I'd hoped you'd feel the same way." I sat on the edge of one bed in the band's room. I'd already wrapped his knuckles in cold, wet washcloths. They would hurt tomorrow.

"Without a doubt, Becki. That's why I think the guys will get this. Not one of them would be willing to stand by and let him get away with that kind of shit just so we could stay on his tour. And besides, we've got one of the best managers on the scene, so I have no doubt we can make this happen—on our own terms."

"Well, I just texted Cyan and asked her a bunch of questions that will give me some inside info I will need to do just that. She doesn't know about the fight yet, and I'm not sure if her loyalty to Max and the guys would keep her from sharing that with me once she finds out. So, I got a jump on things, and it will all be good. I promise. I'll make this happen."

"You're unbelievable. And I can't believe you love me." His voice was small when he spoke those words. Every now and then Calon's tough, sure of himself armor would weaken, and I could see some kind of unworthiness floating just below the surface. It hurt my heart that he might think he wasn't worthy of being loved.

"Absolute."

"Okay, I'll tell the guys the news about the tour, but let me take a call in my office, first."

"Your office?" He looked around the guys' messy ass hotel room.

"The bathroom, silly. They will be busting in here any second, and I need some privacy to make this happen." I grabbed my phone and scrolled to a number I had logged in from Cyan's contacts. Nobody slept in this town. This was the perfect time to connect with people in the industry. Besides, at midnight, they'd most likely be a little buzzed, which could work in our favor.

"You have to take a shit?"

"No, dork! I have to make some calls." Guys were so gross! Like I'd take a shit in *his* toilet.

"Oh, for real? Oh." He looked puzzled but shrugged and grabbed a beer from the fridge.

No sooner did I get inside and lock the door, all hell broke loose in the room. The guys got wind of the fight much quicker than I'd imagined, so Calon was going to have to fill them in on that part. I knew I would round out the announcements with something that would make them forget they even wanted to be on tour with Max.

I made about six phone calls in the hour I had myself locked in the bathroom. I took notes, jotted down names and phone numbers, and filled in dates on the little appointment book I'd picked up in one of the eclectic stores Cyan had introduced me to. I even took a call from Mr. Barnes, who was royally pissed off. I made it clear to him that if he gave us any trouble about the breach in contract, I would personally walk the Smiling Turkeys sexual harassment story into every tabloid office in Los Angeles myself. And that didn't leave him any leverage. He apologized for Max's behavior and wished us luck.

I burst from the bathroom into a room filled with stinky guys lounging around; feet up, beers in hand. No one looked the least bit pissed that we'd lost the tour.

"You didn't tell them, did you?" I pointed at Calon with my pen.

"Of course, I did." He almost looked hurt that I'd assumed he was going to let me do it.

"I didn't hear any yelling, no one swearing, no Bones tantrum… what gives?"

Bones stood up and walked toward me with his arms out. Spider and Manny fell into a single file line behind him. *What the hell are they doing?*

"Becki, what Max did was wrong. None of us would ever let you stand in harm's way just to play a tour. We dig you, babe." Bones wrapped his arms around me and nuzzled into my shoulder. I looked over his shoulder at Calon with my hands out to the sides. He smiled, and I closed my arms awkwardly around Bones and patted him gently.

"Thanks, man. That means a lot." He headed toward the bathroom, and Spider walked up to me next.

"Becki, you're one of us. We're a team. No one gets left behind, and no one's dignity is sacrificed for the sake of a couple shows. Got it?" He hugged me too, but his hug wasn't nearly as uncomfortable as Bones's was. "Want a beer?"

"Hell yeah. Thanks." Spider nodded, headed to the fridge, and Manny brought up the rear of the line.

"Listen, we're all in this for personal growth and for satisfying our souls' longing to play. We aren't in this to make it to The Grammy's. Got it? We should have done a little more research into the members of Smiling Turkeys before agreeing to play with them. I'm sorry we put you in harm's way. It won't happen again, Becki. I promise. None of us are the least bit mad about this situation. Maybe a little jealous that we didn't get to see Calon fuck Max up but…" He threw his arms out to the side and enveloped me in a big, sweet Manny hug.

"Damn girl!" Bones burst out of the bathroom. "She was in there for an hour dropping a load, and it didn't stink at all when I walked in!"

"I was on the phone, not taking a dump, dork!"

"Well, good. Because, I gotta piss." Manny headed toward the bathroom, and Bones giggled. The door shut and Manny yelled a few obscenities.

"My stench, on the other hand, has the wallpaper curling." He howled again. I rolled my eyes and waited for Manny to come back out to share the new development in our tour. I curled up on the bed with Calon. He sat with his back against the headboard, which reminded me of my hands gripped around them when he had me naked for the first time. My breath hitched a little just thinking about it.

Manny came out, and I jumped off the bed to make my announcement.

"Gentlemen, it's not much, but I have four shows lined up for you in the next ten days, along with a rehearsal space. You should end up netting a couple thousand dollars." They all sat up straight and looked around at each other with huge smiles on their faces, which told me I done good. "But, you're still paying for this hotel room. So, I can pay for my own room. But, we are going to have to bring in more than that to cover this one."

"No problem." Bones raised his hand like he was in a classroom. I giggled and motioned for him to continue. "Before we left, my brother donated to the AT fund. I've just never deposited the check. We've got a pretty decent buffer until we start rakin' in the cash."

"Perfect, Bones. Let's get that in the bank before you lose it."

"You got it."

"Now, it's just four shows I've got lined up, but while you're practicing and playing those I will be lining up the next ten days' worth."

"Now, who's the rock star?" Calon pulled me down onto the bed and rolled over onto me. His hair was in a ponytail, and I found myself actually missing the curls tickling my face. He put his face right next to mine and whispered, "I love you, absolute, Becki Mowry."

I reached up and took the hairband from his hair, and all his beautiful locks fell forward onto my face. Fuck, he was hot. "Let's go down to my room."

"No, stop! Please, don't take her away from me!"

I woke in my hotel room to Calon's choking sobs in his sleep. We must have fallen asleep as soon as we hit my bed, exhausted from all that had happened at Paisley.

I was completely stunned by the pain in his voice. My heart jumped into my throat, and I was frozen. I didn't know what to do. He settled for a moment, and I sat up to turn the light on the side table on dim, so it wouldn't wake him, just enough light so I could see him.

"Jesus, no." His voice was a hollow whisper, and he sobbed. The tears came like a torrent. I couldn't bear it any longer. I lay down next to him, wrapped him in my arms, and rocked him.

"Shh. Calon, it's Becki. It's okay. Everything's going to be okay." I rocked him for a long time. The sobbing stopped, his breathing slowed down, but he still whimpered every couple minutes. Without warning, he sat straight up and yelled, "Kate!"

"Calon, babe, it's me, Becki. You're having a nightmare. Calon. Are you awake?" His eyes were open, locked on something that wasn't there, and one last tear rolled down his cheek. I wiped it away and kissed him where a trail was left behind. He turned his head slowly and let his eyes focus on mine. He blinked, breathed deep, then closed his eyes and fell back, flat on his back. He brought his hands up to his face and hid from me, as if he was embarrassed he had a nightmare.

"Becks, I'm so sorry. I'm so, so sorry." He rolled toward me. His breath was staggered, and he was still sniffling.

"Calon, good lord, what was that dream about? Just relax, that's all it was, just a dream." I brushed his hair from his forehead. He'd broken into a cold sweat. He stared past me.

"It wasn't just a dream, Becks. I watched her leave in a car, and I never saw her again. She cried, Becki. She screamed for me, and I could do nothing. I couldn't move. Her little face was so red, so wet from tears. The last thing I saw was her chubby little hand pressed against the car window as it drove away. The bracelet I'd made her still on her wrist. They said it was for the best, but she was terrified."

I was stunned. My heart shattered over a story I didn't yet follow. My heart broke for Calon. I knew I needed to keep my cool. I needed to be gentle and careful not to pry or have the wrong reaction. I needed him to realize he could unload anything to me and I wouldn't flinch. I'd learned early on that when you trust someone enough to open up to them and they shriek or gasp at what you've told them, you retreat into yourself like one of those little origami-folded notes from junior high—all your secrets neatly tucked on the inside.

"Calon, listen, I'm here if you want to tell me what your dream was about, but I'm not going to pry. I want to help you, but I don't want to ask the wrong question or make you feel obligated to tell me something you're not ready to. Help me help you, Calon."

"The memories make me physically ill. Her little hand. Becki, my heart breaks every time I think of her little hand reaching for me." He wasn't quite lucid, still in somewhat of an odd state of consciousness.

"Who, babe? Whose little hand?"

His mouth opened and closed a couple times in an attempt to let the story, or part of it, out one more time, but something kept stopping him. He threw his hands to his face and pressed his clenched fists into his eye sockets. He slowly shook his head from side to side.

"I don't know if I can, Becki. It fucking hurts so deep."

How could this beautiful soul, so kind, so gentle, struggle with the torment of a demon no one knew was inside him? Calon never seemed to hold anything back. When something hit his heart, he'd get choked up, but I'd never seen him shy away from that pain. He would typically push through it, feel it. More than once we'd talked about tragedies and horrors innocent people had experienced. I watched him process the pain; however, I knew this was different. Whatever happened broke him.

I held him as close as I could get him. I cradled his head with the arm I rested on and rocked him as best I could while lying down. He whimpered then broke into choked sobs. His body shook, his tears soaked the sleeve of my t-shirt, and there was nothing I could do for him. I had never felt so helpless in all my life. Tears stung my eyes, my gut wrenched, my heart physically hurt. He fell asleep, but I didn't let go of him. I held him tight, as though it would keep his demons at bay.

"Becks? I need to tell you about Kate." His voice startled me a little, but this time he spoke in a calm but serious tone with a hint of caution. "The little hands belonged to a baby named Kate."

I blinked back tears, completely overwhelmed by what I feared he would say. All the thoughts that floated aimlessly in my mind connected. He and Chloe had a baby before she died. I didn't want him to say it. It would change everything. A couple tears fell, and I couldn't react fast enough to hide them.

"Sorry." I wiped them away and cleared my throat. I sat up straight and wrapped my arms around my bent legs.

"Why are you crying?" His demeanor changed instantly. He went right into protective mode.

"I think I know what you're going to say, and I don't know what to do with it. Dammit, Calon. I just let my guard down and fell in love with you, and *now* you decide to tell me you and Chloe had a baby?" I hid my face against my knees and held my breath so the sobs couldn't get out.

"Chloe and I didn't have a baby. Kate was… is my sister, not my daughter." He picked up my face toward his, scooted up onto his knees and sat back on his heels. He kissed me gently and smiled. "Babe, if I had a child, you would know. Kate is my sister."

"I'm sorry! I'm so sorry for jumping to conclusions, Calon." I had a hard time catching my breath. I was so relieved but at the same time hated that had my assumption been correct, it really may have changed everything.

"Becki, my baby sister Kate was born when I was three. She was the best thing that ever happened to me. She took my mind off the lack of connection I felt with my mom. I remember my mom being real frustrated with Kate as an infant, and by the time she was a toddler, my mom's nerves were rubbed raw. She had no more patience and didn't even try to understand her own daughter. Kate had Down syndrome. She was a gorgeous baby; big blue eyes, blonde hair, and a wide smile that would melt your heart. But, she needed more than my mom could give her. My mom gave up. She just gave up." Calon looked down and took my hands in his.

"One day, we had a little party for seemingly no reason. Kate kept asking if it was her birthday. I knew it wasn't. I was old enough then to realize it was the middle of the winter and Kate had been born in the summer. I remember thinking if I ignored the terrible feeling in my gut and just kept smiling and making Kate laugh, I could stave off the impending disaster I felt waited just around the corner."

I rubbed Calon's hands with mine and watched new tears form and then just hang on the edge of his long, dark lashes. He blinked, and they fell into a steady stream. He looked down at our hands again and back up at me.

"What happened?" I felt my heart stutter. This story was going to rip me apart, and Calon was going to need me to be strong, because I could feel his body start to shake. He bit his lip before he continued.

"Fuck! It wasn't her birthday. Before our little party was over, two older ladies with clip boards knocked on the door. I remember Kate being so confused and asking where her presents were. She kept saying, 'I a good girl, Mama... where my presents? I a good girl. Good girls get presents, Mama.' My mom ignored her and signed a whole stack of papers while I kept distracting Kate and making her giggle. There was nothing I could do to keep it from happening. God, her giggle. It was my favorite sound. I never heard it again after that day."

"Calon, oh my God, I can't imagine carrying this with you all these years." I wrapped my arms around his neck and pulled him as close as I could get him. His body was stiff; he was somewhere else. He wasn't twenty-two-year-old Calon the rock star. He was a six-year-old little boy who was terrified and lost.

"No one explained to me what was happening. I didn't understand. When they bundled her up in her pink winter coat and headed outside, I could see the fear in Kate's eyes. Becks, she was so scared. She reached over the woman's shoulder and screamed for my mom, 'I a good girl, Mama! I a good girl.' She started to flail and shriek, like someone was hurting her." He threw his hands up to his ears, as if he could still hear her cries. "Her little voice got so hoarse so quickly, and by the time they got her in the car, she was spent. She let her head fall back against the car seat, and she turned toward the open door. I was standing on the sidewalk with my mom. Snowflakes melted on my cheeks in the stream of tears. We were so close I could have jumped in the car, but I was terrified they would take me, too. I could have saved her, I was such a coward!"

"Calon! Stop! You were six!"

He grabbed two handfuls of hair and started to rock a little. "Almost seven. I was old enough to at least try to stop them. I didn't even try." He hung his head and sobbed. I ran my hands over his shoulders and down his big, strong arms. He crumbled into me and slid down until his head was in my lap. I raked my fingers through his hair and rubbed his back.

"Calon, listen, there was nothing you could do. Those women were sent there to take your sister out of harm's way. Your mom signed papers. You couldn't have stopped it. Calon, you can't blame yourself."

He stopped crying, and his body stilled. "I was standing on the sidewalk, and my mom's arms were draped over my shoulders. Kate was doing that quiet sob thing, you know, after you cry for a long time and you're left gasping between breaths. Her body wrenched with each gasp, and her little head turned away from us. When she looked back, she didn't even look at my mom. Her eyes welled up with tears, and she called out, 'Brother'. She was so exhausted, it was all she could to do raise her little arm and reach for me. The rainbow-colored, braided friendship bracelet I'd made with her that day when I was trying to distract her, hung loose on her chubby wrist. I tried to take a step toward her, but my mom's grip tightened around my shoulders. My heart was racing, and the tears kept coming. All of a sudden it was like it sunk in and she knew neither my mom, nor I, was going to stop what was happening. She dropped her arm into her lap and spoke as clear as day, 'I see you again, brother. I be good girl then.' The caseworker shut the car door, and Kate's little hand pressed up against the window. Tears covered her little red cheeks, and they drove away. I didn't take my eyes off the car until it turned a corner and disappeared.

"It's the reason I just can't ever have kids. If another part of me is stolen away, for any reason, I wouldn't live through it."

I sank back down to the bed and tried to gather as much of Calon as I could into my arms. His rapid breathing slowed, and his eyes were closed. I thought about the extreme emotions that had just run through his heart and out of his body in just explaining what had happened to Kate that day. I *cannot* imagine actually experiencing that glimpse into Hell, especially not at six years old. He'd been holding this inside his heart for so many years. I rubbed his back. His arms tightened around me, and he nuzzled his face into the side of my neck. Within mere moments he fell asleep, heartbroken and spent.

His body jerked, and he raised his head up. His eyes were bloodshot, heavy, and his voice was hoarse. "Becks, I can't do this again. I will always talk to you about anything, but could we put this part of my past to bed? I don't want to go there again? Please."

"Okay. Whatever you need, Calon. I love you."

"Me too, Becks. Thank you."

I held him close, and I knew at that moment, no matter what, I'd never ever let him go.

ten

Calon

WE CHATTED WITH Gracie over FaceTime right before we went on stage Friday night. She was the main attraction at Mitchell's for the very first time. She practically bubbled over with excitement, it was adorable. I really did miss her and hoped to someday share the stage with her again. She was incredibly talented.

Becki kicked ass planning gigs for us. We'd crushed our first four shows of what we were unofficially calling our solo tour since leaving the Turkeys in our dust. Becki had learned a lot in the little time she spent with Cyan, and we benefitted from it completely. We got to play some pretty cool venues, and it seemed as though our fan base was increasing exponentially, which was so damn cool. The last gig we played, we walked out the back door and right into a swarm of fans armed with Alternate Tragedy merchandise and Sharpies. We signed autographs on CDs and t-shirts for over an hour. Becki was so excited to see the fruits of her labor both in the reception we were getting at the places we played and in the amazing designs she created for the re-released *Fallen* CD cover and t-shirts. She manned the merchandise table during our shows, and we sold out of everything at every one. She wore many more hats than we'd originally planned, and we couldn't pay her what she was actually worth yet, but she jumped in head first and hadn't come up for air since. She was in her element and nothing could be sexier. But, I could tell she needed a break.

"I'm cool with doing three or four shows, then working a three day break into our schedule to regroup and rest up." I hoped she would agree. I knew the guys could see she was exhausted, and there were certain days during the week that were slow days for live music. "Even if we did a couple nights back-to-back then a couple days off then back-to-back shows again, it would still give us time to rest and stay healthy."

We'd adopted FRESH, a sushi place right around the corner from our hotel, as our conference room. Playing into the single digit hours had us sleeping late and eating unorthodox things for breakfast.

"Yeah, you're right, but I need you guys to be a constant hype now. This is when you get your most devoted fans, in the beginning, because they want to take the ride with you… follow you all the way, ya know?" I couldn't take my eyes off her. I winked at her, and she smiled just as she threw a piece of veggie sushi in her mouth.

"What if we played certain clubs on certain nights regularly, then people would know where to come see us. They wouldn't have to look it up anywhere." Spider was always thinking. He was basically our manager before Becki came on board. He was the one to get us gigs and make sure our shows were listed on all the UTK entertainment sites, but he never could have handled all that Becki was doing. I wasn't sure how she did it. I watched her fumble with her veggie rolls.

"That's a great idea, Spider. So, let's brainstorm a list of venues that would be your top ten places to play. I'll call around and see if any of them are looking to fill gaps in their schedules, and we'll go from there. We could let that determine what nights you play and what nights you have off. Sound good?"

"You not hungry, Becks?" The girl could eat any of us under the table and still rock a smokin' hot body. It was odd to see her plate look virtually untouched.

She shook her head. "Just can't talk and eat, that's all." She winked at me and seductively placed a sushi roll in her mouth then licked her lips. I shook my head and smiled. She was all mine.

"Cal, did Malcolm leave you a message?" Spider scratched his head.

"Malcolm Phoenix? No, he didn't. He called you?" I shook my head. The guy was an ass. He'd called me just before we left Knoxville to offer his management services, and I turned him down. It's safe to say he doesn't take rejection well.

"Yeah. I told him he could stop calling since we'd each said 'no thanks' to his management offer at least three times."

"I heard that guy's slimy." Becki turned up her nose. "But, hey, if you wanna give him a try—"

"No!" We all yelled at once.

"Well, good. That's the unanimity I like to feel as your manager. You guys rock." Becki bowed as best she could from her seated position.

"Anyone wanna hit the gym after lunch–breakfast–whatever this is?" I hadn't worked out since we got to LA, and, with all the last minute preparations to get out here, I couldn't remember when I'd last touched weights.

"I could use a run. I'll come." Becki started clearing our table. In all of our late night talks, the subject of exercise had never come up. I had no idea she was a runner. Just one more thing to make her hotter than hell.

THE HOTEL GYM was insane. I couldn't believe all the machines that were available. It was the biggest hotel gym I'd ever seen.

"Calon Ridge... in tennis shoes. Said no one ever." Becki burst out laughing as she walked through the door.

"You didn't think I was going to lift in my Docs, did you?" I was suddenly strangely aware of my athlete wanna-be attire.

"Well, no. I just hadn't thought this whole thing through. I can see your dick." She winked and nodded toward my black athletic shorts.

"Becki!" I tried to whisper because two younger girls had just walked in and hadn't taken their eyes off me. "These are thin, and I don't have compression shorts under them. One more word out of you and those girls will see my dick, too. And it will be pointing at you, because it will be *your* fault," I whispered as controlled as I could, but I was panicked.

The girls giggled, and I prayed it was just the nervous fan-thing and not because they were completely aware of my growing wood. I quickly sat down at the lat machine and distracted myself with a hundred and twenty-five pounds. The two girls came over to me, and I was so thankful I'd thought to sit. Hiding a boner was way easier with my t-shirt shielding my crotch.

"You're—you're Calon Ridge, aren't you?" The shorter blonde was practically hyperventilating as her friend spoke.

"I am. And you are…" I raised an eyebrow, and the blonde grabbed her friend's forearm for balance.

"I'm Shelly, and this is my sister, Tiff. We're huge fans. We saw you play at Paisley. You're amazing." Tiff teetered and giggled. I was going to have to start getting used to this. Totally bizarre.

"Thank you both, so much. I'm so happy you enjoyed the show. Thanks for introducing yourselves. I love to meet our fans." Now, I was uncomfortable. How do you cut a conversation short when you're not leaving the room and have no other excuse to walk away?

"Could you sign our shirts? Sorry, we don't have anything else with us." Shelly handed me a Sharpie she'd dug out of her duffle bag.

"Soccer champs, huh?" I winked. They proudly smiled down at their matching hot pink tournament t-shirts.

"Yeah, we're from Pennsylvania. We're in LA for a national tournament," Tiff finally spoke. Both girls were smiling from ear to ear as I signed my name across the backs of their shoulders.

"There ya go." I looked up at Becki whose breasts were jogging just as much as she was, and I was quickly reminded of the boner I'd just gotten rid of.

"Thanks, Mr. Ridge."

"Calon. I'm not old enough to be a mister." I smiled and winked again.

They squealed and ran out the door.

I turned back around, reached for the lat bar and realized I had a perfect view of Becki on the treadmill in the mirror in front of me. She had popped her ear buds in, and her lips were moving to a song that I assumed was giving her the even pace she was keeping.

My muscles were stinging by the time I finished my set. I moved over to the chest press and planned to just keep going down the line until I couldn't take the pain anymore. Becki was still running, and the line of machines was perfectly placed so I could continue to gawk.

It had only been a couple weeks since I was an enamored escort that made sure Becki got home safely after our shows. I thought back to the nights I left her without anything more than a 'thank you' or a long hug. It seemed like a lifetime since the days I longed to know what her lips would feel like on mine, yet it hadn't been that long at all.

summer flashback

"MAYBE SOMEDAY YOU'LL write a song about me." Becki took my hand in hers as we walked the familiar path from Mitchell's back to her dorm.

"Who knows. Stranger things have happened." I smiled, and she bumped into me with her hip.

"What's that supposed to mean?" Our clasped hands swung between us, and I couldn't ignore the tingling where our skin touched. I was stoked she'd grabbed my hand, because I was out of practice and terrified to come on too strong.

"Oh, I don't know. Just thinking that's a little too cliché for you." I raised an eyebrow, even though it was too dark for her to see.

"Too cliché? Are you kidding? I feel pretty certain that one hundred percent of all women on the planet have, at one time, fantasized about just that." She squeezed my hand, but I wasn't sure why.

"Well, okay then. I'll have to keep that in mind."

We walked in silence, still holding hands, until we reached the street corner by her dorm. She stopped dead in her tracks and turned to me. She took my other hand in hers and locked eyes with me. She didn't say a word. Her lips parted, and her chest heaved. She licked her lips and leaned in toward my mouth. Her lips hovered within millimeters of mine, and I could feel her warm breath on my face.

I'd been walking her home for weeks, yet our lips had never met. I'd left her dorm more than once with a raging hard-on. I'd even spent many of those nights curled up with her in her tiny twin bed yet, I'd never tried to kiss her. Part of me held Chloe and Gracie's kisses as sacred, but the rest of me knew that one day I would find someone I could move on with. Was Becki the one?

Her hands were on my waist and clutching the untucked flannel she'd told me was a hot wardrobe choice earlier that evening. I dropped one hand to the small of her back and pressed her against where I ached for her the most. Both our chests heaved, and we gasped for air, though neither of us moved any closer.

Becki slid her hands under the t-shirt I had on under my flannel. Her soft, warm hands swept across my sides and up my back until she was holding onto my shoulders from behind. Her nails dug in; not enough to break the skin but just enough to buckle my knees slightly. There was a fire ignited in both of us during those few moments, one that would be nearly impossible to squelch.

"Calon?" She spoke between a couple deep breaths.

"Yeah?"

"I want to kiss you so badly." She pulled back a little and looked up at me.

"Yeah." I was speechless at how far she'd climbed into my soul without even kissing me. "I'd like that an awful lot, but I want you to let me know when you're ready."

"I've never been too picky about the guys I make out with." She rolled her eyes and turned away from me a little as if she was embarrassed.

"Okayyy." I drew out the word and chuckled completely out of discomfort. I had no idea where she was going with that comment.

"No, listen a minute. That gets old. It makes kissing as easy as—as dancing with someone. And, I read somewhere that kissing can actually be more intimate than sex. I think that's what I want. I don't want it to come too soon. I want to ache for it." She blinked away the apprehension I sensed in her voice then smiled my favorite shy smile.

"Do you ache for me, Becki?" Yeah, I did that on purpose; pulled the sexy romance novel line right out of my head. She dropped her head back and groaned. We both burst out laughing, and I continued walking her to the door to the building.

"I mean it, Calon. You only had to turn me down a couple of times to make me reconsider giving away something so intimate, so quickly." She looked away again and shivered a little in the cool night air. I'd never seen her so unsure of herself. She was letting down her walls.

I took off my flannel and draped it over her shoulders then ducked down to catch her offset gaze. "Becki, I want you to know I haven't kissed anyone since Gracie."

"Okay... one, mentioning making out with my best friend just moments after we almost kiss for the first time just docked you a couple points." She poked me in the chest. "Second, dude, that was like two *years* ago. You can't be serious." She shook her head in disbelief then let it fall against my chest.

"Okay. One, I'm sorry for mentioning it. Second, yes, I'm serious." I needed to touch her again, so I wrapped my arms around her and pulled her into me, making it look like it was partially to keep her warm when really it was a sure way to feel her against my body again. "I have no doubt a kiss between you and me, whenever it happens, will be worth the wait. *You're* worth the wait."

I felt her sigh, and she shook her head against my chest, then pushed herself away from me slowly. "Look, smooth talkin' rock star, I've got a huge exam tomorrow, so you need to go home. Now. I won't be able to sleep if you stay here getting all deep and shit."

"Oh, sorry for getting all deep and shit."

"I like your deep shit. If I didn't, I wouldn't ask you to take me to dinner tomorrow night."

"Right." I chuckled at how weird she could be. "Okay, then go! Go study. I'll see you tomorrow. For dinner."

We shared one last way-too-sensual hug, then she bounced through the door and she was gone. I floated home, just me and all my deep shit.

"SO, SWEATY PANTS, what are you thinking?" She stood behind me, breasts right behind my head as I finished my last set of abs.

"I was thinking about the night we had our almost-kiss."

"Oh, our almost-kiss?" She smiled knowing exactly what I was referring to.

"Yeah. Very hot." I took a slow deep breath, so I could calm what was in my shorts and finally stand up.

"Very, very hot." As soon as I stood and turned, she leaned into me. Her breasts were covered by just a sports bra, her nipples were alert and pressed against my chest.

"Becki. You can't—"

She grabbed my face and crashed her lips into mine.

"Are you going to make out with me, right here? In the hotel gym?" I put my hands on her small, bare waist and pulled her hips into me. It was futile. I was not getting out of that gym with a limp willy.

"Yeah, I am." She put her hands on my biceps and used them to steer me backwards toward the unisex restroom by the door.

Once inside, we tore at each other's clothes and threw them on the floor. The whole one wall was a vanity with a mirror. I took her by the waist and lifted her up onto the edge of the ceramic counter.

She sucked in a sharp breath. "Shit! That's cold." She wrapped her legs around my hips and thrust her hands up through my hair. "Make me scream, Calon."

"God, Becki." I shuddered at how sexy her voice was when she said those four words.

I plunged deep within her, and she called out my name. Her heels pressed into my ass and pulled me into her as soon as I'd pull out. She pressed her hands down beside each of her hips and leaned back against the mirror. Her head was back, and her mouth open. I ran my hand up her stomach, to her breast, and up her neck, until I dipped my thumb in her mouth. She moaned and sucked hard.

She let go of me with her legs and put her feet up on either side of her ass on the edge of the counter. The view she created for me was my undoing. I grabbed her hips and thrust into her over and over and over, each time something extraordinary built within me.

All of a sudden and without a warning, she came. It was loud, and she bucked and writhed against the mirror. I slowed my pace to let her come down a little, but I couldn't walk out of the bathroom without coming. Something else was going to have to happen to get me off because there was no hiding what she did to me.

"Don't stop, Calon. Harder!"

I was dizzy and out of breath. Sweat dripped down my back as droplets formed all over her chest and stomach. I did what she asked and took her higher with each pump. There was something about the rigidity of the counter under her that made the sensation of being inside her so intense. My knees started to buckle, but I straightened them as best I could, and I took her until a wave came over us, and we both lost it. We were both vocal, calling each other's names and grunting as we came to the end of what was definitely one of the most intense things I'd ever experienced.

I leaned forward to hold onto the counter. She was still shaking with her legs wide open to me. I leaned down and kissed her pussy. She panted. She smelled like me, but tasted like my Becks.

"God, Calon. You are what women dream of, do you know that?" She slipped off the counter and rifled through the clothes on the floor.

"I don't know about that. However, I do know…" I pulled her into me. "That was hands-down the most indescribable thing I've ever experienced. Ever."

She smiled wide and kissed me. "Me, too."

A quiet thunder rumbled under our feet. The vibration of something getting closer and closer. The gym door slammed open against the wall of the restroom, and what sounded like a hundred squealing girls flowed into the room. Their voices and giggles getting louder as the room filled up.

Becki and I were both wide-eyed. I reached over and quietly turned the lock on the door and rolled my eyes at our careless oversight.

It suddenly went silent.

One girl called out, "That's not funny, Tiff! We believed you!"

"Guys, I swear! Look! He signed our shirts! Calon Ridge was here."

"So, where'd he go?" A high pitched squealer begged.

"I don't know, but he was here. I promise you. He touched me. His voice. God, I almost came in my shorts!"

Becki and I covered our mouths. We laughed so hard I thought we'd pass out.

"Ewwww!" A chorus of complaints erupted and was followed by insane laughter.

As soon as we heard the door latch and the room get quiet, we finished getting dressed and quickly headed up the back stairs to Becki's room, since it was closest. No sooner were we inside, and we heard the familiar crescendo of foot thunder.

"Someone said they just saw him on this floor. Come on girls! Knock on every door!"

This whole touring band ride we were on was about to hit a new level, and I knew then there would be surprises around every corner. I just hoped they came one at a time and not as a whole team next time.

eleven

"COME ON, BECKI! Tell us already." Spider wasn't one to complain, but I'd just gotten a really amazing tip from one of the contacts I'd made over the last month of us being on our own. I needed to tell them the news before they took the stage.

"Apparently the interview you did on KALA radio went viral on some rock website. You guys are getting a lot of attention these days. So much so that it's rumored a big record label will be here tonight to check you out." Their eyes all bugged out simultaneously, like little boys who just opened a new bike at Christmas. I giggled. I loved my job.

"What label?" Of course, Calon thought I was just holding back more news. But, I wasn't.

"Actually, I really don't know which one. My contact didn't even know who it was, just that one of the 'big guys' would be at The Moondance tonight."

It was our fourth show in ten days, and the guys had been on fire. They were at the top of their game. It was amazing to watch. Calon was so attuned to the fans and what they wanted to hear. Bones, Spider, and Manny played like I'd never seen. I'd taken a couple videos on my phone and texted them to Gracie. She was in awe. We thought we saw them at their best just before the news about the Smiling Turkeys tour came through, but damned if they hadn't upped their game significantly.

I'd gotten them some live radio interviews and even one short segment on a UCLA campus talk show hosted by two adorable and very high strung Alternate Tragedy fans. So, to say we were tired and run ragged was an understatement. The guys played three kick ass, high energy shows so far, and on the nights they didn't have a gig we went to check out other venues to play. During the day I made calls and filled in the master schedule with new interviews and gigs while they did radio shows or rehearsed. We were beat.

"Listen, we need to focus, be on our A-game, and play a fucking awesome show. Not just because of the label being here, but have you seen how packed this place is? People are coming out in droves, and we need to give them all we got. They'll be back if we do it right." The guys all nodded and fist bumped each other. Calon threw his guitar strap over his shoulder and winked at me. Like a team captain, he always gave the pre-game pep talks. He was adorable. Yet still humble, even though the demos we'd mailed out had gotten tons of air time on not only small radio stations, on big stations, too. It was rumored that 'Fallen' had gotten rave reviews in twenty-one states already.

"You guys are on in two minutes. You good?" One of the stage hands ran past with a headset on and didn't wait to hear the answer to his question. There was no doubt, they were ready.

The music from the DJ booth turned from dance funk tunes to an electronic whammy bar kind of thing. Then a very deep voice that seemingly came out of nowhere introduced the guys.

"Ladies and Gents, finally the band you've all been waiting for. All the way from their home in Knoxville, Tennessee, the one and only, Alternate Tragedy!" The announcer had to yell their name over top of the roaring crowd.

Calon turned toward me with a smile that would light up the darkest chasm on the planet. He was living his dream, and I was thrilled to be able to watch from the wings. I stood on my toes and took his face in my hands. "Calon James, I couldn't be more proud of you then I am at this moment. You deserve this. Go get 'em, rock star." I kissed him deeply and then shoved him toward the stage.

The roar of the crowd got louder and more fierce as the boys took the stage. Calon looked back over his shoulder as he walked to his mic. He gave me one of his 'I *cannot* believe this' smiles. I blew him another kiss and made a motion with my hand telling him to pay attention to the crowd, not me.

"Well, thank you." Calon chuckled and looked around at the rest of the guys, who were trying hard to play it cool so they didn't seem as overwhelmed by the response as they were. Spider marked a double beat with the foot pedal on his bass drum. Little by little the pounding got louder. It sounded like a heartbeat. It was a stunning intro and gave me goose bumps every time. The crowd quieted as the pulsing beat got louder and louder. They opened with "Tried", a very unique but obviously punk inspired song, which matched the vibe of the crowd that was there.

I sucked down the last of my beer and fanned myself with my hand. The lighting on the stage made it feel like I was sitting in the Caribbean sun. I didn't want to leave the wings of the stage. I wanted to be as close to Calon as I could. I got so incredibly turned on when I watched him, but I needed to head to the merchandise table. I snaked through the packed house and headed to the back of the club where I'd set up the t-shirts, stickers, CDs, and posters ahead of time. A scantily clad waitress grabbed the empty bottle from my hand, but didn't ask if I wanted more. I really just wanted some water.

During the last three shows, after all the merchandise sold out, I'd make my way up to the second or third row and literally pretend that I was just a groupie and not Calon's girlfriend.

I watched him like I used to when Gracie and I would go to Mitchell's and see them, with fantasies running through my mind of all the things I wanted him to do to me if I ever got the chance. Recently, when I'd fantasize about still being a groupie, I tried to put myself in the mindset that he and I had yet to meet. When he would leave the stage, walk right over to me, and literally sweep my off my feet, the bottom of my stomach would drop out. By the time we'd get to my hotel room, I could feel my heartbeat in my panties. Then he'd make love to me like only he could. After he'd made me come over and over and we'd just lay next to each other trying to catch our breath, I would let myself come back to reality and realize how incredibly lucky I was to hold the heart of Calon Ridge.

"Excuse me. Are you Calon's girlfriend? I saw you kiss him off stage just before they came out." A tiny girl with long raven hair and bright red lips was pressed against the table waiting to pay for the t-shirt in her hands.

I remembered hearing once that if fans thought a musician was spoken for it could actually inhibit their rise to fame. I wanted the world to know that at night, I was bare ass naked with the hot thing stomping out the beat on stage, but I needed to show some decorum and respect her right to fantasize.

"Well, Calon and I go way back. He's a good friend."

"Oh, so that was a friend kiss?"

I smiled but gritted my teeth behind my tight lips. "That's twenty-five dollars, hun." She didn't budge, just watched me. It was slightly creepy.

People called out sizes of shirts and handed money and credits cards over each other. Soon the raven-haired groupie was gone, which was probably for the best, or I may have let the cat out of the bag about me and Calon just to deflate her inappropriate thoughts.

At the end of their first set, I felt like I'd been working the table for twelve hours. A wave of exhaustion came over me, and I could barely stand. Like she fell from the sky to save me, Cyan showed up behind the table.

"Honey, go get some water and take a break. You look like you're ready to drop."

"God, Cyan. Thank you so much. I don't know what's wrong with me. It just hit me all of a sudden."

"You take something?" She was mindlessly running credit cards and handing over CDs and posters as if she literally had two brains, one that did the math and one that talked to me.

"Take something?" I didn't have a headache. I wasn't sure why she asked that question.

"You know… downers or something?" She said it like she was asking if I'd had dinner, which come to think of it I hadn't. The guys shared a pizza, which was so greasy it turned my stomach, and we ended up not having enough time to grab something else before getting to The Moondance.

"No, just a couple beers while the guys set up."

She shrugged and then grabbed the wrist of some guy who tried to walk off with a t-shirt.

I scooted out between antsy fans waiting for their shit. I was immediately waited on by a tall blond, tattooed god behind the bar. He gave me a pitcher of ice water instead of a glass, which made me like him even more. The club was a nice one, so I just knew there'd be a couch or something in the ladies room, which was good because all of a sudden I felt so nauseous I couldn't see straight.

I hit the stall door with one hand and held my water pitcher with the other. The door slammed into the wall, and I braced myself for what I knew was coming. I set the pitcher on the back of the toilet and pulled my hair back just as I lost what seemed like everything I'd eaten since we arrived in LA. I knew that wasn't possible, but I had no idea where all of it came from.

Someone handed me a box of tissues from the counter, and I thanked them without turning away from the toilet. I wiped my mouth and the mascara that ran down my face. My body wracked with convulsive shivers, I longed for the heat I'd been complaining about just an hour earlier while in the wings off the stage.

I made sure there were no remnants of the contents of my stomach anywhere in the stall and turned to wash out my mouth at the sinks. For no apparent reason, I got a panic sensation in my gut but it took me a moment to decide where it came from. Quiet. There was no sound coming from the bar. No music. I rinsed and spit a couple times then checked myself in the mirror. I needed to get back out there. The music that was audible in the bathroom had been ear-splitting but suddenly was silent. I heard a low rumble. The crowd was booing. There were a few slurred expletives thrown out from very drunk patrons. I wiped sweat from my forehead with the back of my hand, rinsed out my mouth one more time, and grabbed a mint from the countertop candy dispenser. I washed my hands and checked my reflection again. Aside from looking exhausted, I was pretty sure no one would be able to tell how sick I'd just been. I headed out and prepared myself for the worst.

I hurried over to Cyan, who now had a crowd of patrons facing away from her. Every pair of eyes in the bar was fixed on the frantic guys up on stage. I watched Calon and Bones untangle some cords while Spider and Manny inspected the amps.

"What the hell?" I tapped Cyan on the shoulder.

"I have no idea. All of a sudden it went silent."

There was nothing I could do to help fix whatever was broken, but I could at least make the situation a little less tense for the guys. I ran over to the DJ booth, flashed my VIP pass, and climbed up the stairs.

"Hey! Are your acoustics shot, too?" I pointed aimlessly, not knowing a whole lot about the wiring for sound.

"No, you want me to play?" He grabbed his headset and a couple vinyls. He was going to old-school it.

I hadn't answered him, but the pumping sound of his signature DJ beat resonated through the bar. I headed through the crowd as best I could toward the side stage entrance. The bouncer at the door recognized me and opened the door before I had a chance to say anything. I ran up the couple stairs and stood just off the stage to see what was going on.

Calon, who usually kept his cool, was ripping at cords and flailing his arms as he talked to the other guys. They all shook their heads and headed toward me in the wings.

"What—"I didn't even finish my question.

"I have no fucking idea! We were rocking the place, and then all of a sudden it was like the soundboard was disconnected. Everything goes quiet. We looked like fucking idiots!"

Bones held a cord for his bass that hooked to the amp. Everyone's instrument appeared to still be connected to their amps. "We're all plugged in. Nothing's melted or cut. What the hell?"

Calon rubbed his face hard with both hands then put his hands on his hips and took a couple deep breaths.

"I love you, Becks." He said it like he was thanking me for being something positive in the midst of a shitty situation.

"I love you, too." I wrapped my arms around his waist and squeezed. He kissed me on the top of the head and sucked in another deep breath.

Ronaldo, the owner we'd met when we first arrived at The Moondance earlier that evening, popped up on stage. The guys told him the problem. Ronaldo scratched his head, and he headed back down the stairs and out into the bar.

"He said they have extra cords we can try. He's going to bring us what he's got in the storage room." Bones yelled over all the techno music to where Calon and I stood.

"Fuck! We look like amateurs, and that label is supposed to be here." He mumbled under his breath then cupped his hand next to his mouth and called out to the guys who had gone back out to fiddle with the cords. "Can someone go tell the DJ to make an announcement?"

Bones nodded and jumped down off the stage and out into the crowd. He was mobbed by girls, which I'm sure was part of his plan.

"Calon, it will be okay. Ronaldo will be right back, and then you guys can go back out and give them even more than what you planned. They'll think it's awesome." I rubbed his arm hoping to ease the tension I could see spreading to every part of his body. Just then the DJ faded the music.

"Ladies and Gentlemen," it was a girl's voice over the PA system, not Bones, "it appears as though Alternate Tragedy has called it a night. I guess they have another gig to play this evening." The crowd was flipping out. "I know, I know. But DJ Jax has enough talent to keep you rocking long into the night. Let's Party!"

Calon lunged past the curtain as if he was going to rebut what the woman, whoever she was, had just said. But the lights had gone out on stage once the DJ amped up his playlist.

"Cal, listen…" Spider, always the voice of reason, patted Calon on the shoulder and then squeezed it as though reassuring him it was going to be fine. "When Ronaldo comes back with those cords we can set this all straight. It's all gonna work out."

I felt my phone buzz in my back pocket. When I looked down at the screen a wave of dizziness came over me again. I leaned into Calon and felt my legs get weak.

"Whoa, Becks. You okay? Honey, what's wrong?"

"Just stressed. I'm okay." I smiled up at him, not wanting to worry him. And also as a feeble attempt to keep myself from worrying.

He didn't need one more thing to be concerned about. I was just tired, hot, and stressed. I hit the *accept call* button when I saw Ronaldo's name on my screen. I plugged my other ear just as Calon scooted a stool from back stage around the corner and motioned for me to sit while, unbeknownst to him, the once chill club owner was ripping me a new asshole. I hung up. They were not going to like what I was about to tell them.

"That was Ronaldo. He said the closet's been cleared out since he'd been in it last and there are no cords."

"Fuck!" I think all four of them spoke simultaneously.

"Guys," I didn't want to finish Ronaldo's message. "He also said he was deeply disappointed at the lack of professionalism in the announcement that cancelled the set. He said he made it clear that we were to play a full two hour show. Then he asked us to leave the premises... immediately."

"WE didn't make that announcement!" Bones yelled as he joined us back stage.

"Who was that?" Manny pointed out toward the DJ booth.

"I have no fucking idea. I didn't even have time to get to the booth." Bones shook his head in frustration.

"Look, I think it's best we just pack up and head out quietly, and I will smooth things over tomorrow when I call Ronaldo to tell him what actually happened. If I can figure out what actually happened."

The guys started to pack up the stage in the dark, so they could haul everything out the back door and into the van. I headed back to the merchandise table where Cyan was convincing some customers that all sales were final. I couldn't believe people were trying to return t-shirts because the guys had to stop playing. I was so frustrated I could spit. It wasn't like we could somehow let everyone know what happened without taking the mic from the DJ and making an announcement that would inevitably sound like a whole string of excuses. Especially since someone else took it upon themselves to make up a pretty shitty one.

"What the hell are they doing, Becki?" Cyan folded piles of t-shirts into boxes as she spoke.

"Something happened to silence the band and then someone made that unauthorized announcement." I shook my head.

"The girl you sent to borrow my VIP pass is the one who made the announcement. I assumed you told her to."

"What? I didn't send anyone to you." I grabbed the crate we used for CDs and started piling them in so we could close up the table before more people came to return their purchases.

"Oh, shit! Some girl said she needed to borrow my VIP pass to give to you because you lost yours and the bouncer wouldn't let you back stage." She cocked her head a little.

"Cyan. I've had mine the whole time. I didn't ask anyone to come borrow yours."

"Well, the girl who took my VIP pass is the one I saw making that announcement. Becki, what the hell is going on?"

"I have no idea, Cyan. What did she look like? Would you recognize her if you saw her again?" I wasn't sure what difference it would make if I knew who she was. It's not like I could find her in the masses inside The Moondance.

"She had long dark hair, real thin. She was wearing a crop top and leggings. Slutty looking. But, that's all I remember."

"She's the one who asked me if I was Calon's girlfriend. This doesn't make any sense." I stood there holding the crate of CDs trying to figure it all out.

"Becki, I am so sorry. I should have texted you to confirm that you actually needed it, but it was so crazy back here. I was so scared if I got distracted people would start stealing stuff off the tables."

"It's not your fault, Cyan. But it's obvious she wanted your VIP pass to convince the DJ to let her make the announcement that made us sound like total assholes. Shit."

"I'm really sorry, B."

"No worries. There's nothing we can do about it now. Unless you can come up with something that will help us keep this from becoming a huge rumor that snowballs out of control. This place was packed tonight because Alternate Tragedy was playing. And, now, all these people think they're dicks for shutting down the stage and leaving for what they think was another show."

"Let me make some calls, Becki, and I will see what I can do. I may not be able to get ahold of anyone tonight, but I'll call you sometime tomorrow to let you know what I come up with."

"That would be amazing, Cyan. Thank you so much."

She gave me a hug, and we grabbed a couple bouncers to let us out the employee exit and help us carry the boxes to where Spider had the van waiting for us. We packed everything in, and I stayed outside the van to thank Cyan one more time for whatever she was planning to orchestrate for us. We rode in silence toward the hotel. I dozed off a little but was startled by the buzz in my pocket.

Cyan: B! I was wrong. Got ahold of a friend at B103. They can do an afternoon interview on Friday, during their Rock Block. And...

Me: Cyan! THANK YOU! And... what?

Cyan: I did a little digging. Our slutty announcer is Malcolm Phoenix's daughter.

Me: Malcolm Phoenix? The sleazy band manager?

Cyan: That's the one.

Me: Why would SHE do that?

Cyan: No idea. Will keep digging. Gotta go.

Me: *You rock! Thx.*

"Guys! Cyan got you an interview Friday with B103. You can set everything straight about whatever the hell it was that happened tonight."

"Thanks, Becki. You da bomb!" Spider flashed me his gorgeous smile in the rearview mirror.

"And, she also said the girl who made that announcement is Malcolm Phoenix's daughter."

"What the FUCK?! That guy's an ass!" Manny slammed his fists on the dashboard.

"He was pissed that we didn't sign with him last year. I bet this was his chicken shit way of getting revenge." Calon rubbed his forehead. "Well, we can't prove anything. So, we just gotta move past it."

Spider cranked the stereo. Pearl Jam's "State of Love and Trust" was a good song to pull us out of our funk. We all sang at the top of our lungs to rid ourselves of the tension from the evening.

twelve

Calon

I WAS SO pissed I could barely breathe. Becki told us some girl asked Cyan to borrow her VIP pass. Something just seemed messed up about the whole night, but I couldn't make sense of any of it. My blood boiled. I couldn't wait to refute the unauthorized announcement that made it sound like we'd just stopped after the fourth song and left. If the faulty wiring was going to shut us down it could have at least happened mid-song, so the whole crowd could tell it wasn't part of our plan to just cut out. Fuck. That whole thing made us look like huge dicks.

I threw my head back against the headboard of Becki's hotel bed and sucked back the last of my beer. A loud crash that came from the bathroom startled me, and I dropped the empty bottle to the floor.

"Becki!" When I flew through the door, the first thing I saw was blood dripping down the side of the tub. The curtain rod was hanging off the wall on one end. There was water pouring down over the curtain and out onto the floor. I couldn't make sense of what was going on until I realized Becki was lying at the bottom of the tub, unconscious and bleeding from a large gash on her forehead.

"Oh, God!! Help! Becki! Someone help!" It was just us in her room, and I knew no one could hear me. I turned the water off and tried to get my hands under her arms, so I could lift her, but the soapy water made her skin too slippery. My phone was in the other room. As I was trying to decide if I should call 9-1-1, her eyes fluttered open, and she winced.

"Ow. My head. What happened?" She pushed herself up on her hands and looked down at the bottom half of her body still entangled in the shower curtain. Blood dripped from her forehead onto her chest and ran down between her breasts. "Calon! What happened? Why am I bleeding? Calon!"

"Shh. Becki. Let's just get you out of this tub and decide if we're taking you to the hospital or not."

"Hospital? No fucking way. I don't do hospitals. I think I just passed out. I had the water super hot."

"Well, let's just get you dried off and cleaned up and see how you feel." I helped her up, handed her a washcloth to hold on her head, wrapped her snuggly in a big white fluffy towel, and carried her out to the bed and propped up all the pillows against the headboard. "Just sit back and give me a sec to get you all cleaned up and see what we're working with here."

She smiled and then winced when she pulled the washcloth from her head and saw it was soaked with blood. My hands shook. I didn't do emergencies well at all. It brought back way too many memories of what I went through when my mom started dating Carver, a nasty son-of-a-bitch who used me as a punching bag when my mom wasn't around.

Soon after she gave up Kate, my mom pretty much lost her marbles and fell off the edge of reality. I spent the next ten years fending for myself and trying to stay out of the way of Carver and a handful of other violent drunks. But, more than once that I pissed one of them off so badly that it landed me in the hospital bloodied and bruised.

Carver was the most convincing liar of them all, and he wasn't stupid. It always ended up looking like an accident, something I'd carelessly done to bust up my face or break both my wrists. He and my mom were a blip on the doctors' and nurses' radar as soon as we would walk into the ER. Gnarly looking dude carrying a busted up kid and a crying mom standing off to the side with her arms folded and her head down. Classic abuse case.

When they'd ask what happened, Carver would come up with these elaborate scenarios that meticulously described each bruise and cut in a way that made it virtually impossible to be suspicious. And like all abused children feel, my mom's life was at stake. If I told anyone what really happened, he'd have killed us both. Hospitals are the only thing that can throw me into a panic attack. And I have huge trust issues with medical staff, since no one saw through his charade like they should have.

"Ow! Calon! That hurts." She tried to push my hands away from her face.

"Becki, just let me wipe the blood away, so I can see how bad this cut is. What happened in there anyway?"

"I remember getting real dizzy and nauseous, so I bent over to try and sit down. That's all I remember. I guess I passed out and fell the rest of the way down, taking the curtain and curtain rod with me." She smiled and rolled her eyes.

"Well, if that's how it happened then this cut is from the faucet, which means you didn't hit it as hard as you could have if you'd have passed out standing straight up. The cut isn't all that bad. I was more concerned that you had a concussion from hitting the edge of the tub or something."

"I've been dizzy and faint all night. I puked up my own and someone else's guts at the show tonight. I guess the stress got to me, and then the heat in the shower with no food in me is what caused me to faint. I'm so sorry I scared you, Calon." She sat still long enough for me to get a Band-Aid from the complimentary toiletries stash. I carefully placed it across her cut, and she leaned forward and wrapped her arms around my neck. Water droplets from her arms soaked through my thin shirt and gave me chills.

"You puked? Honey, are you okay? Are you coming down with something?" I rubbed her face with the back of my hand and kissed her gently. "You don't taste like puke."

"I brushed my teeth, Calon! And, yes, I'm fine. I used to throw up all the time in elementary and middle school when I'd get really stressed over something. School plays, chorus concerts, and any kind of event that had a lot of details mounting up to the final presentation. Always… that last day I'd puke over the moon."

"That's hot." I laughed and kissed her again. "I hate that what you're doing for us made you sick. We have to figure out how to remedy that."

"I just need to stay off the stage. It's too fucking hot up there. And, I didn't eat dinner. I need to have a water bottle with me when we are out and I'm publicity-ing."

"Pub-what?"

"You know what I mean." She giggled and yawned. "Staying cool, drinking lots of water, and making sure I ate is what got me through high school without so much as one puke fest. Even though I had to take public speaking and curate my own art show, I kept it all under control."

"Okay, well that sounds like a plan. Now, since I'm positive you don't have a concussion, I think we should both get some sleep. You need to get some rest. I've read that you're more likely to have anxiety if you're tired, and we've been running you ragged." I helped her get under the covers. "I'll go refill your water bottle." She smiled up at me with that smile that melted me from the inside out. I couldn't believe she was mine. I couldn't believe I could possibly deserve something as perfect as she was. I was in awe of what we were together. It felt so good. Just being in the hotel room with her wiped away all the hell from earlier. Albeit, temporarily.

"You okay if I take a quick shower?" I handed her the water bottle and started to strip off my sweaty clothes from the gig when I realized I'd need to reattach the curtain rod, before I could even think about washing the night's sweat from my skin.

"I'd like to take one with you." She winked and smiled another sexy smile.

"I'd like that, too, but you are banned from showers for the night. I'll be quick, and then I will wrap myself around you and keep you safe all night. Deal?"

"Deal."

She was sound asleep when I came out with the other fluffy white towel around my waist. She looked so peaceful. I had just stopped shaking. I didn't want her to know how badly her fall had freaked me out. I was afraid she'd start keeping things from me if she thought it would upset me. She was everything to me, and if anything ever happened to her because she was trying to protect me from discomfort, I would never forgive myself.

"What are you thinking?" Her voice stopped my heartbeat for a fraction of a second, and I sucked in a breath so sharp it choked me.

"Geez, Becki." I shook my head and climbed under the covers with her. I knew I had to keep my promise and always answer that question honestly, but I didn't want to. I'd already burdened her with enough of my demons just telling her the story of Kate.

"Come on, what's going on in that pretty head of yours?" She rolled to her side and tucked her arm under her head.

I took a deep breath and rolled over to face her. I gently laid my hand on the side of her neck and rubbed her cheek with the pad of my thumb. She was so incredibly beautiful, and if I told her what I'd been thinking about, the soft gaze she blanketed me with would turn to sorrow and pity. But I'd promised.

"Becki, there's been a lot of abuse in my life, and, as much as I want to share all of me with you, I think it may be better if those details stay within me. I don't want to put those images, the things I wish I could forget, in your mind."

"Calon?" Worry lines spread across her forehead. "The abuse. Who was abused?"

"Becki, do we really wanna go there? This has been a really shitty night. I'd really rather not open up this topic after everything that's happened tonight. Ya know?" I knew she wouldn't let it go. Becki was terrible at patiently waiting... for anything.

"Calon, just tell me. I can't put it out of my head unless you answer my question. I don't need you to give me details. I just want you to answer what I asked. Who was abused? Please." She ran her fingers through my hair, which was something she could do all day long, and I'd never tire of it. My whole body relaxed, and I took a deep breath and closed my eyes for a couple seconds.

"After Kate left, my mom just wigged. She was a mess. She started dating this guy, Carver." Just saying his name lifted the hair on the back of my neck. "Carver hit me and my mom when he'd been drinking. Mostly me because I always tried to keep him from getting to my mom."

"Shit, Calon."

"Yeah." I slid my right arm under the covers and around her waist. The fluffy towel that covered her body was warm and inviting. I wanted to rip it from her and make love to her, but I knew she needed to sleep. "Babe, you need to sleep. Let's get some sleep, all right?"

"Okay." Her voice was barely a whisper, and her eyes fluttered closed. She took a deep breath and wiggled herself as close to me as she could get. "Calon, I'm sorry he hurt you."

I pulled her in close, and her head tucked into my neck. Her breath on my neck and chest was enough to win me a pair of blue balls for the evening, but I could be satisfied with just holding her for now. She fit so perfectly in my arms. It was like she was made to be mine.

As I lay there, lyrics formed in my mind. It was how I wrote the music for the *Fallen* album. I would just lie awake at night and get inside an emotion. My heart would just spurt words and phrases, and I'd write them all down on a pad of paper I kept next to my bed. I propped myself up and looked around the room. There was tablet with a few sheets of hotel letterhead and a pen on the side table. I reached over Becki and grabbed it. Becki rolled away from me and snuggled into her pillow. I rolled over and just started writing.

So much of my life has been darkness
But you handed me the sun
Brought to me as a gift
Baby, you're the one.

Your heart came at me like the tide
Each wave coveting more
Now you're completely inside
And, I'll never leave your shores.

I want to be your habit
I want to be your vice
I want to lose myself inside you.
Be the reflection in your eyes.

So much of my life has been darkness
But you handed me the sun
Brought to me as a gift
Baby, you're the one.

The one who lights my fire
Who turns me inside out.
The one whose body tempts me
Leaves me breathless and spellbound

So much of my life has been darkness
But you handed me the sun
Brought to me as a gift
Baby, you're the one.
I want to be your habit
I want to be your vice
I want to lose myself inside you.
Be the reflection in your eyes.

I want to be
I want to be
I want to be your habit
I want to be your vice
I want to lose myself inside you.
Be the reflection in your eyes.

I laid the pad and pen back on the table and pulled Becki into me again. She mumbled something I couldn't understand, tilted her head back, and pressed her back into me. Even in her sleep she loved me.

summer flashback

JUST BEFORE WE played on the main stage at Summer Fest, we announced we were headed to LA to go on tour with the Turkeys. Becki jumped up on a bench or something and said she'd be our publicist. We kind of hired her on the spot, right there while we were still on stage, more as our manager than publicist. Of course, for her to tour with us she needed to take a leave of absence from UTK, pack up all her belongings and put them in storage until she returned. That was kind of a big deal for a spur of the moment decision. It was then that I knew she wasn't just diggin' me for my hair.

We'd talked for a long time in her sparse dorm the night before we left, because I needed to make sure this was the best decision for her. I wanted to know she'd thought about all the pros and cons. But that night, as she sat cross-legged on her bed in huge sweats and a tank top with her hot pink bra straps distracting me, I made a move I hadn't made thus far.

"Calon, I'm really excited about this opportunity, please don't think I'm making a rash decision." She cocked her head to the side and smiled.

I walked over and sat across from her, one foot on the floor and one folded in front of me. I took her hands in mine. "Becki, listen. It's a big deal for you to drop everything and head across the country in a van with a bunch of guys you barely know." I rubbed her hands with my thumbs.

"Look, Calon," she tore her hands from mine and shot up off the bed and began to pace and wag her finger at me, "if you aren't interested in having me as your manager then just say so. Grow a pair. Don't sit there and make it sound like you're doing me a favor by second-guessing your public decision to hire me on the spot. That's a dick move!" She was pissed and something about that made *my* dick move. *God, this girl.*

"Becki, listen—"

"No! You listen, rock star! Don't make this about me when you just don't want me tagging along. I get it. Having me along for the ride would put a damper on all the groupie-fucking you were looking forward to."

"Becki, it's not like that!"

"Shut up. Listen. Let's just call it a mistake, and you can walk away, no hard feelings. I'm sure I can get an internship locally or something, so I don't have to go through the mess of undoing all the leave of absence paperwork."

"I want—"

"I really thought we were moving toward something, Calon. You had me snowed. Completely. And FUCK if that doesn't piss me off! I don't let my guard down, but you seemed different. You seemed—"

I grabbed her face and crashed my mouth into hers. She gasped, and I felt her rigid body go slack. I closed my eyes and moved my lips against hers, as if I was trying to memorize them. I kissed each corner of her mouth. She let out a soft whimper and slowly started to kiss me back. I slid my tongue between her teeth, she bit down gently, like she wasn't going to let me any further. That lasted less than a second. Our tongues softly explored each other's mouths. What started slow and gentle turned fevered and then back to tender over the next handful of minutes. When the tiny pecks slowed enough that she could speak, she whispered in true Becki form.

"That is the hottest way anyone has ever told me to shut up." She continued to kiss me softly.

"I don't want to leave you behind, Becki. I want nothing more than to have you on this journey with us—with me. I mean that with all my heart. You've got to believe me."

"Well, I do, *now*. Next time, can you just start with that, please? It would save us a whole hell of a lot of trouble."

thirteen
Becki

IT WAS THE day of the B103 radio interview, and I felt like hell. I didn't know what was wrong with me. I thought back to everything I ate the day before. A soft pretzel from a street vendor while the guys rehearsed, a couple pieces of sushi from FRESH on my way to the post office to mail out more demos, and nothing for dinner. Apparently, the vendor guy at FRESH sold me some nasty ass food.

I lay perfectly still so the nausea would subside. I breathed in through my mouth and out through my nose and tried to think of anything but running to the bathroom. I thought about my sweet Calon's face and his soft perfect lips. I pictured us walking hand in hand on campus, and I wiggled at the thought of the sexy looks he gave me from the stage. I held it as long as I could, but there were no winners in this situation. I flung the covers off and ran to the bathroom just in time for the hot, sour liquid from my stomach to hit nothing else but the inside of the toilet. Pulling a towel down from the rack on the wall behind me, I had just enough strength left to drape it over my shoulders.

"Becki?" Calon stood at the door to the bathroom with both hands on his head. He looked panicked and unsure of what to do.

"Water. Please." My voice barely made it out of my throat before another involuntary heave caused me to wretch once again. The muscles in my stomach cramped, and a moan of pain escaped me. My legs were folded under me and the cold tiles made imprints on my shins. I scooted over to the bath mat for some semblance of warmth underneath me. And then the chills came. By the time Calon came back with a bottle of water from the vending machine, I shook uncontrollably. He knelt down behind me and wrapped his warm body around me as best he could. I reached up to flush as I puked again.

"Aww, Becks. What the hell did you eat?" He took the hairband he always kept on his wrist and pulled my hair back into something like a bun to keep it from falling in the toilet.

"I had a pretzel and sushi yesterday, but that's it. I thought the veggies tasted funky, but I just assumed they'd added something else to what they normally put in my vegetarian ones." My stomach cramped again, and I dropped my head down onto my arm, which lay across the toilet seat.

"So, we mark FRESH off our list of places to eat. Dammit, I'm so sorry, Becki." He gently kissed my cheek.

"Ew, Calon, I just puked." I couldn't imagine putting my face that close to someone whose stomach contents had spewed from their lips only seconds ago.

"You didn't puke out your cheek—and I held my breath." He chuckled a little. "We have that radio gig today, maybe we should cancel it, so I can stay here with you. Or, I could just send the guys without me."

"Don't be an idiot, Calon. If you cancel, you will fuel the reputation you got Wednesday night of being unreliable. You need to go. All of you need to be there. I'll be fine. It's not like I've never thrown up alone before." I smiled, but it hurt to open my eyes, my head pounded.

"We'll go but under one condition. You call me if you need me to come back. Promise?"

"Promise. Now, go run upstairs and see if the guys are up. You all need to hash out what your answers will be to the questions that could come up regarding the episode at The Moondance."

"Hey, sick girl, take a sick day. Relax. We got this." He stood and then leaned back down and kissed my head. "I'm going to throw on some clothes, I'll be right back."

"Just go, Calon. Get dressed and go upstairs. I'll be fine. I promise."

"You sure?"

"Go!"

He hustled out of the bathroom, and I could hear him mumbling to himself as he rifled through the drawers he'd filled with a couple changes of clothes, since he slept with me most of the time. He cursed a couple times, I think from stubbing his toe. He peeked in on me one more time. When he saw I had changed from hunched over the toilet to sitting on the side of the tub, he smiled and gave me a thumbs up.

I was scared to take another shower for fear I'd pass out again. I looked up at the rod above my head. I must not have actually broken anything, just pulled it down because Calon had obviously fixed it at some point. That was good, because now that we didn't have a management company paying for our room, we were trying to make the check from Bones's brother last as long as possible. I was glad we didn't have that repair billed to us.

I brushed my teeth and washed my face, threw on some sweats and a t-shirt from my 'this isn't dirty' pile on top of the dresser. I climbed back into bed and looked at the clock. I was sure she'd be up.

"Hello?" I didn't realize how much I missed Gracie until I heard her voice. And, like a stupid jerk, I started to cry.

"Hi." The one single word I spoke broke through my lips alongside a sob so forceful it made me snort at the same time, which made me laugh. *Idiot.*

"Becki? Are you laughing or crying?" She giggled.

"Both. I miss you, Gracie Ann." I wiped the few tears that had escaped and cleared my throat. I grabbed a piece of gum from my purse on the side table in hopes that the mint flavor would settle my stomach some more.

"Aww, I miss you too, Becki. Wow, Calon's got you all mushy and sensitive. I never thought I'd see the day." I could feel her smile across the phone.

"No, he doesn't. It's been a tough thirty-six hours, and I'm just spent. Some shit went down at the show Wednesday night that made the guys look like assholes. I passed out in the shower and split my forehead open that night. Yesterday was uneventful but I woke up this morning puking my guts out. Ya know, just that." I rubbed my head and squeezed my eyes closed to attempt to rid my brain of the dull ache that resided there.

"Geez, what the hell did you drink?"

"Nothing at all! Just water. I think I ate some bad sushi."

"You're eating sushi now?"

"The veggie kind, nothing with faces."

"I was gonna say." We both laughed. Gracie had sat through enough 'what really happens on a farm' documentaries with me to know that eating meat was not ever going to be an option. Ever.

"How's Jake?"

"Perfect."

"Yuck."

"Stop rolling your eyes at me! How's Calon?"

"Perfect-er!" I shook my head at myself when I said it.

"Becki! You fell."

"I did. Deep, girl. I'm in so deep. My head is definitely over my heels."

"Oh my word, Becki!" She squealed so loud I had to hold the phone away from my ear. "I couldn't be happier! For both of you. So…"

"Yeah. We did it."

"Beck." Her voice came out deep and raspy as though she imagined that scenario in her head.

"Watch where your mind goes, girl. That's my rock star penis, *not* yours."

"Well, shit, Becki! How can my mind *not* go there when you call it a rock star penis? Don't worry, I'm not going to ask for the nitty-gritty. Calon and I are too close for me to know what he's like in bed. Although—"

"Stop right there!" I threatened, and she howled, which made me laugh out loud, so hard it hurt my sore puke muscles.

We spent a long time just catching up with each other. We talked about the fucked up situation at The Moondance. Then she told me the trial dates for the Sigma Chi brothers wasn't set yet, but she, Ashley, Chelsea, and a couple other girls had already met with their lawyer to go over the details of each of their attacks. She cried a little as she spoke about the details the lawyer mentioned after he watched the video of her rape. My heart hurt for her that she had to know those details, but I understood the prosecution wanted to be thorough.

"So, playing at Mitchell's is still going well?" I yawned and realized my queasiness had significantly improved.

"Oh, Becki, I love it. Yesterday Jake and I had lunch there, and we were talking to Buzz. He was telling us all these awesome stories about musicians getting discovered, people proposing, stuff he's seen over the years. This morning Jake and I were just lying in bed talking about how amazing it would be to stay here in Knoxville after graduation and open a bar. With his business background, he'd be perfect to open and run his own establishment. And I could still play on the weekends and work during the week at The Extension School."

"Extension School?" I snuggled down under the covers and pretended Gracie and I were just hanging out at her apartment chatting the day away.

"The internship I'm doing right now is at The Knoxville Extension School. It's a school for students who, for one reason or another, just can't make it in a public school setting. Most are special needs, but some struggle with anxiety, and some are severely depressed or suicidal. It's a residence setting for the more severe diagnoses; those kids live there all year round. I'm the life skills coordinator. I do activities with them, work with their therapists, and in some cases, their county case workers."

"Wow, Gracie, you're touching lives. I knew social work was the major for you. I'm so happy for you."

"Yeah, we're both living our dreams, huh?"

"Except you'll have a degree next summer, I'll still be a drop out." I winced a little when I said that word.

"Beck! You withdrew so you could travel with the band. You'll finish your degree. Who knows, maybe you could do it online while you guys are on tour."

"We'll see. I love what I'm doing, but I miss the writing I was doing in my communications classes. I don't write anything now. I just make phone calls and set the guys' schedule for interviews, gigs, and other appearances."

"So, write."

"Write what?"

"I don't know, but find something that keeps that part of you inspired. You're an amazing writer. I was your editor for all those writing classes, remember?"

"Yep, somehow I should have shared those grades with you!"

"Just come back soon and see me! I really miss you, and I'm doing some really cool stuff at The Extension School. I wish you could come to some of our events." She sighed.

"Maybe I can schedule in a break in the next couple months, so we could all come home for a little. The guys could play at Mitchell's. Like a surprise concert. We've been looking for a name for the tour. Maybe we will just call it—"

"The Surprise Tour!" We said it at the same time and squealed. Then we laughed our asses off.

"Gracie, could you give Buzz my number and have him call me? I'd like to get a date set for this, so we can plan on seeing each other sometime soon. I really, really miss you." A wave of nausea came over me unexpectedly, and I bolted to the toilet again.

"Did you just puke again?"

"I did. I'm so sorry. That was really gross."

"Becki, maybe you should go to the doctor's." Gracie was always telling me to go to the doctor's for something. It's just the way her mom was. She took her to the doctor's for everything; hangnails, cramps, cold sores. My mom didn't take me unless I was half unconscious with a hundred and six degree fever.

"I'll be fine, G. It's just whatever Hung Dong put in my veggie sushi roll yesterday."

"Hung Dong?"

"I don't know his name. There was an odd flavor, but I was starving and just assumed it was a different kind of sauce than what I was used to. Something was probably spoiled. I just have to get it all out of my system. I'll be fine. Promise—Oh, God, I gotta go. Round three."

"Feel better, Becki! Love you."

I hit end call just before I dry heaved again into the toilet. I texted her that I loved her, too, then set the phone on the vanity while I rested my head on my folded hands, elbows still on the toilet seat.

It had been almost two hours since Calon had gone upstairs to hash out their plans for the B103 interview. I went into manager mode and texted him.

Me: *Calon, you guys have to be at the B103 studio by 3*

Nothing.

I brushed my teeth and climbed back into bed. I sucked down the last of my water and grabbed the pad of paper from the side table to take my mind off how shitty I felt and to make a list of places I needed to call to set up some more gigs and appearances.

Calon's handwriting. At first, I thought maybe I shouldn't read it. But then, I realized he'd been jotting down lyrics. I could tell by the slant of his letters that he'd written them quickly, like his mind was going faster than his hand, which is usually how it all happened. His heart took over, and his hand just had to try and keep up. I loved to watch him write.

My eyes glided over each verse of his newest song. One I knew nothing about. The way he paired the words and phrases infused so much life into the emotion those words held. I could feel the longing in his heart, the uncertainty within his soul and the fire of a love just beginning when I read his words.

I remembered, not too long ago, telling him that maybe one day he'd write a song about me. There was no doubt in my mind that the words I was reading were written for me. With the words scrawled across the paper I held in my hands, Calon had sculpted an emotion far more intense than I could have described. But it was an emotion I *felt*. He loved me. He really, really loved me. And I, finally, trusted someone with my heart.

Tears.

I heard the hotel door open, and my beautiful man peeked around the corner, as though he was worried he would wake me. When I looked up at him, tears fell from my eyes and rolled down my cheeks. I saw his eyes go to the tablet in my lap. He smiled and walked over to my bedside. He sat on the edge of the bed, took the tablet from me, and held my hands in my lap.

"Becki Jane—*you* do *that* to me. You."

"Wow."

I leaned into his shoulder. He kissed the top of my head and rocked me until I fell back to sleep.

THE BUZZ THAT was specific to Calon rang in my head and jolted me from a peaceful dream.

Calon: *Becks turn on 103 at 3:45*

Me: *I love you*

Calon: *And I love you. Absolute.*

Me: *Turning it on now*

Calon: *Gonna be awesome!*

I turned on the clock radio next to the bed and turned the dial until B103 came in clear as a bell. I tore off Calon's "Vice" lyrics and laid them carefully on the side table, as though they were a precious artifact. To me, they were. I then used the tablet to start a list. I jotted down everything that came to mind.

THE SURPRISE TOUR
CALL BUZZ—OCTOBER SHOW DATE?
LOOK FOR CHARITY EVENTS TO PLAY
CONFIRM DATES FOR UPCOMING GIGS
DEPOSIT CASH FROM MOONDANCE

… and the list continued to spill out of my brain.

At quarter to four on the dot, the B103 DJ spoke loud and clear and pulled my attention from my work.

"Welcome to the afternoon Rock Block. I'm Jesse Severson, and I'm thrilled to come to you live with my new friends Calon, Spider, Manny, and Bones—the talented members of the newest talent on the rock 'n' roll horizon. Please, welcome Alternate Tragedy! Thanks for comin' in, guys. It's great to have you here."

"Thanks for having us, Jesse." Calon's voice was even hotter over the radio. *Sheesh*. I squeezed my thighs together.

"So, how many gigs have you guys played since you've been in LA?"

"I've lost count, but we've done a lot. Big and small shows. We're having a blast in this town."

"Great. Great. You all hail from Knoxville, Tennessee."

"We do. Go Vols!" Bones. What a dork. I wasn't sure he'd ever even been to a UTK sporting event. He'd been at all the tailgates, but I was pretty certain he'd never actually stepped foot in our stadium.

"I've spoken to numerous people in the industry and no one can seem to explain your rise to the top. Spider, you guys aren't even signed, right?" Jesse's excitement about the interview was evident in his voice. It was a cool thing to hear.

"No, we're not." Spider chuckled. "And, believe me, we're just as stunned. We'd never complain about the attention we're getting, but it's just as much of a mystery to us as it is to everyone else."

"So, then what's with the little mishap Wednesday night at The Moondance? You've got some pretty pissed off fans. What happened?"

My phone rang, and it was one of the bar owners I'd called a couple days before. I had to answer it, but I was so mad I would miss Calon's explanation.

But once I heard what the call was about, I was too stoked to care. I knew I'd get the play by play from the guys anyway.

I had to text Calon. I knew he wouldn't get the text until later, but I would've exploded if I'd kept it in.

Me: *You guys are playing The Jungle Room Thurs, Fri, & Sat next week*

I turned the volume up a little to be sure to at least catch the end of what he said about the Moondance gig.

"I tell you, Jesse. The pieces of The Moondance puzzle just don't seem to fit. Something strange and unexplainable happened. From the stage losing power to an unauthorized announcement and a stolen VIP pass, it just doesn't add up. But you can be sure we will be double checking all of our equipment before we go on stage from now on. And to make it up to our fans that felt dissed Wednesday night, we will be at The Jungle Room Thursday, Friday, and Saturday next week—thanks to our amazing manager, Becki Mowry."

I could hear the smile on his face when he said my name. I giggled like a little girl.

I really did heart Calon Ridge. He hearted me right back.

sigh

fourteen
Calon

BECKI ASSURED ME she was fine, but for the last couple weeks she seemed distant, not exhausted. Her sudden illness, if you could call it that, only slowed her down for a couple days, since then she'd been going a hundred miles an hour. She'd lined up at least two gigs but usually four or more a week until Christmas. She'd argue that she could handle stress well; however, her job as manager took a toll on her. I knew she wasn't back to her old self, and I assumed she was still feeling rotten, just hiding it well. I remembered she'd once mentioned that she'd been sick as a little kid and had to have chemo. I couldn't help letting my mind wonder about her health. I knew what I had to do. She'd be so pissed at me, but I needed to put her first and not worry how mad she would be.

"Calon, hey, it's Cyan. I wanted to let you know, I found the perfect manager for you. She's got experience. Interned with the manager of The Killers for a while until they started doing more in-house planning. A real go-getter kind of style. I did background checks, called references, and it all looks good. I said you'd be in touch, so if you'd like to run your own interview, just call Danny directly." She spouted a number for me to call and then ended her message, "Okay. Call me if you need anything else. See ya."

Me: *Our hotel room around dinner would be perfect to meet w Danny*

Cyan: *Done.*

"Who was that?" Becki's head rested on my shoulder as we rode back from rehearsal to the hotel in preparation for a new week of gigs. I knew if I told her we were trying to get her some help to lighten her load, it would get her all fired up. So, telling her in the van with the guys was probably not the perfect plan, but if I tried to blow off her question, she'd lose it. She'd been more than a little moody lately, so I opted for the better of my two shitty options.

"Becks, now, don't get mad." She sat straight up and pursed her lips.

"Aw, shit." Bones attempted to keep his reaction under his breath, but he sucked at being subtle.

"What? Who was it? And why do you look so nervous to tell me." She smacked me hard on my thigh and made me jump. I grabbed her hand, so she didn't go any higher than my thigh.

"Becks, listen. Over the last two months, your responsibilities as manager have grown exponentially compared to what you were doing when we first came out here. And it's wearing you down. I've never seen you so out of it. Over the summer, you were the one keeping *me* up during our all-nighters. You used to do fine with little to no sleep."

"You're firing me? Are you fucking—"

"No! No! No way! We love what you do. You're damn good at it. We just feel like it's not fair for us to expect you to carry the load for us."

"Would you just spit it out already? What am I not supposed to not get mad about?"

"That was a voicemail from Cyan. I called her a couple days ago to see if she'd help find us an assistant for you, so you could cut your responsibilities back a little without losing your creative control." I spoke with barely a breath. I wanted to get it all out before she blew a gasket. "You're kick ass at being our manager, but you could share some of what you do with someone else, so you'd be able to pick and choose what you wanted to handle and push the rest onto your assistant. You see?"

"Calon, I'm fine." I was shocked at how calm she stayed. I really expected a fight. "Whatever made me sick a couple weeks ago just hit me hard. I'm tired, but I'm just starting to get back my vim and vigor. You shouldn't have to pay someone else. I should be able to handle it."

"I have no doubt you *could* do it. I just don't want you to *have* to. I want you to love what you do and lately, you're not enjoying it."

"So, who is this person you'd be hiring?" I was glad she was so open to the idea. It made me think she may not have been comfortable asking for help.

"Cyan found a guy named Danny. He used to intern with The Killers. He comes with great references, and hiring him seems like a no brainer. We're going to meet with him tonight, so you can have a say in who you'll be working so closely with. I want it to be a good match for you."

"Wow. You've got it all figured out, don't you? And you got me a guy. Nice." She smiled at me, and I grabbed her face and kissed her. She took hold of my nipple right through my shirt and twisted.

"Listen, Ridge, how about next time you talk to me directly, instead of pussy-footing around the subject and making plans without me. Okay?"

"Okay, I'm sorry, Becki. Can I have this back, please?" I pushed her hand off my nipple and rubbed the pain away. No doubt, that was gonna leave a mark.

"Thanks, guys, I appreciate the help. A lot. I really do. But, if you three let him go behind my back again, I'll kill ya all. Got it?"

Shit. The guys were silent.

"Becki, there's one more thing."

"Oh, shit." Bones shook his head. "Quit while you're ahead, dude. Quit while you're ahead."

"Calon James, you were scot-free. You could have come out of this unscathed. What the hell?"

"I made a doctor's appointment for this afternoon."

"Nope. I don't do doctors. Cancel it."

"Becki—"

"I don't need you to decide when I see a doctor. I'm fine, just stressed, that's all. I know my body pretty well, Calon. I know what it needs. I'm not going into my whole health history with some stranger just because my resistance is down. Cancel it."

"Becks—"

"Cancel it!" She yelled so loud, Spider hit the curb on the way into the parking garage under our hotel.

"No, I won't." I tried to take her hands again, but she pulled away from me.

"Then you can go because I'm not." She started to get up to get out of the van, and I pulled her back down. "Calon!" She shot a look at me I'd not yet been the recipient of. It shook me a little.

"Uh. We'll see you guys upstairs, okay?" Manny tried to smile, but it came out as an awkward grimace.

"Listen, Becki—"

"No, *you* listen, Calon. You don't get to do this. You don't get to make decisions for me. You're my boyfriend, not my parent."

"I didn't make the appointment because I'm your boyfriend. I'm trying to take care of you. I want you to feel better."

"Does this have something to do with Chloe, Calon?" I couldn't read her tone or her body language. It was like she was apathetic.

"No. Well, I guess a little. But—"

"Calon, I'm exhausted, not dying." As soon as she said it I saw her cringe. "I'm sorry. That sounded insensitive. I didn't mean it like that. I just meant I think you're taking this all too seriously. You can't put your experience with Chloe on me. You can't assume the worst whenever I don't feel good."

"Becki, wouldn't you feel better to know what's actually wrong, instead of just assuming it's exhaustion and stress?" My voice was shaky. I think mostly because I was reliving conversations I'd had with Chloe. Becki looked at her hands folded in her lap. I got the feeling she wasn't just being stubborn.

"Calon, my mom wasn't big on going to the doctors. But I'll never forget the time she drove me from the school nurse's office to my pediatrician. That's the last day I was a healthy kid. A day later I was diagnosed with Leukemia and fighting for my life. I went through it all.

Cancer is a fucking nightmare. I swear it's Hell on earth. Well, once I'd been cancer-free for five years, I decided it was going to take a hell of a lot for me to voluntarily go back to a place that hands out death sentences." I pulled her into my lap, and I turned and stretched my legs out on the length of the bench seat in the back of the van. She laid her head on my shoulder and bit her thumbnail. I'd seen Becki nervous before but nothing like this. She was terrified of getting slapped in the face with a diagnosis she was least expecting.

"Look, the doctor can see you later today. I'm not going to force you to go, but let's just wait it out a little and see how you feel later. We can always cancel it." I rubbed her back, and she tucked her face into my neck. I felt a couple tears, and it broke my heart. Was I making my own diagnosis just because of what I'd been through with Chloe? Would I always assume the worst? I didn't want to upset Becki, but I thought it would put both our minds at ease to know for sure it was just stress.

"Calon, I'm sorry. I'm not trying to be difficult. I just don't want to see that look again. I didn't understand it then, but I'll never forget his somber gaze. He knew the words that would fall from his lips would change everything for my mom and me. I don't want to have something like that thrown at me again." She wiped her face with her hands and took a deep breath.

"Let's go grab something to eat and take it up to the room."

"Sounds good."

"Calon, I'm going to cancel that appointment. You know that, right?"

"Yep." I smiled down at her, and we headed to grab some takeout.

We knocked on the door because our hands were too full to reach for or even swipe a key. Bones swung the door open and waggled his eyebrows like he did when he was about to hit on someone.

"Get outta the way, Bones. I'm gonna drop all this food."

"Hey, guys, Cal and Becki brought dinner. And, Cal, someone's here to see you."

Becki and I sat the bags down on the table at the same time and stood stoic next to each other due to the leggy blonde in cowboy boots perched on the edge of our dresser. She had big curls that fell around her face and down over her shoulders. One of the curls actually disappeared between her breasts. She wore a lacey peach-colored dress that came just to the middle of her thighs, but her legs looked to be nine feet tall, so her dress appeared way shorter than it probably was. A pair of Ray-Ban's sat on the top of her head and a smile that could stop traffic spread across her face. She uncrossed her ankles and walked over to Becki and me with her hand extended.

"Calon. Becki. I'm Danny. Cyan said this was a good time to come meet you guys. I just wanted to introduce myself before we made any plans for a discussion on what services I could provide the band." She winked and shook both our hands.

I waited for some snide comment from Bones on the *services she could provide* for him. He said nothing, but Becki's body language told me I should be more concerned about her reaction to Danny than his. I took Becki's hand in mine and lifted it to kiss her knuckles, making it perfectly clear that flirting with me was not in Danny's best interest.

"Nice to meet you, Danny. I hope you like Mexican food. You're welcome to join us for dinner, and we can chat while you have all of us here." I motioned toward the food.

"Sounds great. I'm a Mexican food whore." Her voice was sultry and deep. But she had a sweet air about her, too.

We spent the next couple hours getting to know Danny, and it seemed she really knew her stuff. As long as she and Becki could stay on good terms with each other, I knew they would make a phenomenal team.

"So, Danny, you would be working as my assistant, which means, as manager, I would give you your weekly responsibilities and you would fulfill them to the best of your ability. What strengths do you have that you feel would be an asset to us?" Becki spun a pencil between her fingers and then tapped the eraser end on the table, as though that was the cue for Danny to answer. There was a subtle cockiness in Becki's attitude. It was obvious she was pissing on her territory and letting Danny know she wasn't going to be disrespected. Manny and Spider both looked over at me and nodded their approval of how Becki was handling the situation. We all glanced over at Bones who was staring, mouth agape, as Danny licked her fingers free of dripping salsa, as she readied herself to answer Becki.

"That's a great question, Becki. Look, I'm here to assist you, plain and simple. Are there tasks and details that I enjoy better than others? Sure. But, my job is to make your job easier, and that's what my focus would be. I'm a very detail oriented person. I'm a bit OCD, which lends itself well to getting a job done right, the first time. I'm also a people pleaser by nature—"

"Shit, yeah you are." Bones's hand slapped over his mouth, and he spoke through his fingers. "Shit! Did I actually say that out loud? Fuck. I'm an idiot." He motioned with his hand for Danny to continue. The rest of us just shook our heads.

"Thanks for the vote of confidence, Bones." Danny laughed. "Becki, you and I can sit down and make a list of the things you would rather not be bothered with, and I won't overstep the boundaries you set. I'm meticulous with following directions and I won't let you down. I really think we'd make a good team."

"Sounds promising. Now, Danny, can you tell us a little about yourself? What would you like us to know about you other than your job-related skills?" Becki jotted some things down on her tablet. I looked over her shoulder and read the words she'd just written…

A BIT TOO PERKY, BUT I DON'T HATE HER YET.

I had to rub my face and clear my throat to keep from laughing out loud.

Danny took a sip of her water and wiped the corners of her mouth with a napkin. I had to kick Bones under the table to keep him from being so obvious with the inappropriate thoughts he was having about Danny as she spoke.

"Well, let's see. I was born and raised in Texas. I'm a country girl through and through. I sing. I'm a huge romance book addict. I run every day, and I'm trying so hard to curb my instinctive reaction to Muppet-flail right now because I'm sitting in a hotel room with the hotties of Alternate

Tragedy." Her voice went up like three octaves as she spoke that last fact, and I could almost feel Becki's eyes roll.

"You said you sing." Becki's voice had a 'bring it on' tone to it. She didn't even give Danny a chance to respond. "Not to put you on the spot, but can you sing something for us?"

"Um, sure." Danny scooted her chair back and shot Becki a look that spoke volumes about her lack of intimidation. Man, chicks were brutal. She smoothed her dress, cleared her throat and put one hand on her stomach. She closed her eyes, hummed quietly, and took a deep breath. She tapped out a beat with one boot and slapped the top of her thigh on the offbeat with her free hand. And like she was standing on an audition stage, she belted the most hypnotizing rendition of Sara Evans's "Suds in the Bucket" I'd ever heard. Her voice was strong and sultry with just the right amount of rasp. I slowly and discreetly rolled down my flannel sleeves. Becki would punch me right in the junk if she noticed the goose bumps that raised on my arms. *Shit, she's amazing.* Her voice did the perfect country twang trill in all the right spots and soon her hips were dipping up and down, back and forth as we watched her lose herself in the a cappella moment.

She sang the entire song, complete with a 'yee-hoo' that just about threw Bones to the floor. She finished, smiled a shy smile, and blushed a little then sat back down in her chair and took a huge bite of her over-stuffed taco. She glanced up at the rest of us, mouths still agape, and giggled.

"Wow. Holy hell, Danny. You're crazy good. Wow. You gave me goose bumps." Becki's eyes were as big as saucers as she spoke her sincere words. Danny was incredibly talented. No one could dispute that. "Well, even if you're only half as talented at assisting, then we would be lucky to have you. You guys agree?" Becki looked around the table at the rest of us, and we all nodded in unison.

"Oh my Gawd! I won't let you down, I promise." She high fived each of us.

"One last question, Danny…" We all looked over at Becki as she smirked at each of us one by one. She was about to add something to this interview, but I had no idea where she was going with it. "Are you free next weekend?"

"Halloween weekend? I've had a couple of party invites. They're nothing I can't respectfully decline, though. What's next weekend?"

"We are headed to Knoxville for the first stop on our newly-titled SURPRISE TOUR; Mitchell's Pub, where these guys have played for years, is having their masquerade ball, and we will all be showing up in costume. It'll be a surprise to everyone except Gracie and Buzz."

The guys howled.

"Becki! That's amazing, but how are we going to do that? It took us days to get out here from Tennessee, and we certainly can't afford to fly." I didn't want to put a damper on what sounded like an incredible plan but I couldn't figure out the logistics.

"Well, believe it or not, Buzz was so excited about the idea he figured out how to make it work. He's a former executive at an airline. Go figure, who would have thought of the grizzled barkeep in a three-piece suit? As part of his retirement package, he gets a decent number of travel vouchers each year. He never uses them because he's too busy running the bar. Lucky for us, he can gift them. It's one of the perks of being an executive. He told us to let him know anytime we need to fly. He's wetting his pants and has all kinds of ideas for hyping the event without actually revealing who will be taking the stage."

We all whooped and yelled at the same time.

Becki grinned and nodded.

"Becki! This is incredible!" I wrapped my arms around her and gave her a loud smacking kiss on the neck. As much as I'd always imagined travelling with the band, I had recently realized how much I missed the small town celebrity thing. I loved checking out all the new venues in LA and meeting new fans each night. But, even with all the exciting things happening, I missed Mitchell's, the college scene, and our close-knit family of fans. I'd never realized what a hometown boy I was.

We were going home. It was only for the weekend, but it would fill our tanks.

"So, I've never been to Tennessee. I'm assuming by y'all's reaction, this is going to be a great time." Danny smiled and seemed to welcome the adventure.

"Hell yeah, it is. I would be honored to be your own personal tour guide, Danny." Bones spoke with sincerity. I waited for the punch line, something that would give her a peek into his inappropriate thoughts, but there was none.

"Thanks, Bones. I'll probably take you up on that." She smiled coyly and winked.

"So, now that it's past happy hour, how about we all head out for the night to celebrate Danny joining our crazy little team and because we're going home next weekend? Who's in?" Manny's party meter must've been running low.

"Danny, you wanna come upstairs with me? My room is a little less smelly and more girl-friendly for primping." Becki seemed quite comfortable with this new assistant idea. Especially for being surprised by the fact that Danny wasn't a dude.

"Sure, Becki. Thanks."

Becki came over and kissed me, and then the girls left the room, and the four of us took turns fist bumping each other.

We did a couple shots and talked about our pending Tennessee trip while we waited for a text from Becki that they were ready to head out. When we got her text, we took a couple minutes to throw the untouched food in the fridge.

"Shit, Cal. The threesome you could have with those two. Woooo, shit! I'd pay to watch that!" Bones made a jacking off motion in front of his crotch.

And there it was. He'd held it in longer than I'd ever known him to, but it all caught up with him and wham, he had me naked with Becki and Danny.

"Shut up, Bones!" I cuffed him on the back of the head, and we all cracked up. I knew each of us got a small glimpse of what that would be like just because of Bones's comment. I shook my head as an innate reaction to rid myself of that image.

"Yeah, you got a visual for that, too, didn't ya, Cal? You're gonna have to do more than shake your head to get rid of that beautiful piece of porn." He nudged me with his elbow as we headed out of the hotel room.

I laughed and pushed him into the elevator and hoped he would keep that little comment to himself once we met up with the girls.

Shit, Bones.

fifteen
Becki

"GRACIE!" I DROPPED my bags and ran as fast as I could and literally tackled my bestest friend in the whole world, right there in the middle of the airport. We rolled around on the floor hugging and giggling while people stared. We didn't care. It had been way, way too long since we laid eyes on each other.

"Becki, you're super skinny. What the hell is up with that? Calon not feeding you?"

"Hey, now. You know I'll always take care of your girl, G." Gracie jumped up off the floor and into Calon's arms. If it was anyone else with their legs wrapped around my boyfriend, I'd throat punch her. Not Gracie, though.

"Calon, you're all scruffy and rock star-y. Wow. Look at you." She rubbed the scruff on his chin.

"Yeah, I don't feed her, and she doesn't let me shave." He laughed and put her down. "You look beautiful, Gracie. You look happy, really, really happy."

"How could I not be? So many of my favorite people are standing right in front of me!"

"Where's Stacy? I thought she'd come with you." I hadn't talked to

Stacy the whole time we'd been gone, but I hadn't realized it until just that minute.

"She's studying. She doesn't even know you guys are coming." She spun around to the other guys. "Bones, Manny, Spider, come here! Give this girl some lovin'." They all fulfilled her request and lifted her up off the ground. When they put her back down, she turned toward Danny.

"You must be Danny. It's really nice to meet you. Becki's told me a lot about you." Gracie gave her a big hug. Gracie was just precious, always making sure no one was uncomfortable. I'd told her about my few, but insistent, reservations about Danny in the beginning. After a month of working with her, they'd all melted away.

"I've heard a ton about you, too, Gracie, from all these guys. You sure are loved." Danny smiled almost in a sad way, which made me wonder more about her background. We all come with shit in our past. Danny and I hadn't gotten into any of that yet.

"Everybody hungry?"

"Starving." We all said in unison. It was actually the first time I remember being hungry in a couple weeks. That's all it was. I just missed home.

Gracie drove us to her apartment building in Jake's new car. On the ride, she had me hand out dark glasses and knit hats from a big bag in the back seat. In order to keep it a secret that Alternate Tragedy was who was behind the costumes at Mitchell's that night, the guys all needed disguises. They all got a kick out of the hats she picked. I looked into the back of the car and cracked up. It looked like Gracie, Danny, and I had picked up four thugs on our way home from the airport. Ridiculous.

When we got to Gracie's apartment, she put her finger up to her lips and shushed us. She silently unlocked the door and carefully pushed the door open. Stacy sat on the couch with her back to the door, bopping her head to the beat of whatever was pumping through her ear buds.

We all walked up to the back of the couch and just stood and waited for her to notice she was being watched. Her reaction was priceless. She squealed and hugged me, shook hands with all the guys and Danny then immediately grabbed me by the wrist and dragged me back to their bedroom and shut the door.

"Shit, Becki. You gotta give me something. You have to tell me what he's like in bed." Stacy sometimes reminded me of Bones.

I cackled, probably a little too loud, rolled my eyes, and zipped the imaginary zipper across my lips.

"Come on, Becki. God, his eyes, that body. Hell, even his feet have got to be hot. Please, give me something, just a little something for me to hold on to. Please?" Stacy slapped her hands together like she was praying.

"Okay, but you have to shut up about it. No telling anyone."

"No telling anyone about what?" Gracie walked in and closed the door behind her.

"Becki's gonna spill it about Calon." Stacy bounced up and down in front of me.

"I'm not spilling anything. You asked *for a little something to hold on to.* That's all I'm giving you."

"Uh. I don't know if I wanna hear this. It's Calon. He's my good friend." Gracie was already covering her ears as she spoke.

"No, you probably don't want to hear about him inducting me into The Mile High Club, do you?"

"BECKI!" Stacy squealed, and Gracie fell down on Stacy's bed and covered her mouth and kicked her feet and flopped around.

There was a knock at the door, and I heard Calon's muffled voice.

"You can come in, Cal. We're all decent. Promise." However, I couldn't promise the girls' reaction to seeing him after what they'd just heard would be decent.

The poor guy opened the door, took a step inside the room as Gracie and Stacy squealed and giggled. A look of fear crossed his face, and he backed up. "I was just coming to tell you the pizzas are here. Uh. Carry on." He was gone as quickly as he arrived.

I fell down on the bed with my BFFs, and we laughed until our stomachs hurt. There was a small part of me that felt bad leaving Danny out there with all the guys when we were obviously having our own private girl-time. But these were my girls, she'd live.

GETTING TO MITCHELL'S Halloween night proved to be a feat even James Bond would've been challenged by. There were collegiate trick-or-treaters everywhere. All the fraternities had drop-in parties, where you got shots at the door instead of candy, and all of the bars had their own Halloween events. The line outside of Mitchell's was insane and put all the other parties to shame. Buzz apparently did a great job promoting the masquerade event, but I knew we'd never get to the front of the line when we couldn't pull the 'we're the band' clause.

"Buzz, we're here with the guys. How do we get in?" Gracie nodded her head. "Yep. Okay, perfect. Headed there now. Thanks, Buzz."

Then she just took off running down the alley, yelling for us to follow her. She was in charge of renting the costumes for the guys, so they were completely unrecognizable, which is exactly what they were. No one would suspect that the giant apple, bunch of green grapes, bunch of purple grapes, and the weird-looking leaf all with white plastic faceless masks were actually the members of Alternate Tragedy. More like Fruit of the Loom Tragedy. Danny and I jogged behind the guys to make sure no one tagged along.

Buzz waited for us around the other side of the building, the daytime entrance to the restaurant portion of Mitchell's was virtually deserted. The night went off without a hitch. The crowd went wild when they realized who it was behind the masks. All it took was for Calon to take the apple headpiece off and shake out his gorgeous curls for the girls to lose it. They changed into normal clothes after the first set, and by then, the place was mobbed. I saw tweets and Facebook posts with pictures of them, so it felt like the whole town was there in no time.

It was so hot near the stage that I kept moving further back toward the stairs, hoping some of the cool night air would fall down the stairwell from the street level door. Eventually, Gracie and I sat at the bar. Maverick handed me glass after glass of ice water. We joked around and laughed the whole time.

"Hey, Gracie. Where's Jake?" Maverick leaned across the bar and slid a bottle of Rolling Rock her way.

"He's on his way. Buzz texted him to pick up some stuff they're running out of because of all the people that are here. This is crazy."

"Seriously, I'm pretty sure we're past max capacity tonight. Hope the fire marshal doesn't show up." Maverick spun around toward a whistle and headed over to a gaggle of squealing girls.

"Becki, you okay? You don't look so good." Gracie rubbed the sweaty hair from my forehead.

"It's just so effing hot in here, Gracie. I feel like I can't breathe. I want to stay until last call, but I feel like I'm melting. I may not make it." I shook my head and tried to suck in a breath even deeper than the last hundred I'd taken. Somehow it just seemed as though the oxygen wasn't getting to my head.

"We can go home, Becki. Becki?" Gracie's voice trailed off and sounded like she was under water. I looked up at the stage, and I could see Calon's mouth moving, but it was like my ears closed, like they do from a sudden increase in altitude. I shook my head and rubbed my eyes.

"Maybe I picked up a cold or something on the plane. I'm fine, just feel super out of it all of a sudden." I leaned back against the bar and held onto my barstool with both hands. I had to concentrate on keeping my focus from blurring into oblivion.

"Becki, you're scaring me." Gracie was ultra-nervous about everything. She'd always been prone to anxiety, even before the hell she went through with Noah. I saw her look to the stage more than once.

"Don't you dare make Calon worry. I think I just need some fresh air." I blew strands of hair out of my face.

"Or the urgent care office on the corner." She nodded her head like it would make me agree with her.

"Gracie, relax. Can you just walk up to the sidewalk with me?"

"Mav!" She called so loud it made me jump. "I'm taking Becki upstairs for some fresh air. If we don't come back down soon, will you come check on us?"

"Absolutely. You okay, Becki?"

"I'm fine, but I'm having trouble convincing my collegiate-age mom of that." I rolled my eyes. Gracie looped arms with me as we headed toward the stairs that led to the sidewalk. I could breathe better by the fifth step, it was like we were ascending above a thick cloud of heat and into thinner, cooler air. It's exactly what my lungs craved. I sucked in as many deep breaths as I could, so that when we got to the sidewalk, Gracie could tell I was fine and just needed some fresh air.

"How's that?" She let go of my arm, and I let my body fall back a couple inches to the wall, which made Gracie gasp and grab at me like I was headed to the ground.

"I'm fine, Gracie. Good God! You will be an awful mom. You'll make your poor kids as nervous and anxious as you are."

"Becki Jane! That's a terrible thing to say! You know how badly I want kids."

I laughed at her panic and obvious horror at what I'd just accused her of. "I'm just kidding, Gracie, you'll make a good mom one day." She smiled and nodded her satisfaction.

I felt a flutter in my chest that felt like the onset of an anxiety attack, which made me pissed at Gracie for freaking out. Then my heartbeat sped up and began to race so fast I slid down the wall to sit and clutched my chest. Gracie took my face in her hands, and she was saying something. I couldn't focus on her words, though, I had to focus on breathing and staying conscious. As if someone turned a switch, I lost my peripheral vision until everything went black.

I COULD HEAR Gracie's voice. I struggled to open my eyes. Through one eye, I could see two figures standing in a doorway, but it was so fucking bright there was no way I could convince my eyes to open any further.

"We're just going to run some tests. It sounds like a classic panic attack, but we want to be sure. Could you try to fill these forms out as best you can while she sleeps? We're going to run some tests on the blood we took and see if we can't get a better idea of what her body's telling us."

"Thank you." Gracie's voice shook.

"Gracie?" I was so exhausted I could barely speak, but I needed her to know I was awake.

"Becki. You shit! You scared the hell out of me! Dammit, Becki!"

"I changed my mind. You'll make an okay mom, but you'd suck as a nurse, yelling at your patients like that." I forced a smile to let her know I was joking.

"Becki, you passed out, right there on the sidewalk. Maverick carried you here."

"Where?" I rubbed my face with my clammy hands.

"The urgent care office. They took like a hundred vials of blood. I didn't think you'd wake up. I feel like we've been here for hours, and it's been probably thirty minutes."

"Calon?"

"Jake called. He just got to Mitchell's, so I asked him to wait until the guys were done playing to tell him what happened."

"Thanks, Gracie. I'd hate if they cut out early. The nightmare of The Moondance gig would start all over again." Everything was coming back into focus, and my eyes had adjusted to the lights, so I could see the glistening tear tracks down Gracie's cheeks. "Are you crying?"

"I know he will be pissed that no one told him right away, but what was he going to do but pace in here while you slept? He'd make me even more nervous than I already was? And, yes, I'm crying. Are you surprised? Becki, you know I'm not good at this kind of stuff!"

All I could do was giggle. No sound came out as I squeezed my eyes shut and my body shook with laughter.

"If you're convulsing, I'm not even helping you because you're laughing at me while you're doing it." Gracie folder her arms over her chest and looked away from me.

"Well, while you're ignoring me, could you please figure out how to prop me up?" I thought about what I'd just asked her to do after I pissed her off. "But BE NICE! Don't hit the eject button or anything. You hear me? My heart can't take that much excitement, yet."

"I think I can control myself." She leaned down and hugged me, boobs pressed against my neck and her arms awkwardly placed around my shoulders. She stood, stuck her tongue out at me, and hit a button that slowly lifted me to a sitting position.

We spent the next thirty minutes filling out the medical history forms. Gracie wrote as I answered questions from my exam table—bed thing. This, of course, meant I had to relive my Leukemia diagnosis and chemotherapy, which was the least favorite of all my childhood memories. I had no answers for my dad's side of the medical history, so that cut down on the time it took us to finish the stack of questions on the clipboard Gracie held on her lap. She was staying very calm, but I knew she had to be freaked out. I was proud of her for holding it together as well as she did.

There was a quiet knock at the door just before the knob turned and a tall gray-haired man walked in. He had the typical balding man comb-over thing going and big grandpa glasses but the kindest eyes I'd ever seen on a doctor. I could tell just by looking at his face that he was tuned into the fact that I was a real person that came to the office with a whole host of things going on, not just some drunk co-ed. His smile calmed me. He peeked over Gracie's shoulder toward the clipboard and then walked over and put his hand out for me to shake.

"Becki, what beautiful eyes you have. I'm glad to finally see them. I'm Dr. Webber. Gracie and I have met, and I see you've been helping her fill out your medical history for me." He patted the outside of my hand with his other hand.

"Thank you, Dr. Webber, and, yes, she's been a big help with all those questions." I smiled.

He took the clipboard from Gracie and adjusted his glasses. He skimmed the pages one by one.

"You're twenty-one and already a cancer survivor. You must be a fighter. Good for you, Becki."

I folded my hands in my lap and a wave of panic came over me. I never told anyone but almost every day of my life, at some point during the day or while I lay in bed at night, I worried one day my cancer would come back. It's a sneaky little bitch, and you don't have to watch too many healthcare commercials on TV to understand that one day you're fine then the next you're talking chemo and radiation. *Fuck.*

"Well, Becki, we're still running some of your blood tests, so we can determine what's gotten into you. Was tonight the first time you've had a dizzy spell?" He flipped the stapled packet over and poised his pen to jot down what I said.

"No, I had some bad sushi a while back, and it just seemed like I haven't snapped back fully after being real sick for a couple days. I just started a new job. It's very busy and sometimes stressful. I don't get a lot of sleep, so I guess I've just assumed I was run down." I cleared my throat to hide the fact that I needed to take a deep breath to calm my shaken nerves. I watched him scrawl some notes over the back of the packet.

"Well, that could be exactly what this is. Now, tell me what your diet is like."

"I'm a vegetarian, so it's pretty much bread, cheese, beans, and rice. Well, besides all the vegetables and fruit I eat."

"Do you drink?" He smiled when he said it. Dumb question.

I chuckled. "Uh, yeah, I do. Not every day, but my job has me in bars a couple nights a week, so I have a couple beers when I'm there."

"What kind of job do you have that you can drink while you work? I may need to look at my options." He smiled and waved his hand from side to side to let me know he was kidding.

"I'm the manager for Alternate Tragedy, and we have a couple gigs a week. While they play, I man the merchandise table, deal with any issues, and throw back some beers or a couple shots to take the edge off the stress. Then all the scheduling and publicity stuff is done during the day while they rehearse."

"Sounds like you're definitely exhausted. Well, I can tell you that I'm thinking this could be a couple things. There's a very good possibility your episode tonight was your body deciding it was time to shut down for just a little bit, so it could rest. But, quite often when we see vegetarian students, we find they're anemic but had no idea. It's quite easy to just cut out meat. But, the problem with that is, your body needs protein for strength, to keep you healthy and to rebuild muscle. Anemia will leave you with little to no energy, you'll become pale, you'll get dizzy often, and even the rapid heartbeat you experienced tonight is a symptom."

"I'll kiss you if that's all this is." I stopped wringing my hands.

"Well, that's the best offer I've had all day… not very professional for me to take you up on that, but I'm flattered." He smiled, and, for a second, I could see Dr. Webber as a young man. I could look past the gray hair and see him thirty years younger. I had a feeling he had been quite the stud.

"I'll take your history, review it a little closer, and be back when your tests are done. Do you have any questions for me?"

"Nope. I just want to go home."

"Let me go check on your tests, and I'll be right back." He smiled and walked out into the hall. When the door clicked shut, I took a deep breath and a choked out a sob I didn't even know I'd been holding back.

"Becki. What's wrong?"

"Gracie, for a couple minutes I thought for sure he was going to tell me that it was classic Leukemia relapse. I'm just so relieved. It doesn't sound like he expects that at all. He didn't even mention it."

"Oh my, Becki. I hadn't even let that enter my mind." She lunged at me, hugged me tight, and sniffled. "Move over." She hopped up onto the weird table-bed thing, and we both just lay there looking at the ceiling. Silent.

"Do you ever wonder when God's just gonna throw you a curveball?" As soon as I said it, I realized what a pussy I sounded like. I looked over at her, and our noses almost touched.

"I think we survive curveballs every day. Some are just worse than others. But, I don't think God is up there tossing them around at people, if that's what you mean." She smiled a little.

"If he's not responsible for passing them out, why wouldn't he stop bad things from happening to good people? Do you ever wonder that?" I rarely got into spiritual or religious conversations with anyone, but Gracie grew up in a two-parent, church-going home, so I knew she wouldn't judge me or laugh at my questions.

"Well, my mom always says that God's plan is just so big that we have to get all the way up to Heaven to look down on it. Then, and only then, will we be able to see the whole thing laid out. I picture it looking something like a puzzle. One of those 'if this didn't happen then *this* wouldn't have happened' kind of riddles. Ya know?" She shrugged and picked at her nails. That was always a sign something triggered a thought of Noah. I didn't want to pry, so I just continued the conversation and figured she'd share if she needed to.

"Your mom's pretty cool. She just seems like one of those moms that always has an answer that'll take the weight of the world off your back."

"Yeah, she has a knack for that." Gracie got really quiet and introspective. She tipped her head to the side and smiled. "When I told her I was falling in love with Jake, do you know what she said to me?"

"I have no idea." I loved Gracie's mom. I wish I had utilized her advice more over the past couple years.

"She said, 'Now, do you see how a huge negative can lead you to something beautiful that you didn't even know existed?' She was talking about Noah. If I hadn't met Noah that summer at Murphy's, there's a good chance I'd never have met Jake. It sounds cheesy, but I didn't even know this kind of love existed or that I was worthy of it. And I wouldn't be where I am today without walking through shit to get here."

"Your mom said *shit?*" Gracie's mom never swore.

"Becki! No. That was my translation. Her point was, sometimes the negative things we go through open us up to things more beautiful than we could ever imagine."

"I love your mom."

"Me, too."

"She's the reason you'll be an amazing mom one day, Gracie."

A quiet knock at the door startled us both and pulled us from our sappy BFF moment. Dr. Webber walked in holding his clipboard to his chest. He smiled and took his glasses off.

"Gracie, would you mind waiting for Becki in the waiting room?"

My stomach fell to the floor. I grabbed Gracie's hand. "No, she's staying. If you're going to tell me I'm dying, I need her here."

"Well, Becki, I'm certainly not going to give you a death sentence. The medical privacy act requires me to talk privately to all my patients.

But, it's up to you if you'd like her to stay, and if she'd like to stay."

"Yes." We spoke in stereo, holding each other's hands.

"Well, okay then…" He smiled, grabbed a stool, and sat down, which made an uncomfortable hiss sound from the seat cushion compacting. "It appears as though we were right about a couple things. You are definitely anemic, and your blood work shows that the anemia and your rapid heartbeat could be connected."

"Okay. Exhaustion?" I bit my lip. *Let that be all this is.*

"Well, actually, yes. Your exhaustion plays a part, as well."

He continued talking, but I spoke over top of him. "I know what you're going to say. You want me to start eating meat. Well, that's not—"

"Becki, you're pregnant."

My heart stopped, I felt it. It slammed inside my chest so hard that I had no pulse for a fraction of a second.

Pregnant.

Gracie stared at Dr. Webber and didn't move.

A baby.

I shook my head.

Inside me.

"But the chemo. They said I'd be sterile."

"Well, apparently, the baby's a fighter like its mom."

Mom.

Dr. Webber kept talking. I heard him say all the other tests came back normal. He said something about iron supplements. He handed me a packet of papers, and I heard him say something about the Obstetrics suite at the hospital.

I blinked my eyes and looked back and forth between Gracie and Dr. Webber.

"Becki, it's going to be okay. You're a healthy young woman. You're in great shape." Dr. Webber put his glasses back on.

"No, it's not okay. This was never going to be part of my life. I never expected…" I couldn't even say the word *pregnant* at that moment.

"Becki, I've given this news to many college students. It may not be what you were expecting me to say. It's a shock. I get that. I've seen the same look on probably a hundred faces over the last couple years. You have options, Becki. It's your body, and you and the father will need to weigh all your options. You have time. You're at the beginning of your pregnancy. I would estimate you are about nine to twelve weeks along. That would make you due…" He flipped through a mini calendar on the counter. "… sometime in May or June."

"I don't want this." I was sweating, and my body shook.

"Well, like I said, you have options."

"No! Fuck! The option I want isn't an option. I want the option of erasing this scenario from my life. I don't want to do this. This situation. I don't want to do this situation. This wasn't supposed to happen. I never thought I could…"

I crumbled into Gracie's body. She sat frozen next to me on the table until my full body weight was on her. She wrapped her arms around my shoulders and rocked me.

"Shh, Becki. We got this. You'll get through this. Calon will be such a great support system. You've got me, you've got Calon—"

"No! Gracie. You've got to promise me you won't tell Calon. He can't know. Promise me." I grabbed onto her shoulders and begged her.

"Becki, what—"

"Gracie! No! He can't know! This wasn't supposed to happen. This will ruin everything for him. For us. Don't tell him. He can't know."

Gracie just stared at me as I sobbed and choked. Tears ran down my neck and onto my chest. "Becki." Her voice was barely a whisper.

"PROMISE ME! Gracie Ann!"

She said nothing.

Dr. Webber cleared his throat and walked to the door. "Becki, I'm going to prepare a packet of information for you before you go. I'll include contact information for each scenario in that packet, so you are comfortable making your final decision. Becki, this has to be the right decision for you. You."

I nodded and wiped the tears from my face. I lay back against the incline of the bed and stared up at the bright lights above me.

"Becki, you have to tell Calon."

I closed my eyes and wished it all away. Instinctively my hands went to my flat belly. I looked down at my hands and shook my head.

"I can't. I don't want you to, either. You're my best friend, and in this situation, you're all I've got."

"Why do you keep saying that? Calon would be an amazing –"

"Gracie, his mom's boyfriend beat him to a pulp. Regularly. We've talked about it. He's terrified of becoming a parent. Terrified he'll carry that curse with him. Besides, he's on tour. They're making it, Gracie, really making it. I can't. I can't destroy his life like this. He can't know."

"So, you're going to get an abortion?" Her voice barely squeaked out the final word of her question.

"No. I couldn't. I can't."

"Then what?"

"I just have to let Calon go." A sharp pang hit my chest. It was no rapid heartbeat. I knew what that felt like. This was a sensation I'd never experienced.

My heart was broken.

sixteen

Calon

"DAMMIT! WHY WON'T they answer their phones? Becki and Gracie's keep going straight to voicemail." I shoved my phone into my back pocket.

"When did she leave Mitchell's?" Danny tripped a little on a lifted part of the sidewalk, probably because the girl drank like a fish. She grabbed my hand to help keep herself steady as we headed to Gracie's apartment. We'd already decided that Danny would stay with Becki at Gracie's, and the guys could bunk at my place, since they had sublet their apartment for the time we'd be gone on tour. As much as I wanted Becki next to me every moment, I knew she needed some Gracie-time.

"I have no idea. I didn't see them leave, and no one told me they'd gone. I should have been watching her. I knew she wasn't feeling well." I shook my head and ran my hand through my hair.

"Well, maybe she went back to Gracie's to get some rest." She tripped again. This time she fell against me so hard I stumbled up against the wall of one of the little shops on College Avenue. My back was against the cold bricks, and her ample breasts pressed up against my chest. She flipped her hair to one side and gave me a daring grin. She turned her head to the left and yelled, "SELFIE!" Her one arm straight out in front of us, and the flash blinded me before I even realized what she was doing. She tried to kiss me for the picture, which seemed out of character, but luckily, she missed.

"Come on, Danny, I need to find the girls." I helped her stand up straight, steadied her, and then shoved my hands in my pockets.

I could have sworn I heard voices coming from Gracie's apartment up until I knocked. Then everything on the other side of the door was silent.

"Gracie! You in there? Gracie?" I knew I was a little louder than I should be considering the time of night, but I had already started to panic. I couldn't figure out why neither of them had called or texted to let me know what was going on. I thought back to the story Gracie told me about how Noah had dragged her out of Mitchell's against her will. I'd been on stage that night, too, and never saw a thing. My heart raced. I grabbed my phone and called Jake.

"Hello?" I could tell he was still at the bar by the noise in the background.

"Jake. It's Calon."

"Hey, how's Becki?"

"I don't know! Where is she?" My heart pounded in my chest. Just the fact that he asked me how she was and I had no idea had me a mess.

"Hang on." Jake took the phone away from his face and yelled for Maverick to take his customers.

"Calon? You there?"

"Dammit, Jake! What the hell happened? Where the hell is Becki?" I wanted to reach through the phone and shake him.

"Shit! Cal, I'm so sorry I didn't catch you before you left. Before I got to Mitchell's Gracie took Becki outside for some fresh air, and she passed out. Gracie called Maverick to come help her and he carried Becki to the urgent care on the corner. Gracie asked me to tell you when your set was over, but we got slammed. I didn't even realize you were gone."

"The urgent care is closed. I just walked by there. I'm standing at Gracie's door. No one's answering the door." I spun so my back was against the wall and tipped my head back. How the hell could this have happened? How could I not know where she was? Danny texted away on her phone. She was completely relaxed, which annoyed me.

"Calon, let me call you right back. Okay? I think I can help you."

I started to ask how he could help me, but Jake hung up before he heard me.

"So, they're not here? Where the hell am I going to sleep?" Danny rolled her eyes and shook her head.

"Sleep? Fuck that, Danny! Becki is sick enough to go to urgent care, and then she vanishes, and you're worried about getting to sleep?" I was livid. I knew she could see the volatility of my anger because she backed away from me and stood against the adjacent wall. "I'm sorry, Danny. I've just had too many people disappear on me, and I'm losing my mind with worry."

My phone buzzed. Jake.

"Hey. Did you find them?"

"They're at Gracie's but didn't hear you knock –"

"Okay, great! Thanks—"

"Calon, wait. I got the feeling that something's wrong, so tread lightly if you're pissed. Just wanted to give you a heads up."

"Yeah, thanks for the warning, but fuck you for not finding me before I left," I said it in jest. I knew Jake was just trying to help.

He chuckled. "Sorry, man. Good luck."

"Thanks, Jake."

I knocked again, this time a little louder as panic now had its fingers wrapped tightly around my throat. I looked over at Danny, who was visibly uncomfortable.

"Danny, I really am sorry about flipping out on you—"

"No worries, Calon, Becki's real lucky to have you." She smiled, and I could see the sincerity and something like longing in her expression.

I heard the lock click, and the knob started to turn. Gracie stood in the crack of the doorway in a long sleep shirt and mascara smudged under her eyes. She looked up at me and an entire conversation passed between us, even though no words were spoken. She stepped back and opened the door to let Danny and me in. I started toward her bedroom, where I knew Becki was, but Gracie grabbed my hand and silently pleaded with me to stand still. It was like exhaustion had over-taken her, and she reserved her energy to speak.

"Danny, I called Sam, Jake's roommate. You and I are sleeping up there tonight. Would you mind waiting in the hall for me?"

"Not at all." Danny looked to the floor and quietly walked back out into the hallway. She left the door open a crack, which I didn't blame her. She was in a strange building in a strange town. She was just being safe.

I pulled my hand from Gracie's and wiped the make-up from under her eyes then held her face in my hands.

"Gracie, you are scaring the hell out of me. What is going on?"

"Calon, it's not my place to say. But, I want to thank you from the bottom of my heart for the way you love my best friend. She needs you more now than she's ever needed anyone, and I'm glad she has you." She took my hands from her face and pressed them together. "Love you, Calon." Then she turned to meet Danny in the hallway.

The bedroom door was closed, but the light that spilled out underneath told me Becki was awake. The four steps I took to that bedroom door took an eternity. My arm felt like it weighed a thousand pounds as I lifted it and turned the knob.

Sweet, sleepy music was a gentle backdrop for the sadness in the eyes that met mine. The eerie but relaxed tempo helped me remember to breathe as I crossed the room and took the broken shell of a girl into my arms. Becki fell against my chest and threaded her arms under mine until they were around my waist. She was dressed in Gracie's flannel pajamas, which swallowed her up, since she'd lost so much weight.

I felt her tears soak through my t-shirt, but she didn't make a sound. I took a couple staggered deep breaths then brushed her hair back off her face and kissed her on the top of her head. She squeezed me tighter, and I swore I felt part of her soul seep into mine. Something so deep troubled her at the same time it drew us even closer, yet I had no idea what she was about to tell me.

"Becks, you're scaring me. Talk to me." My voice cracked, and I pressed her body into mine. My hand on her lower back rubbed in tiny circles, trying to relieve the tension I felt in her core. She remained still, saying nothing. I knew I needed to let her open up when she was ready and not press her. I just needed to be there. Having her in my arms was helping to calm my anxiety, so we just stood and held on for a while.

Her body began to sway to the music. The tone of the song had sort of entwined itself into the vibe Becki projected as she gently moved against me. We moved in the slowest of slow dances. I focused on taking in every second. I felt every nuance of her body when she moved and breathed. I breathed her in; her scent a mix of vanilla and musk. Her hair against the underside of my chin was silky soft. I was so afraid of what she would tell me, I needed to fill myself up with everything she was before she opened up to me. Something in my gut feared she was preparing to walk away.

She chose that moment to step back and look up at me. I wiped the tears from her cheeks and brushed away the damp hair that had matted against the cheek she'd had pressed into my chest. She laid her hands gently on my chest and took a deep breath. Her lips parted then closed a couple times before any sound was made. She finally spoke.

"I love you." The sound of her voice lit a nervous flutter that started in my stomach and lurched into my chest when she choked out a sob. I took her face in my hands and ducked down a little until we were eye to eye.

"I love you, too, Becks. Whatever this is, I'm not going anywhere. It's you and me against the world, baby. Talk to me." I searched her face for just one single emotion, but there were so many it made me gasp a shallow breath. I saw pain and fear and confusion tied together with a level of discord I couldn't imagine. She was terrified of something.

"Calon, I…" Her mouth continued to move, but her words stopped there. "I don't… I can't…"

"Tell me. Let me help you with whatever has you so tongue-tied. I'm here. I'll listen."

"Then listen…" She pointed toward Gracie's iPhone dock where her phone was plugged in.

Everything from that moment on moved in slow motion. When I switched my attention from Becki to the music, a wave hit me that I wasn't prepared for.

Natalie Merchant's voice sang of baby blankets and baby shoes. I'd heard the song "Eat for Two" by 10,000 Maniacs more times than I could count, but its references to an unplanned life growing inside a woman wasn't something I could connect with… until that very moment.

"A baby?" I let out a burst of breath and then took another captive.

A single tear fell from each of her eyes, and she nodded so slightly it was no secret she was wishing the discovery away. I couldn't move. My hands squeezed her shoulders, my mouth gasped for air that refused to fill my lungs because too much of a brand new emotion clogged the space next to my heart, trying to make its way inside.

"You're… pregnant." There was no description for the jolt my heart took when reality struck. Another shallow gasp.

Becki searched my eyes for moments on end as I absorbed a truth she'd already had a couple hours to begin to sort out. A baby.

"Say something." Those two words were flung at me in a panic. She wanted a reaction I wasn't sure I could give. My hands dropped from her shoulders to her hands, and she caught them and squeezed.

"What can I say?" I wasn't sure how to say what was in my mind and in my heart, because they were two completely opposing feelings. My head told me I carried the curse of a criminal for a father on top of every other male role model in my life having been abusive, and my fight or flight instinct sparred against what I knew was right. While at the same time, my heart was touched by a feeling of honor and a notion of being blessed beyond measure. There was a war between sheer panic and uninhibited elation. How do you put that into words?

"We can't." When her lips spoke those two seemingly innocuous words, reality hit me at a velocity that knocked me back onto the bed we stood beside. Again her eyes searched mine for a hint of any emotion other than consternation. Again, I gave her nothing but.

"We have to." The words left me before I knew what I was saying.

"What? I thought you'd be scared." Her breath came easier now, and she spoke quickly and without hesitation. She sat down next to me and clutched both my hands in my lap.

"Scared? I'm terrified. A baby. My—our baby. Becks, we made a baby." The flowed easier when I stopped trying to orchestrate what I said. I stopped worrying how I could comfort her, and instead, I just spoke. "I'm not ready for this. I don't know how to do this. I don't even know how to describe what I'm feeling."

"Try." She tilted her head to the side and another tear dropped into her lap.

"No baby asks to be born. It's a decision that's made without consulting the tiny soul that comes after. We did this. We created a life, and now we need to step up. No matter how scared and lost we feel, this baby wants us. This baby needs us. *Our* baby needs us."

"Calon." Her eyes fluttered, and a meek smile pulled at the corners of her mouth.

"Becki." I took her face in my hands and kissed her so gently goose bumps raised over my whole body. "I love you. Absolute. In case you forgot, that means I love you purely, unconditionally, and without limits and restrictions. And it means I'll love you while you grow our baby." I reached out and put my hands over her toned stomach. She gasped and laid her hands on top of mine.

"I love you, Calon James... more than you could ever know. I'm amazed at the size of your heart and the steadfast way you live your life." She choked past a sob. "I love you. Absolute." She touched my cheek with her hand, sucked in the deep breath, and a peaceful smile spread across her face. "I don't know how we are going to do this. What about the tour, the—"

"Shh. We do this one day at a time. That's it. Trying to take it all in, all at once is entirely too overwhelming. I believe with every fragment of my being that we can do this. I know we can. Will it be easy? Hell no. Will it be worth it? Absolutely." I wrapped my arms around her and pulled her into me. Elation paired with fear filled my soul. We had been given a life. A life. That one simple thought brought tears to my eyes. I pushed her body back, so I could see her face again. "We created a life, Becki. Life is a gift. He or she is a gift, and I promise you I will never take this responsibility lightly and you will never do this on your own. We're a team. I'm in this with you. And nothing is going to change that, I promise."

"I'm so scared, Calon." She sniffled a little, but her smile didn't waver. "I'm not sure anything is scarier than a cancer diagnosis, but being pregnant, for me, is a similar kind of fear, because it's something I never thought would happen to me, and it's going to happen to my body whether I like it or not."

"I'm scared, too, but we've got each other. It's the three of us against the world."

"Three. Wow. What did we do, rock star?" She shook her head and buried her face into my neck.

"We made a family, Becki." I squeezed her and dropped to my knees in front of her and parted her legs, so I could inch closer and be face to face with the place that held our little miracle. "And you, little one…" I put my hands on Becki's belly, and she covered my hands with hers, "you shocked the hell—I mean, heck, out of me. So, listen, I know we've only known each other for a very short time, but every one of those minutes, I've loved *you*, absolute."

"Calon?"

"Yeah, babe?" I looked up into the face I was convinced was the most beautiful I'd ever see. She was glowing. Her eyes were deep pools of various emotions, but the biggest one was love. It was the love that overflowed.

"Make love to me."

I stood and pulled her up with me. I took my phone from my pocket and poked at the screen then put my phone on the dock in place of hers. I turned up the volume a bit so she could hear every word of the song as I made sweet love to her.

Acoustic guitar and piano flooded the room in a smooth melody then the voices of Glen Hansard and Eddie Vedder joined in singing Bruce Springsteen's "Drive All Night". It was perfect for the moment.

"I love this song." She looked up at me and smiled.

I unbuttoned the three oversized buttons on the flannel pajama top she wore, and it slid from her arms and onto the floor. She took the bottom of my t-shirt and pulled it up over my head and let it fall. I hooked my fingers inside the elastic band of her bottoms and pushed them down until they joined the rest of our clothes on the floor. I undid my jeans, and she pushed them to the floor as well. I stepped out of them and then went to my knees one more time. I splayed my hands across her tiny belly and kissed a spot right next to her bellybutton.

"Close your eyes, baby. I'm going to make love to your mommy."

Glen and Eddie sang of the heat of the night, shivers down their spine, and holding someone tight. If there was a soundtrack for the last hour of our lives, it would be that song. I stood and pulled Becki's warm body against mine. We swayed like we had when I first entered Gracie's room, but this time there was no hesitation, no secrets. I softly sang a couple verses of the song to her as my hands drifted across her back, down her hips, and back up under her arms. When I took her breasts in my hands, she tipped her head back, eyes closed, and her lips parted. My mouth crashed into hers, and our tongues intertwined slowly and softly with deep passion and something that stole my breath.

I slowly laid her down on the bed, and I climbed on with her, carefully hovering over her body. I dipped down and rubbed noses with her then kissed my way down her neck and over her breasts. I rolled to the side and touched her belly again then slid my hand down between her thighs, right to where I knew she wanted me the most.

"Becki, you're wet for me."

"All for you." She pushed my shoulders back. The pillows stacked behind me kept me in an almost upright position. She straddled me, and the warmth between her legs rested on my dick. She moved her hips and guided herself toward me then away, sliding along my length. I held onto her hips, allowing her to move to the rhythm she needed.

Her breasts were full and hung in front of me, taunting me. She'd been feeling bad for so long, we hadn't been intimate. I guess I hadn't noticed their growth, but the way they moved as she slid around on me drove me insane. I took one in my hand and directed her breast toward my mouth. My tongue circled her taut nipple, causing her to moan my name. Then in one smooth move, she slid up to my belly, and tipped her ass in the air, letting my tip slip right inside her. She gasped a little then pressed herself back toward her heels slowly until I filled her completely.

"Oh God, Calon, it feels so good."

With my hands on her hips, she started to move faster and harder. Her breasts bounced, and it was all I could do to hold on just a little longer so we could come together. She pressed her hands into the pillows on either side of me, her hair hung all around her face, her eyes rolled back, and her lashes fluttered. She was close.

"Slow, Becki. Go slow."

She rode me with the same inaudible cadence, but her motions were more staccato than they had been. She slid herself forward slowly then forced me back inside her with a sharp motion. The sensation was unbelievably intense. Her mouth opened, and my toes curled. Every muscle in my legs tensed as a means to control the onslaught that was about to hit us.

"Calon, I'm gonna come. Calon!" When she called out my name, her hands moved to my abs, and I watched her body. Her fingernails dug into me, her breasts bounced, she began to breathe through clenched teeth, and then her head fell forward, and she made a raw guttural sound that sent me over the edge.

"God, Becki, yeah. Come, baby. Come!" I couldn't control anything anymore. My body was wracked with an intensity that had me gripping her hips and bucking mine. She continued to ride me hard, and I could feel her squeeze me as she worked through the first wave of orgasm with me. The second wave hit close behind with a magnitude that I was sure would launch us from the bed. She fell forward, and I used my arms to press her as tightly into me as I could. She continued to rock against me, using my body to massage the tiny nub that could work her into a state of abandon.

Together we surrendered to the intensity and both came hard once again. I opened my hands across the small of her back and slowed her rhythm as she pushed herself back up to a sitting position. Her body shook, and her breathing was staggered.

Her face was framed beautifully with her damp golden-brown hair. As she tried to catch her breath, her eyes shined. She slid herself off me, falling to my side. I pulled the blanket that was partially under us up over us, and we fell into our typical sleep position. Her legs entwined with mine, her head against my chest, and our arms wrapped around each other. Our breathing slowed and exhaustion set in. Just before I let sleep take over, she spoke.

"Calon James, you're my dream come true. Never in a million years did I think I'd find the unconditional love you've shown me. Thank you for loving me the way you do. And thank you for not running tonight."

"Becki Jane, you're stuck with me. Always and forever. We are a team tied together by something so small yet so large at the same time. This is it. You are it. And, just so we're clear, you don't ever need to thank me for something that my heart just does naturally. I will always love you."

"Calon?"

"Yeah?"

"Gracie's going to kill us for doing it on her bed."

We had a good, cleansing laugh then fell asleep with nothing between us except love.

True love.

seventeen

Becki

THE FALL BROUGHT a bountiful harvest, which was the perfect time to be eating for two. I'd visited the doctor before we left Knoxville and got the low down on nutrition for vegetarian moms-to-be along with a prescription for prenatal vitamins with extra iron for our growing babe. Bones, Manny, and Spider were completely freaked out by the news of the baby, but warmed up to it eventually.

Danny and I had the guys set up with gigs, some back to back, throughout November. We enjoyed a small, familial Thanksgiving, just the six of us, at the hotel restaurant. I wasn't sure why Danny didn't go home to her family in Texas, but I didn't ask. It was nice to just enjoy each other the day. Right after dinner, we hit the road again to make it to a Black Friday midnight madness concert in Vegas. The guys were making it. They'd flown to New York for a live performance and interviews on MTV and the Today Show. The guys even brought back a tiny little 'I want my MTV' onesie for the baby.

Danny's assistance was immeasurable. She was really talented and had ideas that were kind of off the beaten path. Creative marketing was definitely her thing. We worked like a tag team. When exhaustion hit me, I'd turn the controls over to her, and she'd run with it.

Once December hit, my sick days waned, and I was taken over by a new level of energy. It was a little like being on speed, I assumed. Never touched the stuff, so I didn't know for sure, but I could get a million things done in one day. However, the nights out behind the merchandise table with blaring music and large, insistent crowds had become long and daunting. The guys had padded their bank account even with mine and Danny's decent salaries, so they decided they would take a month long break in Knoxville between Christmas and the end of January. That way we were home for the holidays. I was thrilled, although I had to wonder if it wasn't Calon's idea and one more way to be sure I would rest.

They planned on working in the studio most days, writing new songs, and recording the ones that were ready. And Buzz worked out a schedule where they could play with Gracie on Friday and Saturday nights for the whole month. Buzz also hooked us up with a flight home again, sans Danny this time. Calon and I rented a car since the van was in LA, and I drove us the whole six hours from Knoxville to Martin, my hometown. The guys headed to their respective families for the holidays.

"Are you sure you know where you're going?" Calon seemed concerned. He was more nervous about how far from civilization we were than I was about introducing my mom to the rock star that had gotten me pregnant. I had chickened out and told her the big news over the phone. She wasn't thrilled but had been in my shoes at the same age, so she didn't do the whole 'you're ruining your life' speech.

"Of course, I know where I'm going, dork." I laughed hard.

"We've seen nothing but trees for almost three hours, Becki. It feels like we're out in the middle of nowhere. You know, like where they filmed *Children of the Corn*."

"Funny, you'd think they'd need corn to film that." I laughed harder.

"I just mean there's literally nothing here." He tapped his foot, and I wondered whether it was to the beat of James's "Laid" that played on the radio or out of nervousness about meeting my mom.

"Are you nervous about meeting Joan?"

"Joan?"

"My mom, Calon. Her name is Joan. You *are* nervous, aren't you?"

"A little." For a moment, I saw him as a little boy; big green eyes, pudgy cheeks, and big pouty lips. My heart swelled. I was so in love with him that even the image in my mind of him as a little kid melted me. That's when I realized I'd never even seen a childhood photo of him. I wondered if he had any or if his mom, whom he hadn't had contact with in years, was the only one who would have any.

"Calon." I reached over and took his fidgeting hand in mine and rested them on his thigh. "She's harmless, babe. She had me when she was twenty-one, so she gets it. She's not going to react like Gracie's mom would if Jake knocked up her baby girl."

"But you said she wasn't happy when you told her." He frowned, like he'd internalized my mom's disappointment as his fault.

"What mom would be happy that her daughter got pregnant before graduating college?" I squeezed his hand, and he nodded in acknowledgment. "She wanted the planets to align for me, just like any parent hopes for their child." I was still getting used to saying things like that and including myself in the broad umbrella term of parent.

"What do you hope for our baby, Becks?" He picked at his fingernails in his lap.

"Well, I hope he or she is happy, healthy, and kind. I hope he or she has good friends and even better role models. I want the best of everything for her along with just enough disappointment to keep her grounded. I want her to stay away from assholes like Noah and his Sigma Chi brothers, and I hope she finds the cure for cancer."

"She?"

"What?" He caught me off guard.

"You started out with *he or she* and then ended only saying *she*. Is our baby a girl?" I would have thought he'd been hoping for a boy, mostly because I just assumed all guys wanted their firstborn to be mini-men. The smile on his face told me otherwise. Calon was hoping for a girl.

"We'll find out when we get back to Knoxville. I'll finally have the ultrasound that could tell us the sex. So, you *want* to know?" I hadn't really considered *not* finding out what we were having but realized I hadn't asked him. It was nice to finally have a huge block of time to talk, just the two of us, without Danny and the guys around or appointments to keep.

"Hell yeah, I want to know. I've got work to do."

"Work to do? Here I thought I was the one doing all the work." I smiled and blew him a kiss.

"I want to turn my office in the apartment into a nursery. So, I need to know if we're having a baby girl rock star or a baby boy rock star."

"Shit, Calon. You're the girl in this relationship."

"WHAT? That's not cool—" He got all defensive, and I couldn't help but laugh.

"I just mean, I've never been that girl that had names picked out for all my kids by the time I was twelve. I never expected to have kids. A nursery never even crossed my mind. If you'd have ditched me, I'd probably come home from the hospital and realize I had nowhere for the baby to sleep."

"Well, after your shower, you'll have tons of shit to clue you in to that kind of stuff."

"Shower?"

"FUCK!"

"Calon James, Gracie is going to kick your ass!" I cackled so loud my ears rang. I didn't give a shit that he'd just mentioned something that was supposed to catch me off guard and take me by surprise. I cracked up because he was so pissed at himself in that moment.

"Becki! Shit, Becki! You can't tell her you know. Please, don't tell her you know, just play along and be all surprised and stuff. Please, I had one job. That's what she kept saying, 'Calon, you have one job. Just keep the shower a secret. That's it. One thing,' and she repeated herself so many times I called her Rain Man." He shook his head and growled at himself then mumbled, "One job, just one job."

"Now, who's Rain Man?" I howled. When I looked over at Calon he had pushed his bottom lip out and was looking at me through the curls that had fallen from behind his ear. A pang in my stomach and the precious look on that beautiful face had me looking for the next rest stop for just another taste of Calon James.

"IT'S VERY NICE to meet you, Mrs. Mowry." My mom met us in the stony driveway of our tiny brick house. Calon handed her a small bouquet of flowers from the last gas station we stopped at on the way. I explained to him earlier in our ride why my mom changed both our last names to her maiden name after her divorce. It was simple. Her daughter 'deserved to carry on a name that came with a long line of dependable, responsible ancestors, instead of a long line of assholes', and she kept the 'Mrs.' to thwart the notion that she was a spinster.

"And it's very nice to meet you, too, Calon." My mom was in a daze. Calon, in all his beauty, had left her almost speechless. She held onto his hand longer than you should when someone shakes your hand, which made me laugh.

"Mom." I motioned toward their hands, and she got all frazzled and pulled hers away.

"How about some dinner? You two must be starving."

She was a phenomenal cook. I hadn't realized how much I missed her cooking until I shoved the first piece of grilled zucchini in my mouth. She always made meat but knew I'd never touch it. So, she was thrilled when Calon piled half a cow on his plate before adding a few green beans, so I wouldn't yell at him for not eating veggies.

It was strange. I looked around, and the house was exactly the same way it had been for as long as I could remember. A painting of a snowy cornfield hung over the piano we'd inherited, but no one knew how to play. A portrait of my grandparents sat next to the vase-shaped lamp on the little table next to the plaid couch. Calon saw me looking past him and into the living room. He cautiously turned around to try and see what had caught my attention before he went back to small talk with my mom.

In all the time I'd been away at college, never had I been homesick for my little house, and now a feeling of nostalgia that I didn't quite understand hit me, causing me to get all teary. There was no hiding it from Calon or my mom, so all of a sudden they were handing me napkins, fawning all over me, and asking me what was wrong.

"Nothing's wrong. Something just hit me about how familiar everything is here. There's a peaceful comfort here that I guess I never slowed down long enough to notice. Thanks, Mom. Thanks for keeping such a nice home for us. I'm sorry I'm just now realizing how much I truly appreciate it. I'm sorry I never thanked you before." I reached out and rubbed her soft hand.

Tears streamed down her face, and we all laughed.

"You'll have to excuse all the estrogen in this house, Calon. We should probably apologize ahead of time."

"It's nothing to apologize for. Being real is nothing to apologize for." He smiled and shoved a huge chunk of cow into his face. My mom looked at me and raised her eyebrows, knowing I would interpret what question she was asking.

"Yeah, mom, he's real." I patted Calon on his leg. He didn't follow our silent conversation, so he looked lost and a bit nervous.

"Wow." My mom rolled her eyes and got up to start clearing the plates.

"Please, Mrs. Mowry, let me get it. You and Becki go sit and relax."

Calon took a big swig of the beer Mom had handed him just minutes after we arrived. He stood up from the table and started stacking dishes. He walked over to where she stood with her mouth agape and took the small stack she'd already collected from the table. She was frozen with her hands poised as though they still held the stack of dishes and looked back and forth between me and Calon.

"Come on, Mom, let's go sit on the porch." She took my hand and walked toward the door. Calon gave me a quick kiss before she and I headed out into the chilly mid-fifties weather, which felt incredible. I had been so hot lately, the chill was a welcome shock to my system.

My mom sat on the porch swing and patted beside her. I felt like I was ten again, and she wanted to tell me where babies came from. It was obvious we both knew I was well aware of that lesson.

"You're going to be a mom." She stared straight ahead and took my hand in hers.

"Yeah." I took a deep breath and blew it out slowly through my pursed lips.

"I should ground you for making me a grandmother before I'm fifty, you know?' She squeezed my hand.

"You did it to Grandma. I'm just carrying on the Mowry tradition." I raised an eyebrow and peeked at her out of the corner of my eye to see if she was amused by my reference to our dependable ancestry.

"Becki Jane, this is no joke. He's a touring musician. How do you expect to have the normal life you need to raise a baby?" She shook her head and looked into her lap. Her tone was more concern than anger or disappointment.

"Mom, it will be *our* normal. Just because I won't be sitting at home watching PBS all day in sweatpants and no make-up, doesn't mean we can't be a happy family."

"People do it all the time. I know that. But, it's just not what I pictured for you, honey."

"Do you think Grandma pictured you and Daddy splitting? Do you think she pictured you being a single mom for most of my life?"

"No."

"And this was *our* normal. It's all I know. I like to think I turned out okay. Well, until the rock star knocked me up." We giggled, and she nudged me with her shoulder.

"I didn't knock you up." Calon walked out with two cups of hot tea and handed them to us. He pulled up a deck chair and sat across from us.

"Well, ya kinda did." I smiled at him. The father of my baby. Wow.

"Look, I hate that term because it insinuates a lack of commitment and not giving a shit... I'm sorry... I mean, not giving a second thought to what it means to bring a baby into the world."

He looked directly at my mom and cleared his throat and sat up straight. "Mrs. Mowry, I never thought I'd be a dad. I didn't have one. The men in my life just caused me pain. When Becki told me she was pregnant, something came over me that gave me a peace I never associated with being a parent.

"I am so in love with your daughter, Mrs. Mowry. I feel as though that sense of peace I felt was a sign of completion. Now, my life is complete. I have the woman I love, and we made a miracle. Not everyone is that lucky in life. I'm humbled to have been chosen to have this gift handed to me." He smiled at her then turned his attention to me.

"Becki, I didn't knock you up. We took what our hearts were telling us, and we made a baby. Something real. This is real. This is absolute." He stood up and walked over to where I sat. He bent down, slid his hand around the back of my neck, kissed me gently, and whispered, "I love you. Absolute."

I waited for the flutter in my chest to quell before saying anything. Even then all I could get out was his name in barely a whisper. He took my breath away.

He smiled and stood. "Ladies, I'm going to head out for a bit. Gonna explore this little town and hit the grocery store. I want to make something special for the two of you for breakfast tomorrow, so you both can just relax and enjoy Christmas without having to lift a finger. I'll be back in a bit."

He hopped down the steps, his curls bouncing all over the place. He smiled at us just before climbing into the car and pulling out of the driveway.

"I think you're going to be okay, sweetheart. Calon is an amazing man. Wise beyond his years, it seems."

"Yeah, he's been through a lot in his life, things I wouldn't wish on my worst enemy. But, it's made him so strong and steadfast and sure of himself, which, I guess, is the positive that comes out of all the negative stuff that's been thrown his way." I took a sip of my tea.

"Well, that's a beautiful way of looking at life and all its ups and downs. I'm proud of you, honey. You're going to be a great mom."

We hugged and then chatted about all kinds of stuff until it got too cold to sit on the porch. After we headed inside, I curled up under my favorite blanket on the couch and drifted off to sleep. I woke slowly and didn't open my eyes right away. I heard voices coming from across the room. I peeked through one eye and could see Calon and my mom sitting at the table drinking coffee. They were both smiling and nodding along with whatever their conversation was. I drifted back to sleep with a contentedness I wasn't sure I'd ever felt.

When the urgency in my bladder woke me, I opened my eyes and struggled to get to the bathroom without pissing myself then said goodnight to them and moved myself up to my old bedroom with the intention of climbing under the covers. Walking through that door it felt like stepping into a time machine. I instantly felt like I was in high school again.

I walked over to my dresser mirror and touched every curled photo I'd placed there over the years. As my gaze glanced over the photos, I thought about how I hadn't seen any of the people in them since graduation. The realization crystalized how transparent and fleeting those friendships were.

A piece of glass topped my dresser and everything that most girls put in scrapbooks or photo collages was shoved under that piece of glass. There were movie tickets and dried rose petals, cut out cartoons from the Sunday paper, and a couple of birthday cards. Tracing my finger over each item, I pondered how literal that piece of glass was. I could see everything I held dear during my teen years, but I couldn't touch them. They were set. I wondered what I would have said if the fortune teller downtown had predicted I'd be pregnant with a musician's baby before I graduated college. I laughed out loud thinking about it. This would never have been my expectation for my life either.

I glanced up at the only part of the glass that was covered and slid my jewelry box to the side to see if I'd stuck anything underneath that corner. My hand flew to my chest as my breath deserted me and dizziness clouded my brain. A photo of my dad and me sitting on what looked to be a rock in a green grassy field shouted at me from under the glass. I touched the glass delicately, almost afraid to lay my hand so close to the person I'd tried so hard to push out of my mind. The man who put doubt in my heart about my worthiness to be loved all this time stared up at me. He was dressed in a short-sleeved white dress shirt and khakis. His dark wavy hair tousled over toward one side. My hair was in high pony tails with big red ribbons and there was a small American flag in my hands on my lap. His arms were around me; his head gently leaned against mine. A split second of my life, one I wished I could remember, caught through a lens but not made permanent in my heart. My fingers brushed my mouth as I looked at his. We had the same smile.

I remembered the day my mom gave me that photo, and I remembered shoving it under the glass and setting my jewelry box on top of it. Not until that moment had I ever considered the devotion it took for my dad to stay with my mom throughout her unplanned pregnancy. I'd always focused on the fact that he left us and not on how long he stayed, trying to make it work. She once told me he worked three jobs to help them get by so she could be home with me. He was devoted to me and my mom, but their relationship just wasn't strong enough to weather the storms.

What Calon had just said to my mom a couple hours earlier on the porch, about creating life and it being a tangible miracle that was proof of the depth of our love, made me wonder if my parents ever knew that kind of love, and if they had, why couldn't they have made it work? The man in my mind, who left his only child behind, never to return, did not have the same look in his eyes that the father holding his daughter in the picture had. Prior to that moment, I imagined my dad as a grumpy, hands-off kind of dad, but I realized he wasn't hands off. He was providing for his family, which happened to keep him away from us more than I would have liked. I looked back down at the picture of us. There he was, holding me, hugging me, and loving me. Sadly, all that was left of that love was a faded photo stuck under glass.

"Nice digs, Becks." Calon nodded as he looked around my room. He shuffled over to me with his hands shoved in his pockets and a grin on his face that told me he was fantasizing about the teenager who used to shut the door to hide her secrets.

"Are you making fun of my room? There's a lot of my life in here. And I know you're not making fun of me. Do you realize how dangerous mocking a pregnant woman is?" I turned and walked until I bumped into his chest and wrapped my hands around his waist.

"I would never make fun of you—Cheer Captain Becki." His last three words came out high pitched and obnoxious in a sad attempt to sound like a cheerleader. I looked up at him with a growl as he smirked and nodded his head toward the pompoms that hung on the headboard of my four-poster bed.

"Jerk." I stomped on his foot. Not as hard as I could have, but he flinched. I felt it.

"So, what's got you so quiet and pensive in here?" He briefly squeezed me to him then walked over and sat on the edge of my bed.

"This." I lifted the back corner of the glass just enough to pull the picture out from under it. I walked over and sat on Calon's leg, resting my feet between his on the floor. His hand slid around my hip, and I leaned my body into his embrace. I held the picture up for him to see. A couple seconds ticked by in which neither of us said a word.

"Your dad?" He hugged me tighter.

"Yeah."

"Been a long time since you saw that picture?" He looked back at the picture.

"I forgot I had it. I moved my jewelry box just a couple minutes before you came in, and there it was, directly underneath. Hidden."

"What are you thinking?" Calon squeezed me a little.

"I'm thinking what an amazing dad you're going to be." I kissed him on the tip of his nose then stood and pulled my shirt up over my head, unhooked my bra, and slid my sweats down.

Calon's eyes darted back and forth between me and the door that was slightly opened.

"So, shut it."

"You're... you're not wearing any underwear." He crossed the room and painstakingly shut and locked my door so carefully he could've qualified for a position on the bomb squad.

"Haven't been all day. Nice of you to notice." I slid under the covers and smiled at him with a shy sexy smile. As I looked at the man before me, clad in a tight gray Johnny Cash t-shirt, well-worn jeans sitting low on his hips, and black boots, I realized this man could distract me from just about anything.

"Your mom won't care that we're both sleeping in here? Together?" He slid off his boots.

"Calon. It's no secret that we have sex. She's not the overbearing kind of parent. She would think it was weird if you *didn't* sleep in here." My body squirmed a little just thinking about him starting to undress before me.

"So, this is where you slept growing up? It's kind of sexy to be in here with you. Feels taboo or just a little wrong in all the right ways." He undid the button on his jeans but then stopped. The wheels turned in his head, and I knew his horny brain was up to something.

"Yeah, Calon. This is where I slept every night of my life before going off to college. Well, the nights I actually came home." I winked at him because I knew he was turned on by the bad girl side of me.

"So, did you touch yourself in that bed?" He crossed his arms, which pulled up his shirt just enough that I could see his dark hair that grew just below his belly button. He leaned back against my dresser and crossed his ankles.

"Nope. Not once." I kept a straight face.

As the sudden look of disappointment fell across his face, I burst out laughing.

"Yes, Calon, of course, I did. All girls do it, just most of them lie about it. Hell, girls probably do it even more than guys do." This conversation had my body in knots. My legs squirmed as a dull ache settled deep in my core.

"Will you do something for me?"

"Anything." My lips stayed parted. This was so hot.

"Imagine we are far away from each other and you're thinking about me before you fall asleep. Can you do that?"

"Been there. Done that." I was determined to make him as hot and bothered as he was making me.

"What do you mean?" He looked sincere in his question.

"Calon, I told you this before; the nights we lay on my bed and talked until we could barely hold our eyes open—as soon as you'd leave I'd—well, I'd fantasize that you hadn't gone home."

"How?"

"Like this." I slowly let my eyes close and tilted my head back. One hand slid under the covers and down my bare stomach. The other reached up and took hold of one of the rungs on my headboard. Picturing him in my dorm pulled up all the feelings I'd had when we were just getting to know each other, the excitement of being turned on by him, having to hold back that excitement, and the longing for him to touch me.

Calon sucked in a deep breath when he saw the blankets that covered my hand move. I slid my hand between my legs and squeezed my thighs together. I was so wet for him already. I knew I'd have to back off on the fantasy thing because I could come in just seconds if I kept doing what I was doing.

"Calon," I whispered his name and slid my middle finger to the tiny spot that needed more pressure. My skin was so slick, I instinctively started the small circular motions that I knew would propel me further into the sensations that would cause me to unravel in no time. A moan slipped from my lips without my consent, and my eyes flew open and locked on Calon's. He placed a single finger to his lips shushed me.

"How about some music as a buffer?" He tapped a little on his phone and walked over to the side table. "You're driving me insane." He put his phone on the side table before I heard any instruments, Calon sang the a cappella first line of OneRepublic's "Counting Stars" as he shed his clothes. By the second verse, he'd climbed under the covers and hovered over me. "Sorry, Becks, I couldn't wait to touch you. The images in my head of you touching yourself while you think of me sends me over the edge."

"Then make love to me, rock star." I put my hands on his hips. He dipped down and took my bottom lip between his teeth. He bit down just enough to make me gasp as the gentle pain in my lip shot like lightning down to my core. I wrapped my legs around the backs of his and tipped my hips up. His curls hung around his face and those fucking sexy green eyes stared down into my soul.

"God, I'm so in love with you." With that he slid inside me. His head flung back, and his mouth fell open as he felt me clench around him. I slid my hands across his back and down to his ass. Hottest ass ever. He clenched it under my fingers as he made sweet, hot love to me in my bed.

We fell asleep sweaty, naked, and sated. I was aware of his hands on me throughout the night. When I rolled over for him to spoon me, he took my hips and dragged them toward him until my ass was firmly against his dick, as though he needed me there. His strong arms around me all night made all my stress melt away.

I woke to an empty bed but a smell that practically lifted me from it. Squinting in the early morning sunshine that poured into my room as I searched for something to throw on, I grabbed black leggings and my favorite oversized Nirvana t-shirt simply because I could get them on quickly while I walked toward the door and out into the hallway.

The house was quiet, except for some noise in the kitchen and Calon's humming. I couldn't place the tune, but he hummed the same short tune over and over again. I stood just outside the kitchen archway to listen some more. He melted me.

"Merry Christmas." I touched his back and he jumped at the sound of my voice. I giggled.

"Merry Christmas, beautiful." He turned and kissed me on the nose then walked a bubbly casserole dish to the table and tossed the hot pads on the counter. I let my eyes drift across the table. The fruit salad looked like something gourmet you'd see in a cooking magazine. There was just about every color of the rainbow chopped and sliced in a big ceramic bowl. There were bagels and scones, cream cheese, jelly, and even a small jar of lemon curd. The casserole in the center of the table looked amazing. Cheese, eggs, and big chunks of sourdough bread all mixed together in a giant brick of heaven. My mouth started to water, and I looked at him in awe.

"You are amazing. I'm so lucky." Yeah, it was sappy, but it was the truth and the truth was sometimes mushy. I wrapped my arms around him, and we hugged and swayed next to the table.

"Morning, you two. I'll get the juice." My mom smiled at us and winked at me when she walked past. "So, Calon, what is that heavenly smell?"

"Well, it's something my mom used to make all the time. It's strata. Bread, cheese, and eggs all stirred together and baked. You let it soak in the pan overnight, so the bread sucks up all the moisture. You can put just about anything in it, but I was a little limited to meatless ingredients." He smiled and pulled me closer into his side.

"Wow. Was your mom Martha Stewart.?" I cringed on the inside at her question, because I didn't know where that would take Calon in his mind.

"Not really, Mrs. Mowry. Quite honestly, I've been cooking since I was five. So, it was simply the ease in preparation that inspired her to share this recipe with me. That way she didn't have to get up to make us breakfast." I rested my head against his chest and pulled him to me. His smile was pained, but he had been respectful in his portrayal of his mom. I wondered where she was, if she was better, if she knew of her son's talents and success.

I looked up at my mom and made a face. She needed to respond somehow. Calon didn't open up to many people.

"Calon, I'm sorry. I—"

"No worries, Mrs. Mowry. It was a long time ago. Now, ladies, are we going to eat or what?"

After a couple hours of eating and storytelling, we were all too stuffed to move. Calon got up and brought the presents from under the tree to the table.

Neither of us grew up doing big Christmas mornings like the ones you see on TV where the room is filled with piles and piles of gifts. My mom always taught me that giving gifts wasn't about the amount of gifts you bought someone, it was about the amount of thought that went into that one perfect gift.

At a street fair in LA, Calon and I'd watched a man hand-dye a silk scarf. The design was very abstract, but the blue and green splotches of color reminded me of Hydrangeas, which were my mom's favorite flower.

"I love this. It looks like Hydrangeas. Thank you both, so much. There was no need to spend money on me. My gift was you two coming home for the holidays in the middle of a big tour." She looped the scarf around her neck and fluffed it here and there to make it just right.

"Well, I guess it's my turn. I got you two a joint gift." She reached across the table and placed an envelope in front of us. Calon motioned for me to open it. It was a five hundred dollar gift card for BabyMe, a baby boutique just outside Knoxville that had everything we'd need to welcome our little one home.

"Thank you so much, Mom. This is amazing." I got up and walked around the table to give her a hug. When I turned to head back to where I'd been sitting, Calon was behind me, waiting to hug her. Their hug lasted a little longer than I would have thought, and neither of them spoke. Not out loud, at least.

I was so excited to give Calon what I'd had made for him. There was this cool shop down the street from the hotel that sold handmade jewelry, tapestries, leather bags, belts, and cuffs. Leather cuffs were a rocker thing. A single wide strap and a snap, like a bracelet. I had the guy that made them hand-stamp something and dye Calon's a little darker than he usually did. He'd looked at me like I was crazy when I wrote down what I wanted stamped into it. I told him to just make it look good. He made the letters smaller than he usually did so all the words would fit and it turned out beautiful. I knew Calon would love it.

When he pulled it from the bag, he read it out loud.

"Without limit, infinite, no catch, no fine print, no holds barred, no ifs ands or buts, no joke, no strings attached, pure, unconditional, unlimited, and unrestricted." Unshed tears floated in his eyes. He reached for my chin and pulled my face to his. "I've never owned something this personal. Thank you so much, Becki. I love it. I really, really love it." He kissed me gently then snapped his cuff around his arm and, like a little boy, grabbed the finely wrapped small, flat box from in front of him and handed it to me.

It didn't take long to unwrap, and, to be honest, I was a bit nervous to open it. I had a feeling it was something as personal and meaningful as what I'd given him. When I pulled the lid off, I smiled. It was a bracelet, too, a narrow silver bangle. And it was also hand-stamped but with the last stanza of the song I'd read on the pad of paper by the hotel bed.

"I want to be your habit. I want to be your vice. I want to lose myself inside you. Be the reflection in your eyes." I slid it on my arm and held my arm out for my mom to see. She turned it as she read it.

"Now, how did you two do that? Your gifts are almost identical?"

"Good minds, Mrs. Mowry." Calon flashed her a priceless smile.

"Calon, so that song really *was* about me?"

"You doubted me?"

"I don't know. I just thought maybe it was a song about love more so than about a specific person."

"Nope. It's all you. And there's another small part to my present." He got up and walked into the hallway. I heard the coat closet open and close. When he walked back into the kitchen, his acoustic guitar was hanging from his shoulders. He smiled, and I realized what he was going to do.

Calon put his foot up on the seat of his chair and rested his guitar on his thigh. He looked up at us and chuckled. My mom and I must've looked like a couple crazed fans just waiting for him to notice us. He winked, shook his head, and then started to play. It was the melody I'd heard him humming in the kitchen.

So much of my life has been darkness
But you handed me the sun
Brought to me as a gift
Baby, you're the one.

Your heart came at me like the tide
Each wave coveting more
Now you're completely inside
And, I'll never leave your shores.

I want to be your habit
I want to be your vice
I want to lose myself inside you
Be the reflection in your eyes.

So much of my life has been darkness
But you handed me the sun
Brought to me as a gift
Baby, you're the one.

The one who lights my fire
Who turns me inside out.
The one whose body tempts me
Leaves me breathless and spellbound

So much of my life has been darkness
But you handed me the sun
Brought to me as a gift
Baby, you're the one.

I want to be your habit
I want to be your vice
I want to lose myself inside you
Be the reflection in your eyes.

I want to be
I want to be
I want to be your habit
I want to be your vice
I want to lose myself inside you
Be the reflection in your eyes.

Tears rolled down my cheeks, and I just sat there, silent and still. What in the hell did I do in my lifetime to deserve this amazing man? What made him love me the way he did? My mom squeezed my hand, pounded it a little on my leg, then stood and walked toward Calon.

"You're a keeper, Calon Ridge. Don't you hurt my girl, you hear me?" She nodded slightly.

"Never in a million years, Mrs. Mowry. Not ever." His eyes landed on mine as he said it.

"I love my bracelet, Calon."

"I love you, Becki."

"Absolute," we said it in unison. We were so corny, and I didn't care.

eighteen
Calon

"So, how does this thing work?" I was so nervous I could puke. Becki looked down at our clasped hands in her lap and then back up at me. I hated the way doctor's offices and hospitals smelled. You'd think with all the medical miracles, someone could create an air freshener than didn't strike fear into the hearts of its patients.

"I have no idea, Calon. I've never done this before." She smiled a flawless but nervous smile.

"You didn't look it up or Google it or anything?" My knee bounced up and down, which made the waiting room chair squeak. Becki reached out and stopped my leg as she shook her head. "You didn't? You're going in there blind?"

"Not blind, Calon. I've seen people having ultrasounds on TV shows. I know it doesn't hurt, and that's all I care about. I want to get through this entire pregnancy with as little pain as possible. I don't do physical pain very well."

"Um, Becks, I'm pretty sure a twelve pound baby coming out of your... you know... will hurt."

"First of all, I highly doubt I will be having a twelve pound baby, and it's called a vagina, Calon. Say it with me, vuh-jy-nuh. Vagina." She said the second half of her little corrective speech way louder than I would have liked. The snickering I heard from the other women in the waiting room made me more than a little uncomfortable.

"You're Calon Ridge, right?" A very pregnant young woman, not much older than Becki, stood directly in front of me. She was so close that standing up wasn't even an option for me. If I tried, I'd hit her belly, and she'd topple backwards. So, I spoke to her from my seat, which made me even more uncomfortable than I was during the vagina dialogue.

"I am. And you are?" I smiled and put my hand out to shake hers. I hoped she couldn't feel me shaking.

"Violet, nice of you to remember. We met about, oh, I don't know, about seven months ago." She patted her belly and raised one eyebrow. Becki sucked in a breath and squeezed my hand. My throat slammed closed. Violet burst out laughing and held her belly with both hands. "I'm totally joking! Oh my word, that was so funny I almost peed myself."

"Nice." Becki was never one to hold back when someone pissed her off. "So, can we help you with something?" She motioned toward how close Violet stood to us.

"I just wanted to get your autograph and tell you how much I love your music." She completely ignored Becki and handed me a Rolling Stone Magazine turned to the page with a very small piece on West Coast bands. She pointed to a black and white photo of our band in action at The Moondance.

I took the magazine and the pen she'd handed me and scribbled my name across the photo then smiled and handed everything back to her. "It was nice to meet you, Violet."

"Becki Mowry?" A nurse clad in scrubs with little cartoon babies all over them stood holding a chart at the doorway that led to the exam rooms. Violet took a step back when the nurse looked in our direction.

"Excuse us." Becki stood and took my hand. She spoke with a smile, but there was a definite undertone of annoyance in her voice.

Once in the room, the nurse did all the vitals then told Becki to strip from the waist up and handed her a hideous hospital gown. The door shut, and Becki whipped off her top and bra and then slid her arms through the way-too-wide arm holes.

"You're not picky, are you?"

"Huh?" She turned in two full circles, looking over her shoulder as she tried to find the other string to tie her gown shut.

"You didn't even know her name." I shook my head, feigned disappointment, and grabbed the ties she couldn't find and tied them.

"What the hell, Calon? Just talk. I'm too nervous to translate your riddles." She huffed and sat up on the exam table. Her feet swinging with nervous energy.

"I just meant, you didn't know that nurse for longer than a couple minutes and you took your bra off with no hesitation. Never mind, it was a joke." I stood and walked over between her knees, I reached down and placed my hands firmly on her calves to stop her legs and calm her nerves. As I rubbed the tense muscles in her legs, her eyes rolled back in her head, and she moaned. It was a familiar enough sound that my dick did a little jump, thinking it was go time. Unfortunately, the sterile smell of a doctor's office just didn't do it for me, so Walter quickly went back to sleep.

"I guess I'm just easy like that when I'm pregnant." She smiled and leaned forward until her forehead touched my chest. She breathed in a very slow, deep breath.

"What are you thinking?" I ran my fingers through her hair and realized how much it had grown in four months of pregnancy. It was surreal that we were just shy of being half way to the due date. Not finding out until Becki was already three months pregnant cheated us out of the full nine months to prepare.

She looked up at me and smirked. Staying true to her promise to always answer that question truthfully, she let it all out. It came in waves of emotion, one right after the other.

"What if I'm not good enough? What if I really can't do this? What the fuck are we doing? Calon, I don't even know how to change a diaper, and I skipped school on the day they watched the birth video in sex ed, because I had no interest in watching some woman's crotch stretch its way into oblivion." She sucked in a couple sobs and wiped her nose with my shirt. *Yuck*. I just let her talk it out and wisely didn't complain about the snot. "I don't want my crotch to stretch to oblivion. When we have sex after this baby you'll have to tie a two-by-four to your ass to keep from falling in the giant cavernous void that once was my vagina."

I tried to hold it in, but I couldn't. I howled with laughter and wrapped my arms around her. I rocked her back and forth until she realized how freaking hysterical that visual was, and then we both laughed together.

"Everything will be just fine, Becks. Please, don't worry unless we have something to worry about." By the time the doctor came in my t-shirt was soaked with all kinds of fluids that found their way out of Becki's face in what had only been about five minutes.

"Hi there, Becki and…" The short, dark-haired woman looked through some paperwork and tried to find my name.

"Calon. Nice to meet you." I put my hand out for her to shake, and then she shook Becki's hand, too. It was nice to still be unrecognizable.

"Nice to meet you both. I'm Dr. Daily. So, Calon and Becki, we're having a baby. This weekend marks the end of your fourth month, and your baby is about the size of a banana." She held her hands up to show the average length of a fruit I'd never considered would be used to measure a human. I got a cold nervous feeling in my chest. I had no idea how big our baby was, but seeing her hands a good six or seven inches apart, made it even more real than just noticing the small bump that used to be Becki's flat, toned stomach. The doctor began the appointment by firing questions at Becki. I stood beside her and held her hand and rubbed her back.

"Have you felt any movement? Would feel a little like gas bubbles."

"I don't think so. I mean, I didn't know I should be feeling anything yet, so I guess I could have. I've had tons of gas bubbles lately."

"That's normal. Just a couple weeks from now, there will be no doubt what is a kick and what is a bubble. You'll be able to feel your baby's every move."

"You haven't gained a whole lot of weight, just slightly over five pounds. Are you eating well balanced meals? Three or four of them a day?"

"I was so sick at the beginning when I didn't know I was pregnant. I lost a lot of weight over the first couple months, so, technically, I have probably gained almost fifteen if you count the weight I put back on after being sick."

"Well, that's good. Good." She flipped through some sheets of paper in Becki's file and mumbled under her breath as she read through numerous typed pages. "I see here that you're a vegetarian. You really want to focus on your iron intake if you're not consuming meat. Iron-rich foods are legumes, soy-based products, spinach, prune juice, and iron-fortified cereals. I saw that Dr. Webber wrote you a prescription for a high iron prenatal. Are you taking those?"

"Yeah. They're fu—freaking huge, but I take them."

"Yeah, they are pretty big. Sorry about that." She chuckled.

"I see some charts have been faxed in from HealthOne in Los Angeles? Do you live in Knoxville or LA?"

"Well, we're back and forth. Calon's in a band, and we have a tour running on the West Coast. We're home until the end of January, and then we fly back out for the rest of the tour. This is the first time we've been back since Halloween, which is when I saw Dr. Webber. I went to an OB in LA last month, because I didn't want to go a whole two months without being checked. But, I did hold off on an ultrasound until now because I assumed I'll have the baby here and wanted the big tests to be done by the doctor who would do the delivery."

"Perfect, Becki. Well, let's get you prepped to see this baby. Do we want to know the sex of what you've got cooking in there?"

Becki and I looked at each other and nodded. We were anxious for the ultrasound, and it showed in our deer-in-the-headlights expressions. Everything Becki had just said hit me like a whirlwind. She was thinking more about the details of this pregnancy than I was. It wasn't that I was ignoring it. I had no idea what was going on inside of her so much so that I didn't even know what to ask. Since this was the first appointment I'd actually been to, I was learning way more than I expected.

"Look, you two. People do this pregnancy thing every day. You're fine. Let's just relax." She rubbed me on the back and tilted the exam table back. "Okay, Miss Becki, make yourself comfortable and pull the gown up right under your breasts."

"Oh shit. I didn't think I'd be this nervous. Calon, come here." It was then that I realized I hadn't moved from the end of the table where I'd first stood since when we came into the room. I took a couple quick steps until I was right next to Becki, who was scared out of her mind. I took her hand in one of mine and rubbed her hair with the other.

"Now, this jelly should be warm, as long as my warmer is working." Dr. Daily took what looked like a bottle you'd find condiments in at a picnic and squirted a mound of warm clear gel onto Becki's stomach. She typed in some information from Becki's chart on a keyboard just under the screen, flipped a switch to turn on what looked like a tiny TV, and reached for the wand. She then made eye contact with each of us, and with a smile she said, "Let's have a look, shall we?"

She pressed the wand around in the jelly and moved it around Becki's belly while staring at the screen, which, to me, looked like a scribbling of chalk on a blackboard. All I could see was white sketchiness on a black screen. I hoped that wasn't our baby, because it looked more like a pancake than a person.

"Is that the baby?" I said it louder than I needed to, but I was freaking out, because I couldn't make heads or tails of what I was looking at.

"Actually, Calon, that's Becki's bladder. Isn't it just lovely?" She smiled, and Becki and I laughed. Dr. Daily knew what she was doing when it came to helping patients relax.

"What's the whooshing noise?" Becki asked, but I had barely noticed it as anything other than a humming of the monitor, but then the musical part of my brain tuned into the syncopated rhythm of the sound. It was even and regular.

"It's the heartbeat. A healthy heartbeat." She looked up at us and smiled. Without warning, my eyes filled with tears. I looked down at Becki, who was looking up at me, and tears rolled down over her temples. Our baby's heartbeat.

The white shapes on the black screen changed quickly as the wand slid around Becki's belly. All of a sudden a large black ovular shape appeared in the center of the screen and in the center of the black was a white shape. It didn't look like anything at first, but when Dr. Daily started pointing to the screen and telling us the parts, I felt my knees go weak.

"Here is the baby's stomach, and when I look over here, we can see the spine." She dropped dotted lines across the screen with her wireless mouse and typed numbers on the keyboard. "Here's the heart and—"

"Oh my God, is that a hand?" Becki's voice was soft, as though she didn't want to spook the baby. I couldn't take my eyes off the screen where a tiny little hand that looked to be splayed out and pressing on the other side of the glass presented us with five perfect little fingers.

"Yes, it is, and here's the baby's head." It was a perfect profile shot, and it took my breath away. There was a chair directly behind me, which I took advantage of. I sat down and pressed Becki's hand between both of mine and tried to hold in the sobs that threatened to embarrass the hell out of me.

"Calon." Becki squeezed my hand, but her gaze remained on the screen. I felt an emotion I didn't know existed within me seep inside my chest. Dr. Daily did more of her measuring and typed in her numbers while Becki and I just stared at the perfect little human inside her.

"Now," Dr. Daily's voice startled me out of my daze, "if I get a good look from this side, you can almost make out a face. Can you see? The eyes, a little nose, a chin?" Although a little creepy and skeleton-like, I could see the baby's face perfectly. She took screen shots. I had to let go of Becki's hand for a moment to wipe my face.

"Calon, are you okay?" Becki giggled, reached out, and ran her fingers through my hair. She lifted my face with her fingers under my chin. She smiled, and her cheeks glistened with tears, too.

"I'm more than okay, Becki. This is the best day of my life. That's our baby. We *made* that." I sniffled and cleared my throat and thought about how glad I was that Alternate Tragedy wasn't yet at the popularity level that would have paparazzi hanging around every corner. Here I was a six foot tall musician in a leather jacket, torn jeans, and Doc Marten's with tears pouring out of me faster than I could wipe them away.

"So, you want to know what you're having, correct."

"Yes," Becki and I spoke in stereo. She gave me both her hands, and I squeezed them inside mine.

"Okay, let's see." Dr. Daily spoke, but it was like everything moved in slow motion all of a sudden. "Here's baby's heart. You can see all four chambers. Here's the umbilical cord, and right between the legs we should be able to find…" She wiggled the wand around at different angles, trying to get a clear shot at exactly what she was looking for. "This." She took a screen shot while Becki and I stared silently at the screen for what felt like five full minutes. Dr. Daily made some notes on Becki's chart and then finally looked up at us and chuckled.

"It's a girl. You're having a girl. Congratulations."

That's when I really lost it. I put my head down on the exam table, took a couple deep breaths, wrapped my arms around Becki as best I could from my seated position, and cried like a baby. A girl. We had made a tiny little human, and she was a girl. We were having a girl.

Becki called her mom to let her know the news. She had been adamant that she didn't want anyone in the room with us for the ultrasound, not even Gracie. I saw the disappointment on Gracie's face, but I knew she wasn't mad. She understood. But I had no one to tell. These were the times I missed having family.

"Yes, mom, a granddaughter! We're due May twenty-second." Dr. Daily had left but told us to take our time. Becki threw her arm up over her face and sobbed with her mom. Her shaky voice squeaked out 'a girl' a couple more times before they said their goodbyes.

Dr. Daily knocked lightly then came back in carrying a load of papers to keep us informed between visits as to what was going on with the baby and what to expect.

"All right. Up until your twenty-eighth week we like to see you once a month, but then after that we will need to see you every two weeks, and at thirty-six weeks you'll be in here every week."

"Oh dear. That's a lot of travelling." Becki looked up at me, and I could see scenario after scenario cross her face.

"Well, HealthOne would be a perfectly fine practice to see for your twenty-four and twenty-eight week check-ups. You could stay in LA for those, if that's easier. But, you'll have to decide where you want to have this baby, here or there. Because, you were right, it would be better to see the doctor that will deliver the baby for those next eight appointments."

"Well, I want to have her..." Becki looked up at me and a smile spread all the way across her face. *Her.* "Here. I want to have her here."

"Then you will have to either run your tour in this direction over the next two months, or you'll need to move home without Calon for the last twelve weeks of your pregnancy. That is, if you don't deliver early for some reason."

"Oh, God. That makes me so nervous." She pulled her hair back into a messy bun and rubbed her face.

"I don't need you to make a decision now, but you'll need to think it over and have a concrete plan before you head back on tour at the end of the month."

"Okay." Becki was thrown, I could tell. Neither of us was ready for this huge event to happen at all, let alone right in the middle of the tour. We had been so busy with gigs and promotional appointments that we barely had time to think more than one day ahead of the one we were living. I knew that was also a defense mechanism for both of us. If we kept our minds busy, we didn't have time to consider all the details of this life-changing surprise. Funny that Becki and Gracie had named the tour The 'Surprise' Tour.

"And, tell me a little more about what you do for the band. What is your schedule like, Becki?"

"Well, I'm the manager. I have an assistant, so we divvy up the load, but it still means eight to ten hour days. I travel with the guys to interviews and appearances, and we have lots of late nights at their shows. About three to four a week, on average."

"Here's my concern. Those hours are not good for someone carrying a baby. You need to delegate more of your responsibilities and start making sure you're getting at least six hours of sleep a night, if not eight." Becki grimaced but nodded respectfully. "And about the three to four concerts a week. Some studies have shown that unborn babies exposed to loud noise over a long period of time are more likely to be born early, have lower birth weight, and some even have hearing loss at birth.

"Your baby can hear what's going on around you. Your voices, music, loud sounds, such as car horns, and she can even startle enough that you'll feel her jump when frightened."

"So, what are we supposed to do?"

"Well, it's your decision, but my suggestion would be this; I would like to see you come back to Knoxville at twenty-eight weeks, that's in two months. I would like you to have your assistant take on enough of the responsibilities that will allow you to get six to eight hours of sleep every night." She jotted what she was saying down on the top sheet of the stack of paper she'd handed Becki.

"What about their shows? They don't have daytime shows." I saw Becki's eyes tear up. She loved the shows. She was a live music girl.

"Let's make a deal, Becki. You can do one show a week, but that's it. You've got to start putting your baby's safety and health above everything. It won't be easy, but you're a mom now." She looked up at me. "And, Calon, you're a dad. You need to keep an eye on this girl and help her keep the baby safe and healthy."

"I had no idea how all this worked. I truly thought you just carried the thing around inside you for nine-months and the real responsibility came after it came out. Oh, yeah, about the coming out part. Does that hurt and will my vagina ever be the same?" Becki giggled.

"Tell you what. About halfway through that stack is everything you will need to know about what you just asked me. And, Calon, you'll be pleased to know that you get some hands-on assignments that you may find enjoyable—if you know what I mean." She elbowed me a little and then turned for the door. "I will look over the measurements we took today and call you if there's anything I need to share with you. You two have a good day, okay? And, do that homework."

"Thank you, Dr. Daily." I was thrilled we ended up with a down to earth doctor who could joke with us but also give it to us like it was. I wouldn't say it to Becki, but I had been concerned that she would blow off whatever the doctor told us. It didn't appear as though she had that attitude with Dr. Daily, and for that I was thrilled.

We walked back to my apartment holding hands, both of us pensive. I risked looking like an idiot and carried Becki's purse now that it had ten pounds worth of paperwork in it. But I couldn't wait to lie in bed with her and read everything we needed to know about being pregnant. Part of me was sad that we didn't know about the baby for so long, it was like we'd been docked a couple months of excitement, nervousness, and research. We really should've been reading up on all of this.

"So, what are we going to do, Calon?" We walked up the stairs and into my place.

"Well, I think Dr. Daily had a good plan. You come back here and stay put at twenty-eight weeks."

"Are you doing that math? We are home, in Knoxville, for four of those weeks. I'd only be back in LA with you for four weeks, and then I'd have to move home. The baby is coming at the end of May. That's all of March, April, and May away from you. Calon! You guys have shows all the way into the fall of next year. I can't do that to you guys. And, I don't want to be that far away from you all that time."

Standing in the middle of my living room, I took her into my arms and let her bag fall from my shoulder. "Listen, I hate the idea of being away from you, but like Dr. Daily said, we have to start putting *her* ahead of what *we* want." I touched her belly with both my hands.

"I'm really just a little too selfish for this, Calon. Why couldn't you just have left your dick in your pants? Ugh." She stomped over to the kitchen and poured herself a glass of water. I followed her.

"Now, *that's* all your fault. If you weren't so unbelievably sexy, I would have had no problem keeping it in my pants. I did pretty well with that for the four years before I met you, ya know."

"I still don't know how you did that. Four years? That's some will power." She took a big gulp of water.

"Or hand power." I made the universal jacking-off gesture, and with bad timing, I might add, because the giant gulp of water Becki had just taken came back out all over me.

"You're such a dork." She wiped off her face and mine while she giggled non-stop. "Hey, I promised Gracie I'd stop by her work and let her know how the ultrasound went. Wanna come?" She laced her hands around my waist and stood on her toes to kiss me, even though she was tall enough she didn't really need to.

"I really should head to the studio. The guys have been there working on shit for hours without me."

"Okay, well, maybe we can have dinner with Jake and Gracie tonight?" She winced a little, as though she needed to beg me to spend time with them. I loved Gracie like a sister, and once Jake realized I wasn't trying to steal her from him, we hit it off. I loved hanging out with them and missed it a lot while we'd been gone.

"Of course, that sounds great. Let's shoot for six-ish? You text me where you want me to meet you, and I'll be there." She nodded against me but didn't let go.

"What are you thinking, Miss Mowry?" I pulled her face to mine.

"You're going to have a daughter, Mr. Ridge." A pang of nervousness hit my stomach so hard I blinked, and it stole my breath.

"We're having a girl." I kissed her slow and deep. Our mouths celebrated with a kiss that left me weak and wanting more. "If she's half as amazing as her mommy, she will be perfect."

A daughter.

My girl.

nineteen

Becki

AFTER I SIGNED in at The Knoxville Extension School office, the secretary pointed me in the direction of Gracie's classroom. The only sound in the hallway was my Converse squeaking on the linoleum tile floor. I walked slowly and looked at all the art hanging on the walls in the wide hallway. There were paintings of trees with bits and pieces of torn green tissue paper glued on for leaves. Then there were larger horizontal drawings of words that had me mesmerized in no time. They were obviously done by older children with a significant interest in art. It looked as though students had traced large letters to spell a word of their choice, and then they used colorful markers to add pattern and designs to each letter. They were beautiful. I whispered each word as I walked.

"TRUST, HOME, FRIENDS, HAPPY, BEACH, LIFE, LOVE, SUNSET…"

I stopped dead in my tracks and walked over to touch the intricate lines on a word that stood out from the rest. The letters were drawn on a black piece of paper, where all the others were on white. The letters were outlined in white, and the designs within the letters were done with expert precision in metallic gold.

"ABSOLUTE." I spoke just above a whisper and took in every

nuance of every line. There was a subtle movement to the design. The design in the 'A' was sparse, just a couple small shapes, almost like the yin yang symbol. Each letter became more dense with design, ending on the 'E' that was so filled with meticulous lines and shapes that the design you saw when you stood back was actually created by a void of lines. The shapes were made up of the black spaces between the designs. The artist's initials, 'SKO', were hidden in the design.

I grabbed my phone from my pocket and texted a photo of the project to Calon. I knew that was probably a rip-off in the art community, but it's not like I was going to sell it or claim it to be my own. I just wanted to share the beautification of that word with Calon.

"Okay, now, I'm going to play you a song, and I want you to sing to your new friend." Gracie's voice was perfect for the social work profession and working with special needs and troubled kids. It was the epitome of peace and calm but somehow strong at the same time. I stood just outside her room, leaned against the wall and listened.

"Miss Jordan, I don't know the words."

I heard Gracie giggle. "Joe Joe, honey, I didn't play the song yet. Hold your horses."

I smiled. If this school didn't hire her after graduation, they were missing out. She was made for this job. I, personally, was always nervous around mentally challenged people. I was too worried they'd think I was staring, or if I laughed they wouldn't know I was laughing *with* them and not *at* them. I was happy to wait out in the hallway until Gracie was free.

I gently dropped my head back against the wall when I heard the music start. "Lips Like Sugar" by Echo and the Bunnymen was our ritual while we got ready for parties in Gracie's apartment. Gracie, Stacy, and I would dance around like idiots while we showered, got dressed, and put on our make-up. I knew Gracie and I were both having the same flashbacks at that moment, which made me smile. But, partying was now a part of my past. You don't see many pregnant girls at fraternities these days. It would've been fun to party a little just with Gracie while we were home for the month, like old times. An attempt at one last hoorah before she and Jake graduate, and we all end up going out into the real world. I pressed my hand to my stomach just as Gracie opened the door and stuck her head into the hallway.

"Becki! I hoped you'd be here. You need to come in and see this." She grabbed me by the hand that wasn't on my belly and tugged.

"Oh, Gracie, you know how this stuff is for me. It makes me super uncomfortable. I'll just wait out here." I struggled against her grip.

"Becki, we're listening to music and hanging out with puppies. You can't find *that* much fun in the hallway. Come on!"

"I'm gonna kill you, Gracie Ann."

"You love me."

She pulled me around the corner and into a room that threw me right back into an elementary school mindset. It smelled like paint, the kid kind of paint. Sunshine filled the room through a whole wall of windows. There were colorful kid-made mobiles hanging from the ceiling, and a huge red carpet that took up most of the entire floor. There were some desks on the carpet but not many.

There were about ten little people sitting on the carpet in a tight circle. They were trying their damnedest to keep up with the lyrics of Echo and the Bunnymen while they loved on what looked to be an entire litter of golden retriever pups. The giggles far outweighed the actually singing, but a more precious scene I'd never laid eyes on.

"Miss Jordan, can you and your friend come play, too?" A little blonde girl with glasses tried to hold her puppy still as she spoke. She ended up getting a mouthful of puppy tongue but couldn't have cared less. It just made her giggle louder.

"Come on, Beck. You can do this. You just have to relax. Look at it as just a group of kids and puppies and try to look past their differences. Try to see them for what they are, happy little people." Gracie whispered, so I was the only one who heard her directive.

"Fine." I was terrified but knew it would make Gracie so happy to have me experience the activity with her and her class.

"Well, make some room, guys." Gracie poked her foot between a dark-haired little boy and the blonde who'd asked us to play. Gracie and I fought against the current of puppies trying to lick us to death as we squeezed in between them and sat down. "Guys, this is my best friend, Becki."

"Hi, Miss Becki." All ten of them sang their welcome in unison. I smiled and thanked them but tried not to make eye contact. My stomach was filled with butterflies, and I couldn't wait for them to be dismissed for lunch, so I could have lunch with Gracie and tell her my big news.

"This is Taryn, Timothy, Thomas, Jenna, Marcus, Gabe, Joe Joe, April, Calla, and Sammy." She knew there was no way I would remember all their names, but she was being polite.

"Hi, everyone. It's nice to meet you." I waved and smiled.

"You guys aren't singing. Come on! Let's sing the words you hear." Gracie glowed brighter than I'd ever seen her. She was in her element. Her heart was so huge, and she gave her love away so freely. I couldn't imagine a better group of people to be the recipients of pieces of her heart. I felt myself relax.

A tired little pup curled up in my lap, sighed a big puppy sigh, and snuggled into me. The name tag on his collar said Sisco and the longer I stroked his fuzzy back, the more relaxed I felt. Soon, I was as close as I'd ever been to looking past the obvious difficulties these children came into the world with. It was their laughter. That beautiful sound dissolved my nervous jitters. There were only a couple kiddos that I couldn't pinpoint their challenge. Almost half the circle was made up of kids with Down syndrome. There was a set of twins with coke bottle thick glasses, who reached for the puppies but didn't appear to be able to see them very well. One little girl had an oxygen tank next to her and clear tubes that wrapped around her ears and went into her nose. She smiled at the puppies and giggled the loudest when the rest of the class sang about *lips like sugar* and *sugar kisses.*

A loud buzz came over the PA system, causing me to jump in surprise. All the kids ran to the bank of cubbies in the back of the room, and all the dogs went wild with the open space to play.

"Becki! Help me get these guys in their crate!"

Gracie and I must've looked like greased pig wranglers because the kids stood at the edge of the carpet and giggled harder at us than they had at the puppies' kisses. Sisco was the last one in, and we locked the crate. The room erupted into cheers and applause. Becki and I bowed and curtsied to the class, which cracked us up as much as it did them.

"All right. All right. Get to lunch. Go on. Scoot." She brought up the end of their single file line out the door. Just then someone from Animals Are Friends, a non-profit pet therapy group, came in and left with the crate of puppies.

"See you next week, Miss Jordan!" He flashed a big smile and a wave.

"Bye, Doc!"

The little blonde girl, who'd invited me to play with her and her friends, ran back in with her lunchbox in one hand and pushing up her glasses with the other. She ran right up to me, put her little chubby arms around me, and hugged me with her cheek pressed against my belly.

"Thank you for playing with us, Miss Becki. You're pretty. I love your hair." She squeezed me so tight it almost hurt.

"Thank you for asking me to play with you…" I looked at Gracie when I realized I didn't know anyone's name.

"Taryn." She spoke her name with a slight speech impediment which made her 'r' sound more like a 'w', which was adorable. She tilted her head back, and I fell into the most gentle, inviting eyes I'd ever seen in a child. It was almost like she was an older soul living in a school age girl's body. My nose burned as a warning the tears would soon fall. I blinked them back. She lay her rosy cheek against my belly again and took a deep breath. She squeezed me too tight once more then skipped out of the room. A tear slid down my cheek.

"Beck?"

"Shut up. I don't know what the fuck is wrong with me. Just today I turned into this blubbering idiot." I wiped the tears away and pulled a chair up to Gracie's desk.

"It's all the hormones. I remember my mom's friends being pregnant, and they cried over everything. That'll be you soon." She giggled and pulled a big Panera bag from the fridge and quickly transformed her desk into a table for two. Once she was done, we had our own little café.

"Oh, Gracie," I said her name in a very sexual tone, but it had to do with the Caprese Panini she'd ordered for me. Nothing had ever tasted so good. I hadn't realized how hungry I was. Luckily, Gracie and I had been friends long enough that she knew it was the sandwich that brought out my sexy voice.

"Okay. Tell me. How was the ultrasound?" She said every word like a goof.

"It was amazing, Gracie. Calon and I cried like idiots. We saw fingers and a perfect little profile." My hand went right to my stomach as I spoke.

"AND?" Her face was priceless. She was on the edge of her seat.

"It's a girl." Tears streamed down my cheeks. Gracie screamed so loud I felt my entire belly jump. I rubbed my hands over my belly and laughed until my sides hurt.

"Gracie, you just scared the shit out of her. I felt her jump. I've never felt her move until just now. You're going to give her a heart attack. I have a baby in me now, you need to be quiet." She giggled, ran around the desk and hugged me then dropped to her knees in front of me.

"I'm so sorry I scared you. I promise to make it up to you as soon as you come out of your mommy's belly. I'm going to spoil you so bad." Gracie winked at me. I laughed at the fact that she was talking to my stomach, but it also made my heart full. Two of my most favorite people on the planet were head over heels in love with the little person who swam in my belly.

"Becki, I still can't believe you're pregnant. I mean, it hits me every now and then, and it floors me. Floors me!" She sat back down with a thud.

"Yeah, me, too. I don't know how to do this, Gracie. I'm scared as hell to do this." I bit into my sandwich to distract myself from the fear in my gut.

"I'm sure that's normal. You're growing a human inside you. You've got to think about everything you do, breathe, eat, drink... everything. From now on, whatever you do, whatever decisions you make will affect that little one inside you." She dipped her head and filled her mouth with steaming soup.

"Oh, well, if that's all, then shit, I got this. You're a jerk, Gracie

Jordan!" I growled and threw my napkin at her.

She looked down and gasped so deep she choked herself. She picked her phone up out of her lap and put it in front of me while she hacked and coughed and cleared her throat, unable to explain. I looked down at the screen. She had clicked on a notification that came from her music news feed on Twitter, and the photo I stared at had the top trending hashtag: #whocalonknockedup

It was from the OB waiting room earlier that day. It was a cropped photo from the second Violet patted her belly and tried to make us think her baby was Calon's. Whoever the asshat photographer was caught Calon's horrified look in the split second it took for him to react to her sick joke. The caption read, *Calon Ridge. News of a baby he doesn't want.*

"What the fuck? That bitch!"

"Who did this?" Gracie cleared her throat and took a long swig of her water. "You know her?"

"Some girl. Violet, I think she said. She basically told Calon she was pregnant with his baby in the OB waiting room."

"WHAT? Becki, that's insane! You have to tweet something."

"No. If I've learned anything on this tour so far, it's the more you entertain idiocy, the more is thrown at you. Right now, I can't tolerate idiots. I have enough stress of my own."

I texted Danny.

Me: *Rumor mill. #whocalonknockedup*

Danny: *Got it.*

"You're just going to let it go? That's not the ass-kickin' Becki I know." Gracie flashed a devilish grin.

"I just texted Danny. She will squash anything that comes her way. Unfortunately, the ass-kickin' Becki had to retire. I have to remain professional. Besides, I'm too stressed out about stuff the doctor said. People can believe what they want, until it starts to affect the band in a negative way, I'm going to stay out of it." I blew my nose and wished I could turn off the waterworks. The crying thing was getting on my nerves. Big time.

"Is everything okay? What did the doctor say?" A look of worry crossed her face as she reached out and grabbed my hand.

"The baby's fine. At least the doctor didn't tell us otherwise. But, she said because the appointments I'll need to go to get closer and closer together as the pregnancy progresses, she thinks I should move back to Knoxville at the end of February or find a doctor in LA and have the baby there."

"You will NOT have her in LA!" Gracie slammed her hands down on her desk, which made such a loud crack the baby tried to jump out my throat.

I grabbed my stomach and rubbed it with both hands. "You've GOT to stop doing that, Gracie." Then I just laughed and laughed at the whole scenario.

"I'm not having the baby in LA. I promise. But being away from Calon for the last three months, do you realize how hard that will be? That's when I'm supposed to take the birthing classes, and he'll be entertaining groupies across the country while I'm heavy-breathing on a mat in a birthing class alone."

"I could be your birthing coach. I mean… well, I don't know if…" Gracie looked all around her desk and fiddled with pens and papers.

"That would be amazing, Gracie. I would love that. You're the only other person I'd trust to be there when someone makes me do dumb shit."

"You never told me your due date,"

"May twenty-second."

"So, I'll have to remember to add her as your 'plus one' on your invitation to our wedding." She made a goofy face and squeezed her fists together as she tried to hold in another squeal she knew would startle the baby again.

Jake and Gracie got engaged over Christmas. They called us while we were still at my mom's. We put her on speaker phone, and she told us the whole goopy, sappy story. The canoe, the moon on the pond, blah, blah, blah. It was a great story, and I was thrilled for them, but it wasn't my kind of engagement story. Perfect for Gracie because Jake knew how to love her the way she needed to be loved. If Calon ever asked me to marry him, I hoped he knew me well enough not to do something that sappy.

After my lunch with Gracie, I walked back to Calon's. I slipped out of the jeans I could no longer button. My stomach pooched out just enough to keep the button too far from the buttonhole.

I stood completely naked in front of the full length mirror on the back of Calon's bedroom door. I turned to the side and studied the shape of my lower belly. I tried to imagine the position of the baby inside. I put both hands on the small protrusion and for the first time ever I spoke directly to my unborn child.

"Hi, baby, I'm your mommy. I wasn't expecting you, like ever, but I'm glad you're here—in me. I'm glad you chose me. I can't wait to meet you."

I threw on one of Calon's huge gray UTK hoodies he wore when he ran in the cold and a pair of old, comfy sweats I'd had since high school. I grabbed all the papers from my purse and climbed between the covers that smelled like Calon. I felt a twinge in my core as I thought how he loved my body in that bed.

The thick stack of papers had me mesmerized in no time. I suddenly craved more and more information about the baby growing inside me. I grabbed a highlighter from the cup of pens and pencils next to Calon's bed and started studying pregnancy stages like it was my job.

My body was so comfortable lying in Calon's bed. Pretty soon the papers I'd been reading were strewn all over the place, and I was out cold. The pillow top king-sized mattress, high thread count sheets, and a down comforter lulled me to sleep. Every time I crawled into his bed I felt like it pulled me into it just as much. It was a whole new level of comfort.

I could tell it was getting dark even with my eyes closed. But I needed to get up unless I wanted to pee in Calon's pillowy paradise. Before my eyes were completely open, Calon came into focus, but he wasn't looking at me. I lay perfectly still and closed my eyes again, but just far enough that he couldn't tell I was spying on him.

He leaned against the frame of the door in nothing but a towel looking at something small he held in his hand. He stood perfectly still, his wet curls clung to his face. My eyes raked over his perfect body, and that twinge in my core came back with a vengeance. Never before had anyone made my body parts ache for them without a single touch. Just looking at him lit me up. I moved my feet under the covers to see what he would do. He spooked and then shoved whatever he was holding into the pocket of the ugliest damn coat he kept on a hook on the door of his closet. I stilled.

He stared at me lying in his bed and smiled. Then, as though it was part of a script, he started to sing. His voice was so quiet I couldn't make out the words. Whatever the song, he sang it like a lullaby. He walked around the bed, and I felt the bed sink down and the covers shift as he climbed in behind me. He was still singing, but he was closer, and I could hear every single word. A beautiful a cappella rendition of "What if" by Five for Fighting. A song that always reminded me of our love story. When we first started our long talks, I remember wondering what it would be like to let him *hold my heart,* and if I'd be able to *wear his scars.* I imagined secrets he would tell me, and, in my mind, I told him mine. There were a whole lot of 'what ifs' in the beginning but not anymore.

We had each other to hold onto, and now we had a baby that tied us together for an eternity. We were through the 'what ifs' and onto 'what's next'.

twenty

Calou

BY MID-JANUARY we had all fallen into a rhythm of sorts. The guys and I wrote and practiced all day then recorded or played at Mitchell's in the evenings. We played with Gracie every Friday, and Buzz was kind enough to switch some bands around, so we could play every Saturday for the whole month.

We finished our first set, and I winked at Becki and Gracie sitting at the bar. I looked around just before I left the stage and took it all in. I loved the feel of the small bar crowd, because it was so much more personal and seemingly relevant to what we were about, more so than the large venues we'd been playing. When we first started out with Max and his crew, we were thrilled to be playing for crowds two and three times larger than any we'd played for at Mitchell's and that seemed to be inspiring to all of us.

Just before Christmas we were called to open for Tragic Monster, a big band that had just signed a deal with Genesis Records. They lost their opening act at the last minute, and someone told their manager to give us a call to fill in for their Hollywood Bowl show. The Hollywood Bowl is the largest natural outdoor amphitheater in the US, and the night we played it was a sold out crowd, which meant over seventeen thousand screaming fans. Our biggest show ever.

Afterwards, in the limo that Tragic Monster had hired to get us there and back to our hotel, I sat between Becki and Danny, and the guys sat across from us in a rear facing seat. A conversation started about what it felt like to play for that many people.

"It blew my mind to see that many faces staring up at us, ya know? But, to say it was overwhelming would be an understatement." Spider tossed back a shot of whiskey and winced as the burn made its way down his throat.

"But, overwhelming is good, right? Don't the big timers usually talk about that in interviews and stuff? I've heard bands mention how freaked out they were in the beginning when they started playing for big crowds. Right?" I wrung my hands to try and stop the trembling. I didn't know where my mind was on the subject of huge crowds, but it wasn't the thrill I thought it would be. Quite honestly, it felt contrived and I felt disconnected.

"It's probably normal to feel that way, Calon." Danny patted me on the leg and smiled.

Manny poured us each another shot, and we all downed them before he began to speak. "Listen, guys, y'all remember the Pearl Jam documentary, right?"

"PJ20?" Bones piped up and poured himself his fifth shot.

"Yeah. Remember when they showed them playing at some outdoor gig in the Netherlands, I think it was?" Manny threw back his shot.

"Pink Pop. Nineteen ninety-two." Bones was our in-house trivia dork.

"That's it. Do you remember Ed taking Polaroid shots during the show? When they interviewed him afterwards he pulled the pictures out of his pocket and said it was overwhelming to play for such a big crowd because at that point, they'd never played any place that big. I don't remember how many people they said were there—"

"Sixty thousand."

"Thanks, Bones. Okay, so it was significantly more than what we saw tonight, but it was the biggest show for them at that point in their career, and it overwhelmed them. Ya know? I think it's natural to feel the nerves we're feeling." Manny closed his eyes, and I couldn't tell if he was too drunk to keep his eyes open or just reveling in the size of the crowd we'd just rocked.

"Yeah, but, do you question whether that's what we want?" Becki squeezed my hand when I spoke, and I knew I'd just opened a can of worms, but I had to make it known that I needed to make sense of the path we were on.

"Fuck no!" Bones choked on his spit and hacked up a drunk lung then continued. "Dude, that's what we're in this for, right? To make it big. Play big places. Do interviews and have documentaries made about us. Right? Aren't we in it for the fame?"

"I don't think that's what I focus on, Bones." I looked over at Becki, and she smiled. She knew I tried to stay grounded and recognized that the speed we were going, it could soon be difficult to keep our hearts in the right place and not get sucked into the fame circus.

"Come on, Cal! Don't minimize what this was for us. Don't get all philosophical. We just fuckin' played The Hollywood Bowl, and people were loving us."

"I know, Bones. I am so humbled that a crowd of that size welcomed us as freely as they did."

"Hell, yeah, they did. Because we fuckin' rocked their world. Doesn't that give you a boner, man?"

Becki giggled and took the last sip from her water bottle.

"Listen, guys." Becki's voice was calming. "This is all part of the journey, and that's what you have to focus on right now—the journey. Don't look ahead and try to decide whether you want to play big or small venues, or whether you want to make decent cash or be a household name. There will come a time that you'll be faced with a situation that will set this all straight for you. You'll know what you want when you have to make tough choices. Stay true to your hearts and don't let go of your integrity, and someday you'll know. You'll just know." Becki smiled and nodded at each one of us as she spoke.

I always knew Becki was our sanity, but, in my eyes, she more than proved herself with those couple sentences. She was right. We needed to just take it all in and savor every bit of what we were experiencing and one day, we'd just know.

WE DECIDED TO hang out at a table for a while after we finished playing.

"You guys remember that night we talked in the limo about the size of our crowds?" I poured another beer from the pitcher that seemed to never empty thanks to a star struck waitress who used refills as her excuse to come backstage and flirt.

"Yeah, what's up, Cal?" Spider raised his pilsner into the air, and we all followed suit.

"I just want you to know that I am enjoying the small crowds at Mitchell's, but there's an energy that's missing, and I guess that's one of the things you get only from the larger crowds." I took a swig of my beer.

"I'd have to agree. When I'm in the moment and jamming away on the bass, it's the sound of thousands of people who make me forget how exhausted I am. Ya know? I'm sure there are pros and cons to both. We just need to, as a band, stay grounded about it and not fade into the masses of all those bands just in it to make it big. It needs to be about the music. Always." Bones nodded to himself, seemingly impressed with his change of heart since we'd discussed fame that night in the limo with Becki. The cute waitress was back and filled all our glasses this time instead of just bringing a fresh pitcher. She winked at Bones when she scooted passed him.

"What's your name, sweetheart?" Bones was relentless when it came to women who flirted with him. He always felt it was his responsibility to get them even giddier than they already were. It was just strange to have that level of fandom in Knoxville. We usually felt like the crowd was more a group of friends hanging out with us and not "fans," so to speak.

"I'm... I'm Charlotte." She blushed and batted her eyes at each of us. "I'm a Delta Gamma sister. Tonight is our DeeGee-Waitress fundraiser. We pulled straws to see who got to wait on you guys. It was me. I got the longest straw." She bounced up and down and squealed a little.

"That's funny because, of the four of us, I've got the longest straw, too, Charlotte." Bones mimicked her bouncing, but did it in a way that was funny and not callous.

"Well, Bones, maybe you can show me later." Charlotte winked and turned, wiggling her ass on her way back out to the bar with our empty pitcher.

"What... Did you... Guys!" It was rare for Bones to be caught off guard by a girl coming onto him, but there was something about Charlotte he apparently appreciated more than most. I was relieved she was into Bones, because it was an arduous task having to curtail the flirting and come-ons. Since the Twitter incident and the 'who Calon knocked up' hashtag trended, I'd tried to keep those kinds of fans at arm's length. But the more venues we played, the worse it got, and I wondered if Mitchell's was immune to that sort of behavior.

After the bar emptied out, Buzz fed us like kings while the Delta Gamma girls bused their tables. Jake and Gracie stayed to hang out, too.

"Hey, Calon, Jake and I have a question for you." Gracie looked across the booth at me and a huge smile spread across her face. She was so freaking adorable.

"Yeah?" I threw a couple fries in my mouth and sucked down half my glass of beer.

"Well, the question is really for *all* of you."

"Yesssss, Gracie..." Bones dragged her name out like he was entertaining a beggar. "We will marry you. Sorry, Jake, it's just the rock star thing. You can't compete with that, ya know?" Bones shook his head, as though he felt bad for Jake.

"Thanks, Bones. But, as you recall, I'm already taken." Gracie smiled.

"Shit! That's right! Congratulations, by the way." Bones fist bumped Jake across the table. "That Gracie, she's a good one." Bones winked at Gracie.

"Oh, I'm well aware of how good she is, Bones. Well aware." Jake waggled his eyebrows at Gracie, and when his innuendo hit her, she gasped and blushed, which made us all laugh.

"So, anyway. You all know Jake and I are planning our wedding for August ninth, right?"

We all nodded, mouths filled with food.

"We were hoping you guys would play at our reception. Please?" She clasped her hands under her chin and batted her eyes.

"Well, you'll have to talk to our manager. She does all the scheduling." I put my arm around Becki and pulled her into my side. She laid her head on my shoulder. Poor thing, I knew she was beat and would rather have headed back to my apartment then make the night longer with a food fest.

"I think I could squeeze you in, Gracie." Becki winked in a way that made me think their wedding was already penciled in on our schedule and the asking was just a formality.

"Have you guys picked all your songs? You know, your dance, the father-daughter dance, mother-son dance... all that?" Spider always needed details.

"We have. I'll make sure Becki gives you guys the list. We are dancing to 'Fallen', of course." She smiled and short flashbacks of all the things that tied her and Jake to that song scrolled through my mind. They'd really been through a lot, and I felt humbled to be a part of their story.

"Um. Excuse me, Calon. Would you mind posing for a couple pictures with some of your fans?" Charlotte smiled and popped her hip out to the side.

"Well..." I looked over at Becki who eyed her up and down.

"A couple of my sisters that were here for the fundraiser were hoping to meet you. It will only take a second." She smiled sweetly.

I looked back at Becki, and she nodded with an 'if you must' grimace. Charlotte grabbed my hand and yanked me toward the bar.

"They're in the back room." Still holding my hand, she dragged me past the bar, and into the private party room just off the kitchen. But, no one was there. "Wait, where'd they go?"

"Charlotte, are you sure—" Before I knew what was happening, she shoved her hand down the front of my pants and pressed me up against the wall. I took her firmly by the wrist, probably a little too rough, but I felt sexually violated for the first time in my life, and pulled her hand out. "What the FUCK?"

"Look, I lied. I just wanted to get you alone so I could tell you that I would do anything... ANYTHING... to have just one night with you, Calon."

"Charlotte, that's... umm, nice... and... and thank you?" It came out like a question, which made me look like an idiot, but this girl was off her rocker. Who does that? "But, I'm very happy with my girlfriend Becki out there. Nothing's going to happen between you and me. Ever."

"Cocksucker!" She attempted to knee me in the balls, but I caught her leg before it made contact with Walter's co-pilots. She grunted and stormed out of the room.

I leaned my head back against the wall and made the decision to tell Becki about Charlotte's proposition long after we'd left Mitchell's. She'd kill her. Really. Kill her. I gathered myself and headed back to our table as if nothing bizarre had happened.

I smiled and nodded to everyone like I'd just had a routine fan photo shoot. No one asked anything, and Jake and Gracie's wedding conversation continued. I looked around the bar, but didn't see Charlotte. Not too long thereafter, our little reunion split up, and we all headed back to our places for the night. Becki collapsed into bed fully clothed, and I did an inventory of all she wore to decide if I needed to try to talk her into changing. She had on a white oversized vintage Pearl Jam t-shirt and black leggings, perfect for sleeping. I covered her up to her chin, refilled her cup of water she kept on the nightstand, and went outside to the small balcony off my bedroom to call Gracie.

"Calon? Everything okay?" Her voice was on the verge of panic.

"Yeah, G. Were you sleeping?"

"No. We just walked into the apartment. What's up?"

"Hey. Please don't scream when I ask you this, okay?"

"Um. Okay?" She giggled a little.

"I want... well, I need to... ugh. I don't know how to say this without it making you scream." I ran my fingers through my hair, bent over, and rested my elbow that held the phone on the railing and just went for it. I spoke quickly, because I knew I'd have to say it fast so I could move the phone away from my ear for when she screamed. She was gonna scream. "I bought a ring. I want to ask Becki to marry me, and I need your help."

Yep, she screamed. I heard Jake questioning her in the background, and she just continued to squeal and giggle for what felt like an hour. We decided that we would talk about it later, or neither of us would get any sleep.

I took a quick shower then slid into bed behind Becki and dropped my arm over her. I pulled her close, and she made small noises that let me know she felt me there. She reached back for me, and her hand landed on my bare ass. She made another noise that was more of a growl than anything else.

"Promise me you'll still be naked when I wake up in the morning?" She slurred her words, but I knew it was from sheer exhaustion, since she hadn't had a drink since we found out about the baby.

"I promise." I breathed her in and slid my hand under the covers and to her belly. There was just as small pooch there and just as my hand settled there was a kick. It took my breath away. Our little girl was big enough that I could feel her presence on the outside of Becki's body. I wanted so badly to wake Becki and tell her what I'd just felt, but she needed her sleep. I rubbed her belly and fell sound asleep.

I awoke to small flutters under my right palm. Becki was propped up in bed with a baby names book, and I was still on my side with my hand on her belly. My eyes flashed open and up at her. She smiled.

"She's been trying to get your attention for an hour now."

I stretched and then scooted down toward the end of the bed and Becki turned on her side so my face was right at her belly. "Hello, my sweet baby." She kicked and my heart skipped a beat. She could really hear me. Dr. Daily said she could, but I guess I was a bit skeptical.

"Becki, she hears me. Do you think she knows I'm her dad?"

"I'm sure she does. I play your music to her when you're not here."

"You what?"

"Now, don't laugh, but while you're at the studio, I sometimes tuck my ear buds inside the waistband of my sweats, and she listens to your original *Fallen* album."

"For real?" I don't know why that made me so emotional, but it did. I slid back up to Becki's face and kissed her softly on the lips. She moaned, rolled toward me, and pressed her tongue through my lips. Her book fell to the bed, and she took my face in her hands.

"So, does it say in your book anywhere when we have to stop having sex?" I flipped her gently onto her back and hovered over her, brushing her golden-brown locks from her face.

"We don't have to stop unless it's uncomfortable for me, but it's not supposed to be. I assume we'll have to get creative as far as positions go once my fat stomach is big enough to get in the way." She looked up at me, and her eyes begged me to tell her she'd never look fat to me.

"Becki, what you're doing in here…" I pressed my hand to the side of her belly, "is beautiful. No matter what size or shape you get, I will still think you're beautiful."

"Promise?"

"Absolutely." I leaned down and pressed my dick between her legs. All she had to do was talk, and I would get hard. Everything about Becki Mowry made me crazy, physically and emotionally crazy, and that's how I knew I wanted to marry her.

During our month off, Sundays had become literally our day of rest. Becki would read me chapter after chapter of *What to Expect While You're Expecting*, we'd make plans for our future, and we'd make love then fall asleep. Last weekend we watched classic movies, *The Breakfast Club*, *Grease*, and *Sixteen Candles,* and ordered pizza and Chinese that we ate in bed.

"Calon, I'm nervous for our appointment next week."

"What? Why?" I rolled over and pulled her with me so she was on top, and she laid her head on my chest.

"I don't know. I just got the feeling Dr. Daily was holding back something at our ultrasound appointment. Like there was something she chose not to say."

"Honey, I think you were reading way too much into it. She just has that intensely pensive personality. Besides, there's nothing we can't handle, right? We've got this. I'm sure it's nothing."

She nodded and slid off me back onto her side. I put my hand on her belly and laid my head just above it.

"Calon, you're coming with me, right? You can schedule rehearsals around it, right?"

"I'll be there, Becks. I can't wait to hear her heartbeat again. Could we please pick a name? I'm tired of using a pronoun as her name."

She laughed, which made my head bounce up and down. She propped the baby names book on top of my head and started reading them aloud.

"Alanis, Avril, Axyl…" Her belly bounced my head again as she silently laughed.

"We are *not* giving her a rock star name." I shook my head.

"I was just seeing if you were paying attention."

"How could I not? Between her kicking me in the side of the head and you bouncing me all over the place, I'd have to be in a drunken stupor to be able to zone out. Now, why don't you pick out some names that are more reasonable?"

"Reasonable. Hmm. Let's see. You mean like Sue and Jill and Betty?"

"No, I was thinking classic names, like Emily or Abigail." I looked up at her, and she smiled.

"We have plenty of time to pick a name. She's not getting here for quite some time."

"Quite some time? Baby, we are more than half way there. She's going to be here in no time."

"Shh. We have time." Becki closed her eyes and rolled toward me, which put my face right between her growing breasts.

"Becki, these…" I slid my hands under she shirt and took two handfuls. "These are making me insane. And, by the way, you wearing the low cut tops to the shows is quite distracting. You'll need to invest in some turtlenecks." I pushed her t-shirt up and unclasped the front closure of her bra, which freed the beautiful things right into my face.

"That won't ever happen, rock star. Me. In a turtleneck. Nope. My mama always taught me 'if you got it, flaunt it', and I ain't puttin' these babies away anytime soon."

I cupped one of her breasts with my hand and slid my tongue around her peaked nipple. She sucked in a breath and dropped the baby names book to the floor.

"Oh, Calon." Her voice was low and sultry, which made me harder than I already was.

"So, wanna try something new?" I continued to lick and kiss her breasts.

"Mmm. That's turning me inside out. It's making me crazy, Calon, your tongue."

"I love the way you taste, Becks." My eyes fluttered when I took as much of her as I could get into my mouth and continued to roll her around my tongue.

I repeated everything on her other breast then slid my body up hers until we were face to face. I took her head in my hands and kissed her so deeply her staggered breaths pulsed inside my mouth.

"Calon."

"Yeah, baby?" I was out of breath and throbbing. She would be my undoing.

"I need you to help me find something." She pulled her head away from my hands and winked. That was my cue to just follow her lead. I had no idea what she was about to do, but there wasn't a doubt in my mind it would be *something new* and I would love every second of whatever it was.

Becki scooted to the edge of the bed and pushed me off, which left me no choice but to stand up and wait for her to give me a clue as to what she was looking for. There was no doubt I knew where this would lead. She wiggled out of her leggings, then knelt on the bed and met me eye-to-eye, naked from the waist down. I pulled her shirt and bra up over her head and aimlessly tossed it.

"What do you need me—"

"Shh." She put her finger up to my lips and winked yet again.

She kissed me gently with her round breasts pressed against my chest. My hands instinctively went to her waist. My thumbs dug into her hip bones, and my fingers pressed into the fleshy part of her hips. She pulled her head back and smirked then spun her body within my grasp. My hands were still on her hips, but now my thumbs were pressed into her hips and my fingers into her hipbones. I had an idea of what she was about to do, and if I didn't pace myself, I'd be done in under ten seconds.

"I don't usually do this kind of thing with rock stars, but I couldn't help myself, Calon. Seeing you on that stage just made me crazy. I think I lost my panties in your bed." She tilted her head back onto my shoulder and used her hands to slide mine up to her breasts. She was role playing. Something we'd never done, but it was so hot, I could barely speak.

"Well, Becki, I've never brought a fan back to my apartment either. But, when my eyes locked on yours, I knew I had to have you. Now, let's see if we can find your panties, shall we?"

My hands slid back down to her hips as she tipped her body forward until her hands hit the bed.

"I know they're under here somewhere." She reached under the covers, making sweeping motions with her hands and stretching away from me, which made her ass the highest part of her body. The sight of her at that moment took my breath away.

"I think you need to reach a little further, baby. Just a little." I let go with one hand and wrapped it around my cock. I positioned its tip at her opening and instantly had to distract myself when I saw a drop of her moisture hit my deep red sheets.

"I found them!" She cried out and shoved her body back and directly onto my pulsing dick. She knew what she was doing. We'd never done it in this position, and it was quite possibly because it was so insanely hot I would've come instantly had we not worked up to it.

"Fuck, Becks. You're dripping."

"It's all you, baby. You make me wet. Now, I want it hard and fast. God, please, Calon."

With both my hands holding her in place, I buried myself inside her and then went completely still. I could feel her squeezing me, an involuntary reaction to what I was doing to her. I pulled out, all but the tip, and drove right back in a little harder than the first time. There was no way I was going to fuck her as hard as I knew I could. Regardless of how many times she told me I couldn't hurt the baby, I was just going to be a little gentler with her during these next couple months.

"Oh, God, Calon. You're so hard."

I couldn't stand it anymore. She was on the edge, and so was I. I drove myself into her over and over.

"Come with me, Becks. I'm gonna come inside you." I hissed the words out from between clenched teeth.

"I'm coming, Calon. I'm coming, CALON!"

When my name came out of her mouth in a guttural scream, I lost it and emptied myself into her as she milked me for every last drop. I slowed my pace and jerked the last few sensations from my body then dropped forward with my hands on either side of hers. We fell to the bed, and I slid out of her as she rolled to face me.

"Calon James, you are the hottest creature God ever created. I'm serious. There is no way other people have sex as hot as we do. There's just no way." She put her hand to her heart, as though it would help it beat slower.

"Becki, your ass in the air…" I shuddered, and my eyes rolled back. "You have the power to unravel me, baby."

"You like my ass."

"Always have. But, I had no idea how much I liked it until you bent completely in half and all of you was right there. That's probably the only part of your body I hadn't seen yet, Becks. And the fact that you had no inhibitions out that, made it even hotter—if that's possible."

"Well, Calon Ridge—you may just have a kinky side to you. We may need to invest a little time into all those dirty thoughts in your head." She kissed me on the tip of my nose and raised one eyebrow.

"I don't have dirty thoughts." She didn't buy it. "Okay, let me clarify. I don't have dirty thoughts about anyone but you, Becki Mowry."

We climbed up to the pillows, wrapped our arms around each other, and fell into a mid-morning, post-sex slumber. Yeah, Sundays were good days, and I'd give up all the rock star days left in me for the girl who stole my heart right out from under me.

But I still hadn't told her about Charlotte molesting me. I knew the longer I waited, the worse it would be.

twenty-one

Becki

"WAIT, CAN YOU explain what a soft marker is?" I sat across from Dr. Daily in her mahogany paneled office, bouncing my knees. I looked at the clock on her wall and made a conscious decision to not get pissed unless Calon was more than ten minutes late. A mere week ago he told me I needn't worry about him missing this appointment. I'd called him from the car when I pulled into the parking lot outside the doctors' office wing of the hospital and got no answer, which was his first mistake. I believe somewhere it's carved in stone that when your pregnant girlfriend calls, unless you're dead, you answer the phone.

"I was really hoping Calon would be here for this appointment." Dr. Daily looked down at her watch and tapped her pencil on my file that lay open on her desk. Mistake number two would be making me sit here alone, nervous as hell, because he wasn't watching the clock.

"You and me both." Tears burned behind my eyes, but I refused to let them fall. Never in my life had I been a crier, especially when I was pissed. But this damn pregnancy had my hormones so fucked up, I cried when I was pissed, when I was happy, and sometimes even when I was hungry, which was just stupid.

"Do you think he forgot the appointment, Becki?" I knew she was probably worried about making her other patients wait if our appointment ran later than scheduled. We'd already been through the routine exam, but then she brought me to her office afterwards.

"He knew. He called me around ten from the studio and said they just got a request for a conference call with a record label that saw them play in LA. He assured me the call would be over long before our appointment." I cleared my throat, hoping to stave off the tears even longer.

"Well, while we're waiting, what did you both decide about where the baby will be born? Have you discussed it?" She adjusted her glasses further up her nose. She was naturally pretty, probably mid-forties and Greek, I think. Her hair was coal black and short, and her skin was flawless, not a wrinkle in sight. I wondered if she had kids. I wondered if she was as terrified as I was to have a baby. Probably not.

"We decided to have her here in Knoxville. I'll go back to LA with Calon and the band at the end of January. Then we'll fly back together at the end of February for our next appointment, and I'll stay until she's born. Our assistant manager will take over for me when I'm unable to be on the West Coast with them." I tried so hard to not think about being in Knoxville while Calon was out touring and being mobbed by gorgeous un-pregnant groupies. It was inevitable, but I still didn't want to think about it until I had to.

"That sounds good. I'm glad you'll continue with my practice until the baby is born. Do you two have plans to get married?" That question threw me. Not only was it odd for a doctor to inquire about such a personal thing but Calon and I had never even said the word marriage in any of the conversations we'd had. I had no idea what he was thinking on that subject, and at that moment I felt like an idiot, because it was obvious I struggled to answer her question.

"Um. Well, I suppose down the road we may, if our relationship remains as it is." I smiled when I said it as though I wasn't ready to choke him with his own balls for not meeting me there. I worried that maybe it was the beginning of the end. Calon had been nothing but sweet, gentle, honest, and present. Present for me through everything—so far. But what if all of this was freaking him out? What if being at the studio was an escape for him? An escape from me, from us.

"Becki, the reason I asked you about the direction of your relationship goes back to what I started to say about the soft markers. When I did your ultrasound, I noticed an abnormal amount of skin at the back or your baby's neck, and her femur measurements calculated out at a little shorter than we'd like to see at this stage in your pregnancy." Dr. Daily paged through some loose papers in my file.

"Dr. Daily, can you excuse me a minute? I'd really like Calon to be here for this. I need to call him." I had no idea what any of what she just said meant, but I knew it wasn't good, and I didn't want to lose my shit alone. Dr. Daily nodded, so I stepped out into the hallway and around the corner, where there was a small waiting area with just two chairs. I dialed Calon's phone number and once again got his voicemail.

"Calon, I'm freaking out. Dr. Daily acts like she's going to tell us that our baby is sick or in danger or something, and you're not here. I can't do this alone, Calon, I can't. Please, please, call me and come to her office as soon as you get this." I hung up and then texted him almost word for word what I'd just spoken. I pictured him on a conference call and not wanting to answer his cell. However, he could read a text without the person on the other line knowing he'd been distracted. Then I texted Gracie.

> **Me:** *Hey. Can you meet me at Parking Lot E at the hospital? Please?*

> **Gracie:** *Absolutely. You OK? When do you need me there?*

> **Me:** *I'm not ok - Calon didn't show. 30 mins?*

> **Gracie:** *Got it. Will text you when I get there.*

> **Me:** *TY*

> **Gracie:** *You're freaking me out.*

Me: *Sorry. Scared.*

Gracie: *Hang on. I'm coming.*

Me: *K*

I walked back into Dr. Daily's office, took my seat, and tucked my phone under my leg so I could feel it vibrate when Gracie got there.

"Will Calon be joining us?" There was a sensitivity in her expression that made me apprehensive. I wished I was anywhere but in an OB office.

"I guess not. I can't seem to get a hold of him. I'm sorry for making you wait." I glanced out the window and saw a couple walking through the parking lot holding hands. The man held one of those baby carrier car seats. He leaned down and kissed the woman then pulled her into his side. For the first time since all of this happened, I worried I might be going it alone. If I was totally honest, which I hadn't been to anyone as of yet, I would have to admit that I was not a hundred percent into being pregnant and becoming a mom at twenty-one. I cried some nights while Calon slept, thinking of all of the plans I had that I could never accomplish now that I'd have a kid. I couldn't travel to Brazil alone like I'd always dreamed. I wasn't even sure how you could be the manager of a band and have a kid. Do they just go everywhere with you? Do you hire a nanny? Some days, I was less than thrilled to be in the situation I was in and half mad at God for all of it. And now, to top it all off, because of his absence, I was starting to doubt Calon's commitment to us. I certainly wasn't happy about the notion I could one day be a single mom. That's when I lost it.

"Becki, don't cry. Listen, I know this news is frightening, especially without Calon here, but I want to reassure you that you don't need to be fearful."

"I'm sorry, Dr. Daily, I'm super upset that Calon missed this appointment without even calling me. And I'm completely lost as to what you're trying to tell me about the baby. I'm freaking out, and the hormones aren't helping. Can you just use layman's terms and tell me what your findings mean?" I didn't want to hear what she was going to say.

Everything in me told me to cover my ears, but I knew that was ridiculous. Freaking out wasn't an option. It's not like I could run away from a pregnancy.

"Becki, there's a possibility your baby may be born with Down syndrome. Do you know what that is?" I held my breath and nodded in what felt like slow motion and saw little Taryn from Gracie's class smiling in my mind. Dr. Daily's voice sounded a million miles away and the edges of my vision became fuzzy. My heart beat so hard I could hear the blood pumping through my ears. I couldn't breathe, so I gasped for air. This couldn't be happening. This was a cruel joke, a bad movie. Girl who's not supposed to get pregnant falls in dumb love with a rock star and then gets knocked up. The rock star abandons her and their mentally challenged love child. And they lived happily ever after. Not! I know it was harsh to think that way, and I know everyone says how every child is a blessing, but this news was bigger than I could have imagined. Blessed was not how I would describe what I felt at that moment.

My phone buzzed, and I glanced at it through an ocean of tears. BLOCKED. I didn't know anyone with a blocked number, so I certainly wasn't about to answer.

"Becki, breathe. The information I collected from your ultrasound was skewed but on a small level, which is why I didn't mention it at your ultrasound appointment. I shared it with a colleague of mine at an institute on the East Coast. I wanted to wait for him to tell me his thoughts before I mentioned any of my concerns to you. Typically, I would have mentioned something at the ultrasound, but like I said, it was such a small deviation, I didn't want to mention anything until I got a second opinion."

"I had cancer when I was younger and I heard the doctor tell my mom I'd be sterile. Did this happen because of the chemo? Is there something wrong with her because of my cancer?" I sucked in a breath and placed my hand on my stomach. *Did I do this?*

"No, Becki. Down syndrome occurs when a person has an extra copy of the twenty-first chromosome. It's a genetic disorder, not something you could have caused. However, I'm surprised your doctor didn't follow up with some sort of fertility testing once you were old enough to be sexually active."

"I've tried my hardest to stay away from doctors once I was handed the 'no evidence of disease' status. I don't ever remember hearing anything about a fertility test."

Dr. Daily walked around her desk and sat in the chair next to me, which only reminded me again who should have been in that chair. She took my hands in hers. "Honey, listen, I know this is a lot to take in, and I know you will need time to process it all. The fertility testing is inconsequential now. But we do know that your chemo didn't cause this."

"So, I have to wait until she's born to know if she'll have the disorder?" I slid one hand from between hers and wiped the tears from my cheeks. She handed me the tissue box from her desk. I wondered how many other moms had used the same box when given similar news.

"I'd like your permission to do an amniocentesis. Do you know what that is?" She tilted her head and gently smiled.

"The long needle?" I exhaled slowly through pursed lips.

"Yes, we can go to one of the exam rooms and do it today, before you leave. An amniocentesis is almost one hundred percent accurate when done after the fifteenth week of pregnancy."

"Okay." What was I going to say? No? I needed to know what we were facing with our baby.

"I'm glad I will be the one guiding you through this pregnancy. I have a lot of experience with Down syndrome." She reached for a frame on her desk and turned it around. I stared into the eyes of the most beautiful dark-haired version of Taryn. Her smile was so genuine it brought even more tears to my eyes. I took the frame from her and held it in both hands.

"Is this your daughter?" I ran the pad of my thumb over the glass right where her pudgy cheeks held a dimple.

"Yes, this is my Maribelle. I know what it feels like to get this news. You're terrified. I was, too. I remember it like it was yesterday. But, what seemed like devastation six years ago has become my greatest blessing. I wouldn't trade her for a child without Down syndrome ever. You'll get there, Becki. I promise. You've been blessed with the miracle of life, and I don't know what your beliefs are, but I believe God chose this exact baby for you because He knew you would be strong enough to handle whatever she brings with her. And I will be the first to tell you that I feel lucky to be Maribelle's mom." She reached out and pulled me in for a big hug.

My phone buzzed, and I broke our hug with an apologetic smile. "Sorry. This might be Calon."

It wasn't. Gracie texted that she was in the parking lot which was good. There was no way I could drive myself home; I was too shaken.

Me: *Dr wants to run another test. It could take a while.*

Gracie: *Want me to come in?*

Me: *No. I'll be okay. Thx*

Gracie: *I'm not going anywhere. I'll just work on schoolwork til you're done…*

An hour later I was ready to leave. The procedure, although terrifying, was virtually painless and pretty quick. Then they had to monitor me and the baby for a bit to make sure everything was fine. Dr. Daily walked me out to the desk where I'd schedule my next appointment.

"Thank you, Dr. Daily. I'm a mess, I'm sorry." I had a handful of tissues and tossed them in the trashcan by the appointment desk.

"You don't need to be sorry, Becki. I've been there. You don't have to hold back any emotion from me. I felt them all when I was in your shoes." She walked over to a large filing cabinet and rifled through some hanging files. "Here's a packet of information and a DVD about Down syndrome. I will call you when we get the results, and I will be open and honest with you the whole way through. Okay?" She put all the papers, DVD, and a box of tissues in a recyclable bag with the hospital logo on it and walked me to the door.

"Thank you." I didn't know what else to say.

"You're welcome. Call me if you need anything. I mean it."

I smiled and nodded then turned toward the waiting room. I stepped onto the elevator in a daze. I felt guilty that I'd been picturing our baby girl with very different features from the ones she may be born with.

When the elevator doors opened on the ground floor, I saw a sign for the chapel. And something drew me in the opposite direction of the exit. I gently pushed open the wooden doors with small stained glass windows and stepped into a small, warm room with organ music playing very softly in the background. There were fresh bouquets of flowers at the front of the room, beyond the few rows of pews. I started to cry before I even sat down. I do mean cry. I sobbed. I was alone, so I didn't hold back. I needed to digest what Dr. Daily had just told me, and I wanted to get some of my emotions out before I had to tell Gracie. And Calon.

I dropped the bag of Down syndrome information and rested my elbows on my thighs. My face fell into my hands, and my shoulders shook with sadness. I sobbed for the baby I thought I was having before I walked into Dr. Daily's office, and I sobbed for the baby I may give birth to. But, I sobbed especially from the guilt of being so distraught over the news, and I prayed out loud to a God I hadn't spoken to for a long time.

"God, if you're really up there, and you can hear me, I need clarity. I don't want to go through this pregnancy in fear of what my—our—baby will be like. I don't want to be fearful of the child you've placed with me." It was weird that all of that poured from my mouth. I didn't even know what I wanted to pray when I bowed my head, but I suppose my subconscious did. "God, I'm asking you for reminders of the gift she is, even when I'm feeling burdened by all the 'what ifs'."

The door to the chapel whined, and I heard footsteps behind me. I turned, hoping it was Calon, but it was a woman with her face in her hands. Another woman, who could've been her mom, held her upright as she walked. The younger woman's knees buckled, and she wept. Her mom helped her into a pew and caught her as she fell into her lap. Her cries were pained. I wiped my face and tried not to stare. I was heartbroken for this woman who maybe had just lost a father or a husband.

I stood, wiped my face again and said a quick, silent 'Amen' then left to give them the same privacy I had. I stood right outside the doors and reached into my bag for more tissues to clean myself up before I walked out to Gracie's car. A man with bloodshot eyes walked up and tried to see through the stained glass windows into the chapel.

"Did a woman with dark hair and a red sweater just go in there?" His voice was gravely and hoarse.

"Yeah. Is she okay?" I knew it was none of my business, but I felt compelled to ask.

"We just…" He took a couple staggered breaths and pressed his lips into the back of his hand. "Our son, Julian, won't be with us much longer. We were hoping for a miracle, but I guess God needs him more than we do." He nodded and walked through the doors.

I placed my hand on my stomach and felt her kick twice. She was our miracle, and I took that as a reminder, the sign I'd specifically asked for. In that moment, I decided to try my damnedest to work through my emotions and see her as just that, a miracle.

Gracie met me at the doors. Her expression distressed.

"Becki, what is it?" I knew she wouldn't be devastated when I told her the news. I knew exactly what she would say.

"There's a chance the baby will be born with Down syndrome." I tipped my head to the side and a single tear rolled down my cheek. I felt so guilty for being sad.

"Oh, Becki." She hugged me so tight I could barely breathe. "I know this is scary for you now, but if she does have Down syndrome, she will still be perfect. You'll see." She hugged me again.

"Of course, she won't have a dad, and she'll be born in jail, because I'm going to kill Calon for putting a conference call ahead of our appointment," I declared as we walked toward her car.

"That's not like him. Not like him at all." She shook her head, but I could see the wheels turning. She tried hard to find the same loophole I'd been searching for. Something that would keep Calon on his pedestal.

"I'm worried, Gracie. What if all this is too much for him? And, now, I've got to tell him there's a chance she'll have a serious disorder?" I flopped down into the front seat of Jake's car.

"Becki, do you really see him reacting that way? If anything, I see him taking the opposite path and being so overbearing you'll want to strangle him." We both laughed. That's the Calon I expected to meet me at the appointment.

My phone buzzed. I answered it without looking at the screen, I knew it had to be Calon.

"Calon?"

"Becki!" It was Bones.

"Bones, where the hell—"

"Becki! The cops just came for Calon."

twenty-two

Calon

"THANK YOU FOR coming in. Mr. Ridge."

"Calon. You can call me Calon."

"Okay, Calon. We have a few questions for you regarding a young lady you met at Mitchell's two weeks ago. The detective that took his good ole' time to get to the interview room sat across a table from me.

I was trying to keep my cool, but I was getting anxious. At the studio he said I just needed to come down to the station to answer some questions. I figured a couple questions wouldn't put me in jeopardy of missing the conference call or being late to meet Becki for our appointment with Dr. Daily. But no one said anything about waiting a half an hour in a room by myself. Now I could quite possibly miss both.

"Listen, I'm going to be late for an appointment, and I have no signal in here. Is there a phone I could use before we get started?"

"You can use the one on the wall." The detective pointed to a phone that looked like it had been there since the nineteen sixties. I quickly punched in Becki's number. It rang three times and went to voice-mail, and 'I'm at the police station. I've been called in for questioning' isn't something I wanted to leave in a message. "Dammit." I hung up and walked back to my seat.

"Calon, a young lady filed a formal complaint this morning that she had been attacked by you at Mitchell's Pub two weeks ago." The officer paged through a file and continued to look me up and down. "She said you were drunk and unruly and you assaulted her in a back room. She had photos of bruising on her wrist that she claims was from you. Do you have any recollection of this?"

"That's bullshit! Look, there was a girl Mitchell's who asked me to take some photos with her and her friends. When we were out of eyeshot of the rest of the bar, she shoved her hand down my pants, but I absolutely did not attack her. I removed her hand from my pants, which could be where the bruises came from. I feel bad for hurting her, if I did, but I was completely freaked out."

"So, you're saying she came onto you." He jotted something down.

"Yes, I am. She told me she just wanted to get me alone so she could tell me she'd do anything to be able to have just one night with me."

"So, you didn't put your hands on her?" He tapped his pen.

"I did. But only to get her hands off my dick." I took a couple deep breaths and looked at the clock. "Is that clock right?"

He nodded. I started to sweat.

"Give me a minute, I want to run something by my partner. I'll be right back." He headed toward the door.

"Can I try that phone again?"

"Sure. But, just so you know, it will show up as a BLOCKED number on caller ID." He shut the door behind him.

That's why she didn't answer. There was no sense in trying again.

Shit! Shit! Shit! I rubbed my face in my hands and started pacing. This was not going to go down well at all. Becki was going to kick my ass. Not only was I missing the appointment she was worried about, but I was at the police station being questioned for something I hadn't even told her happened between me and Charlotte. I walked over to the window, hoping to get a signal on my cell phone.

NO SIGNAL

I looked down to the streets below and wondered about the lives of the people I saw walking around. Where were they going? What obstacles had life thrown their way? I thought about how blessed my life really was and all I had to be thankful for.

I looked around the dingy, stale room and thought about how easy it would have been for me to end up in jail if I would have followed the stereotypical path. Single mom and her dysfunctional relationships with various men along with the beatings I endured at the hand of more than one of them. Then you factor in the gaping hole in my heart for Kate, the baby sister I'd never see again, and Chloe's death. I could have landed into the rock star scene without as much as a blip on the screen, just another junkie. Maybe I would have made headlines when I overdosed on crack or beat the shit out of my girlfriend, but that wasn't who I was. Despite the hell I'd been through, my heart was too sensitive to bring pain to anyone, except for assholes like Max. But, at the same time, that sensitivity threatened to rip me to pieces when I tried to digest what the hell Becki and I were doing… becoming parents. I was scared out of my mind.

I must've stood there thinking for quite some time because when I looked at the clock, panic shot through me. The appointment had to be over, or close to it.

"Well, Calon, all I need from you is a written statement, and then you're free to go."

"Thank God!"

The detective told me to write out the scenario exactly how it happened and sign it.

"Thanks for your cooperation, Calon. I know this isn't how you planned on spending your day."

"No worries. You're just doing your job. Have a good day."

I decided to take my motorcycle to the station as a means to calm my nerves before being questioned. But, I had no idea that nothing would be able to calm what was going on in my head when I left the building. Nothing but wrapping my arms around the woman who held my heart and hoping she could forgive me.

No sooner did I throw my leg over the seat and all the missed calls, voicemails, and texts I missed while I didn't have service started buzzing in my pocket.

I didn't bother scrolling through them. I hit the call back button next to Becki's name. It rang twice and stopped. She picked up but didn't say a word. My stomach flipped over itself.

"Becks?"

"What the hell, Calon?" She barely got the entire question out before she burst into tears. She tried to talk through her sobs, but I couldn't understand a word she said. Then the phone went dead.

I called her back.

"Calon?" It was Gracie's voice.

"Gracie, she's going to kill me, isn't she?" I dropped my head into my free hand.

"Unless I get to you first. Calon, where are you?"

"It's probably better if I tell her that in person. Can you just take her to my place?"

"Sure. Calon?"

"Yeah, G?"

"Don't screw this up. She needs you now more than she's ever needed anyone in her life." Her voice was muffled, like she was trying to keep her words just between us.

"Thanks for being there for her." The line went dead which I deserved.

Just then a text came in.

Bones: *Nice move, dick. We lost the opp with Blue Note Recording bc you ditched the call.*

"Fuck!" I let my bike slowly roll into the street and fishtailed when I gave it full throttle. My heart was in knots. I was leaving one unexpected situation and walking into another. And I was sure Becki had been through even more with me missing the appointment and her having no idea why. It was a bad day for both of us. The excessive speed of my bike barely touched the stress I'd hoped to relieve but had me home in no time.

I pulled into my driveway and saw Gracie and Becki leaning against the back of Jake's car. They linked arms and walked toward me. I could read Gracie's face, and it plainly said, *You better have a good explanation for this, or we're both going to kill you.*

"Becki, I am so sorry. Let me explain." This is exactly why I should have told her about Charlotte the night it all went down, not two weeks later when I'm made to look stupid guilty. I opened my arms to pull her into me, and she punched me in the gut for all she was worth.

"That's for not answering your phone when I called you."

She stomped on my foot before I had fully straightened up from the sucker punch.

"And that was for missing the appointment. What the hell, Calon?"

"Becks, listen. The police needed me to go down to the station and answer some questions because someone made a bogus claim that I assaulted them."

She slammed her palms into my chest and pushed me away from her. Hard. "And that's for being a convict!"

She was definitely pissed, but knowing I'd been brought in for questioning and not just delinquent in making the appointment took the edge off. I hoped.

Gracie offered to have Jake drive the rental car back to my apartment later, so Becki and I could just hash out everything that was going on in our lives at the moment.

Becki waved as Gracie climbed into the car. Becki's eyes flashed up to mine, and she held my gaze just long enough for me to see the depth of sadness she carried in them. But she said nothing.

We climbed the stairs to my apartment, and she walked right into our bedroom. Silent. She sat on the edge of the bed and folded her hands in her lap. She bit her lip, which I'd learned is what she did when she was trying not to cry. *Shit.* I hated that I'd disappointed her.

"I am so sorry, Becki." I sat down on the floor in front of her and folded my arms across her legs. "You know how badly I wanted to be at the appointment with you."

"Not bad enough to actually be there." She looked past me and blinked a couple times.

"Becki, honey, I told you. Someone tried to press charges against me for assault."

"Who, Calon? Who would do that?" She slapped her hands beside her on the bed.

"I need you to hear me out, okay? I need you to stay calm until I tell you the whole story." As soon as it was out of my mouth, I realized there was probably a better way to have opened up the conversation.

"Calon James—"

"Two weeks ago at Mitchell's. The sorority girl who asked me to pose with her sisters for a couple photos. Remember?"

She nodded.

"Well, that was a scam. There was no one in the back room, and she propositioned me with her hand down the front of my pants."

"WHAT!" She stood up so fast it knocked me off balance, and I fell backwards onto my ass. She started to pace.

"Babe, listen. I don't know why she went to the cops, but she told them *I* attacked *her.* You know that's not true, right? You *know* I would never hurt a girl."

She stopped pacing and just stared out the big window at the far end of the room. She was somewhere else. I wasn't even sure she heard what I said. Her arms fell from being crossed across her chest, and her hands cradled her round belly. Her body swayed slowly, and her hands rubbed in small circles. She looked down at her belly and smiled but then winced and fell to her knees and sobbed.

"Becks! Baby, what is it?" I ran up behind her, got down on my knees and took her into my arms. I curled around her. She shook and choked and cried. I was so scared.

"The baby." She drew in a couple staggered breaths and turned to face me. Her mascara ran in streams down her cheeks, and she wiped it all onto the back of her hand. I took her hands in mine, but I couldn't speak. I wanted that moment of not knowing whatever she was going to tell me to last a lifetime. I wanted the worst news of the day to be a false accusation, not something about our baby. Something happened at her appointment that she'd been holding in this whole time, and

I wasn't sure I was fully ready to hear it.

"You're scaring me." The words came out intermingled with a breath that was forced from me out of sheer panic.

"There's a good chance the baby will have…" She took my face in her hands, and her expression changed from fear to something that hung between guilt and sympathy. She took a deep breath. "Calon, the baby may have Down syndrome. She's got what they call soft markers. Parts of her have abnormal measurements that led Dr. Daily to consult a colleague, and they both agreed she may have the disorder. So, she did an amniocentesis today. It's almost a hundred percent accurate in diagnosing Down syndrome. She's going to call us when she gets the results."

My mind shot back to watching my baby sister wave at me from the car. Her little bracelet we'd made together bouncing around on her wrist. I was overcome with emotion. Kate was the best part of my life for the three years I had her as my sister. She was perfect. She was sweet and kind and could make me laugh louder than anyone. Then she was gone.

Maybe it was the connection between Kate and what Becki had just told me, but I was flailing through a whole slew of emotions. Would our baby be a constant trigger for the sadness I still felt for losing Kate? Would I look at our baby and feel blessed, but sad for a sister I no longer knew? I didn't even know what kind of parent I was capable of being. My mother surely wasn't capable, or at least she wasn't strong enough to believe she was capable. What if I would inherit her feelings of defeat when faced with the same situation?

"Calon, talk to me. What are you thinking?" Becki tilted her head and for a moment appeared to forget her own panic in an attempt to carry mine.

"I'm scared shitless, Becks. But I'm thinking she's going to be perfect, just like Kate was." I tried to catch my breath.

"I'm scared, and I feel like that makes me a bad mom."

"I'm terrified I won't be a good dad."

"I'm afraid kids will make fun of her." Becki frowned at giving voice to that fear.

"I'm worried she'll have health problems." I knew Down syndrome came with a whole host of possible issues.

"Worrying about all these things doesn't make us bad parents, does it?"

"Well, if it does, then I think that would make every parent on the planet a bad parent. Right?"

"I'm not worried I won't be able to love her, or that I'll be disappointed for the child we've been given. All my worries lie in my own capabilities."

"Every parent holds that same fear, I think. Because every child comes into the world with issues and difficulties. Some have learning disabilities, some have OCD, some need glasses, some can't behave, and some are painfully shy. There are kids born with the potential for high IQs and those that have delays. One day those kids will be labelled by a doctor or psychologist. We're lucky because we know what to prepare for ahead of time, before she's even born." Everything that tumbled from my heart and through my lips was sent from something bigger than me because that was the first time those thoughts had entered my mind.

"I love her so much it hurts, Calon."

"That's absolute love, Becks." Becki wrapped her arms around my neck, and we cried together. Our tears celebrated the beauty of our baby girl and all that she was and all that she one day would be. It would be a lie to say we didn't also cry in response to a fear of the unknown. But, we agreed we were blessed beyond measure already, and she wasn't even here yet.

WE SAT OUT on the balcony and watched the sun go down after we depleted our bodies of all our tears then we came inside and climbed between the covers together. It was cathartic and refreshing to get out all our fears and sadness. It was like it made more room for all the emotions our baby would bring into our lives. Quite possibly emotions we didn't even know existed. I snuggled up behind my sleeping Becki.

"Did Charlotte actually... touch it?" Becki's voice made me jump. She'd been so quiet and still, I was certain she was asleep.

"What?"

"Walter. Did Charlotte touch Walter?"

"Kinda." I cracked up laughing. "Well, just through my boxers."

Becki rolled over, smacked me in the chest and growled. Her fists clenched against me.

"But only for a fraction of a second because I grabbed her hand. I swear." I spoke so quickly and panicked, I wasn't even sure she could decipher everything I'd just said. I just didn't want her to hit me again.

"I'll kill her if I ever see her again." Her voice was barely a whisper as she drifted off.

I felt terrible for disappointing Becki. I felt guilty for keeping the whole Charlotte thing from her. And I was uptight because it seemed someone was always trying to make bad press for us. Worst of all, I felt our return flight to LA looming.

There was something I felt in Knoxville that I didn't feel anywhere else on the planet, and I couldn't explain it. I fought that feeling and chalked it up to an amateurish fear of the unknown; something I was sure all musicians struggled with. I was living my dream. Or was I? Everything I'd ever imagined my life would be was being challenged at every turn. I'd dreamed of touring and watching hoards of fans sing lyrics I'd written right along with me. I loved that, but if I was honest with myself, I felt homesick for Knoxville most of the time. And, now, the baby. That certainly hadn't been part of my big dream. I was twenty-two, and our band was just starting to make it. I was travelling with the love of my life and sharing all the excitement and celebrations with her, but she would soon have to pass the baton to Danny and live in Tennessee without me while I did all of it alone. Well, I'd be with the guys, but I wanted Becki next to me. I wanted her at the Red Carpet events and in the wings of the stage while I performed. But, now, everything was skewed.

"Hello? Did you hear what I said?" Her voice pulled me from my thoughts.

"I didn't, sorry." I kissed her gently.

"I think I like your idea of a classic name." Her eyes fluttered from exhaustion.

"Oh, yeah?" I kissed her again.

"What do you think of Abby? The first two letters of her name are the same first two letters in *absolute*."

"Abigail." My heart swelled. It matched the sweet baby girl I knew she would be, perfectly.

"Abigail Kate?" Becki's voice saying her name was more beautiful than any song ever written. Her eyes filled up, and her wide smile knocked the tears to her cheeks.

"Abigail Kate. I love it." Tears streamed down my cheeks. I missed my baby sister every day of my life, but somehow I missed her more at that moment. I wanted to be able to tell her that my baby carried her name as a tribute to how amazing I thought she was. It meant so much to me that Becki had chosen to use her name before I'd even thought of it.

Our little family. Absolute.

Becki's hands were on her belly when her eyes closed and I could tell by her breathing she was out.

I decided to end the day from Hell by succumbing to sleep. I fell in and out of consciousness thinking of proposal ideas. My mind kept going back to the show we were playing on Valentine's Day. Maybe a public proposal would be it for us. I doubt she'd suspect a thing.

Most everyone in the industry will tell you that appearing to be single and allowing your fans to believe they still have a chance with you is good for sales. I didn't fucking care. I wanted the entire world, especially all the Violets and Charlottes, to know I was taken. My heart belonged to Becki Mowry. The end.

twenty-three

Becki

I'D BEEN TERRIFIED of flying prior to this whirlwind I'd come to know as Calon Ridge. The flight attendants reminded us to have our trays in the upright position for takeoff. I took Calon's hand in mine, closed my eyes, and relived the last two days in my mind.

I felt like I'd barely seen Manny, Bones, and Spider the whole time we were in Knoxville. I saw them when they played at Mitchell's, but that was really it. Calon spent the nights with me, and the rest of the guys went out and did what rock stars do in college towns. Their apartment was no longer being rented out, so they just bunked there, which was nice for me and Calon.

It had only been two days since they said good-bye to the Mitchell's crowd by doing a song they'd never covered before. Calon picked it, and I told him he'd have people in tears, but he doubted me. They sang "Crash" by Sum 41 which is a 'see ya later, this is over' kind of song. It gave me goose bumps, because the vague references to death reminded me of Calon's accident right after he met Gracie. The severity of his injuries were haunting, and I hated to think I could be living my life without him or that someday, something so terrible could happen to our little family. I was right, though, by the end of the song, girls were in tears, and it took us almost two hours to get out of the bar because of all the band rats who wanted advice from the guys about 'how to make it big'. The guys were sweet to hang out and entertain all their questions.

Just before we left that night there was a huge crash in the kitchen. Gracie, Jake, and I ran back, and it was Buzz. He'd fallen somehow and was unconscious. We called an ambulance, locked up the bar, and then spent the rest of the night at the hospital. None of us had known Buzz had no family. We knew he wasn't married, he always said the bar was his wife, but we were shocked to find out he'd only had one sibling, and his brother and parents passed away more than just a couple years ago. If we didn't stay with him at the hospital, he'd be all alone. After all the help he'd given the guys over the years, how could we not stay the night until the doctors gave him some answers?

"Buzz, I just want you to know how much we appreciate the help you've given us with our flights. It's really too much. I'm starting to feel guilty." I smiled at him and patted his arm.

"Now, stop that. You guys have spent more on beer over the last three years than what those vouchers would cost. It's my pleasure to be able to help you out." He smiled, but he looked tired. "Just go, kids. I'll be fine."

"Buzz, we're not leaving." Calon put his hand on Buzz's shoulder. "Now get some sleep, old man."

"Don't you boss me around. I know your landlord. I'll have you evicted." We all got a good chuckle out of that, considering Buzz owned the duplex Calon lived in. Calon lived upstairs, and the bottom floor was rented out for football weekends. I was sure Buzz made more money off those weekends than what Calon paid in a year.

It was Monday, and Buzz was still in the hospital. We had an early morning flight back to LA, but the doctors assured us they would be releasing Buzz after he met with his team of doctors. Buzz never gave us any explanation for his collapse and none of us wanted to ask. I hated to leave him while he was still in the hospital, but I knew Gracie and Jake would keep an eye on him, and Calon and I would be flying home in a couple weeks for my next doctor's appointment. I shook that thought from my mind, because that's when Calon would fly back to LA without me. At least we'd get to celebrate Valentine's Day before we'd be separated by so many miles. I decided to focus on that.

"You don't have a show on Valentine's Day, do you?" I wasn't sure if he was sleeping or not, so I spoke quietly.

He made a face, like a wince, and didn't even open his eyes but spoke in a hushed voice. "We'll have to ask Danny."

I closed my eyes again and fell sound asleep until we landed at LAX. But because we were unexpectedly bombarded by reporters asking questions about Charlotte's accusations and my baby bump, it took us longer than usual to get to the line of taxis to take us to the hotel. None of us could fathom how the false accusation got from Knoxville to LA so quickly. We were stumped.

"CALON, I KNOW your fans would love your explanation for your arrest that's been trending on the internet." Jimmy James, BMX-FM's smart ass DJ waggled his eyebrows at Calon, like he was trying to trap him on live radio. *Asshole.*

I stood behind the glass that separated me from where they all sat with headsets on. I snapped a couple pictures of all of them in their dorky headphones. Bones made stupid faces at me, and I giggled.

"Listen, Jimmy, I wasn't arrested. I was asked to go to the police station for questions regarding a report that had been made. I have no explanation for the accusation other than some people will do anything to have their name coupled with a rising star in the news and tabloids." Calon rubbed his chin and stared back at Jimmy, challenging him to push further.

"Yeah, but you didn't answer my question. Sources say you may have…" Jimmy looked up at me and winked. "Well, they say you forced yourself on a sorority girl in a back room of the bar you guys play in Knoxville."

"I did no such thing." I saw his jaw clench.

"Was she the same girl whose 'hashtag who Calon knocked up' tweet ended up getting, what was it?" Jimmy flipped through the stack of notes and tabloids on the desk in front of him. "Forty-two hundred retweets?"

"Jimmy, come on, man, you're smarter than that. Do you believe everything you read? I don't. If I did, I'd think you were transgender." This time Calon raised his eyebrows at Jimmy.

"Wow. You are just dodging every one of these bullets. Let's see if you can go three for three. How do you explain this?" He held up a tabloid for the guys to see. I couldn't see the picture, and he didn't turn it my way but all four guys' eyes got as big as saucers. All eight eyes flashed up at me. I shrugged. I couldn't react if I couldn't see what they were gawking at.

"That's one of our managers. She had a little too much to drink that night, so I walked her home. She caught me off guard and took a picture of us. It looks a lot worse than it is. She'd tell you herself, if she were here." Calon smirked, and it was obvious Jimmy wasn't getting what he wanted. I caught a glimpse of the photo on the cover when Jimmy tossed the paper onto the seat next to him. A selfie of Danny and Calon. *When was that?*

The questioning went back and forth in a similar manner for the full thirty minutes. Jimmy eventually moved his attention to Manny, Spider, and Bones when catching Calon in something scandalous didn't work out for him.

Jimmy was cocky and just about throwing a tantrum because he hadn't stirred up any trouble during his show that was usually controversial and R-rated. So, when a devious smile slowly crossed his face, I worried just a little.

"Well, well, well. What do we have here? I just got a text from my producer that it's rumored your manager from the photo has ties to Malcolm Phoenix." He raised one eyebrow. "Calon, you have anything to say about that?"

I texted Cyan immediately.

Me: *Hey. Is there any connection between Danny and Malcolm Phoenix?*

Cyan: *Not that I know of. Why?*

Me: *Jimmy James is digging deep to try and find dirt on the guys. He said there was some connection.*

Cyan: *Malcolm's a dick, I hope she's not messed up with him*

Me: *Me too. Thx*

All I heard of Calon's answer to Jimmy's question was, "Jimmy, I'm sorry I'm not giving you whatever it is you want, but, quite frankly, I couldn't care less what the tabloids, or Malcolm Phoenix for that matter, throw at us. I'm not a vindictive person. It's just not something I choose to waste time on."

"I don't know about all you listeners, but I'm starting to wonder if Calon Ridge is bad ass enough to be a rock star. You don't let drunk girls have their way with you, and you don't want revenge for false accusations that could ruin your career." Jimmy shook his head, and Calon rolled his eyes. He looked up at me and rolled them again.

"Well, thanks for having us, Jimmy. We've gotta hit the road." Spider smacked his hands on his thighs and scooted his chair out from the desk.

"It's been great. Ladies and gentlemen, Alternate Tragedy. Keep an eye out for them. They're playing all over the city these days."

"You can find us at the El Rey Wednesday, Thursday, and Friday this week. We're back at The Hollywood Bowl on Saturday and then The Wiltern Monday, Tuesday, and Wednesday of next week. And..." Bones looked around for help from the other guys. I was floored at the number of upcoming shows Danny had booked.

"We're at the House of Blues Saturday the thirteenth and Sunday the fourteenth." Spider cleared his throat. "After that, you'll have to check our website."

I rolled my eyes at Calon and walked out into the ground floor lobby of the radio station. That schedule was ridiculous. I'd need to look at it all written out, but from what I gathered as Bones and Spider rattled off their gig dates, it seemed as though Calon and I might get three or four days together in the next two weeks. That meant, they'd be rehearsing most of the afternoon and playing at night while I stayed in the hotel twiddling my thumbs and sleeping away the mornings. I knew I was being selfish and unprofessional, but I needed Calon more now than ever. I started to wonder what the hell I'd even flown back for.

Strong arms slid around my belly from behind and clasped across the front. "Have I told you lately how absolutely stunning you are, Miss Mowry?"

That's why I flew back. This man.

"So, what's with not taking Valentine's Day off?" I spun within his hug and poked him in the chest.

"What? When's Valentine's Day?" He looked like a deer in headlights.

"Are you fucking serious right now, Calon Ridge?" I smacked him hard in the chest.

"Relax. It's our first Valentine's Day together, how could I forget it? But, we've been talking about playing the House of Blues for forever, and they had a last minute cancellation, so Danny pulled some strings and got us in. It sucks that it's on Valentine's Day, but I thought that would be considered a sappy holiday in 'The Book of Becki'. Besides, I promise I will make it up to you." He tipped his hips into mine and moved them from side to side.

"Damn straight, rock star. We might have to find out just how kinky you are to make up for this one."

"Oh." His eyes widened with intrigue.

"Now, let's go spend the twelve minutes I have with you in the next two weeks, doing something fun."

"What did you have in mind, Becks?"

"Well, I could eat the ass of a horse right now. So, first you have to feed me."

His head flew back, and he laughed so loud it echoed off the marble tiles that lined the never ending hallways just off the BMX-FM lobby.

We walked hand in hand to a little vegetarian café on a bustling corner. We sat at an outdoor table and looked over the menu. Just the two, well, three of us.

"How did we not know this place was here? Calon, I can eat anything on this menu."

"I know. I thought you'd like it here. Every time we pass it on the way to the studio, I think of you." He smiled and winked then looked back down at his menu.

"Well, how nice of you." It came out harsh and bitchy, but I was exhausted from the flight the day before, and I was starting to get uncomfortable with my growing body.

"What's wrong?"

"Can I get you guys drinks?" The waitress just about fell over when she looked up from her order pad and saw Calon. Here we go again.

"Oh. My. God. You're Calon Ridge. You're Calon Ridge!" Tears welled up in her eyes, and I was just about to stab her in the head with my fork when she cleared her throat and calmed herself down.

"I think I'll have a Rolling Rock." Calon smiled and licked his lips, as though he was in a desert, and she was about to hand-deliver the oasis. I think she had her own thoughts of what his tongue sliding over his bottom lip meant.

"I'll just have a water. With lemon, please." I wanted to do something, anything to get her eyes off him. Good God, it was like she already had him naked in her mind. Her. Teeny. Tiny. Little. Fucking. Mind.

"You're an ass." I slammed my menu on the table when she left, which threatened to knock the salt and pepper from the little tray they sat on.

"What the—" Calon scrambled to right the shakers.

"Calon, you can't lick your lips like that when a stranger is gawking at you. Don't you know everything you do will have girls reading into your intentions?" I thought back to when Gracie and I used to dissect every nuance of his performance to convince ourselves he wanted one of us.

"You're crazy. That's your hormones talking." He rolled his eyes.

"Gracie and I had a whole thesaurus written in our minds for what each of your movements on stage meant."

"Your Rolling Rock, and your water." Teeny Tiny Mind interrupted us and looked as though she'd hiked her skin tight pencil skirt up two inches before coming back with our drinks. "Are you both ready to order?" She said it to both of us, but she hadn't looked at me once.

"I'll have the house salad but without onions. Onions make our baby hiccup, and it's a really bizarre feeling." I patted my belly and reached across the table for Calon's hand. He shook his head, and his curls danced around his face, his perfectly gorgeous face. Her eyes were as big as saucers, and I knew at that moment it was a stupid trick to have pulled. It'd be all over the internet as soon as she went back to the kitchen and tweeted with the hashtag 'who Calon knocked up'.

"And I'll have the Greek salad with no onions… you know, so she, the baby, doesn't get hiccups." He smiled politely like what he'd just said wasn't ridiculous. She giggled, jotted his order down, grabbed our menus, and left our table without saying a word. And also without the huge flirting grin she'd been spilling all over us before.

"I'm so sorry, Calon. That was so stupid! Danny's going to kill me for that." I rubbed my forehead. I felt like my life was a giant tornado of emotions. At that very moment, I wanted to jump across the table into Calon's lap and ride him like a cowgirl. I was still working through the fear of giving birth to a special needs child, and I was on the brink of tears, because the number of hours we had left before we'd be separated by more than a couple states were dwindling. In addition to that, I was fed up with sharing Calon with every horny woman on the fucking planet. It's not like I didn't know what I was getting myself into. It was no secret that there wasn't a uterus in the seas of concert-goers that wasn't craving his seed. I knew what dating a semi-famous rock star meant, yet I wanted to slit the throats of every fucking woman who looked a little too long at him. The fact that the typical stare started at his face and ended on his crotch didn't help.

"Becks, I couldn't care less what people think about me or our relationship and the baby. I love you, I love our baby, and I love playing music. What other people think is completely irrelevant." He squeezed the hand I still held across the table.

"Danny keeps telling us that you guys will lose fans if girls know you're taken." I took a sip of my water.

"If there are people out there who love Alternate Tragedy on the condition that its members stay single, then they really aren't loving our music. They're loving the *idea* of us; an idea they've created in their own minds. And that's just bullshit. Telling the media that we're having a baby will just weed out those people just riding the bandwagon. Ya know?" He picked up his Rolling Rock and held it up to make a toast. "To our beautiful baby girl, Abigail Kate, may the next fifteen weeks fly by, so we can meet her in person."

That number, fifteen, knocked the wind out of me. I knew I was a mother the moment she was conceived, but I would be a legit mom when she was on the outside of my body. Then I'd have to know the difference between her hunger cries and her gassy ones. I'd have to get up with her throughout the night and walk her around when she was inconsolable. A level of fear I hadn't experienced yet came over me. I felt a hundred pounds heavier in the little wrought iron café chair that held my already growing ass.

"Becks, whoa. What in the world? You're as pale as a ghost." Calon slid his chair out from under him, like he was going to swoop me up in his arms and carry me to the hospital.

"Sit down, dork. I'm fine. It's just when you said 'fifteen weeks' I realized how soon she would really be here. All the things I've been reading in that book flew into my head all at once. The Braxton Hicks contractions, the possibility of pissing myself with no warning, the labor. Oh, God, Calon, did you know some women are in labor for days? Days! Then there's everything we have to know after we take her home. Feedings and diapers, fevers, and crying." His face went white, and I was sure the weight of our reality hit him as hard as it had just got me.

"So, this is what's got you all keyed up. Wait! Did you say, days?" He was obviously thrown by the labor thing. "How the hell am I supposed to know what to do for you?" He dropped my hand to rub his temples.

"We'll have to sign up for birthing classes." Then it hit me. "Shit! How are we supposed to do birthing classes while you're out here and I'm home? Maybe they can just cut her out." My panic level shot up into dangerous territory.

"Becks, I'm pretty sure there's a way we can do it. Would you be okay with Gracie being in the room with us? You know, while you're having the baby?" I loved that she was the first person he thought of.

"Of course, and maybe she could take the birthing classes with me if you're be in LA. As long as you're okay with it. You wouldn't care would you?"

"Not at all. So, Gracie can take the birth classes with you, and she can be just as much my coach as yours when the big day comes. She'll just tell me what to do, and I'll do it. You know, the ice chips and the weird breathing and stuff." Seeing my big, tough, sexy rock star rattled about the birth of our child, somehow relaxed my entire body. Everything would be okay. I knew it at that very moment.

"You've been reading the books by the bed, haven't you?" My heart fluttered.

"Well, of course, I have. You don't think I was going to just sit there and watch, do you? I even know what to do with the olive oil." He lifted his eyebrows and winked.

"Olive oil? What the hell are you talking about?" I couldn't wait to hear what part of the book he'd misinterpreted.

"Becki Jane Mowry, do I know something you don't know?"

"Calon, seriously? I can't fathom what you think you're supposed to do with olive oil. Please, do tell."

"It was in the papers Dr. Daily gave us, and I have a feeling it's what she was referring to that one day when she said there were things I could help with. So, anyway, it said that because your... uh... you know, your parts..." He nodded in the direction of my crotch   that was completely out of his line of vision thanks to the table between us. "Your parts are gonna stretch like crazy, and the baby's head could rip you up—"

"Calon!" I instinctively pressed my thighs together, and I immediately understood why guys buckle just at the thought of getting hit in the nads.

"No, I'm serious. The book said if you rub olive oil there regularly, it will keep your skin elastic and significantly lower the chance of it tearing. I can do that." He nodded and finished his beer in one final gulp, and I pressed my thighs together for a completely different reason. He was so hot.

"Your salads." Teeny was back, and her skirt was pulled back down closer to her knees. Hooker. "Can I get you two anything else?"

Calon looked at me and smirked. "Yeah, the check and a small to-go container of olive oil, please."

twenty-four

Calon

"SO, DO YOU really think there's a connection between Danny and Malcolm?" Gracie looked up at me from her plate of fries.

"Actually, there's a connection between Malcolm and a lot of the negative shit that's happened since we left Knoxville." I shook my head, still in disbelief that someone would go to such lengths to try and kill someone else's success.

"Really? How?" Gracie looked back and forth between me and Becki.

"Well," Becki cleared her throat. "Malcolm was blackmailing Danny with information he supposedly had that connected her... intimately... to a big name artist who was married."

"What? That's insane." Gracie shook her head.

"And," I continued when Becki took another huge bite of her salad. "Apparently Malcolm found Violet and Charlotte on an Alternate Tragedy fan site. He saw all their posts in the 'I'm the biggest Calon fan' thread and contacted them when he realized where they lived. He created a unique story for each of them to get them to do his dirty work. We've heard through the grapevine that Malcolm had been using the site to get proof for the shit he sells to the tabloids, too. When Charlotte was questioned by police for her false accusation she admitted to connecting with him on that website. We can only assume that Violet also got paid for the photo of me at the OB's office." The whole thing gave me a headache.

"So, what's Malcolm got against Alternate Tragedy?" Jake looked stunned.

"Malcolm's been losing his pull in the industry, and I guess he panicked. We turned down his numerous offers to be our manager, and it pissed him off, so I guess he orchestrated the hashtags, the photos that were supposed to be incriminating, and Charlotte's police report."

"And, we still haven't figured out why we lost power at The Moondance, but we do know that Malcolm's daughter is the one who made the bogus announcement. So, we assume Malcolm was behind that, too." I watched Becki's fists clench on top of the table.

"Are you firing Danny?" Gracie liked Danny, and I could tell by the look on her face she was hoping for the best for her.

"No. We've got nothing against her. She's a great girl, just got in a little over her head. Malcolm was the reason Danny took that selfie that looked like we were about to kiss. He sold it under a fictitious name to the tabloids. When she realized it wasn't just her he was manipulating, she went to the police with his texts and emails, and pressed charges." I closed my eyes and took a deep breath to clear my head.

"Can we talk about something else? This is really bringing me down." Becki laughed and started telling Gracie and Jake a funny story from our trek in the van to LA.

It was a gorgeous Sunday afternoon, and Jake and Gracie flew in for our Valentine's Day show at The House of Blues. I didn't remember ever being as nervous as I was then, and the show was still a good seven hours away. But, the countdown to my proposal was so close I could taste it.

Gracie and Jake were going to be a huge part of my plan. I needed to make sure Becki made it out that night, and I needed her close enough to the front of the crowd for me to have her join me on stage. Her safety and comfort were the biggest uncontrollable factors in my plan.

Gracie had also been planning Becki's shower since the moment she found out Becki was pregnant, but she hadn't picked the date. Although, she knew she wanted it to be at Mitchell's. Friday nights were still Gracie's nights to perform, and she'd been readying the crowd for the event knowing how Becki loved things done big. The Mitchell's crowd was a close-knit bunch, and Gracie knew the fans who embraced Alternate Tragedy would love to celebrate the baby. All these surprises were making me a nervous wreck. I hated having to keep secrets from Becki when I was used to sharing everything with her. Recently, I'd had to break our 'what are you thinking' rule a couple times, bullshitting my way through the answer each time, which I hated.

"What are you thinking?" Becki interrupted my thoughts.

"I'm thinking there's a lot to see in LA. We need to get movin' and show these guys around, or we'll be late for the show." *Dammit.* Lied again.

We spent the day taking Gracie and Jake around the city, and showing them all the famous places you hear about or see on TV and in the movies. Becki was a good sport. I knew how tired she was; I could see it on her face as the day went on, but she stayed lively. A couple fans came up to us just to talk to Becki about the baby.

After the amniocentesis results came back positive, we decided we would be open to the public and the press about the fact that Abigail would be born with Down syndrome. We talked a lot about all the good we could do by raising awareness. Even Spider, Manny, and Bones brought up the possibly of supporting The Knoxville Extension School as our own personal philanthropy. It wasn't a Down syndrome facility, per se, but much of the student body happened to have Down syndrome.

When it was time for the guys and me to head out to The House of Blues, Gracie and Jake knew it was up to them to get Becki there by nine and have her as close to the stage as they could get her for our encore. I'd alerted the bouncers at our show the night before what was going down and who would be asking for their help to get down front. All in all, everything was going according to plan, but I was a fucking nervous wreck.

"Dude, you sure you wanna do this?" As much as Bones loved Becki and was excited about our little girl, marriage scared the piss out of him. I was pretty sure he would be a career playboy and never settle down.

"Yeah, I'm nervous as hell. But I'm more than sure, I'm positive." Manny and Spider clapped me on the back and then shook my hand.

Bones shrugged and gave me an awkward hug. Sucking in a deep breath, I leaned past Bones to see out into the crowd from the side of the stage where we were hidden. The crowd was even bigger than the night before. Danny had gotten word that there were at least two record labels coming, the 'missed conference call' label being one of them. Both were interested in approaching us with deals.

"Relax, man. You got this." Danny pulled me in for a hug.

I nodded and squared my shoulders.

I'd always thought the guys who looked so scared just before they were about to propose, were afraid their girl may say no. Well, I knew Becki wouldn't say no, and I was still shaking in my Docs.

"Ladies and gentleman, gracing our stage for the second night in a row, please welcome Alternate Tragedy!" The voice bellowed from the rafters, and the crowd went wild. We always waited just a little longer than most bands before we walked out on stage, just to keep the hype up; however, my feet felt like lead tonight, and I struggled to move them when the guys made their way onto the stage. They always insisted I be the last one out, because that's when the crowd's energy skyrocketed. I didn't get it, but they were right. The second I got my feet to move and my body hit the edge of the stage, the crowd lost it. I could do nothing but chuckle, and I felt the natural peace I always felt on stage drown out my unnecessary jitters.

"Wow!" I hoped my voice would last. The crowd was insane. "Thank you all for such an amazing welcome. We are Alternate Tragedy, and we're ready to party. Y'all up for the challenge?" They went wild again, and there was no way they would hear me over the roar, so I took that time to scan the scene for Becki. The crowd was huge and unlike the smaller clubs we played, there was no bar within my view. Being pregnant, Becki was more comfortable sitting at the bar than she was getting down into the mix. I wasn't sure how I would find her. I had to let that go, though, and trust Gracie and Jake to do what we'd planned.

We rocked the house. There was nothing more surreal than seeing people singing every word to songs you'd written. It was the best compliment, and the emotion that came from it was indescribable. We invited Danny out, and she sang a couple songs with me then blew the crowd away with her own rendition of "Criminal" by Fiona Apple. It was a sexy song, and there was little about Danny that wasn't sexy especially in skin tight jeans and cowboy boots. She was an amazing performer and had a great head on her shoulders. She knew the music industry forwards and backwards. The guys and I had talked to her about being our opening act at venues that would allow us one. She was thrilled. I'd been almost afraid to run the idea past Becki, but she echoed our excitement. It was a great set up.

We left the stage after our third set, and I knew with all of my heart and soul that what I was about to do was not only the biggest decision of my life but the best.

"You ready, lover boy?" Danny, still trying to catch her breath, put her hand on my shoulder and squeezed.

"Danny, you killed that!" I gave her a high five. "And, I'm fucking nervous as hell, but I've never been more ready for anything." I sucked in a big breath and felt all the emotions of everything Becki and I had been through in the short time we'd been together well up just under my heart, which was about to pound out of my chest.

"This is good, Calon. You guys are the epitome of love. Y'all have raised the bar for me as far as what I'll expect from a relationship from here on out. You're a great catch, and I couldn't be happier for my girl, Becki."

"Thanks, Danny. That really means a lot." I gave her a big squeeze. "And thanks for your help with the undercover ring shopping. I don't know how we dodged Malcolm's ulterior motives that day."

"Could have been your ridiculous disguise. You looked like an eccentric hobo." She threw her head back, and we both laughed hard. "Here. Take this and go make all her dreams come true." She shoved her hand into the front pocket of her jeans and handed me the white gold, one carat emerald cut solitaire she assured me Becki would love. I'd kept it in the pocket of my favorite coat that hung on my closet door for quite some time. From a security stand point, it probably wasn't the smartest place to keep it, but I knew it was one place Becki would never find it. She hated that coat and wouldn't have touched it with a ten foot pole. "It's ugly Calon. You just need to throw that thing away."

I waved at the guys to head out on stage, took a deep breath, and put the ring in my pocket. The crowd went nuts when we walked back out onto the stage. I took the mic stand in one hand and laid my other hand across the mic to feign calm, but my insides buzzed. I waited a minute, then put one hand up to squelch the crowd as best I could.

"Dammit, you have got to be the best crowd we've performed for yet. What do you think, guys?" I turned to Manny, Bones, and Spider, and they all nodded, which made the crowd even louder. I waved again for them to quiet down.

"Calon, I love you!" I shrill squeal from a blonde in the front row cut through the dull roar that was still rumbling.

"Well, thank you." I winked, and she leaned into the guy next to her. He shook his head and rolled his eyes.

"Now, we've never done this song outside of the studio, but it's got a special purpose tonight. Has anyone seen my beautiful girlfriend? Becki! Are you out there somewhere?"

My eyes landed on her, and she stole my breath. Her hair was up and sitting in a twist at the back of her head. Golden-brown tendrils swayed by her ears. The silver hoops that hung from her ears sparkled almost as much as her eyes, and I fell in love with her all over again.

"Becki, baby, this one's for you. I changed some of the words, so it would be just perfect. I hope you love it." She smiled and wiped tears from her cheeks then shook her head, frustrated by the emotions she could no longer hold in. The one thing she disliked most about her raging hormones was one of the things I loved the best.

"This song is inspired by 'The One' by Static Cycle." I steadied myself with both hands on the mic and my feet planted on either side of the stand. The song was written as though someone is walking away from a relationship, so I adjusted the words to illustrate us walking into love together. The first line was the one I wanted Becki to hold onto forever.

I've been loved before.
It's just never felt this way.

Over and over I sang to her that she'd always be the one. I didn't take my eyes off her for the whole song, except the few times I was overcome by emotion and my eyes forced themselves closed. When the song ended on the title words, I put my hand out toward her, and the bouncers closest to her lead her and Gracie to the wings.

She stood in the wings for a moment and looked as terrified as I felt standing in the same spot just moments earlier. She walked out when Gracie nudged her, and she took my breath away.

She was dressed in a white Alternate Tragedy t-shirt she'd cut up and assured me was fashionable. The sleeves were cut off and it hung down off her one shoulder revealing the strap of the black tank top she wore underneath. Both the shirt and the tank stretched down across her growing belly, and that's when I realized both my girls were joining me on stage. The frayed jean skirt and combat boots just about sent me over the edge. The bangle bracelet I'd given her for Christmas hung around her wrist and as she walked toward me, I was convinced she was the sexiest, most beautiful woman on the planet. And, as fate would have it, she was mine. She put her hand out, and I took it in mine and pulled the mic from the stand with the other. Her hand trembled.

She mouthed, *What are you doing?* I pulled her close and kissed her mouth softly, which resulted in a communal sigh from what sounded like all the women in the crowd. And I'm sure a collective eye roll from all the men they came with.

"Happy Valentine's Day, Becki," I whispered her name into the mic, and the crowd went silent. And, I mean silent. I placed her trembling hand over my heart and pressed it against me with mine. "You've stolen my heart, and you've rocked my world. A more perfect soul I'll never know. After our first kiss, just six months ago, I knew I'd never find anyone more perfect for me than that one crazy girl in the crowd; one I'd had my eye on for a while. I love you,

Becki Jane Mowry, but I'm really not that crazy about your last name."

She gave me a look like I'd just poked her in the forehead, and it made me laugh so hard I had to hold the mic away from my mouth a little then clear my throat to continue.

"I'd like to change your last name, if that's okay with you." The crowd gasped.

I watched her body absorb what I tried to say, and she sucked in a deep breath at the same time I did. I held onto her hand and knelt down on one knee in front her. We were no longer in front of thousands of fans. It was just us.

"Abigail Kate, I love you, baby girl." I leaned in and kissed Becki's belly. "I want to marry your mommy. I hope that's okay with you." I felt Becki's body shaking. I looked up, and her cheeks glistened with tears. She tried as best she could to wipe them away with her one free hand.

"Becki, I've been loved before, but it's just never felt this way. I want to feel this way for the rest of my life—if you'll have me. With all my heart and all my soul, I want to spend the rest of my days on this planet by your side. I love you more than words can express, and I want to make you my wife. Becki Mowry, will you marry me?" The crowd lost their mind.

She nodded and said, "Yes." I had to read her lips because the roar of the crowd was deafening. She covered her mouth and sobbed. I pulled the ring from my pocket slipped it on her finger, and then I stood and wrapped my arms around her waist, crashing my mouth into hers. Lifting her off the stage, I kissed her for the first time as my wife-to-be.

"Calon James, you are the most amazing man on earth. I can't believe you just did this in front of all these people. On Valentine's Day! You really *do* love me." If her lips hadn't been right next to my ear, I'd never have heard her.

"I'll love you forever. Thank you for saying yes." I kissed her again and set her down gently on the stage then turned toward our fans.

"Gracie!" I spoke into the mic and searched the wings and the crowd for her but couldn't find her. "Now the shower can be a baby shower *AND* a bridal shower!"

"CALON!" I heard Gracie's voice even over the still-screaming crowd. And at that same moment, Becki cracked me in the arm with her open hand.

"SHIT! Gracie, I told you I was bad at this." I threw my hands into the air. There was nothing to do but laugh.

"Thank you all for being witnesses to one of the most magical moments in my life. The next magical moment will happen in a little over three months." I reached down and patted her belly again. "Now, do you all agree that Becki Jane Ridge sounds way better?"

There were cheers and whistles, and Becki giggled. I put the mic back in the stand, waved good-bye to the crowd, and hello to a new chapter of my life.

I STEPPED INTO the shower with my fiancée and pulled her to me. Our bodies slick and warm in the stream of hot water. I took her face in my hands and kissed her deeply. She groaned into my mouth, and her hands splayed across my lower back and pressed me into her. She finished our kiss and pulled her face from mine.

"You know, marrying me means sex with me, only me, for the rest of your life."

"Yeah?"

"That doesn't freak you out at all?"

"Nope." I ran my hands up and down her warm, wet back and over the bulge of her belly. "Why? Were you not done having sex with other people?"

"Calon, baby, what your body does to mine, I am perfectly happy with just you for the rest of my life."

"Well, good." I smiled and kissed the tip of her nose.

We washed each other thoroughly, and it was, bar none, the most sensual, intimate thing I'd ever experienced without actually having sex. It was like another language. It was beautiful.

We dried each other off, and I carried her to our bed. I laid her down gently and hovered over her body, covered in goose bumps.

"Tonight, I'm going to make love to my fiancée all night long if that's okay with you."

She batted her eyes at me and breathed out the words, "Please do."

twenty-five
Becki

"BECKI, PLEASE! I really can't run this whole thing by myself!" Gracie's voice was a little too whiny for seven thirty in the morning on a Saturday. Calon didn't budge. We'd taken a red eye to Knoxville after Alternate Tragedy's Friday night show in LA and climbed into our bed just a couple hours prior to Gracie's call. We had another doctor's appointment on Monday. It would start off the week Calon would go back to LA without me. So, we decided to make a whole weekend of it and spend as much time as we could together. Now, my best friend was panicked and begging me to leave his bed and come help her with some carnival out at The Extension School that benefited the Special Olympics.

"All right, Gracie, but I don't think I can be there before ten." I yawned and rubbed my eyes then watched my big diamond sparkle in the morning sunshine.

"Becki, that would be amazing! It doesn't start until then, so that's perfect. I'll be at the registration table, where my assistant was supposed to be, but the flu had other plans for her."

"It's funny, that day I spent with you at the school, I was so uncomfortable. But, I'm looking forward to spending time with those same kids today. Is that weird?"

"Not at all. You're going to be the mom of a special needs kid, and everything within you is getting you ready. I really think that kind of thing happens naturally and can't be forced."

"Can I bring Calon?" I looked over at him, catching his deep green eyes looking back at me. He smiled.

"That would be awesome. You two can run a couple of the carnival games with Samantha."

"Did I meet Samantha when I was there?" I stood up and walked to the kitchen to start a pot of coffee for Calon, who I knew would be ready to pass out by lunchtime. In rock star world it was still night time until about three in the afternoon.

"No, Sam is nineteen. She was an accelerated student and graduated earlier than most special needs kids. She's who I turn to when I need to count on something to get done quickly. She helps me in the classroom sometimes, but she wasn't there the day you were there."

"Sounds good. I think I hear Calon moving around in the bedroom. We'll be there as soon as we can be."

"Just be here by ten. The kids will love that a real rock star is running the carnival games." She giggled. "Oh, crap, I gotta go, one of the food trucks is parking in the wrong spot. See ya when you get here."

Calon and I leisurely got ourselves ready, ate some breakfast, and decided we would walk out to the school grounds. It was a gorgeous sunny day, and Calon's schedule didn't allow him a lot of daylight. I knew he'd enjoy it immensely. Besides, there weren't many things hotter than Calon in a pair of Aviators. That sight stole my breath.

We walked hand in hand down the sidewalks and crossed campus into the little residential neighborhood that bordered it. We came out of the tree-lined streets and stepped onto the grounds of The Extension School. The green expanse of the grassy lawns spoke volumes about the care that went into the school. The actual building was at the back of the property, and Gracie's carnival was set up in front of it.

"Wow. She planned this all herself?" Calon was like a wide-eyed child headed toward his favorite place on earth.

"The faculty helped her and local businesses offered their services for free, but the planning and coordinating, that's all Gracie. She loves this place. She even said she'd like to continue working here after graduation. I think she and Jake are considering staying in Knoxville. Couldn't you see them living in one of those little Cape Cods we just passed?"

"Definitely. What would Jake do? He's a business major, right?" Calon helped me hop over a puddle.

"Yeah, I guess he and Buzz are trying to work something out. I think he's talked to Jake about possibly running the place."

"That would be great." There was a twinge of sadness in Calon's eyes that I didn't quite understand.

"What are you thinking?" I squeezed his hand and stood on my tippy toes to steal a kiss.

"Don't get mad at me, but there's always been a part of me that sometimes wished we hadn't made it so big, so fast. I really love Knoxville. I love playing at Mitchell's. I love the campus town feel. Ya know?"

"I do." I'd been feeling the same way, but was so afraid to say anything to Calon for fear he would make a rash decision and sacrifice his dream just so I was as happy as I could be. I wasn't willing to let him do that, but it was comforting to know he felt the same way about Knoxville that I did. Besides, I was pretty sure most bands would tell you that they second-guessed their search for fame in the beginning of their careers taking off.

"Guys! You couldn't have gotten here at a better time. Not only did my assistant leave me, but I've had two people call in late." Gracie had three or four pencils sticking out of the messy bun that sat on the very top of her head. She held two clipboards and had a walkie-talkie clipped to her jeans.

"Just tell us where you want us." Calon put his hands on her shoulders in an attempt to settle her nerves.

Gracie smiled and took a deep breath. "I just sent Samantha over to the games area, but she's going to need your help lifting some of the partitions into place. Calon, could you help her with that?"

"You got it." Calon jogged over to a short blonde girl trying her damnedest to lift part of a structure into place. I could see her wide smile when she saw him coming her way. She dropped the piece she had been holding and ran up to him, wrapping her arms around his waist.

"She's a huge fan." Gracie smiled and watched them through the introductions we couldn't hear. Calon's demeanor was so relaxed. Samantha had Down syndrome.

"She's beautiful, Gracie." I instantly pictured Abigail in her teens. I smiled, knowing I'd be proud of her from day one. I was already proud of her for being such a fighter and beating the odds in a womb that wasn't supposed to work.

"She really is, inside and out. She's one of the higher functioning students with Down syndrome we've had, and she has more energy than anyone I know." Someone squawked over the walkie-talkie, and Gracie handed me her clip boards. "Becki, I just need to you check off the students' names as they arrive. They all should have name tags, but make sure they all stop to check in. It's part of their Life Skills class to follow appropriate directions when out in a crowd."

"You got it. Now, go, BFF, do your thing!" I was so proud of her. The administration at The Extension School would be stupid not to hire her full time after graduation.

I eventually got to go work the games with Calon and Samantha. I couldn't remember the last time I had so much fun or laughed so hard. The kids who came through were just adorable, and we gave out prizes to everyone. It was Gracie's rule. "Everyone wins for their attempt," is what she told us.

"So, Samantha, what do you do for Gracie?" There were a couple times when things were happening on the main stage that the games area was kid-free. I used that time to get to know Samantha. Her personality was so inviting, you couldn't *not* want to know her.

"I'm her assistant on Wednesdays. Wednesdays are the days I read to the kids and do special art projects with them. I love the kids. I love to make them happy, because they make me so happy." She smiled and went back to organizing all the darts according to color. Then she started laying out the replacement balloons for when the next round of students came through her Balloon Pop game.

"Do you live at the school?" Calon asked as he picked up a couple balloons the wind had blown off the counter.

"Thank you, Calon. You're very nice." Calon smiled and nodded his thank you. "No, I don't live here. I live in one of those houses over there with my mom." She pointed to the houses that bordered the school property. The ones I imagined Gracie and Jake living in.

"Just you and your mom?" Questioning whether she had siblings or not came from my subconscious because until that moment I hadn't thought of the fact that I probably would never be pregnant again. This pregnancy was such a miracle, there was a good chance Abigail would be an only child.

"Yep. She's a nice mom, and she's super funny. Maybe you can meet her today. Wow! Your ring is very sparkly!" She took my hand and inspected my ring thoroughly.

"Thank you. Calon and I are getting married." I loved saying that. Calon winked at me and smiled.

"That's sweet." Samantha patted my hand and smiled as some more kids walked up to her with tickets to play her game.

I shuffled back to my station and blew a kiss at Calon, who was helping a little boy at his station hold his putter correctly to make a hole-in-one. Everything about the day was perfect. The man of my dreams, my best friend, and my newly found comfort level with kiddos with special needs; something that came out of nowhere but cut my fears of becoming Abigail's mom in half.

It was a long day, but one I felt honored to be a part of. Even though my feet hurt, and I was sure I had blisters, I didn't want the day to end. Each and every one of the children that came through was beaming with joy.

"You guys want to do dinner? Jake just called, and Buzz isn't feeling well again, so he's gotta run the bar tonight. I thought we could grab a pizza out somewhere or something."

"Sounds good." I was starving. Gracie, Calon, Samantha, and I stood at what had been the registration table and watched the last of the groups leave through the carnival gates.

"Samantha, you coming?" Calon winked at her, and his invitation stole her breath.

Samantha wrung her hands, looked at Gracie and stuttered her way through a, "Yes."

Gracie had thought of everything. She knew how exhausted she'd be at the end of the day, so she had a whole team of janitors from the school volunteer to break everything down and get it all back to the places that had donated it.

"LOS ANGELES HAS a lot of great things, but I have yet to find pizza as good as Brother's Pizza." I spoke with my mouthful and grease dripping down my chin, but I didn't care. Five more minutes and I may have passed out from starvation. Calon grabbed me some funnel cake about half way through the day, but that wasn't even close to being enough sustenance for a woman with child.

"Becki, you eat a LOT!" Samantha giggled when she said it, which made everyone else laugh along with her.

"I know. I really do. Do you know why?"

Samantha shook her head and sank her teeth into the tip of her next slice of pizza, knowing I was two pieces ahead of her already. Her eyes bounced back and forth between me and Calon.

"Because, I'm feeding two people with this pizza." I smiled and waited for it to sink it, not completely sure she would understand.

Samantha ducked her head down and looked around like she was about to dispel a secret. She whispered as loudly as you can and still call it a whisper. "You're having a baby?"

"We are." Calon smiled and puffed his chest out like a stereotypical proud papa.

"A baby. I've never held a baby before." She smiled shyly.

"Well, you can hold Abigail. I'm sure you'll be a natural." Just the thought of her with a baby in her arms was precious.

Samantha smiled at me from ear to ear and took another bite of pizza.

I thought about the things I'd read in the literature Dr. Daily had given us. I understood that Samantha was mentally a young teenager, and that she was comforted by order and structure. I'd become quite the Down syndrome encyclopedia over the last month, knowing our baby would have the condition. I guess it was our first glimpse into the natural adaptation parents make for their children.

"Do you work anywhere else other than Gracie's class, Samantha?" I smiled at Gracie, knowing she was reveling in my comfort level around Samantha.

"I work in the cafeteria at The Extension School on Mondays and Fridays and with Miss Gracie on Wednesdays." She smiled and wiped her hands on her napkin. "What do you do, Becki?"

"Well, I was the manager for Calon's band, but now that I'm having a baby, I'm going to stay in Knoxville, so I'm close to my doctor. Someone else will be taking over my job with Calon, so I won't have a job until I find a new one." I was going to die of boredom. So, Calon and I decided it would be a good idea to explore jobs I could do from home. That way I could have an income before the baby came. And after she was born, when I felt up to it, I could continue to work from home. It seemed to be the best plan. Babies were expensive.

"Gracie!" We all jumped when Samantha's voice hit a more-than-a-whisper volume. "Gracie! Can Becki come work at the school? Please, Gracie?"

"Well, actually, in a staff meeting last week they were mentioning the need for a website with information and articles about the school, the events we run, and maybe even interviews with current and former students." Gracie looked at me and smiled, and I knew exactly what she was thinking. "Becki, it's pretty much a publicist's job but without the high salary I'm sure being a rock star's publicist plays."

"Well, technically, I was Calon's manager. He didn't pay me as much as I was worth, but I let him work it off…" I stopped myself before saying he paid me in sex, when I realized Samantha probably didn't need to be privy to the same information Gracie was privy to. Calon squeezed my leg under the table and smiled. He'd been really quiet, just saying a couple words, the whole time we'd been at Brother's. So, when Gracie and Samantha started discussing the job opening at the school, I turned to Calon. He was watching every nuance of Samantha's movements. He was completely still.

"Calon, what is it?" I whispered, not wanting to draw attention to his apparent uneasiness.

"It's Samantha. I'm missing Kate. My heart hurts and I have that nervous homesick feeling in my stomach. I can't shake it." He rubbed his forehead and looked around to make sure no one picked up on his anxiety.

I squeezed his hand and laid my head on his shoulder. Instantly, I was filled with worry that Abigail's birth would send Calon back to the heartbreak of losing Kate. As a stressed, new mom, I was going to need him to be my rock, and if he was crushed by his memories of Kate, I was going to have to walk myself through being a new mom while I walked him through the grief process. I was fully willing to do whatever I needed to so he could heal the wound I knew had been gaping for most of his life, but I wasn't sure how well I could do it while learning how to be a new mom.

"Babe, I know you miss Kate—"

"Kate? Whose name is Kate? That's my middle name!" Samantha was squealing and bouncing around on the vinyl seat cushion. I felt bad for drawing attention to my conversation with Calon, I thought I'd whispered her name.

"Samantha Kate?" Calon's voice was monotone, like he was far away. "That's a beautiful name."

"Yep. Samantha Kate O'Brien. That's me. I like my name." She smiled from ear to ear.

Calon pulled his phone from his pocket and put it up to his ear. "Hello? Yeah. Yeah, whatcha need, dude?" He put a finger up toward us as an "excuse me" when he got up from the table and headed out the front door. I watched him walk to the corner and lean against a light pole. Whoever was on the phone was taking up the entire conversation, because Calon's mouth wasn't moving.

"Oh, gosh, look at the time. Samantha, I told your mom I'd have you home before six thirty. We need to go." They stood, and Gracie took the check up to the register.

"Can you tell Calon I said it was nice to meet him? He's real cute." Samantha smiled and craned her neck to see him on the corner.

"Why don't you walk out with me? Gracie will catch up. You can tell him yourself." She smiled and took my hand.

"My heart beats so fast when he's so close. Is that because he's so cute?" She pressed her open hand against her chest and tried to steady her breathing.

"Yeah, he does that to my heart, too." Calon lifted his head when we stepped out onto the sidewalk. He didn't say a word to whoever was on the phone but stuffed his phone in his back pocket and his eyes locked on us. The way he was acting made me wonder if he'd just used his phone as a way to escape for a little while. Samantha let go of my hand, ran up to Calon, and grabbed both of his.

"I am so happy to meet you, Calon. I hope we can have pizza again soon." She stood up on her toes and hugged him tight then took his hands again.

Calon looked down at her hands in his and a big smile spread across his face. Gracie walked up and bumped her hip into mine. We could finish each other's sentences, and there was no doubt in my mind what she was thinking... we were forming a bond that would be a lifelong friendship with someone who is the older version of the baby I carried. I smiled at Gracie and nodded. But, when I looked back at Calon, his whole demeanor had changed. He seemed pensive. He and Samantha walked over to the bench just passed me and Gracie. They sat down, still holding hands.

I watched him, not knowing whether I should interrupt and quietly suggest he deal with his emotions somewhere other than in Samantha's presence or just let them have their moment. I was so afraid he was freaking her out.

"Becki? What—"

"I don't know. Should I make him stop?" I hated to do that, but Samantha may not be comfortable with whatever it was he was doing.

"No, it's okay. Samantha is a strong girl. She's been through a lot of emotional stuff. If it gets too intense, she'll tell him. She has boundaries, and she'll let him know if he's making her uncomfortable. This is actually good for her." Gracie never took her eyes off Calon and Samantha as she spoke.

"Calon, can I tell you a story?" Samantha's voice was soft, and she squeezed Calon's hands and rubbed them with her thumbs.

Calon nodded, and, at that moment, I wanted to read his mind. With everything I had, I wanted to take away all his pain. All the loss he had experienced was still so intense in his huge heart.

"Calon, I have something that makes me smile even when I'm really, really sad. You look really sad right now, and I wish you weren't." She smiled and waited for a response.

"Thank you, Samantha. I just miss someone very much, and I've thought about her a lot today." He looked up at me and tried to smile, but his lips denied him the happy shape.

"That's exactly how I feel, too. I get really sad sometimes because…" She took her hands from Calon's, reached up inside her sweatshirt, and pulled something toward her wrist. From where I stood I couldn't see what it was, but when Calon's mouth fell open, I started to piece it all together. "The boy who gave this to me went away, and I never saw him again. He was my brother. He made this bracelet for me before he went away."

Calon took her wrist in his hand and lifted it so I could see. An old, worn, rainbow-colored friendship bracelet hung around her wrist. It was obvious it had been lengthened over and over again to fit a growing girl.

"Samantha, where did you hear that story?" Calon's eyes were wide, and I wasn't sure if he had breathed in the last three minutes.

"I didn't hear it, silly. I remember him. Now stop interrupting me." Calon's faint smile pushed tears out onto his cheeks. "I was trying to ask you if you wanted to wear my bracelet until you feel better. As long as you promise to give it back when you're done. It's been on my wrist since I was three."

That comment sealed the deal, and there was no doubt in my mind that Calon had just been reunited with Kate. Gracie reached over and squeezed my hand, then blinked back tears.

"That's very nice of you to share your bracelet, Samantha. Why don't we take Calon and Becki with us to your house? I bet your mom would love to meet them." Gracie walked up next to Samantha and put her hands on her shoulder. I had shared Calon's story with Gracie soon after he told me. When she realized what was happening, she was quick on her feet to invite us to meet Kate's mom.

"You can keep your bracelet on your wrist, Samantha. All of my sadness went away when you shared that story with me. Thank you." Calon wiped the tears from his face.

"Oh." Samantha looked around at all of us and shrugged. "That's sorta weird but whatever." She stood and walked away with Gracie. I took Calon into my arms and stood on my toes to get as much of him in my hug as I could.

"Becki," he whispered, "It's her." He laughed and sobbed at the same time. It was obvious that it was not our place to decide when was an appropriate time to explain the story to her.

Gracie had pulled Calon aside at the beginning of our walk, and asked Calon if it was okay that she share what had just happened with Samantha's mom. Of course, he said yes. Gracie was on her phone ahead of all of us as we walked along the tree-lined streets. Samantha took Calon's hand again and swung it between them as we walked.

Samantha's house was exactly like the one I pictured Gracie and Jake living in one day. It was a white stucco Cape Cod style house with pale blue shutters and two dormers that jutted out of the roof. Samantha's mom came to the door with her hand across her mouth and tears in her eyes. She went right to Calon and wrapped her arms around him and whispered into his ear.

"I swear if I'd have known how to, I would have found you. I didn't get any information about any of her family through the adoption agency. They said, at the time, that it was in her best interest." She took Calon's face in her hands, "I wanted to find you all these years, but I didn't know how. You have to believe me."

"Mrs. O'Brien, please, don't apologize. There's no reason to feel regret. This is a good day. This is a really good day."

"Well, come on in." She hustled everyone inside, and Gracie introduced me, which resulted in another huge hug. I looked over at Calon, and we both smiled at Samantha sitting on the couch with her hands folded in her lap.

"Can someone, please, tell me what's going on?" She tapped her foot like an impatient little kid.

Mrs. O'Brien smiled at Calon and nodded. "I believe you have a story to tell. I trust you to tell her the happiest parts." Calon didn't need her to tell him there were parts Samantha didn't need to know, but I knew he understood her need to say it.

Mrs. O'Brien came over to Gracie and me and scooted in between us with her arms around our waists. We did the same and held each other's hands behind Mrs. O'Brien's back. Calon walked over and sat next to Samantha on the couch. He turned to her and took her hands in his once again.

"Samantha, about sixteen years ago I lost the most precious thing in my life. It tore my heart apart. I was six, and there was nothing I could do but trust the adults in my life that it was something that needed to happen."

"Is that what was making you so sad outside the pizza place?" Samantha looked at him with the face of an angel, and it was evident in her expression that she longed to take away his pain. Little did she know she had already eased the ache.

"Yeah, it is. But, that's not the end of the story I want to tell you." Calon looked up at his audience of three and smiled a smile that had a story all its own. The one person that was taken from him that he could actually get back was sitting right before him. Samantha hung on his every word. Her anticipation of what he would say was prominent in the room.

"Samantha, my sister's name was Kate, Kate Samantha."

Samantha gasped.

"The day we were separated I gave her something, so she'd never forget me or forget how much I loved her." A single tear ran down each of Calon's cheeks.

"What did you give her?"

"I gave her a rainbow-colored, braided friendship bracelet."

Samantha's hand left Calon's and her fingers nervously twisted the bracelet on her arm, but her eyes never left his. I watched what Calon had just said sink in, and I watched all the breath leave her body. Her cheeks got pink, and her eyes filled with tears.

"Calon. What are you telling me? I know what I want it to be, but I'm afraid to get my hopes up. I really need you to say it. Please, say it." Both her hands were back in his, and he squeezed them before he spoke. He wiped the tears that dripped from his chin with his forearm.

I watched the man I loved with all my heart prepare to tell his baby sister that her brother was back in her life. Tears streamed down my face. I looked over at Gracie who had her hand over her mouth and tried desperately to hold in the sob that loomed in her throat.

"Samantha, I gave you this bracelet. I gave you this sixteen years ago as a way for you to remember me. I'm your brother, and my heart is so full right now because you found me. To see that your heart is still as big as it was then makes me the proudest brother on the planet." Calon pulled her in for a hug. She cried on his shoulder.

"Brother. I called you, 'Brother'. I didn't know. You're my brother. I love my brother."

"I love my sister." Calon's eyes flashed up to mine, and there was a sparkle in them that I'd never seen. As beautiful as those eyes were something had been missing the whole time I knew him, but it was back.

"Calon?" Samantha pressed her body back, so she could see Calon's face. "How did you know I had a big heart when I was so little?"

Calon smiled. "The day I made you this bracelet..." He twirled her bracelet between his fingers. "I put it on you, and you smiled. You waddled over to the table where all our string was and picked up a handful of loose rainbow-colored strands. You held that string in your hands until the grown-ups told us it was time to say good-bye." Calon took a deep breath. "You were crying because you didn't want to go. Just before you left, you handed me the wad of colorful, sweaty string and smiled as best you could through your tears. You needed so badly to make sure you had something to give me, too. You understood, and because of that we would stay connected, literally by strands of string, all these years."

Calon reached for his wallet. He opened it and pulled out a tangle of colored string. "I've been carrying this string in my wallet ever since that day. Today, I got all of you back. I no longer need the string in my pocket to feel close to you. You're right here. *We* are right here, together. I'll never leave you again, Kate. Never."

I don't think either of them caught the fact that he'd just called her Kate instead of Samantha. It was just natural for him to call her that.

There were a lot of questions that I'm sure Mrs. O'Brien would need to prepare for, but what Calon was able to do for Samantha's heart would far outweigh any painful memories she may uncover.

We spent the next couple hours around the O'Brien's kitchen island eating our weight in cookies and listening to Samantha and Calon try to outdo each other with silly stories of their misbehavior growing up. My sides ached from laughing so hard.

Gracie and Calon walked to get Jake's car at the school. I didn't have the energy to walk, and Calon didn't want Gracie walking alone. I was perfectly happy on the couch talking while I waited for them to come back for me. Samantha tried to talk me into working at her school while I waited for them to return for me. And, if I wasn't exhausted before our pizza dinner, I sure was exhausted by the time we said our good-byes.

Calon practically carried me up the stairs to the apartment and tucked me into bed. Before my eyes closed for the last time, I watched him sitting in the corner chair going through a shoebox of photos I'd never noticed on his bookshelf. I watched his face light up, and I watched tears drop into his lap. It had been an amazing day, and it felt as if everything was where it was supposed to be.

Until Monday after my appointment, when he'd fly back to Los Angeles without me.

twenty-six

Calon

I LAY IN bed, Becki cuddled up next to me, and tried to calm the butterflies in my stomach. It was our twenty-eight week appointment with Dr. Daily. I wasn't sure what I was nervous for, but I was. I was pretty certain we knew the extent of the issues we faced with Abigail's health and development, so I was uncertain as to what was causing the unsettled feeling in my gut. I looked at the clock, and my brain instinctively did the math for how many hours I had left before I had to be at the airport. That's where the anxiety was coming from, leaving my girls.

I fell back onto my pillow and ran my hands through my hair. Dammit, I was so overwhelmed. In the last month I came to terms with the fact that our child, who was a huge surprise, would be born with Down syndrome, I asked Becki to be my wife, and I found my sister after sixteen years. My phone buzzed. It was Bones.

"Hey. What's up?" I whispered, so I didn't wake Becki.

"Dude, we just got the call." Bones's voice was so loud I had to hold the phone from my ear.

"What call?" I pulled my arm carefully out from under Becki and walked quickly, but quietly, to the kitchen to brew some coffee and heat up water for her tea.

"Dude, Fire Box Entertainment and Ugly Stereo Records were at The House of Blues on Valentine's Day and they both want to sign us!" Each word he spoke got louder, and by the end of his sentence, he was literally squealing like a little girl.

"Are you fucking serious?" My heart pounded, and my body temperature increased by about ten degrees. I leaned back against the counter and put my head in my free hand. I was stunned. We had been down this road a couple times before, but each time was with a record label that was just starting out. Fire Box and Ugly Stereo represented some of the bands we did covers for, big, well-known bands.

"Shit, yeah! So, here's the deal. Fire Box wants us in their office tomorrow morning, and Ugly Stereo has us penciled in on Wednesday. You gotta fly back tonight."

"Tonight? Shit." The flying back and forth from Knoxville to LA wore me down. Becki and I had a couple days in LA after our Valentine's Day proposal show. Jake and Gracie flew back to Knoxville the day after that show, so Gracie could get ready for her Special Olympics event. Becki and I enjoyed a couple days of newly-engaged bliss in our hotel room then flew back to Knoxville the day before event, which worked out well. We didn't have any shows scheduled that weekend, and we had a doctor's appointment on Monday. It was a bittersweet weekend, because when I flew back, Becki wouldn't be joining me. According to Dr. Daily's schedule, Becki needed to start bimonthly appointments, and flying back and forth so often would be too much for her body to handle, since our due date was just eleven weeks away.

"Unless you want us to kill you, yes, you need to fly back tonight." Bones seemed frazzled, which was understandable, since I knew he could hear the hesitation in my voice. I had considered surprising Becki and Samantha staying for the week and taking a red-eye back to LA Thursday night for our Friday rehearsal before another weekend of scheduled gigs.

"I know, man. Just messing with ya. I'll be there."

"Good. See you tonight."

"Yep."

I ended the call and set my phone on the counter. I rubbed my face and tried to stop my brain from spinning. Everything I'd ever wanted was coming at me all at once, along with a few things I hadn't *known* I wanted, which made the possibility of a record deal quite overwhelming, more so than I'd ever imagined it would be.

"Hey." Her hands touched my bare chest at the same time she spoke. My body exploded with the sensation only she could give me.

"Hey." I pulled her into me, and she laid her cheek against my collarbone and wrapped her arms around my waist then breathed me in.

"Who was on the phone?" Her voice was quiet and sleepy, and it made me smile. She was my peace. Becki's touch had the power to hush all the unsettled feelings within me. Happened every time. And, now, I had to go back to LA without her.

"It was Bones. Two record labels want to sign us." There was something that didn't sit right deep within me, but I couldn't pinpoint why this news didn't have me one hundred percent stoked. I had always imagined what it would feel like to have a label we'd actually heard of interested in us. But, there was hesitation in my gut, and it was interfering with me being excited about the news.

"TWO? Calon! Are you kidding? What labels?" Becki's hands pressed into my chest as she leaned back and searched my face. "And why are you not bouncing around the kitchen? Come on! Two labels?" She smacked my chest and bounced around for me.

"Ugly Stereo and Fire Box." I winced because I knew she would smack me again because of the history both labels had. It really did warrant some bouncing.

"Calon James!" She smacked me again. Three times.

"Becki! Geez. That one left a mark." I pointed to the hand-shaped welt on my chest.

"Calon! This is huge. What's your deal?" She quieted her voice when she sensed my calm vibe wasn't just part of a rouse to catch her off guard with the news. She put her hands on either side of my face and tipped my face toward hers.

"I don't know, Becks. I just feel… it's like I'm…" I sighed. I didn't even know how to explain the emotion I was dealing with.

"Listen, you've got a lot on your plate right now. We're pregnant with a special needs baby, we're newly engaged, and you found Kate. Then this news of a possible record deal? It's a lot to grasp for *me*, and I'm not the rock star. What you're feeling is completely natural. It's a lot of emotion. A lot of noise. Don't try to force the emotions you thought you'd have. Just wade through the ones you're getting hit with as they come and try to stay above the noise." She squeezed me tight.

"How do you do that?" I kissed the top of her head.

"Do what?" Her breath on my chest is just one of the many things I would miss tomorrow.

"How do *you* tell *me* what I'm feeling when I can't even articulate it?"

"I'm pretty intuitive. And, Gracie gave me lots of practice. Sometimes, she can be as thick as a brick about what her emotions are telling her." She rubbed my back with open hands and nuzzled into my chest then started kissing it. She kissed a small path up to my collarbone and then to my neck. Another thing I would miss tomorrow.

I breathed in a slow, deep breath. "I have to leave tonight."

She said nothing, just squeezed me as if she was trying to slide me inside her, so I couldn't go. We stood there and held each other, savoring every scent, memorizing the feeling of each other beneath our fingers. I didn't want to go, but I couldn't let the guys down. I struggled with the notion that if I'd been a solo artist, I may let go of everything just so I'd never have to leave Becki again. Then I imagined what these good-byes would feel like once Abigail was born. Tears pricked behind my eyes. I tipped my head back to hold them in.

"At least you're here for my appointment. You're still coming to my appointment, right?" She looked up at me, eyes glistening.

"As long as I can get a flight later today."

"Well, get that flight so we have a whole day together before you have to leave. What do you want to do?" She grabbed two coffee cups from the cabinet and poured me a cup. She poured hot water in hers and dunked her tea bag a few times. Three times, like she always did. I watched her walk over to the fridge and pull out the creamer. She poured a small amount into my cup and stirred, added another splash until it was the exact color I would've prepared. She licked the spoon seductively and winked at me.

"As long as I'm with you, I don't care what we do." I watched her walk to the windows by the kitchen table and stretch. The early morning sunlight shone through her long sleep shirt and revealed the perfect silhouette of her body, and when she turned to the side, I could see my daughter's shape as well.

"Well, what do you say we call Samantha and see if she'd like to join us in whatever we decide to do?" Becki smiled, and her eyes flickered with sheer happiness. She was glowing. I couldn't believe how lucky I was to have such a supportive counterpart. It was no secret how tough my schedule was about to get, and not one time did Becki falter in her support of my dream. She was along for the ride.

"I love that idea. I'll call the airport about changing my departure day, and you see if you can get a hold of Samantha, then hop in the shower." I leaned back against the counter, crossed my ankles and started to dial the airport.

"Sounds good. But, Calon?" She walked back over to me.

"Yeah, Becks?" I looked up from my phone.

"Can you make that phone call quick, so you can join me before we run out of hot water?"

"Now, how could I say no to that proposition? I'll be there in five." I winked at her, but she wasn't looking at me.

She waggled her finger that pointed at the crotch of my loose pajama pants. "What's goin' on in there?" I looked down.

"Well, Walter heard your invitation. What did you expect? He's not a very sound sleeper."

The look on Becki's face went from sweet to sultry. She pinned me against the counter with her hands on either side of my hips. I uncrossed my ankles and rested my hands on her shoulders. She looked up at me and smiled but with only one corner of her mouth. Becki could be devilishly sexy without even trying.

Her hands moved from the counter to my sides. She brushed them up over my chest and down across my stomach to the waistband of my thin cotton pants.

"Whatcha got in here, rock star?" She hooked one finger around the elastic just below my belly button and pulled it toward her until she could peek down inside. "Ah, goin' commando, huh? Do you know how hot that is?"

My hands slid from her shoulders and went back to the edge of the counter. I swallowed hard and shook my head, unable to speak at that moment. I curled my fingers around the lip of the cool laminate and moved my feet apart just a little to steady myself.

"Well, it's really hot. Really, really hot." She slid her hand inside and wrapped her fingers around me. There was no doubt she could feel my pulse.

"Becks."

"We need to get rid of these." She slid her hand around to the side, grabbed the opposite side of my waistband with the other and lowered my pants painfully slow. I didn't take my eyes off hers. She lowered her body as she pulled my pants to the floor. I stepped out of them, and she tucked them under her knees when she knelt before me. She put her hands on the outside of my thighs, and I could feel her breath on me as she took in the sight of how excited I was to have her there.

"God, Becki." I tipped my head back and squeezed my eyes. The longing for her to touch me was so intense it was almost painful. I panted as I waited.

When I felt her mouth slide onto me, I sucked in a breath so deep I felt it in my toes. Her hands slid around to my ass, and she took as much of me into her mouth as she could. I could feel the back of her throat press against the tip of my cock. A soft growl left my throat, and I dropped my hands to her head.

She spoiled and teased me for what had to be a good twenty minutes before she took me to a new level of ecstasy. There was this thing she did with her tongue that buckled my knees and stole my breath. I had to put my hands back on the counter, or I was sure she'd take me to my knees.

"Becks, I can't stand anymore. My legs are shaking."

She looked up at me from her kneeling position, one hand wrapped around me, and her lips wetted with a mix of the two of us.

"Fuck. That's hot. I… I need to sit."

Becki smirked and nodded as I hopped up onto the cold countertop. She stood and moved between my legs. She then started the whole process over again. The gentle flicking of her tongue. Her hands cupping and gently massaging my balls. She held me on the edge for so long I was sure I would lose my mind. Then all of a sudden she stopped, and her touch left me.

I opened my eyes, and she was reaching into the freezer. She walked back to me slowly and used an ice cube like she would lip gloss. Slowly letting her hot lips melt it. Drips fell down and dotted her gray nightshirt. She took the whole thing in her mouth and rolled it around with her tongue then spit it in the sink and went down on me once more, and that was my undoing.

I throbbed so hard it hurt. I pushed my fingers into her shoulders as she increased the speed in which she sucked me. She moaned each time my cock grew thicker in her mouth and soon her nails dug into my hips as her head bobbed up and down between my legs. I was on the edge and was sure I would unravel beneath her at any second. Just then she slowed. Slower. Slower. The pressure of her lips on me lighter. Lighter.

She stood up and took my face in her hands then kissed me deeply, her tongue circling mine in the same pattern it had just been circling my tip. I could taste myself on her. I squeezed her between my thighs and groaned. The edge of ecstasy was a pained pleasure. My cock throbbed, and there was a dull ache that rocked my core. I needed to come like I needed my next breath.

"Fuck. You're killing me. Becks, I need to come. Make me come. God, please, make me come."

A satisfied smile crossed her lips, and she lifted her nightshirt over her head. Her heavy breasts bounced a little when the shirt pulled them up with it. She slid her finger down between her legs and moved her hand in a circular motion. Her eyes rolled back, and she slapped her other hand down on my thigh. She sucked in air through her clenched teeth then bit her lip.

"I want to come with you, Calon." Her words came out breathy and staccato.

"Oh. My. God." My voice was hoarse. She took me in the hand that wasn't between her legs, and then pressed me through her tightened lips. I could see every muscle in her tense and she moved her head up and down along my shaft with the same rhythm she rocked her hips into her own hand.

"Becks. Oh, God, Becki, I'm gonna come. Fuck! Becki! Becki! I'm coming!" And with that I let go, and, apparently, she did too, because she called out at the same time I filled her mouth. The warm liquid dripped out from her parted lips and back down onto me as she thrust her fisted fingers down the length of me, milking me for all I had. She grunted and whimpered and came again, this time harder than the first. Her body slowed, and she leaned into me and grabbed the dishtowel from the counter to wipe her mouth.

Our breathing slowed, and her head fell against me.

"I love you," she whispered it against my chest.

"I love you, too." I rubbed every part of her I could reach with my open hands. Her skin was so soft and goose bumps raised across it as I slid my hands to every corner of her body.

WE EVENTUALLY MADE our phone calls and took our showers separately, simply because I wasn't sure I could handle that intensity twice in the same hour, and headed out to meet Samantha for lunch at Brother's. I walked a little cockier down College Avenue and secretly spoke to every guy we passed, *Yeah, my fiancée's hotter than your girlfriend. Dudes, you have no idea!*

We had lunch with Samantha, and then asked her if she wanted to come to our doctor's appointment with us. Once we convinced her there would be no blood and she wouldn't have to get a shot, she agreed. After she found out she'd get to *see* the baby, she was giddy with excitement.

"Okay, Samantha, are you ready?" Dr. Daily was thrilled for us. We'd given her the Cliff's Notes version of the reunion between me and Samantha. She was also thrilled that the three dimensional ultrasound had an extra spectator.

"Ready." Samantha smiled from ear to ear and gave Dr. Daily a thumbs up.

The wand moved around Becki's belly and the black and white fuzzy images came up on the screen. I saw Samantha's face contort as she tried to make sense of the shapes she saw.

"Don't worry. That's all Becki's inside parts, she doesn't have it pointed at the baby, yet. When she gets there, you'll see her." Samantha grabbed my hand and squeezed. A jolt of electricity shot up my arm, and my mind went back, once again, to that chubby little hand waving at me from the car window. I moved behind her and put my arms around her shoulders. She took both my hands in hers and bounced with excitement.

"Now, do you know what a profile is, Samantha? This is the baby's profile. See her forehead, her nose—" Dr. Daily didn't even get to finish her description.

"I seeeeeee herrrrrr." Samantha elongated each word she spoke, as though she was speaking in slow motion. She sucked in a deep breath.

"Okay, everyone, hold onto your hats, this is where it will blow your mind." A switch flipped, and the screen went black. When it came back on, it was like we were all peering through a window into Becki's belly. Dr. Daily had turned the screen to a three-dimensional view.

Abigail's face was round and chubby. She had a sweet little button nose. Her hand came up to her face, and she snuggled into it.

"Calon! Look at her. She's perfect." Becki sobbed "Shit! Why do I have to cry at everything?"

Dr. Daily laughed, and Samantha scolded Becki for swearing in front of the baby.

"I think she sees me." Samantha was convinced, so none of us told her any different. When Abigail's hand looked as though it was pressing against the window we peered through, Samantha squealed and hopped up and down. "She waved at me. Did you see her? She waved!"

"Everything looks good. She's growing nicely, and I don't see anything that would make me think she'll have any birth defects or health issues. Your baby girl is beautiful.

"I also wanted to tell you about a support group here at the hospital for expectant and new parents of babies with Down syndrome. I'll give you some literature on it when you leave. It will be something you'll enjoy and get a lot out of, I think." Dr. Daily continued moving the wand over Becki's belly, so we were seeing all of Abigail's expressions and even a big yawn. I was in love.

"Oh, don't you worry, I'll tell her everything there is to know about being a kid with Down syndrome. We're the coolest kids around, you know." Samantha puffed up with pride.

"Well, Aunt Samantha, it sounds like you'll be ready for her when she gets here." Dr. Daily wiped the gel from Becki's belly and printed out some pictures for us to take with us.

"Aunt? I'm going to be an aunt? I'm Aunt Samantha? I love this day! This is the best day, I tell you!" She turned and hugged me for all she was worth. I was almost as excited for Samantha to meet Abigail as I was for Becki and me to meet her.

"Samantha, I couldn't have picked a better aunt for Abigail. I'm so happy she'll have you." Becki reached out for Samantha's hand and looked up at me and smiled.

The change in Becki from the day we found out about Abigail's diagnosis to that moment was remarkable. She was no longer fearful, and like any expectant mother she was already one hundred percent in love with our baby and unbelievably excited to meet her.

Samantha came with us to the airport, still holding the ultrasound pictures. She and Becki walked me to the gate, and we started our good-byes.

"Samantha, when I come home the next time, what do you say you and I go on a brother-sister date? We could go shopping or to a movie. Whatever you want." I hugged her hard.

"I would love to do that, brother." She looked up at me and smiled, and then she hugged me just as tightly.

"Now, you take good care of Becki while I'm gone, okay?" I poked her in the nose and kissed her cheek.

"You got it." Samantha gave me a thumbs up and then spotted a baby in a stroller just a couple feet from us. She went over and started telling the family everything that had happened at the ultrasound earlier. I was glad she had the pictures with her to share with them. They kept looking over at Becki and me and smiling.

"Becki." I pulled her into me and held her as close as I could get her. "There are no words for how much I'm going to miss you. Especially, after this morning." I rolled my eyes and tilted my head back. "Just kidding. What happened this morning has nothing to do with why I will miss you so much. I've just really gotten used to being with you non-stop, and I like it a lot."

"Well, rock star, I'm not looking forward to all the good-byes we have ahead of us. After you sign with one of the labels, there'll most likely be many more. But, I'm willing to raise Abigail as a true rock star's kid and tote her along to as many shows as we can make." She smiled, but I could see she was holding back her sadness.

"I would love that. Becks, no matter what, you and Abigail come first—above everything." I took her face in my hands and dipped down so we were eye-to-eye. "Do you understand?"

"I do. Thank you, Calon. You don't know how much that means. I want you to know, I will never make you choose between me and your career. When I marry you, I marry everything you are, and I know what that means." She kissed me softly.

"That's right, we have a wedding to plan." I could feel my eyes get as big as saucers.

"One thing at a time, babe. Let's hatch this baby and see what's up with those labels, first. Then if you still love me and want to be with us..." She laughed. "Then we can plan a wedding. Besides, I'm pretty sure I could just borrow all Gracie's *What to do When You're Engaged* notes, and it'll be a cinch." Her eyes twinkled. She was going to be my wife. I was still in shock that I could be so lucky to have found her.

"Can Gracie be both my Best Man and your Maid of Honor?" I

chuckled, but if it weren't for Gracie, it was possible Becki and my paths may never have crossed.

"Well, considering she'll be getting married first, she would then be my Matron of Honor." Becki winced when she said *Matron*.

"Yeah, she's going to make you change her title. I don't see her diggin' that word as a reference to her status."

"You're right." She folded into me and nuzzled against me, like she wanted to crawl inside me.

"Flight 327, now boarding for Los Angeles."

I felt Becki's body tense. "Don't go." Her voice was barely a whisper.

"Becks…"

"I'm sorry. I don't want you to go, but I do. I want to allow you everything, but I'm going to fucking miss you." She rubbed her face against my flannel.

"I'm going to fucking miss you, too." I squeezed her tight and smiled

"Call me when you land, okay?" She looked up at me with puppy dog eyes.

"I promise."

"Bye, brother. I'll miss ya." Samantha leaned into me, and I hugged both my girls.

"I'll miss you, too, sister. You two take care of each other, okay?" I took a couple steps toward the gate.

They both nodded, and Becki put her hands on her belly then blew me a kiss. I literally had to force myself to turn and walk up the ramp. I couldn't look back. I knew I should, but I was afraid if I did, I'd never get on that plane. I needed to work through the uncertainty in my gut before I made any rash decisions. Being a rock star seemed so inconsequential compared to everything else that was going on in my life at that very moment, but it had always been my biggest aspiration.

As far as I was concerned, fatherhood would soon trump that life-long dream. I pulled out a pen and paper and scribbled down lyrics that came out of nowhere.

Absolute

My soul's no longer my own
It has two more occupants
And I willingly surrender
To a love that's left me entranced.

All my dreams on hold
Isn't that what life's about?
To give until it hurts
To love your heart inside out.

A prayer sent up
And it waits its turn
Hold 'em tight, keep 'em safe
Until I return

And should time run out
This message isn't moot
Make sure they always know
I love them, absolute.

twenty-seven

Becki

"I MISS YOU, too." I rubbed my temples to thwart what felt like an oncoming migraine.

"Let me know how Buzz is by tomorrow, if things aren't any better I could be in Knoxville by mid-day. We have a week or so to look over all the details of each label's contracts, and we don't play again until Sunday night." I could hear the exhaustion in Calon's voice. He was tired. Tired of a lot of things, I was sure. But we were all worried about Buzz.

"I don't want you to do that, Calon. The more travelling you do, the more I worry something will happen to you." I looked up at Gracie, and she smiled.

"Nothing's going to happen to me. I want to be there if his situation stays as grim as you say it is." Calon never put himself first. That was sexy and worrisome all at the same time. I knew the back and forth flights were wearing him down. All the energy he spent worrying about me and the baby over the last three weeks had him on edge and losing sleep.

"Okay. I'll call you tomorrow. Try to get some sleep."

"I just hate sleeping without you." His voice made my toes curl.

"I know. Me, too." I tried my hardest not to sound sappy and whiny with the audience I currently had in the hospital waiting room. I had my elbows on my knees and my chin tucked into my chest, trying to keep our conversation private.

"You know what would really help me sleep?" His voice went deep with a bit of sultry.

"What's that?" I smiled a flirty smile as if he could see it and lifted my head to see if anyone was looking. Most everyone was half asleep or on their phones.

"If you could do that kitchen counter thing again."

"Hmm. You enjoyed that?" I glanced in Gracie's direction. She flipped the pages of a People Magazine and rolled her eyes. She smiled at me and shook her head.

"Enjoyed it? That was the hottest thing you've ever done. I slept the entire flight back to LA that day. I barely had enough energy to carry my bag. I could use that kind of sleep again." I heard him sigh.

"So, pretend I'm there." I cupped my hand over my mouth when I said it. I knew Gracie would know exactly what I was suggesting.

"It's not the same. Trust me." Calon chuckled. I squeezed my thighs together at the thought of him touching himself.

"I miss you, Calon. Your bed is super big when you're not in it."

"Our bed, Becks. You're going to be my wife. You need to start saying *ours*."

"Mmkay." I couldn't wipe the goofy grin off my face. "Listen, I need to go. Gracie and I should go back and check on Buzz. And, you need sleep. I'll call you tomorrow."

"I love you, Becki Jane."

"I love you, Calon James." As much as I wanted to keep talking, I knew how badly he needed sleep.

Gracie and I tossed our cold, rancid hospital coffee in the trash as we left the waiting room. Jake had called Gracie around nine to tell her an ambulance had just taken Buzz to the hospital. She told him to call in another band for her ten o'clock show because she was headed to see Buzz. Luckily, there'd been a band bugging Buzz to give them a spot, and they jumped at the chance to cover for Gracie.

She picked me up in Jake's car on her way, and we'd been checking on Buzz and roaming the halls ever since. It was three in the morning, and Jake had just left Mitchell's. Maverick was giving him a ride to the hospital.

"So, did you hear anything from Jake about the new band?" I was anxious to see how Gracie's last minute replacement worked out. They were a young band, new to the bar scene, but I'd heard great things about them. They had a fresh, unique sound.

"His exact words were, 'Friday nights are my favorite nights of the week because I get to watch you shine, but if I had to watch someone else, Decent Breath would be it.'"

"Gag." I pretended to put my finger down my throat, and we both cracked up.

"Really? And 'pretend I'm there' didn't make *me* want to barf? You and Calon are two of my best friends. I don't need to picture you guys… you know."

We got to Buzz's room just as one of the nurses jotted something in his file then hung it back on the end of his bed.

"Hi, girls. I'm sorry, but there's been no change." The nurses had been so cool to us. We were the closest thing Buzz had to family, so they didn't make us adhere to the visiting hours, and he had signed papers saying the doctors and nurses could share details of his health with us. Buzz had cancer.

It was tough to see Buzz so helpless. He was a big man with a big personality, so seeing him hooked up to machines was surreal. No one knew he was sick until the night he collapsed in the kitchen. Since then, he'd been in and out of the hospital, and up until last night was pretty tight-lipped about what was going on.

But now that we knew it was cancer, and he was opting out of the suggested chemo regimen, we planned to take shifts with Jake, Mav, and some other guys from the bar. There would be someone by his side around the clock. When he was awake, he was still making everyone laugh. We kept his TV on ESPN, so he could keep track of his March Madness bracket. His love of basketball seemed to breathe life back into him, even if it was just for the length of a game.

Gracie turned the volume down on a repeat of one of the day's games, and we each curled up in our chairs with our white hospital blankets the nurses had provided.

"I can't believe all these years we never knew Buzz didn't have anyone. No family." I shook my head at the thought and let my eyes close a little longer than a blink.

"I know, it's really sad. We could have been checking in on him all these years, making sure he was taking his meds and stuff." Gracie looked over at the once bigger-than-life man we all adored. He was pale, pasty white, and his eye sockets were dark and sunken.

"Maybe that's *why* he made sure we didn't know. We would have driven him crazy."

"Damn straight, that's why I didn't tell no one. You all would have camped out on my front lawn." Buzz's deep voice made Gracie and I jump. We stood and walked over to the side of his bed. His eyes were still closed, and it didn't look like he'd even moved.

"Buzz?" Gracie's voice was soft, and she laid her hand on his.

"Yeah, Gracie?" His lips moved, but he still didn't open his eyes.

"Jake said Decent Breath was awesome. He was really pleased with their show tonight." She rubbed his hand gently without touching the spot where the IV went in.

"Well, they're no Gracie Jordan, that's for sure. You've got the voice of an angel, sweetheart. You're my favorite performer we've ever had." He peeked out of one eye and looked from Gracie to me. "But, don't tell that hairball boyfriend of yours I said that. I'll deny it." He smiled as best he could and then went silent again.

"Buzz, do you need anything?" I reached out and touched his arm.

"A new lease on life would be good."

I didn't know what to say. His head tipped to the side a little, and he stilled. Thankfully, the machine next to his bed continued to beep with each of his heartbeats, so I knew those weren't his last words.

We walked back to our tandem chairs and curled back up in our blankets. "God, Becki, I hate this. I don't know why he just wouldn't get the chemo." Gracie started to cry.

"Gracie, you've seen what chemo does to people. Sure, it extends their life, but it's Hell just living through the side effects. If the doctors know it won't cure you, so they're just slowing it down, there just doesn't seem to be any quality of life left at that point, ya know?" I rarely put myself in other people's positions, but at that moment, I did. I had to admit that'd be a tough call.

Something started beeping rapidly, and Buzz's body jerked a couple times. I grabbed Gracie's hand, and we both stood to go get someone. A whole team of nurses ran in and asked us to leave. My heart pounded so hard I could hear the blood pulsing in my ears. Gracie and I held onto each other for dear life and headed out into the hallway.

No sooner did we get out there, when the sharpest pain I'd ever felt hit me just above my pubic bone. I cried out and leaned back against the wall.

"Becki! What is it?" Gracie grabbed me by my biceps and stood right in front of me. "Becki, look at me."

I had a hard time focusing on her face simply because my brain was spinning with thoughts of what a pain like that could mean. I took a couple deep breaths and slowly straightened up until my back was flush against the wall.

"I'm okay, Gracie. It was just a really sharp pain, but it's gone." I placed my hand on my belly and felt Abigail move. "She's moving all over the place. Maybe she just kicked and hit a nerve. I'm okay."

"Are you sure?" Gracie was as pale as a ghost.

"Gracie, let's get you some water and somewhere to sit." We took about three steps when another nurse ran by us and into Buzz's room. I was scared. It probably sounded selfish, but if he was going to die anytime soon, I really would have preferred it be on someone else's watch. I thought about Chloe and how haunting the images of her last moments must have been for Calon all these years. I couldn't imagine.

As much as I didn't want Calon to have to fly home, he needed to know something was up.

Me: Hey. Something just happened w Buzz. Will let you know when we know more.

Calon: *Ok.*

Me: *You're not ASLEEP?*

Calon: *LOL. I love you. I'm trying.*

Me: *I love you, too.*

Gracie saw Jake step off the elevator down the hall. She ran to him, and I decided to take that seat I'd suggested we take just a few minutes prior. I put my hand on my belly again for a reassuring kick, and I didn't have to wait more than a couple seconds for it.

"Becki, you okay?" Jake came over and sat next to me on the bench outside Buzz's room.

"Yeah, I'm good. Just a weird pain. My books say that's normal." I wasn't sure that was exactly the truth, but I thought it would take the attention off me when it was really Buzz who needed it.

A nurse walked out of Buzz's room, and Jake stopped her.

"What's going on? Can you tell us how he is?"

"He's still here. We will send his doctor down to you as soon as he gets here. He can fill you in on his status." She smiled and headed to the nurses' station. One by one the rest of the nurses left, and the three of us ducked in.

Buzz didn't look any different than he had before the nurses kicked us out, but the beeping had stopped which terrified me. I looked up at his screen, and there were still pointed blips jumping across it, so I assumed they'd just muted the sound.

"Hey, Buzz?" Jake walked over and put his hand on Buzz's shoulder. "Buzz, the band was great. The lead singer is funny as hell and was just as entertaining as their music. They play twisted up versions of songs you forgot you knew. The *Gilligan's Island* theme song, stuff from classic commercials. It was a blast. I penciled them in on the dates Gracie needs off and a couple open Saturdays, too. I hope that's okay." Jake's voice was so calm and strong. It was probably good for Buzz to hear that, instead of

Gracie's and my shaky, sad voices each time we talked to him.

"You guys should get some rest. You've been here for hours." Buzz's doctor spoke when he walked in. He grabbed Buzz's chart from the foot of his bed. "I'm Dr. Stevens."

"I'm their respite." Jake nodded. "They're going home."

"Well, not many of our patients get such amazing care from non-family members. I'm impressed with your stamina over the last couple times Mr. Stanley's been admitted. He's a lucky man to have all you devoted young people."

"Buzz is a great guy." Gracie's voice was small and sad.

"Can you all come into the hall with me?" Dr. Stevens tipped his head toward the door.

We fell in behind him and stepped out into the hallway. My body started to tremble. It was obvious, at least to me, what Dr. Stevens wanted to tell us.

"Well, here's what we're looking at. Mr. Stanley's cancer has gone so long without chemo that it's now in his bones. Without any treatment, the calcium from his bones will leach into his blood stream, which will cause him to go unconscious, and then he will pass quickly."

"How long?" Jake spoke, and Gracie held his hand and pressed her face into his shoulder.

"Well, that's not something I can tell you. There are a lot of other factors that come into play that make that impossible to estimate. Each case is different." Dr. Stevens looked down at his feet and then back up to us. "It's good that you're here. I'm not sure if he will regain consciousness, but, he still may be able to hear you, so just keep talking to him. He may acknowledge you, or he may just lie still, but don't let that deter you from reliving old stories or talking to him about what's going on in your lives now."

None of us could speak. We just nodded.

"I'm going to do my rounds, and I'll be back in a couple of hours. You two should get some sleep." He pointed to Gracie and me, then walked down the hall and into the next room. I felt bad for Jake, though, he'd just ran a bar into the wee hours of the morning and *he* was supposed to be relieving *us* from our post.

"You two take my car and go home and rest." Gracie still had tears still streaming down her face. Jake pulled us both in for a big, tight Jake-hug. I loved him for knowing I needed one of his hugs just as much as Gracie did.

Gracie and I got to Jake's car and decided it was silly to drive all the way home. We grabbed a couple blankets from the back seat and laid our seats all the way back and fell asleep within seconds.

We woke to the sound of Gracie's Pearl Jam ringtone. The sun was coming up and the sky was blue.

"Jake?" Gracie gasped and covered her mouth, tears fell down her cheeks. I quickly texted Calon to come as soon as possible. "We're coming now."

When she hung up, I took her hand. "Gracie?"

"Jake said Buzz's breathing is labored, and it stops every now and then. Dr. Stevens just came in and told him he should call us to come in. Jake assumed that meant he won't be here much longer." She sobbed into her hands, and I pulled her into my shoulder. Tears streamed down my face as I thought of all the laughter we all shared with our sweet friend, Buzz.

"Come on, we should go up there." I threw my blanket in the back.

"Becki. I don't want to see him die. I'll never get that out of my head." A wave of guilt washed over her face.

"Gracie, you do what you need to do. If you can't be in the room, that's fine. Buzz wouldn't be offended. He would hate it if you did something for him that caused you pain. No one is going to fault you for that." I was nauseous. I didn't want to be in that room when Buzz took his last breath either. I'd be happy to live my whole life without experiencing something that painful.

When we got up to Buzz's room, Jake stood by his side with one hand on his arm. We stopped and stood in the doorway. The volume of the heart monitor had been turned back up so I knew he wasn't gone.

"I'll take good care of everything, Buzz." Jake wiped his eyes and sucked in a deep breath. "I promise I will honor all your wishes." Jake picked up some papers off the side table, folded them and stuffed them in his back pocket. It was obvious Buzz wasn't conscious.

"Jake?" Gracie walked in, and I followed.

Jake pulled Gracie in for a huge hug and waved me closer. He wrapped his arms around both of us, and we all sobbed. It was strange how easy it was to take someone else's life for granted. Buzz was an always present entity. I couldn't ever remember a time I was at Mitchell's that he wasn't there. It never even occurred to me that one day Mitchell's would open its doors to the public, but Buzz wouldn't be the one opening them. A huge wave of emotion came over me, and I slid out of Jake's hug and into the chair I'd slept in multiple times.

The sound of a roaring crowd came from the TV and drowned out the steady beeping of Buzz's heart monitor. Jake and Gracie looked up at the screen just as I did and saw the score as the sports casters relived the previous night's game.

Penn State Nittany Lions 53
UT Vols 54

"He had money riding on that game." Jake chuckled and shook his head. "He told me he just wanted to see them win one last time. He fell back to sleep just after they replayed the winning three-pointer."

"He was awake?" Gracie and I spoke in stereo.

"Yeah, after you girls left, he woke up. Eyes open and everything. We had a long talk. He gave me this." Jake pulled the folded papers from his pocket and took a deep breath. "He's leaving the bar to us, Gracie. You and me. And the house Calon rents will belong to the two of you, Becki. It's all right here. He made sure his lawyer knew his wishes. It's just a matter of signing some papers. He was so lucid and even cracked a couple jokes."

My phone rang. It was Calon.

"Hey. You should come home." I didn't even wait to hear his voice. "Buzz won't be here much longer."

"I'm already on my way. I flew out when I realized I'd never fall asleep. I just left the airport. Told the taxi driver if he can get me to the hospital in less than twenty minutes I'll double his fare."

"Tell him to be careful. I need you here in one piece. This is really hard." My voice broke.

"Shh, Becks. I'm coming. Hang on."

"K." I took a deep breath to try to calm my nerves, but it didn't seem to help. My heart raced.

Just then Buzz made a gurgling sound and gasped for air. I stood, but my knees gave out, and I landed back in the chair.

"Calon! Oh God, something… he's… gasping."

"Becks, put the phone up to his ear. Hurry."

I scooted passed Gracie and Jake, who stood at the foot of the bed and held each other, tears streaming down their cheeks. I held the phone up to Buzz's ear.

"He's listening, Calon." I could hear Calon's voice, but I couldn't make out his words. My legs shook, and my tears were audible as they hit the sheet that was pulled up under Buzz's arms.

Buzz's stopped gasping, and he looked so peaceful. For a moment, time froze as I memorized every wrinkle and every freckle on Buzz's face, knowing our time with him was limited. I looked back at Jake and Gracie. We held each other's gaze for what felt like a decade. I could almost see the memories that ran through their minds as we stood readying ourselves to say good-bye to an old friend.

When I no longer heard Calon's voice, I put the phone to my ear, and my head was shot full of a piercing, shrill sound. I looked at my screen and saw CALL ENDED. I put it back up to my ear to try and figure out what that noise meant when I realized the sound was coming from Buzz's heart monitor that stood right next to me. I turned, saw the flat green line, and knew he was gone.

I couldn't move. My feet were stuck to the floor, and my body felt like lead. I sat back in the chair at the window and texted Calon, because I knew I couldn't say the words out loud.

Me: *He's gone.*

twenty-eight
Calon

"BUZZ, IT'S CALON. Look, Jake texted me and told me about your conversation. I can't thank you enough for all you've done for me and the guys over the years." I took a deep breath and tried to hold it together just a little longer. I didn't need to make a speech, but I didn't want Buzz to leave the planet not knowing how much I appreciated him.

"Buzz, the band wouldn't be where we are if it hadn't been for you. It seems like a lifetime ago that four ratty-haired teenagers walked into the upstairs café and told you they were the next big thing and wanted to be on your entertainment schedule for the bar. You may have doubted us, but you never let us know it. We are where we are because we had someone who believed in us when no one else did. And, for that, I thank you."

"Excuse me, sir. This exit for hospital?" Annoyed at being interrupted, I glanced up at the road.

"It was the last exit. You missed it." I felt frazzled. I didn't need to be giving directions to my cabbie, I needed to be focusing on Buzz. He grumbled in another language, and I felt the car slow down. I was nearly bounced out of my seat as we drove over rocks and holes and into the grassy median. Illegal U-turn. *Idiot.*

"Look, Buzz. I know it's hard to leave when you know how many

305

people count on you to keep things running. But, you have to know, Jake and I got this. We won't let you down. You can go home, now. Just breathe."

The car surged and the wheels spun in the grass. Without a warning, the driver swerved, and my head hit the window with a loud crack. Horns blared passed us. I dropped my phone, grabbed the driver's headrest, and forced my body against the pull that tried to bury me in my seat.

As if in slow motion, the grill of a truck filled my line of vision. The driver screamed and jerked the steering wheel again, and the deafening sound of the truck's horn faded as it sped past us and under an overpass. The taxi came to an abrupt stop among the weeds not far from where we pulled onto the median.

"What the fuck?! Dude! You almost fucking killed us!"

"Truck was in spot I could not see when I try and pull out onto highway." His broken English wasn't helping me not want to ring his scrawny little neck. My heart pounded so hard I could see the letters on my OBX sweatshirt thump with an identical cadence to the whooshing of blood in my ears.

"Look! Just get me to the hospital!" I sat back and tried to catch my breath. "And make sure it's clear before you pull out."

"Tough spot. Around curve cars come, and I not see them." He put his head down on his steering wheel and mumbled a prayer of sorts.

I ignored him and grabbed my phone and saw the text Becki had just sent.

Becki: *He's gone.*

Me: *Be there in fifteen. Driver of taxi number 5525 is an idiot. I love you.*

The driver took the car out of park and slowly inched forward then stopped. I saw his head double checking either direction.

I thought about Buzz and how excited he was for Abigail's arrival. He referred to himself as Uncle Buzz whenever the two of us were around him at the same time. I took a deep cleansing breath and looked down at my lock screen, a still from our three dimensional ultrasound. My Abigail.

The wheels spun, then the car jerked forward, and the centrifugal force of the maniacal U-turn pulled my body toward the center of the car, which gave me a close up of another truck coming right at us. I didn't even have time to yell before the impact. A sharp pain pierced my leg and everything went black.

Silenced.

twenty-nine
Becki

"CALON'S FIFTEEN MINUTES away." I smiled at his comment about the taxi driver. Calon could be a bit overbearing when he was in a hurry and not in control of the vehicle he was riding in. I almost felt bad for his driver. I was sure my impatient fiancé was swearing like a trucker.

Me: *I love you! Tell the idiot to hurry, but get here in one piece!*

Gracie, Jake, and I sat in the hospital cafeteria and picked at food we probably shouldn't have even ordered. I was still so nauseous from actually watching someone die. Gracie hadn't stopped crying, and Jake was making phone calls to all the Mitchell's staff telling them to close the bar for the day. He alerted the University, so they could do an email blast to all the students about Buzz's passing. I was glad Jake was here.

"So, we plan the funeral? Right? Since he didn't have family?" Gracie sucked in an involuntary breath every other word. She reminded me of a little kid who'd cried too long for a toy in the store. Her bottom lip quivered each time she did it. God bless her heart. It was so big, and when it hurt, it hurt big. I always told her I didn't think she was born with the wall the rest of us can put up to protect our hearts when we needed to.

308

Not that any wall would keep us all from being sad that we'd lost Buzz, but something about her made me think Gracie hurt deeper than most.

"Yeah, I thought it would be cool to have the team of employees organize it." Jake punched something into the notes on his phone. "Gracie, would you sing?"

"Jake, good Lord, you're going to give her an aneurism. Let the girl catch her breath before you throw her into another emotional melt down." I looked over at Gracie and winked. She smiled back.

"It's okay. I would be honored to sing for him one last time. I have the perfect song. I sang it once for him when it was just him and me in the bar. He loved it. I'd like to sing it again for him. It's called 'Wings' by Birdy." She smiled and closed her eyes. I knew she was remembering that moment between she and Buzz.

Gracie started to sing quietly. Her voice flowed out of her so gently and, like Buzz would say, angelic. God, she was so talented. The words to "Wings" were beautiful. It wasn't one of those songs that would seem cliché because every word was about letting someone go. I imagined being in the funeral home, surrounded by classmates and friends from the bar. In my mind Sam, Ashley, Stacy, Greg, Maverick, Chelsey, Rob, Jake, Gracie, Spider, Bones, Manny, Calon, and I would sit together and comfort one another. People would get up and tell funny stories about all we put Buzz through. Then Gracie would sing for him. Her voice, quite possibly capable of bringing someone back from the other side, pierced my heart. I closed my eyes and listened as she finished the last couple lines of the song.

"Gracie. That was unbelievable. Your voice. Just wow." I truly had no words. I'd heard Gracie sing a billion times. Hearing her sing something that would be engraved into the memories of everyone present at Buzz's funeral forced me to hear her not as my best friend, but as a vessel that could easily pour out an ethereal blessing at a moment's notice. She could stop time with that talent.

"Jake, she's gonna sing to your babies with that voice someday." Jake smiled and looked at her the way he always did, like she was the only girl on the planet.

"And Calon will be singing to Abigail." Gracie smiled and glanced down at my obvious belly.

"He already does. She can hear him. Over the last three weeks that he's been away, each time we talk on the phone, before we hang up he has me hold the phone to my belly, and he sings a song he wrote for her called, 'Absolute'. She squirms all over the place when she hears her daddy's voice." I put both hands on my stomach and took a deep breath. I was exhausted, and it must've been all the standing and walking, but it felt like I was carrying bricks in my belly.

"Shouldn't he be here by now?" Gracie picked up her phone to check the time.

"Turn that up! Can someone turn that up?" One of the doctors from a large table of white coats stood and pointed to a TV that hung in the corner of the cafeteria. He grabbed his phone, held it to his ear, and then spoke to the people at his table as if he was repeating what he was hearing from whomever called. "Looks like an MVA on Alcoa Highway. We're the closest trauma center. Prepare the ER for incoming injuries."

The sharp but sober tone of his voice made the hair on the back of my neck stand up. I looked up at the TV and watched a helicopter's view of an accident just under an overpass. There were ambulances and police cars and a line of traffic backed up for miles in each direction. The footage from the helicopter was so bouncy it was hard to actually make out the vehicles in the accident. There was fire. Flames shot from what looked like a tractor trailer truck. The helicopter zoomed in on the flames, and then I saw it, a bright yellow bumper that jutted out from underneath the trailer portion of the truck.

"Oh my God, it's a taxi." Every muscle in my body tensed to the point of being painful. My heart pounded so hard in my chest I could feel it in my head.

"Becki, relax. There's more than one taxi in Knoxville." Jake spoke so calm, and his steady voice was reassuring. He reached across the table and grabbed my hand.

The room started to spin and a wave of panic crashed down onto me. "But what if…"

I saw ambulances pull away from the scene, a couple with lights and sirens blaring and one without. Debris littered the highway and numerous rescue people milled around in all different directions. Police surveyed the scene, I assumed to prepare an accident report.

"The four victims from the accident on Alcoa are headed our way." The doctor was on his phone and calling out to the other doctors at his table. "One deceased, two critical, and one in serious condition. Get your teams in place. They're fifteen minutes out."

Fifteen minutes. Fifteen minutes. My stomach cramped so hard I cursed out loud. Gracie scooted over to my side of the booth and held my hands while we watched the screen. I saw the volume icon appear in the bottom corner of the screen. Someone finally turned up the volume for the doctor, but he already had the information he'd wanted. The voice of the reporter was all I could hear but couldn't make out a word she said. The camera zoomed in on the yellow bumper one more time. The numbers 5525 came into focus just as one of the reporters interrupted the other.

"Excuse me for interrupting, Bob. But we just got word from one of our reporters on the ground." The male voice drew out his words with way too much time in between each one. "There's a possibility that one of the four victims in this crash is Calon Ridge, lead singer of Knoxville-based band, Alternate Tragedy. We are unsure at this time of his injuries."

All the air was forced from my lungs, and, for a split second, I had hope that everything on the TV had been my imagination running wild. But, all I had to do was look at Jake and Gracie's ashen faces to know everything I'd seen and heard was my reality. Calon was one of four accident victims headed toward the hospital. And one of those four was dead.

"We have to get to the ER. I need to see him!" I scrambled to get out of the booth.

"Becki, listen, that news channel has been known to jump the gun and release false information." Gracie was in her safe place, the state of denial.

"Calon was in taxi 5525, Gracie." My legs were too shaky to even think of running, but I left the cafeteria and followed the signs to the ER.

Gracie and Jake followed. My heart flipped through emotion after emotion, switching up the intensity each time. Sadness. Terror. Anger. Another stabbing pain in my lower belly made me grunt, and I broke out into a cold sweat just as we rounded another corner.

"Becki, listen to me." Gracie caught up to me. "Abby can feel your stress. You've got to try to calm down. I have a feeling she's fierce like you. If you keep freaking out, she's gonna keep kicking you. Harder and harder each time until you chill."

"Gracie, he can't die. He can't." I stopped walking, buried my face in my hands, and shook my head, wishing it all away. Moments with my beautiful Calon flipped through my mind, like I was paging through a scrapbook of memories.

summer flashback

THE NIGHT ALTERNATE Tragedy played at Sid's last summer Gracie and I got tanked. I yelled for Calon to sing something for Gracie when she pulled me onto the dance floor. Who knew he'd play the sexiest song of all time. His panty-dropping looks paired with that sultry stare and seductive voice froze me in my spot as he growled out the words to Finger Eleven's "Paralyzer". Calon and I had met a couple days prior when Gracie and I kind of broke into Mitchell's. We'd watched Calon perform a zillion times, but there was something about that night that flipped a switch for me. I knew it would be hard for anyone who knew me to believe it, but even though I didn't know it at the time, a brick in one of the walls I'd built around my heart smashed to the ground each time he sang, "Your place or my place," with his eyes locked on mine.

When we left the bar after dancing our asses off, Calon caught up to us, being the gentleman that he was, to make sure we made it home safely. He and Gracie fought about whether she needed an escort, and he finally stole her phone and called Jake. He walked me home that night. He held onto me the whole way, making sure to point out the lifted sidewalk squares, so I wouldn't trip.

He walked me all the way to my room, and I invited him in. He walked in with his hands stuffed in the front pockets of his well-worn jeans.

"You wanna stay?" I was sure I knew why he accepted my invitation to come in. I wasn't that girl wasting time fantasizing about the dreamy guy who would steal her heart and live happily ever after, so I was prepared to simply give Calon Ridge a night both he and I would never forget. No strings attached.

And I never *will* forget that night but not for the reason most people, especially the girls standing in my hall when the door closed behind him, would think.

"Becki, listen. Don't think I'm not incredibly attracted to you. I am. I really am. But, I didn't walk you home to give you a one night stand. I just needed to know you got home safely."

"I want to kiss you." I tried so hard to speak those five words without slurring them.

"I want to kiss you, too, Becki. But, I'm not going to." He winked and turned for the door.

"You're a tease, Calon Ridge. I could make this night worth your while." I definitely slurred those words and lost my balance and fell onto my bed.

He walked over to my bed and pulled a blanket up over me. He rubbed the hair from my forehead and smiled. "But, I'm thinking you're worth the wait."

It was a string of ordinary words that people speak every day, but that night it was almost as good as I knew his kiss would be. Almost.

I could hear his voice as clear as day every time I recalled that night.

THE ER WAS eerily still. There were a couple nurses talking behind the counter, a handful of people waiting to be seen and the three of us, standing in the middle of an almost empty hallway looking for something that wasn't there.

"The accident on Alcoa. Have they brought in the victims yet?" Jake spoke when I couldn't

"Are you family?" She almost looked annoyed when she asked me the question.

"My name is Becky Mowry. I'm Calon Ridge's fiancé. I know he was in that accident, and I need to know where he is."

"Let me call a doctor for you. He'll be able to answer any questions you may have. Why don't you have a seat over there?"

I was shocked she believed me. I turned to Gracie as soon as we sat down. "How many girls could just walk in here and say they were Calon's fiancé. Would she just let anyone who claimed him in to see him?"

"People in Knoxville know your face. You've been hyped almost as much as he has around here. You're the local celebrities." She tried to hide her fear, but I could see it.

"Miss Mowry, could you come with me, please?" A handsome Indian doctor waved his hand in the direction of an empty, more private, waiting area.

I nodded and grabbed Jake with one hand and Gracie with the other. The waiting area was made up of three glass walls, which gave us privacy, but, at the same time, made me feel like we were in a fishbowl. Like everyone would be watching to see what reaction I had to the words they couldn't hear the doctor say. Then they'd all text and tweet the assumptions they'd made.

"I'm Dr. Shevaz. Have a seat." He pulled a single chair over and sat across the bank of connected chairs Jake, Gracie, and I sat in.

"Look, don't draw this out. I need you to tell me if Calon is alive." I rubbed my hands on my legs.

"He is alive, yes."

I gasped, and Gracie grabbed my hand.

Dr. Shevaz looked down at his clasped hands. "He's being prepped for surgery now. Calon has had extensive damage to one of his legs along with some internal bleeding and minor head trauma. It could be touch and go for a while, but I assure you, we will do everything we can."

"Can I see him before he goes into surgery?" My throat tightened not knowing exactly what I would see.

"Come with me, I'll see what I can do." He stood and motioned for me to follow him through a set of doors to our right. "I'm sorry, but I can't take you all back. You two will have to wait for her here."

"Gracie, can you call my mom and Mrs. O'Brien?" I glanced back over my shoulder just as she wiped her cheeks. She nodded and slid her hand from Jake's gentle grasp. "Here's my phone. Call Danny and Spider, too. Please." I tossed my phone to her.

I locked my eyes on the back of Dr. Shevaz's white coat and followed him down what felt like a never ending hallway. I didn't want to see anything happening around me. I didn't need to see other people's pain when I had more than I could handle on my own. I pressed my hand into the side of my protruding belly and rubbed her gently.

"He's in here. Now, I need you to know—"

I pushed right passed Dr. Shevaz and stepped into a small room that squeezed the breath out of me. I slowed my pace and took a couple deep breaths. I followed the beeping sounds and rounded the curtain. Two nurses looked up at me, then behind me at Dr. Shevaz. They left Calon's bedside. I didn't look any further than the foot of Calon's bed. I was terrified of what I'd see.

I turned toward Dr. Shevaz, who stood at the edge of the curtain. He spoke in a quiet, calm voice.

"When the OR is ready, we will need to take him for surgery immediately."

"Can he hear me?" I thought of what Dr. Stevens had said about Buzz.

"We can't be certain, but it wouldn't hurt to let him know you're here. Just a couple minutes, Miss Mowry." He turned and left the room. The beeping of the heart monitor split my ear drums, but I silently begged it to keep beeping. I started to shake, but I wasn't about to let myself lose it. I had to hold it together.

I kept my eyes down and walked around to the other side of the bed.

The first thing I saw was his hand, poked and threaded with IVs. A gentle hand that knew every square inch of my body lay still and lax against the white sheet. I took his hand in mine and prepared myself to see the extent of his injuries. I said his name quietly as I lifted my eyes.

"Oh, God." I grabbed the bedside with my free hand and then reached up to touch his hairline. His head was wrapped in gauze, and it covered the scars from his previous car accident. I remember Calon telling me the doctors reconstructed part of his face because it had been peeled back from his hairline when his head went through the window. He lost his memory for a short time. I sucked in a gasp at the thought.

"Calon, baby, don't go anywhere, okay?" I touched his face lightly. The right side of his face was swollen, and there was significant bruising around his right eye and down his cheek. "It's Becki... and Abigail. We need you, Calon. They're gonna take you to the OR and fix you, okay?" I sobbed. "But you hang on! Do you hear me? Calon James, you do not have our permission to leave."

I broke down; my soul weak and my heart preparing itself for an irreparable wound. I couldn't even process the emotions that raced through me. I was sad, angry, lost, hopeful, nostalgic, lonely, and terrified. I needed Calon to be okay. I couldn't imagine my life without him. The connection we held was primal and its depth vast.

"Calon, listen to me. I don't care what bright light shines your way, your life here... with me, with us... is just beginning. Don't you dare pick that light over us. Love us enough to stay here. Samantha needs her brother. Abigail needs her daddy, and I need you. I need you so much it hurts."

I leaned down and pressed my lips to his, gently. I held our kiss and whispered.

"You're my absolute, my forever. Please, don't go."

"Miss Mowry, I'm sorry, but the OR is ready." I looked up and two nurses stood at the curtain, seemingly hesitant to come closer.

I carefully took Calon's face in both my hands and pressed my lips to his again.

"I'll see you soon. I can't wait to see those beautiful eyes... open. I love you, Calon James. I'll see you soon."

I stepped back against the wall and nodded. Tears streamed down my face, and I covered my mouth with my hands to try and subdue the sobs I'd lost control over. I didn't want him to hear me crying.

The song he sang to the crowd at the end of their very last show at Mitchell's slowly dragged through my mind. The lyrics of Sum 41's "Crash" gutted me as I watched them wheel Calon's gurney out of the room.

Please, don't go.

thirty

Calon

I LOVE YOU, too, Becki.

I could hear her voice and feel her touch and her kiss, but my eyes refused to open. My body void of response. I didn't want her to leave my side.

I wasn't aware of the time of day or even where I was. My head throbbed and the sharp, stabbing pain in my leg made me nauseous. There were voices, but I couldn't make out what they said. Nothing was as clear and audible as Becki's voice had been.

I felt a rush of cool air, and there was music. Another voice spoke as clearly as Becki's had.

"Calon, I'm Dr. Shevaz. I'm going to fix you up so you can go home with that beautiful woman waiting for you. So, you stay with me, and we'll get this done. Deal?"

A sensation entered my body that made me feel like I was floating. I became less and less aware of my surroundings. The pain slowly seeped from me, voices became more like white noise, and soon even the music blurred out into nothing.

Nothing.

thirty-one

Becki

"MISS MOWRY?"

Dr. Shevaz's voice and gentle nudge spooked me, and my legs shot to the floor. I sat up as straight as I could. The clock on the wall said twelve-fifteen, and I struggled to make sense of that. I looked around and saw Jake and Gracie asleep, propped up against each other on a bench seat near the corner of the waiting room. We were the only people there.

"I'm sorry to startle you. It's just after noon, and Calon's surgery went very well."

"He's okay? Gracie! Wake up!" I called out. She stirred a little then sleepily rushed to my side. Jake followed.

"Well, he hasn't woken up yet, so we are still monitoring him very closely. The next few hours are the most crucial. He's got thirty stitches in his head and a concussion from the impact of his head on the widow when the truck hit the cab, but there's no bleeding on his brain, so when he wakes he'll most likely just have a bad headache for a while. We had to remove his spleen to get the internal bleeding under control, but that's pretty routine for a car accident victim."

"That's it? A headache and a scar on his side?" I was wide awake.

"Well, no. There was extensive damage to his right leg. It was broken

319

in three places, and the muscle in his thigh was basically shredded by a projectile from one of the vehicles." Dr. Shevaz took my hands. "We had to remove a large part of the muscle, so he will need rehabilitation services to get him back on his feet again and rebuild the muscle that's left."

I reached for Gracie, never taking my eyes off Dr. Shevaz. She squeezed my hand with both of hers.

"But, he will be okay." I purposely said it as a statement and not a question, willing it to be truth.

"Like I said, the hours after surgery are always the most crucial and sometimes touch and go, but we are keeping him closely monitored. I'm not expecting any complications. He may even be awake now, if you'd like to see him." He smiled. "Usually I only let family in, but you two must be pretty close friends to still be here." He stood and motioned for all three of us to follow him.

Walking into Calon's room this time was easier than the last. Gracie and Jake lagged back a little. I couldn't get to Calon fast enough. I took my spot on the window-side of his bed and thanked God he was still alive. His eyes were closed, and he just had a small piece of gauze over his stitches. He looked so peaceful. Dr. Shevaz peeked inside his chart, then smiled, and left the room. I forced my worries of amnesia to the back of my mind.

"Calon. Calon, can you hear me?" I took hold of his hand and squeezed. "Squeeze my hand if you can hear me." My smile faded when his hand remained limp in mine.

"Becki, just keep talking to him. It's probably just the anesthesia. He just needs to come out of it." Gracie walked over to her side of Calon's bed, tilted her head, and sucked in her bottom lip with a frown when she saw all the bruising on the side of his face, which had gotten darker and more colorful since before his surgery.

"Calon? Wake up. Please, open your eyes." I guess I expected him to wake up as soon as he heard me. When he didn't, I started to panic. My heart pounded, and I broke out into a sweat. My stomach tightened again, like Abigail yanked the walls of my stomach toward her from the inside. I bent over a little and instinctively tried to breathe even breaths. I squeezed my eyes shut and put my head down on my hand that held Calon's.

"Becki!" Jake was at my side and holding onto me before Gracie had taken her eyes from Calon's injuries. "Sit down. There's a chair right behind you. Careful." He helped me into the chair. Now *he* looked like he was going to pass out.

"Jake, are *you* okay?" I laughed a little.

"I'm fine. You're just freaking me out with all the gasping and those damn Braxton Hicks contractions." He shook his head and rolled his eyes, probably embarrassed that he knew more about pregnancy than most college seniors. He sat in the chair next to mine. "Sorry, I freaked. I'm exhausted."

"We all are." Gracie spoke but was frozen at Calon's bedside, seemingly not knowing what to do for Jake's and my sorry asses.

"Gracie, I need to catch my breath for a second. I just got super nauseous, and I really don't want to stand up and puke all over the place. Can you talk to him for a minute?" I focused on anything but how sick I felt.

"Hey, Calon, so… we were hoping you'd wake up. So, wake up." Gracie looked at me and shrugged.

"Good lord, girl. That was awkward. Could you at least sing to him? Something?" I put both hands on my belly and patted it when I felt Abigail move. I didn't want to say out loud that I was nervous he wouldn't wake up. But, I was.

"Uh, sure. What, though? What song?"

"Gracie! This isn't American Idol. Just sing something. Preferably something that will make him wake up." I smiled. I needed something to calm my nerves, and Gracie's voice would do just that. So, maybe it was a selfish request, but I knew we'd all draw something peaceful from her voice.

Gracie closed her eyes and instinctively started to pat her leg and keep time with her foot on the floor. Something I'd seen her do a million times. Calon, too. She cleared her throat and closed her eyes and sang "Accident" by Emily Wolfe in perfect Gracie style. Her voice was beautiful from the first syllable out of her mouth. She had the perfect voice of folk-style music, and the song wasn't really about an accident. It was about accidental love. I glanced over at Jake, who just grinned.

I looked around the room as Gracie sang the last couple verses and realized how beautifully blessed I was. The most important people in my life were always by my side no matter how far the distance or how dire the situation. We had a bond that I truly believed would never be broken. I didn't trust the sincerity of most people, and I knew that stemmed from my dad leaving, but I trusted Calon, Gracie, and Jake with every fiber of my being. I never questioned their motives or their advice. In our friendship, I knew there were no secrets, and there would be no surprises or admissions of things held back. This was true family. My friends were the family I'd hand-picked for myself, the people who would never let me down.

"Becki?" My mom's voice pulled me from my sappy reflection. She looked over at Calon and covered her mouth with a gasp that hung in the air.

"Mom, he's okay." I carefully got up, making sure I didn't move too quickly and cause another cramp. "He has a concussion, is missing a spleen, and will need rehab for this leg. But, he's alive. He's still here."

Dammit! There was something about being in my mom's presence that turned me back into a little girl. As soon as I saw her arms open toward me, I rushed to her and fell into her hug and wept. All the emotions of Buzz's death, the accident, Calon's surgery, the fact that he wasn't awake yet, it all tumbled down on top of me, and I could no longer handle the weight.

"Gracie, Jake, thank you for being here for my Becki. You two are great friends." My mom blew them kisses but stood firm, rubbing my back as if I was ten years old again.

"Thanks for coming, Mom." I stood up to gather myself. She handed me a tissue and no sooner did I start to blow my nose, when a gush of liquid left my body. I was so embarrassed I'd peed all over the floor. But when I stepped back, another gush came, which left me in the middle of a large puddle of amniotic fluid.

The baby.

Just then Manny, Spider, Bones, and Danny walked in.

"Um. I think I'm having a baby." The words barely made it out of my mouth before a contraction started.

The whirlwind that ensued within seconds was similar to something from an episode of every hospital show that ever aired. There were nurses, a wheelchair, Gracie and my mom answered questions, and there I sat in the middle of this surreal dream. We were just under ten weeks from Abigail's due date, my water broke, and Calon was still unconscious from life-saving surgery. Another pain I was not ready for hit me low in my belly, and I called out for Calon. I knew he wouldn't hear me, but his name was the first thing from my mouth. Manny, Spider, Bones and Danny stood frozen against the wall, taking it all in.

"Becki, we are going to take you up to Labor and Delivery floor and get you and the baby hooked up to some monitors. We'll see which way the baby is facing, and then we will work up a birth plan—that's assuming you haven't done the birthing classes yet." The nurse was firm but kind, and I was relieved to feel like someone else was going to carry the responsibility of my pregnancy for a little while. I was exhausted and now worried about both Abigail and Calon. She was coming too soon, and he wasn't waking up fast enough.

"She's almost ten weeks early. Will she be okay?" I didn't want to ask because I was afraid of the answer. I had to stop being afraid, though.

Jake, Gracie, and my mom followed the nurse who pushed my wheelchair onto the elevator. They all looked at her and silently begged her to say *yes*.

"Well, there's obviously no way for me to know that for sure. But, I can tell you that we have an award winning NICU, and babies born much earlier than yours have gone home with their parents after just a couple weeks."

"She'll have to be here a couple weeks?" I truly had been taking this pregnancy day by day, so I could breathe and not be suffocated by all the 'what ifs' that started to fill my mind when I thought about her birth. It had never crossed my mind that she may not come home with us when I was released.

"Most likely. She'll need to be monitored around the clock, but as soon as she can eat, breathe and keep her body temperature at a normal level, you'll be able to take her home."

"I haven't even taken the birth classes. I have no fucking idea how to have a baby!" Panic set in. The baby was coming out of me today.

"Becki Jane!" My mom scolded me for my language. I winced.

"It's okay. I've worked in Labor and Delivery for twelve years, I've heard a *lot* worse. Believe me." The nurse rolled her eyes and chuckled.

The elevator stopped, and we got off. Another pain hit me, and I cried out and buckled over, holding onto my stomach. I took a deep breath and then let it out slowly until the pain subsided.

"Look at you! You just did your first Lamaze breathing, and I didn't even tell you how to do it, yet." The nurse patted my back and smiled.

"Becki, you're going to ace this. I just know it." Gracie smiled a cheesy 'everything's gonna be alright' smile, and I shook my head.

"Gracie Jordan, there will soon be a human being climbing out of my vagina. I'm not worried about acing anything. I just wish I could make her climb out yours instead."

"Sorry, friend, that's not happening." She rubbed my back, and Jake looked like he was going to pass out again.

"Jake, you okay?" I looked up at him as I climbed into the bed in the cozy birthing room. He nodded and gave me a thumbs up, but I knew he was freaked out.

"This place is beautiful. It doesn't even feel like a hospital in here." My mom walked in a circle taking it all in. "This is nothing like the delivery room you were born in."

I knew my mom. She was trying to distract herself, so she wouldn't panic. But when I let out another yell and groaned through what I'd come to know as contractions, she went into Super Mom mode. She was at one side of the bed, and Gracie was at the other. When the nurse pulled the stirrups out from the end of the bed, near where Jake stood, and said it was time to check me, I knew we'd seen the last of him.

"I'm going to head to Calon's room and fill everyone in on what's going on. Gracie, you can text me what's happening. I'm really sorry, Becki…" He came over and kissed my forehead. "But this just really isn't something I think I can handle. I'm sorry."

"No worries, pussy—I mean, Jake." He flashed me an evil look then laughed and quickly headed out the door.

My mom smacked my arm and shook her head.

When the nurse was finished checking me, she took off her glove and walked up to the head of the bed and gave me a look. I wasn't sure what look that was, but it was definitely a look.

"Becki? How long have you been having contractions?" She put a big elastic belt around my stomach and turned on a machine that filled the room with the baby's heartbeat.

"I've been having the Braxton Hicks ones since yesterday or the day before, but I assumed that was because of stress. A friend of ours died yesterday, and my fiancé was in a terrible accident not long after. He just got out of surgery. We were down stairs waiting for his anesthesia to wear off when my water broke." I was rambling, but the way she questioned me made me nervous, like I was in trouble.

"Well, it seems as though you have worked your way through most of your active labor. You are dilated seven centimeters and almost fully effaced. Your baby will most likely be joining you for dinner."

"Well, I'm not ready. Calon's not awake. Can you give me something to keep her in? Medicine? A cork? Something?" I begged nervously just as another contraction hit, this the biggest one yet.

"I usually have women begging me to get their babies out, not keep them in." She looked at my mom and smiled. "Now, I do have one down side to a quick labor and delivery."

"Down side?" I held onto the hand rail on the bed and continued to brace myself and breathe as the big contraction waned.

"You are too far along for us to offer you an epidural. We can give you a shot, some medicines will take the edge off, but nothing will numb you like the epidural would. But, the upside is, she apparently wants out of you, so that means a shorter labor for you. We also don't need that birth plan I told you about. Most everything I would have asked you is moot now, considering you are just zipping through this process." She tilted her head and winked. "Now, my name is Mary. If you need anything, hit your call button, and I'll be here as quickly as I can."

"Wait! You're leaving? What am I supposed to do? How will I know how to get her out?" My mom and Gracie laughed at the same time.

"Becki, you'll be in labor for a little longer before she'll be ready to come out. At that time, we'll bring Dr. Daily in. You've got time before you need to start pushing." She winked again.

"Okay." Another wave of exhaustion hit me, and I let my head fall back on the pillow. I closed my eyes and wished for Calon. I never intended to do this without him. I was so thankful for Gracie and my mom.

The next few hours were awful. Not only was Abigail shredding my insides as she prepared for her entrance into the world, but I had to answer forty-seven million questions. I swear every nurse on the floor came in with something to fill out or for me to sign. When the contractions got worse and much closer together, they shot me up with something, but all it did was make me dizzy, so I kept my eyes closed.

Gracie and my mom told funny stories, they watched a little television, and all the while I was contracting and resting, contracting, and resting. I was exhausted, and I hadn't even started pushing yet.

Every time I'd hear the door to my room open, I knew they were here to check my progress. I'd roll to my back and spread my legs. I didn't care if it was the fucking mailman, someone needed to tell me that baby was coming out, or I would leave. Just leave.

Gracie and my mom took turns feeding me ice chips and rubbing my back, which seemed to take the brunt of the labor pains after a while. They told me I could get up and walk around if the dizziness wore off, but with the amount of intense pressure I was feeling between my legs, there was no way I was going to stand up. I was afraid she'd just fall out.

"Gracie, have you heard from Jake?" I breathed through the end of another tough contraction.

"He texted me just a couple minutes ago and said the nurses keep telling him some people just take longer to wake up because of how the anesthesia affects their body."

"Shit. Damn. Fucking hell!" I winced, knowing my mom was going to smack me.

"Becki Jane! That baby of yours is going to come out swearing like a sailor if you don't knock it off. She can hear you, you know?"

"I know, Mom."

I heard the door squeak, and I turned my head. I wished for Calon. It was Mary, coming in to check me again. I rolled over and let my legs fall to the opposite sides.

"Well, don't look so happy to see me. Sheesh." She pushed what felt like her entire arm up me and then pulled it out and smiled.

"Darlin', it's time to push." Mary smiled wide.

"She's coming?"

"She is. I'll call the doctor, and she'll be here soon, but we're going to do a little pushing without her. Are you ready?"

"No! Calon! I can't do this without him! I won't!" A huge wave of panic came over me, and I started to hyperventilate.

Mary got right in my face. "Becki, you listen to me. There's no stopping her from coming. She's ready to meet you. Now, this may not be how you pictured it, but you're going to have to accept this as your reality. Your daughter needs you to push NOW."

I nodded. Wow, she was good. And I was terrified. I was terrified, because I had no idea what to expect. I was terrified that Calon wouldn't wake up. It had been hours since we left his room. But, I smiled because I was about to meet my little angel. She'd soon be on the outside of my body.

"Now, there's the smile I was hoping to see." Mary got everything ready and then gave me a quick lesson in breathing, pushing, counting and repeating.

"I won't really shit myself, right?" That was a disgusting thought.

"Well, it's fine if you do. We see—"

"Oh, it is *so* not fine with me!" I wanted a cork again. Someone give me a cork.

"You ready, girl?" Mary stood at the bottom of my bed and did with her fingers what we'd tried a couple times with the olive oil. It thankfully didn't give me the same sensation as it did when Calon did it. I could only feel the pressure of her finger.

"There's another contraction coming." Gracie had become the monitor translator. There was a long ticker tape that showed my contractions, and she would tell me when each one was about to hit. Like I didn't fucking already know that. My stomach was being wrung out, I could feel each and every damn one, but I just let her do her thing.

"Becki, when you feel this next one, I want you to take a deep breath, bear down, and push hard for ten counts then—"

"I know! I know! Then a quick breath and push for ten more. Get ready!" I took a huge breath and bore down for all I was worth. My body started to shake at seven, and I wasn't sure I'd get to ten.

"Good! You're really good at this. Now quick breath… and push for ten. Push, push, push, push…"

An hour later, I doubted there was anything happening. I'd pushed and breathed and pushed again, but the contractions kept coming and nothing was shooting out of me. I was so ready to just get up and say we'd try again tomorrow after a long nap and maybe a conscious baby daddy. I rubbed the thin silver bangle on my wrist between my fingers and wished for Calon.

"Becki, I can feel her hair. I need another big push with the next contraction."

The door squeaked open. I saw Dr. Daily's dark hair and knew if she was here, Abigail would be here soon.

"Another one, Becki." Gracie alerted me, and I bore down for what felt like the thousandth time and counted to ten. I took a cleansing breath then ten more counts. I was so exhausted I couldn't even hold my eyelids up on my own.

"Becki." It was Dr. Daily's voice this time, not Mary's. "You're a natural at this! Just a couple more pushes until you meet your baby."

I shook my head, then let it fall to the side. I was spent. "I can't. I'm just too tired. I've got nothing left."

"You've got me." A raspy deep voice pulled me from my denial. I lifted my eyelids, and a pair of green eyes stared back at me from a wheelchair next to my bed.

I gasped and sobbed and laughed all at the same time. So did my mom and Gracie.

"Calon, you're awake. You're here!" I reached for him as best I could. I just wanted to touch him and know he was real.

"I wouldn't miss this for the world, Becks. We get to meet our baby girl today."

He was real. All banged up, but real.

Another contraction hit me out of nowhere, and I went into survival mode. Calon grabbed my hand and squeezed while I pushed, and my mom counted aloud.

"Oh, Becki." Calon spoke in a voice that was the definition of awe.

"Becki, stop. Don't push." Mary's voice was sharp and grabbed all of our attention. "Look up, there's a mirror. You're going to see your baby girl the next time you push. Don't take your eyes off that mirror."

The next contraction made itself known, and I took a deep breath and pushed. Calon squeezed my hand and leaned his head against my shoulder. Then her sweet, little, perfect head pressed its way out, and Calon and I both gasped. I gasped at both the sting of pain and at the full head of dark curls that framed the sweetest face I'd ever seen.

"Hold on. Don't push." Dr. Daily suctioned out her nose and mouth.

"Be careful. She's just little." The very first protective mother words quietly fell from my lips.

"This is the hardest part, Becki. The shoulders. So I want you to give me everything you've got on this one, okay?" Dr. Daily nodded with me.

"Deep breath and push, push, push, push…" Gracie and my mom were coaching me along with Mary. Both standing in awe on the other side of me.

A slick, slippery gush left my body, and a pinkish-grey, tiny body was suddenly in Dr. Daily's hands.

"Oh my Lord, Becki. Look what you just did." Calon tried to lift himself from his chair but grunted and winced and fell back to his seat.

Dr. Daily gently laid Abigail Kate on my belly. Her little eyes squeezed tighter, and I held up my hand to shield her face from the light. Calon reached out toward her and touched her little fingers.

"Did you wash your hands?" I elbowed his hand out of the way.

"I assure you I was sanitized before you even knew I was here." He shook his head and smiled then reached for our little girl again.

"Happy birthday, baby girl." A tear fell from Calon's eye. He looked back at me and smiled.

As if a natural instinct kicked in, she opened her little hand and wrapped her fingers around his, which looked giant in her tiny grasp. She was so little. She whimpered and wiggled a little then opened her mouth and let out a quiet cry, which I knew was a good sign.

Dr. Daily cut the cord, and they whisked her away to a little clear bassinette by the wall. She cried louder.

My mom and Gracie cried almost as loud and hugged each other, then bent down and showered me with kisses. I cried at the miracle I'd been given. This perfect little person, whom I loved more than I ever thought possible, had made it into our world, and I was overcome with a sense of welcome responsibility.

"Becks, she's here. She's really here. She's beautiful." More tears fell from Calon's eyes, and I wiped them.

"She's got your hair." I laughed and peeked over his head toward the nurses tending to her.

"Is she okay?" I called out so they could hear me over all the other sounds in the room.

"She looks great." Mary turned and smiled. "She is three pounds, six ounces and eighteen inches long. All her scores are higher than we typically expect for a preemie. She's breathing well on her own. We're going to let you have her for a couple more minutes then we will take her to the NICU, so she can be set up in her incubator. This is a precautionary measure, and we'll be able to tell you more about her condition after we monitor her for a little while."

Mary walked over with our tiny little swaddled package and laid her on my chest again. I adjusted her tiny pink hat. She opened her eyes, and I saw them lock on Calon's immediately.

"Hi, baby girl. I'm your daddy, and I'm so glad you're here."

"Calon?" Our faces were inches apart.

"Yeah, beautiful?" His eyes left hers and landed on mine. The intense connection I'd always felt to Calon increased tenfold in that room.

"Would you sing to her?" There was nothing I could imagine that could make the moment more perfect than to have his voice fill this room and bless all of us in it.

"Good lord, Becki! Are you trying to kill us?" Gracie and my mom practically held each other up. Calon and I laughed so hard it startled Abigail, and she whined out a pitiful cry.

"Shh, baby girl. Mommy and Daddy are sorry." I rubbed her little fist with my thumb.

Dr. Daily came over, took Abigail from me, and placed her in Calon's arms.

He squeezed tears from his eyes, smiled the proudest smile, and took a couple breaths then in his most beautiful deep voice he sang "With Arms Wide Open" by Creed, which lead singer, Scott Stapp, wrote when he found out he was going to be a dad. Only Calon could pull a song like that out of nowhere. The nurses all stopped what they were doing, and Dr. Daily crossed her arms and looked on as my daughter's father sang her into the world.

I thought I'd lost Calon and then worried I'd lose Abigail, all in the same day. Fortunately, there was a force bigger than all of us that knew better. And as fate would have it, we welcomed our little miracle into the world together with arms wide open.

epilogue
Becki

"GRACIE, CAN YOU help me in the kitchen for a second?" I tried to balance a tray of snacks in one hand and a tray of drinks in the other, but I knew I'd never make it out to our living room without one tray crashing to the floor.

"Good lord, Becki! Who are you kidding? Do you *not* recall your waitressing days? This just isn't your thing." Gracie nudged me with her elbow and giggled.

She was right. After she and Jake took over Mitchell's, I thought it would be fun to work with them for a little extra cash, but I didn't pass Waitressing 101 with Gracie. I made decent money at The Extension School as their webmaster and publicist, so I didn't really *need* another job. I just thought it would be fun to work with Gracie.

"What are you doing?" I rolled my eyes as Gracie and I walked out into the living room to watch the big game with the guys and found Calon and Jake standing amid a tangle of cords behind the entertainment center.

Samantha slapped her knee and cracked up laughing. "Who knows. But, they're fun to watch."

"Trying to hook up the new Blu-ray player." Calon blew curls off his forehead.

"We have a new Blu-ray player?" I was confused.

Calon looked up at me with his *don't be mad at me* puppy dog eyes and pointed to some shredded white wrapping paper next to the stack of wedding presents we hadn't opened yet.

"Calon James! I told you I wanted us to open those together!" I stamped my foot.

"We—are together?" He tilted his head and winced his way through a sexy grin. *Dammit.* The guy could get away with anything.

It was the beginning of December. Calon and I had been married for a little over a month, and we still hadn't opened any presents. To say a baby keeps you busy is an understatement. Abigail was eight and a half months old, and she talked almost as much as I do. Of course, she sounded more like I did when I'd go head to head with Gracie at beer pong. She slurred and babbled away all day long.

Calon was taking a couple classes, working as a TA in the music department, and playing at Mitchell's on Friday nights with Gracie. I did all my Extension School stuff from home, so Abby and I were best friends. Of course, Mama was her first word, but followed soon after with Dada so Calon didn't pout too long.

"Becki, I can't believe you haven't opened these, yet." Gracie walked around the decent-sized pile in the corner of our living room. "What if someone gave you something perishable, like a ham or something?"

"Ham?" I set the tray of snacks on the coffee table, knowing as soon as Abby woke up from her nap, we'd have to move it, or she'd make a mess of everything.

"We got ham from one of my aunts for our wedding." Gracie plopped down on the couch and stuck her tongue out at me.

Gracie and Jake's wedding was one of those fairy tale weddings that all other weddings you attend would suffer by comparison. The service was unbelievable. Gracie actually sang "True Companion" by Marc Cohn to Jake during the service. Abby was just five months old, and my hormones were on crack, so, of course, I cried like a baby when I heard her sing the words to Jake.

Gracie was the most beautiful bride I'd ever seen, and that's not because she's my best friend. She truly was. There was a collective gasp in the church when she and her dad took their first step down the aisle. Jake held it together and just beamed at his bride from the front of the church. Calon and the guys played the reception at Mitchell's and sang "Fallen" for the Bride and Groom dance. Gracie was practically sobbing into Jake's lapel by the end of the song.

The rape trial wrapped up the week before their wedding. It was really tough on everyone. Gracie, Chelsea, Ashley, and a couple of other girls took the stand and told stories I wished I could delete from my memory. But, I think they all felt a solid sense of closure when Noah, Travis, Falco, Hank, and Jeremy were sentenced to five years in prison on five counts of aggravated sexual battery, and Noah was charged with one count of unlawful photography. It was over, but I knew it was always something she would have to deal with emotionally. Every now and then something would trigger that memory for her, and she would pull away for a couple days, but those times were getting less and less.

"Go it!" Calon and Jake high fived each other and then did some stupid little dance similar to our star quarterback's touchdown dance but way more awkward. We all cracked up, and Samantha yelled at them.

"You two need to stop! Your dancing is embarrassing me!"

"Well, I'm offended by that. You're my sister, you're supposed to think everything I do is cool." Calon sat down on the couch next Samantha and pulled her in for a hug.

"Calon. Your dancing is not cool. Not at all." She rolled her eyes and shrugged his arms from her shoulders then laughed so hard she turned bright red.

"So, who's the Blu-ray player from?" I picked up the baby monitor and checked the volume, so I could hear when Abby woke up.

"Jake and Gracie." Calon patted the seat next to him, and I joined him and Samantha on the couch. Gracie slid something into the DVD player then snuggled up to Jake on the loveseat.

"I thought we were watching the game." I really wasn't a huge football fan, but when UTK played, I was a football freak.

"Kick off isn't for another hour. We brought something to watch.

Consider it our pre-game entertainment." Jake smiled up at Gracie, who hit play on the remote.

I looked at Calon, and he shrugged. Jake and Gracie were always surprising us with stuff, but they never told Calon any of it. The guy was terrible at keeping secrets. My baby shower and my bridal shower did end up being surprises, which was fun, so Calon was off the hook with Gracie for spilling the beans so many times.

"Gracie! Stop! I am taking a piss for God's sake!" My voice shot from the speakers of our TV. It was shrill and obnoxious, and I couldn't figure out what the hell was on this video.

"But, Becki, you're in a wedding dress, and all I can see is your head. You look like a baby bird in a big white nest." Gracie cackled and a short video clip that matched her description slowly appeared on the screen.

"Gracie Ann! I'm gonna kill you!"

"It's your wedding video! I had one of our tech guys at work splice together all the footage, and it's the other part of our wedding present to you." She grinned from ear to ear, so pleased with herself.

"Oh, so you didn't get us ham?" I cracked up, and Gracie threw a pillow at me.

"Gracie. You're amazing." Calon blew her a kiss, and I ran over to hug her.

"Stop! Stop! Stop! Hug me later. Sit down and watch! You're going to miss it."

I watched Gracie, Stacy, Danny, and Samantha walk down the aisle toward the front of the church, my beautiful bridesmaids in short sliver dresses. Joe Joe, the sweet six year old from Gracie's class was dressed in a gray tux. He was our ring bearer and pulled our sweet Abigail in a wagon down toward her daddy. Abby's dress matched the bridesmaids as best as it could, and Gracie's mom had made her a beautiful little flower crown with the same orange flowers that were in the bridesmaids bouquets.

We went with the silver and orange color scheme, because we were married on Halloween. Not because either of us are particularly big fans of the spooky holiday, but because Halloween marked one year since finding out we were pregnant with Abby. It seemed like a no-brainer date.

"Oh, God." I put my hand to my heart and smiled at my mom walking me down the aisle. The camera angle switched to Calon's face the moment he saw me. The look of wonderment on his face took my breath away.

The DVD was pieced together beautifully, spotlighting the best moments of the evening. It was a riot that I had proof that Spider, Manny, and Bones cleaned up nicely and could definitely rock tuxes like nobody's business. Of course, Bones's black and white Chucks sticking out below his tux pants in every shot made me smile. Jake joined the three of them as Calon's groomsmen. Gracie was honored that she was asked to be both my Matron of Honor and Calon's Best Matron, but then we all decided we wouldn't have titles for any one in our wedding party. They were all equally important.

"Ladies and Gentlemen, I give you Mr. and Mrs. Calon Ridge." The pastor spoke loud and clear, and everyone shot up from their pews in a shower of applause. I watched Calon take my hand and limp down the aisle toward the back of the church, and I thought about how much effort he put into rehab, so he could actually walk on our wedding day.

I squeezed Calon's knee. "You know I'd still love you even if you had to crawl down that aisle, right?"

"That's weird, Becks." He laughed and got up from the couch.

"Anyone want a beer?" He used his fingers to keep track of who said yes, which was silly because Samantha was the only one who wouldn't want one.

"Becki, when is Abby going to get up?" Samantha was always so impatient when it was Abby's nap time. She was the best babysitter. I would never leave the house when she was here watching Abby, but she was a huge help. She'd take the bus to our apartment when her day was done at The Extension School and she'd watch Abby while I made dinner, worked out, or just completed small tasks that were difficult to do with a baby crawling around under my feet.

"She'll wake up soon. You can go get her when she does. Okay?"

Samantha clapped her hands and whispered, "YES!" like she'd just scored for her team.

Calon carried in two ice buckets filled with Rolling Rock ponies and set them on the coffee table just as the *new* Alternate Tragedy took the stage at our reception.

After a long talk with the guys, Calon bowed out of the band, and Danny stepped up as lead singer. It was an amicable decision on everyone's part. Calon struggled through rehab for months and even sang at Gracie's wedding with a crutch tucked under his arm. Touring wasn't an option because of his injury and the rehabilitation he still needed, and he also realized being a family man was a bigger dream than being a rock star.

Danny and the guys signed a deal with Ugly Stereo Records and left for Europe the day after our wedding. We were stoked for them and planned to see them as many times as we could when they came to the states. Calon was still writing music, some for him and Gracie to perform and some for Alternate Tragedy.

"Please, introduce yourselves and then leave a message or some advice for the Bride and Groom." The videographer from the school's Tech department spoke to a whole line of people while he recorded.

"Look! I'm first!" Samantha clapped and bounced up and down on the couch next to Calon.

"Be happy. Just... well, yeah. Just be happy. Oh, and I'm Samantha, Calon's sister." She made the universal 'rock on' sign and threw her head back and forth. We all died laughing.

"Calon and Becki, it's me, Danny. My advice would be to always be honest with each other no matter how hard that truth might be. Why I am telling *you* two that? You taught that to me."

"We're Sam and Ashley, and our best advice is to never call your wiener a squirmy worm. Girls don't dig it." Ashley smacked Sam and then spoke. "That's *his* advice. *My* advice is to love until it hurts. Always. Love you guys."

"I'm Stacy, and this is Greg, and we just wanted to wish you the best in whatever you do and wherever life takes you." Stacy got real close to the camera and whispered. "And, Calon, I'm still a super big groupie. Just wanted you to know." She giggled, and Greg rolled his eyes.

"Yeah, so by the time you watch this I'll be livin' the high life without ya, dude. But, take care of my girl Becki. You know she wants me, right?" Bones gave the universal 'rock on' sign, too, and bit his bottom lip. He reminded me of Jack Black. Calon had to put his hand over his mouth to keep from spitting his beer all over the place.

"Well, I'm Spider, and I've known Calon a long time, so I think it's pretty accurate when I say, Becki, you're the best thing that has ever happened to him. Everything about him changed for the better when he fell for you. He was a great guy to begin with but you pulled something out of him that made him even greater. We're happy to have you in our AT extended family. Take care of our boy. We miss ya, Cal."

I looked over at Calon, and he sucked in a deep breath. He blinked his eyes a couple times then tipped his bottle toward the TV in acknowledgement of Spider's kind words.

"I'm Manny, and I know the two of you will laugh when you hear me say this, but I hope to one day find what the two of you have. Of course, I'll have to amputate myself from these idiots, but someday I'd like to settle down with the love of my life. Guess I gotta find her first, though, huh?" We all chuckled as Manny shrugged.

"Maverick here. Becki you're a tough ass chick, and I love ya. I'm glad you finally got your rock star, because Chelsea was getting a little freaked out by all the stuff you did while you were stalking *me*. Sorry, Calon." He winked and then laughed. "Just kidding! I can't wait to hang with you both at Mitchell's, 'cuz you know I ain't leavin' this town anytime soon."

"I'm Chelsea. Becki and Calon, it's been great getting to know you both. You've got something beautiful going on between you. Don't take it for granted. I can't wait to hang out some more with y'all. Congratulations and thanks for letting us be a part of your special day."

"Dudes, this gig is awesome."

"Yeah, good party, man. And like, congrats and all."

Yaz and Van from The Garage forgot to introduce themselves. We all lost it after we saw what they probably thought was their fifteen minutes of fame. They were stoned out of their minds. I was glad they had a good time.

"Well, I'm Rob, and I feel personally responsible for the two of you hooking up. Oh, wait, no that was Gracie that hooked up with Calon out at Phi Tau that night…" Rob pretended to be embarrassed by is fake slip of the tongue. "Just kidding guys. I'm thrilled you invited me to your big day. It's been a long ride, this time we've all spent at UTK, but we're headin' out into the real world knowing what true friendship is all about. Thank you for that. I wish you the best." He raised a frosty mug of beer and called out, "CHEERS!"

Everyone behind him answered with, "CHEERS!"

The words *Happily Ever After* scrolled across the screen from all directions and in all different fonts. Then instead of the typical *The End* appearing on the screen, the words *The Beginning* ended the video.

"Gracie, that was perfect! What an awesome surprise!" I walked over and hugged her and Jake. "Thank you!"

"You're welcome. You know it was a surprise for Calon, too, because we can't tell him anything that we want kept a secret."

"Yeah, yeah." Calon shook his head and rolled his eyes.

A sweet little muffled cry came through the monitor and before I even turned around, Samantha was headed to the nursery.

Before Calon was released, and regardless of how he was feeling, he never missed a day in the NICU. He sang "Absolute" to Abby each time he visited. Each time I heard him sing that last verse, I lost it.

And should time run out
This message isn't moot
Make sure they always know
I love them, absolute.

And, apparently, the nurses all swooned as they tended to the other little ones in the room. Who wouldn't? Seeing our itty bitty Abby in Calon's arms was enough to make anyone melt. Add the look in his eyes and the sound of his voice… unbelievably beautiful. I made sure I took a couple quick pictures and short video clips on my phone, so I could show Abby one day.

Abby and Calon were released from the hospital within days of each other. Calon struggled for a while with balance and walking without a crutch or cane, but he was an ace at painting from a rolling office chair. Samantha and Calon spent some sweet brother-sister time turning Calon's office into a nursery. He insisted on painting Abby's room and putting together all of the furniture because he could do both while seated. Samantha and I filled the room with all the frilly girly stuff that I swore I'd never buy, and Manny found an old guitar in the back room of Mitchell's and had the guys all sign it. It looked perfect hanging on the wall above the crib.

"There's my girl." Calon put his hands out and walked toward Abigail, who was snuggled into her blanket in Samantha's arms.

She saw her daddy coming her way, her huge evergreen eyes lit up, and her arms shot out toward him. "Dada."

I watched Calon melt into her just as much as she melted into him. It was my peace. Her dark, curly hair and thick eye lashes were simply smaller versions of Calon's. There was no denying she was his daughter. Abigail lay her head on Calon's shoulder and put her thumb in her mouth. Instinctively, my broad shouldered, long-haired rock star husband began to hum "Absolute" to his baby girl.

"Can I hold you, pretty girl?" Gracie clapped her hands lightly and held them out to Abby.

Gracie and Abby had the most special relationship. Gracie was like my own personal Down syndrome dictionary. She'd been to every one of Abby's well-visits and even the eye appointment we'd just taken her to. She was going to look adorable in her new tiny glasses.

Abby smiled from ear to ear with her thumb still in her mouth and leaned toward Gracie from Calon's arms.

"Hi, baby. How was your nap?" Gracie pulled Abby's head into her cheek and breathed her in.

Abby pulled away from Gracie and peered down as though she was looking for something on the floor. We all craned our necks to try and see what she was looking for. Her blanket was in her hand, so I knew that wasn't it.

"What are you looking at, Abby?" Gracie giggled and struggled to keep her from twisting out of her arms.

Abby practically bent in half and reached down with her little hand and pressed it onto Gracie's belly that peeked out below her shirt from all the wiggling. She looked at her own little hand then up to Gracie then back at her hand again.

"Ha bee bee." Her little voice went up in pitch on the last syllable. She smiled and said it again, "Ha bee bee."

"Gracie! She's repeating you. You said 'Hi, baby' when you took her from Calon." I was stunned that she picked up on that so quickly. She was remarkable. She had all her therapists floored at how well she was able to speak for being so young.

"She's definitely *your* daughter, Calon." Gracie shook her head, and laughed. Jake stood up behind her.

Calon and I looked at each other, both wondering what Gracie meant by her comment.

"Don't you see what she's doing?" Gracie laughed so hard Abby bounced in her arms.

"She's a terrible secret keeper, just like Calon."

"Ha bee bee," Abby spoke again and patted Gracie's belly.

Hi, baby. My stomach rolled.

"Gracie?" I exclaimed as I ran over to her and gripped her shoulders. "Gracie Ann!"

"We're having a baby." She beamed. Samantha and I lost it. Jake and Calon shook hands while all the girls squealed and giggled and hopped up and down. Abigail was laughing hysterically by the time we all settled.

Another baby in the family.

"Samantha, you are going to make a killing babysitting for Gracie and me. Oh, this is going to be fun. This is going to be SO fun!"

"Wait! You didn't open my present." Samantha ran over and grabbed a large, flat, rectangular gift from our stack. "Open it! Open it!"

I took the gift and sat down on the couch. Everyone stood around me as I carefully unwrapped it and slid something flat out of a butcher paper sleeve.

My breath hitched when I flipped it over and saw what it was.

ABSOLUTE.

A beautiful black, white and gold design.

"Samantha, you did this?" I saw her initials in the bottom corner.

SKO.

Samantha nodded and blushed a little.

"Becks, you texted me something that looked just like that." Calon scratched his head.

"Calon, this is *exactly* what I texted you." I looked back at Samantha. "I saw this in the hallway the very first time I was in your school. I took a picture of it and texted it to Calon because the word 'absolute' has always had a special meaning to us.

Samantha smiled.

"You know why it's special to us?" Calon leaned into Samantha with his shoulder.

Samantha nodded. "Gracie told me."

"This will be something we will cherish forever, Samantha. Thank you." Calon hugged her tight and lifted her off the floor which made her giggle.

"Now, I *absolutely* want to hold that baby! Sheesh!" Samantha huffed, walked right over and stole Abby from Gracie and we all laughed.

If the love that was held within our little living room that day could be bottled, there would be world peace. But, I'd settle for it simply being our little piece of Heaven.

Absolute.

acknowledgements

I LOVE YOU, Ken Brownlow! Yeah, you're the reason I have the nerve to put my heart on paper and send it out to the masses. Thank you, for encouraging me and supporting me and listening to hours and hours of one-sided conversations with myself as I hash out a plot twist. I'm living my dream because you believe in me.

Thanks to my family for always asking about my progress… it's what keeps me going. Tiff, it thrills me to no end that you love what I do. And thanks, Mom and Dad, for being proud of me, even when I write the "spicy" scenes.

Matthew and Emily, I couldn't have named all the characters and bands without you.

Izaiah, you're only eight and you already "get" what I do. And when you're frustrated with me and yell, "Mom! Just go write your book!" to get me off your back, I have to admit, I love it!

All the artists that make the amazing music on the playlist for this book have the MKB seal of approval (like they need it that from ME). Especially, to the men of Pearl Jam, thank you for making music that touches lives and inspires the soul and thank you for being the inspiration for this series!

Pete Griesbach, thank you from the bottom of my heart for being my very own ROCK STAR RESOURCE! I couldn't have gotten all the details right without you! Sidebar: If you're reading this book and you're a Pearl Jam fan, be sure to check out Pete's Pearl Jam tribute band, LAST EXIT, they're from Long Island, and they're super awesome!

A huge thanks goes out to the bands of State College, past and present; Bones, Man Alive, and Spider Kelly for your inspiration for Alternate Tragedy. And Eric, thanks for being the inspiration for Calon.

Michele, Nicole, and Joe Joe, thank you for all your knowledge and answers to my Down syndrome questions and for the inspiration for Abigail. Love you.

Todd, thanks for being my SWAT COP RESOURCE. You really come in handy. Hope all my texts didn't keep you from hauling in the bad guys.

A huge thank you to all my friends and acquaintances who inspired this series' cast of characters! Ken, Jeni, Lauren, Todd, Mike, John, Shirley, Todd P., Michelle (RIP), cheers to each and every one of you for the parts you've played in my life! I can't thank you enough for your friendship and love.

Ashley Erin, thank you for being Sam's girlfriend! <3

Bruce, thanks for the *badum-ching* lesson a la Gene Krupa.

Thank you to all my fans who ask for more on a daily basis and to all my author friends who answer my questions and breathe life into my creativity when I need it. And thank you to the authors I fangirl over… you inspire me!

And to my BEAUTIFUL BETAS—Jenee Gibbs, Heather Davenport, and Holly Baker—I love you all SO FREAKIN' HARD for the passion you have for romance and the love you have for my little group of characters!

Thanks to Heather at Book Plug Promotions for all the work you put into my launch, cover reveal, release and book tour. You're amazing at what you do, and I'm thrilled we are friends. Thank you, Liz at Book Peddler's Editing, for all the time you spent editing this book. Your editing talents far surpassed anything I expected. And, thanks to Angela at

Fictional Formats for your beautiful formatting talents. It's business owners like the three of you who make our dreams reality! Thank you!

And, of course to the gorgeous "Lorenzo C" for his beautiful face that graces this cover.

Made in the USA
Charleston, SC
19 June 2014